The Story of a New Zealand River

THE STORY OF A NEW ZEALAND RIVER

NR
Mandela

THE STORY OF A NEW ZEALAND RIVER

THE STORY OF A NEW ZEALAND RIVER

BY

JANE MANDER

NEW YORK: JOHN LANE COMPANY
LONDON: JOHN LANE, THE BODLEY HEAD
MCMXX

Press of
J. J. Little & Ives Company
New York, U. S. A.

TO
MY MOTHER

BOOK I

CHAPTER I

"DAMNATION! I wish they would hurry up."

David Bruce stamped his numbed feet upon one of the few reliable planks in the landing-stage, which threatened to collapse under his vigour, and blew upon his hands, rough and contracted by the cold. The only person within hearing, Sonny Shoreman, a lanky youth whose manhood was not yet under way, hung shivering over the side of the black punt that was moored to the rotting piles of the little wharf. His hands were tucked under his armpits. His bottle-green eyes glared miserably up at the horizon, now tinged with a weak glow from the rising sun.

"Are you sure you told them seven o'clock?" demanded Bruce, kicking at a piece of lichen.

"Yes, certain," mumbled Sonny.

The tide, running out fast, made little wakes round the square ends of the punt, which was a huge coffin-like craft full of furniture and boxes partly hidden under a new tarpaulin cover. The creek, here little more than twice the width of the boat, ran deep between lines of mangroves, the dull green of their stiff leaves relieved but little by the flat yellow berries, which seemed to continue the colour scheme of the clay in solution in the river, recently flooded by the spring rains. Walled up to a high horizon on either side was virgin forest from which a mist, getting lighter every minute, was slowly lifting.

The wharf, the punt, and the two men looked as if they had been dropped from the clouds into the depths of that remote ravine. There seemed to be no way in and no way out. But as the fog shifted they could see, about half a mile along another gully, a small white school and teacher's house, set on the side of a hill.

The eyes of both Bruce and Sonny Shoreman now gazed with fierce interrogation upon those humble buildings. As they looked, the forms of a man, two women carrying babies, and a child—all laden with packages—took shape in the mist. Only occasionally as they came on were they seen by the impatient watchers by the punt, for the road, which was carved round the spurs of the range, lay mostly under cover, and it seemed to Bruce that there passed eternities of biting cold before the welcome sound of voices and the squelching of thin mud made music for his urgent ears.

Indifferent as to the personality of the boss's wife and children, who were to be his passengers, Bruce began to loosen the ropes. When the party finally appeared round a ti-tree clump, and reached the creaking wharf, he turned, raising his cap to Roy Harding, the schoolmaster, and his wife, whom he knew well. Then he looked casually at Mrs. Roland.

He was instantly conscious of his deficiencies.

"The devil! Why didn't I shave?" he growled inwardly.

As they moved on towards him he suspected that Alice Roland was what the washerwomen called a "real lydy," and he saw that in spite of a hard black hat, and a rather ugly brown cloak, she was a young and very good-looking one too. He saw that she was tall, and that though she carried a baby and a basket hung over her arm she moved gracefully. He had time to notice her good colour, her straight features, and the coils of chestnut hair upon her neck before the party stopped before him.

As Alice turned her grey, day-of-judgment eyes upon him, with a look that instantly judged him and dismissed him from her consciousness, he realized how much she resented being formally introduced to him as to an equal. He did not know that never before had she been presented to any one who looked as unprepossessing as he did at that moment.

He was only too conscious of the marks of his recent short but reckless whisky drinking. His fine brown eyes were strained and blood-shot, his hands red and dirty, his dark hair uncombed, his hat guilty of indescribable disreputableness, his battered dungarees smelling of river mud, tar and stale tobacco.

It would have taken a connoisseur in types to have realized his possibilities. It was not remarkable that on that particular morning Alice Roland failed to perceive them. She saw only the dirty clothes, the unshaven face, the bloodshot eyes, the shrinking manner, all that she had been taught to connect with the name of pariah; and, forgetting for the moment that she was to be dependent on him on an unknown river journey, she barely acknowledged his presence.

Bruce had scarcely time to flush before Mrs. Harding turned to him, trying to ignore the unfortunate manner of the woman she had introduced.

"We have not seen you for three weeks. How is that?" she asked.

Bruce smiled gratefully at her.

"I've been helping Mr. Roland with the house," he answered quietly.

"Why didn't you come up last night?" she went on.

"We got up late, and it took me till midnight to get the things aboard. We shall have to hurry now. It will take us all our time to get down on the tide."

He turned as he spoke, and as he did so the child of the party, who had been watching him, stepped up to him. Her eight-year-old dignity was offended at having been ignored.

"How do you do?" she said ceremoniously, holding out a hand that was lost in a dark blue mitten.

Bruce stopped short to look down at her. All he could see of her face was a pair of mischievous and inquiring blue eyes, haloed by a voluminous and floppy bonnet. Before he thought, he had taken that friendly little hand.

"Asia," said her mother coldly, "Mr. Harding will help you into the boat."

Absurdly hurt, David Bruce turned quickly away from her. But the child looked after him.

"I will get in myself, thank you," she said to Roy, with a comical dignity.

As Bruce undid the ropes he was vividly conscious of the little scene of embarkation. Helped by the Hardings, Alice Roland finally got herself, her children, and her packages all safely into the punt. Bruce felt sorry for her when he saw by her awkwardness and her uncertainty how utterly unfamiliar she was with travelling of that primitive kind; and, looking ahead for her, he wondered how she would stand the rest of it. In spite of her behaviour to him, he liked the way she thanked the Hardings for their fortnight's hospitality. Something about her attitude, as she stood with her face upturned to them, attracted him to a second glance as he began to shove the punt away from the piles. Then he walked round the side of it, at the back of the family group, and slid down into the tow-boat, where Sonny had the bow seat.

"Good-bye, Mr. Bruce," called the Hardings together. "Come along soon."

"Thanks, I will." He waved his cap back at them.

Then with sweeping strokes, which Sonny Shoreman ached to rival, Bruce swept the tow-boat ahead, and the punt drew away from the landing.

The Hardings stood till the last vestige of Asia's waving handkerchief disappeared round the first bend. Then they looked at each other. Roy shrugged his shoulders.

"Poor thing," said Dorrie. "However will she stand it?"

"The Lord knows. She was rotten to Bruce. She'll have to learn sense."

"She'll alter when she's had a few weeks of that loneliness. And then David will shine beside Roland, once he is clean and shaved." She spoke significantly.

He looked at her.

"Hm! I hadn't thought of that."

She laughed with feminine suggestiveness.

"Well, I have."

They walked back, turning several times to watch the passage of the punt between the mangroves. Tears glistened in Dorrie's eyes. She read into Alice Roland's future things her husband did not think of.

Meantime, in the punt, Alice occupied herself with the immediate problem of coping with the cold, which was to be considered before the remoter issues of this dreaded excursion into unknown wilds. Betty, who was three years old, and the baby, who had just had her first birthday, both chose the occasion to howl piteously at this dislocation of accustomed ways. Alice, who could not bear that anything belonging to her should misbehave in public, exerted all her forces of comfort and cajolery.

Asia heroically helped her mother with "the children," as she always called them. But she burned to investigate this wonderful adventure. Presently, when the baby was soothed to sleep on an improvised bed in a bath-tin, and when Betty was pacified, she felt she was free. Then she darted with the spasmodic rapidity of a squeezed wet bean from one part of the punt to the other, scrambling over the tarpaulin, and calling every few minutes in gasping whispers to her mother to look. Her life, spent so far only in cities, had contained no hints of the wonders of silence and space, of the mysteries of forest depths and rustling trees, of the strange ways of the free creatures of the air and earth. She clasped her hands, electrified and speechless, as startled wild duck rose from hidden places, or ungainly shags flapped an erratic course down stream, or gawgaws croaked from the heights.

Then Alice stood up. The only thing that seemed to belong to her, in that incongruous setting of boxes and mattresses and common furniture, was a piano which was packed in a heavy case. It had cost Bruce an anxious hour the night before, till with the help of chance riders he had got it safely aboard. Against the end of it she now leaned, her proud profile clearly visible to Bruce, who kept looking away from it and back again. He wondered if the scenery was getting her as it had got him the first time he came down that magic river.

He vividly remembered the morning when he had piloted the boss to the kauri forest at Pukekaroro. It had been a case of the blind leading the blind down that winding channel; but, in spite of strandings in the mud and the boss's temper, Bruce had felt the call of the wild, and had accepted the offer to stay. He wondered once, as he saw Alice's face turned towards a gorge in the mountains, if she felt about it all as he had done. He knew that one might well forget the petty facts of life in the midst of that tremendous scenery.

The river was a mere thread at the bottom of the narrow valley, which was walled up on either side by precipitous hills that kept the sunlight out till midday. From the mangrove banks to the sky a great variety of trees in fifty shades of evergreen covered every yard of space. There was a riotous spring colour in the forest, voluptuous gold and red in the clumps of yellow kowhai and the crimson rata, and there were masses of greeny white clematis and bowers of pale tree ferns to rest the satiated eye. Stiff laurel-like puriris stood beside the drooping fringe of the lacy rimu; hard blackish kahikateas brooded over the oak-like ti-toki with its lovely scarlet berry.

Nowhere in the world is there more variety. Here nature hated the very beginnings of monotony. So she scattered a little of everything about those wonderful hills. Towering arrogantly above all else, on the crests and down the spurs, stood groups of the kauri, the giant timber tree of New Zealand, whose great grey trunks, like the pillars in the ancient halls of Karnak, shot up seventy and eighty feet without a knot or branch, and whose colossal heads, swelling up into the sky, made a cipher of every tree near.

Round each bend there was a fresh gully, a new and stimulating vista. And everywhere there was a vibrating silence, a terribly lonely silence, but rarely broken by the note of a singing bird.

In springtime it was a cold, windy, rain-washed land. It lacked the fierce blues and flame colours of Australia. Its days never palpitated with the exciting hum of that tropical land. Its nights were chaste and chilly. No "soft lascivious stars" caressed its rare wandering lovers. Its winds growled harshly or sighed mournfully, blowing ever over dead men's bones. For the river and the hills were one of the gateways to the land of the lost.

The first thing that struck Alice about it all was its appalling isolation. Every mile of it meant a mile farther from even such limited civilization as she had just left behind. Every hour of it meant so much more of life cut off from the only things she knew and loved. Every bend in the river meant another fearful look forward, and another yearning look back. It was just eight o'clock now, and they were to go on like this hour after hour, until two, or perhaps three in the afternoon.

For the last fortnight she had been alternately shirking it and facing it. Each day had further intensified her fear. Once, as she turned, Bruce saw the expression on her face. All sense of hurt left him as he realized that she was horribly afraid.

Only once had her grey eyes rested, carefully expressionless, upon his muscular frame, as it swung backwards and forwards with the ease of a well-oiled machine. She did not appreciate the fact that he was giving a magnificent exhibition of physical strength as he rowed desperately to keep ahead of the tide. To her he was a bushman, one of the lawless oddments of humanity who had either fled from civilization, as the result of evil deeds, or was drifting shiftlessly towards a wretched end. And, as a servant of her husband, and a sometimes drunken one at that, he was outside her speculations.

Each time that Asia, fascinated by the steady sweep of

the oars, stopped at the front of the punt to watch them, she was called back.

"You must not stare at them," Alice said.

"Don't they get tired, mother?" asked the child.

"No, they are used to it."

"They must be very strong."

"Oh, yes, men are."

Presently the children woke up, and had to be fed, kept warm, and played with. When Alice next had time to look around, the face of the world had changed. There were no mountains on the western bank of the river now, and the eastern ones had dwarfed. The river, too, had widened out, swelled at intervals by smelly creeks, sneaking from remote sources away among the hills. They passed fire-swept wastes, and blackened ranges and valleys, where denuded kauri trees, now often standing alone like giant spectres, held up their bleached heads imploringly to the sky. Once a gully opened out upon a dark level wall of stiff kahikateas, and once a break in the ranges revealed, on a distant green hill, a solitary house beside a clump of friendly pines.

Alice and Asia both saw it at the same instant.

"Is that ours?" asked the child.

"I don't know."

Asia bounded to the front of the punt.

"Is that our house?" she called to Bruce.

"Asia!" exclaimed her mother angrily.

Bruce saw that the child had spoken, but he had not heard what she said. He stopped rowing.

"I beg your pardon," he answered.

Upset by her mother's tone, Asia hesitated.

"Go on, you must ask him now," said Alice very low.

"Is that our house?" asked Asia, in a crestfallen voice.

"No, not yet. I'm afraid you won't see it for some hours." He spoke naturally, but he had perfectly understood the significance of the little scene.

He and Sonny Shoreman rowed on without stopping for two more hours. Then they came suddenly upon a broad bay and beach, with a Maori settlement nestled against the low hills behind. Canoes were drawn up on the sand, and the sun shone on fields of young corn and freshly ploughed land.

They had now reached a channel that was permanently deep, and there was no longer any danger of being stuck.

Bruce stopped rowing, backed the tow-boat, put his hands on the front of the punt, and vaulted up on it.

"I have to go ashore here for half an hour or so, Mrs. Roland. I shall anchor the punt here. You will be perfectly safe," as he saw her fearful glance at the shore. "The Maoris are quite harmless. They won't come out to you. They may call, but that would only be friendly."

"Yes," she replied rather stupidly. For the first time she noticed his voice.

He swung out a heavy anchor, Asia watching him, absorbed. Then he jumped back into the tow-boat, and he and Sonny rowed ashore.

Maori children playing on the beach ran up to him, and women, brilliant spots of colour, waved their hands at him from the fields. Alice, interested in spite of herself, and Asia, in another ecstasy, both looked on at the unfamiliar scene.

"We'll get something to eat, Sonny, and have a spell," said Bruce.

Seeing by her watch that it was twelve o'clock, Alice unpacked Mrs. Harding's kit of luncheon. The children, who had nibbled at intervals, said they were still starving, so Alice spread out the sandwiches and the bottles of milk to look like a meal. Warm now under the sunshine of a glorious day, she recovered a measure of cheerfulness, and in an effort to make her children gay she learnt for the first time in her life the delights of a meal out of doors.

They had scarcely finished when Bruce and Sonny returned. Without a word the men got the boats under way again.

Acting on one of her sudden impulses, Asia took up a

packet of sandwiches, and as Alice turned to the baby, who had seized a knife, she scrambled to the front of the punt, and with friendly glee in her eyes she signalled with it to Bruce.

Alice moved round just as she lost her balance, clutched vainly at the taut connecting rope, and went down.

Before she could utter a sound Bruce, who had seen it coming, shot over the stern of the tow-boat, and dived at the sinking blue bonnet. There was an eternal moment of silence when Alice knew they were both somewhere underneath the punt. Then she heard a splash towards the rear.

"All right," called Bruce.

She heard him, but she could not move. She heard the swift strokes through the water beside the punt. She saw Sonny Shoreman haul Asia into the little boat.

Breathing hard and dripping streams of water from his pockets, Bruce struggled in, pulled the rope, and handed Asia, who was spluttering and coughing, but otherwise unhurt and unafraid, over the end of the punt.

Livid and speechless, Alice seized her and looked dumbly at Bruce. He was moved to swift sympathy at the agony in her eyes.

"She is all right, Mrs. Roland. Just change her clothes at once and she will be none the worse." Then he jumped back and went on rowing.

All Alice could feel was the sickening weakness that follows a sudden shock. She stared at Asia dripping before her as at some incredible thing. The first thing to come back to her consciousness was a realization of fresh fears bound up with this new future—new dangers to her children.

The victim of this misadventure, who even at that age had a great sense of the dramatic, coughed energetically, and exclaimed with the air of a tragedy queen:

"Oh, my nice new bonnet! It's just ruined." Then she saw her mother's face. "What is it, mother? Never mind about my bonnet. I'll make the old one do." She did not understand why she was suddenly seized and passionately kissed.

"What were you doing to fall in?" gasped her mother, as she opened a portmanteau full of dry clothes.

Asia looked guilty.

"I was going to give him some sandwiches, Mother. He didn't have any dinner."

Alice stood accused. It had not occurred to her. She flushed.

"Get your clothes off," she said.

As she stood to form a shield round the child she seriously wondered how she was to treat a workman who had performed such service as Bruce had. She was kind rather with the trained consideration incidental to habits of good breeding than with a natural spontaneity that rushed forth to meet human beings. And as a woman born in the ruling class she was inclined to take a good deal for granted in the serving class. She would not have put baldly into words that it was Bruce's duty to save her child, but she unconsciously minimised the value of his action because he was her husband's servant.

Also, in action it always took her some time to decide how far precedent should act as a guide. Faced with a new situation her first sensations were those of indecision and helplessness. After some minutes' thought she took up the remaining packet of sandwiches and moved with it to the bow. She was furious to find herself flushing.

"Will you have some sandwiches?" she asked, looking down into Bruce's steaming face.

He at once stopped rowing and stood up, while Sonny Shoreman kept the little boat end on and steady.

"I beg your pardon, Mrs. Roland." Bruce's fine eyes were as expressionless as he could make them.

She repeated her question.

"Thanks, we shall be glad to," he answered, taking the package. Then he saw that she wanted to say something more.

"I thank you—I hope you won't catch cold," she stammered, looking at his wet clothes.

He wondered why it cost her such an effort to say that simple thing.

"Oh, there's no fear of that, thank you. I'm used to it." Then, as if she could not possibly have any more to say to him, he dropped back into his seat. "Here, Sonny," he whispered, handing him the sandwiches, "eat one whether you want it or not." He helped himself to the other and then took up the oars again.

Alice sat down in the punt feeling that the incident had somehow put her in the wrong.

Sometime over an hour later the punt crawled round a precipitous point on the right, and down a long length of rippling river there stood out, at the end of a line of white cliffs, the outline of a small house against a splendid wall of bush.

The irrepressible Asia rushed to the bow.

"Is that it?" she called, and this time went unreproved.

"It is," smiled Bruce.

"That's it, Mother, that's it!" she cried, whirling about in the limited space.

She grabbed up Betty, who saw all sorts of things, but not the thing she was supposed to see.

With the baby in her arms Alice stood up again. On the right bank she saw hills and gullies, hills and gullies without end, and on the left she saw the waste of low scrub land, brown in patches from last autumn's fires.

Startled wild duck rose from hidden lagoons. Hundreds of curlew, just arrived from Siberia, fed upon the shimmering mud flats. Lines of mangroves marked the course of sluggish creeks. Nowhere was there a sign of habitation; not a clump of pines, not even the yellow line of a road.

As the punt passed in deep water close beside the bank Alice saw peeping out of the fern on a mound above two small enclosures with rough unpainted crosses falling against the rotting palings. Those unknown graves were the last straw. Bruce saw her lips quiver. He saw the look of desperation and despair in her eyes as she sank down out of his sight. And her helplessness put him on her side for ever.

When, at last, Alice raised her head again, she caught her breath. She found herself looking up a slope of grass-land at a solid pack of Scotch firs, horizon high. They evidently hid a house, for there were outbuildings, and cattle and sheep grazing in the field. They had come suddenly upon it all round an eastern headland.

Alice tried to calculate the distance between that friendly thicket and the small house at the end of the cliffs. It did not look more than three miles, but by road it might be four or five. And there would be a woman there, perhaps some impossible, rough, farm-house drudge, but still, a woman. Alice thought of babies to come, the worst nightmare of this future life, and thanked God from the depths of her orthodox soul for that clump of pines and that suggestion of home and neighbour.

As they moved on, they saw that the river turned at right angles into the west. Instead of landing immediately below the house the rowers made a detour to avoid a mud flat, round which the channel ran. This carried them over against the wall of bush to the end of a sand-spit that stretched from the bank below the cottage almost across the river, and that left only a narrow channel to carry the tide into a little bay that formed the heel of the bend.

As they approached the spit, whose rocky end made a fine landing-place, a short thick-set man with a bristly moustache, reddish hair, and a skin tanned to the toughness of leather, left the house, and walked rapidly down the bank and along the spit, where two men waited with a sledge.

Bruce observed that no handkerchiefs were waved at this end of the journey, that the babies were not held up and told to greet their father, and that even Asia displayed little enthusiasm.

When the punt finally grounded against the shells there

were no signs of eager greeting on either side, but only an obvious "Well, you're here" from the boss, and a composed acquiescence from his wife.

Tom Roland at once led the way along the spit and up the hill. He did not offer to carry anything, nor did he walk beside his wife, but sprang nimbly up the slippery grass slope in front of her, and waited impatiently now and then till she caught him up.

Asia trudged on behind, holding tightly the hand of the cross and tired Betty, who was not equal to the bumps and stumbles, at which she wailed miserably.

"What's up, you baby?" roared Roland from the top.

Bruce, following, dropped some of his load, picked up the tired child, and carried her to the door.

Crimson with humiliation, Alice gave him a short look meant to convey the appropriate amount of gratitude.

Too mentally sick to be interested, she mounted the rough block steps and entered what was to be her home. Only the two front rooms were finished sufficiently to be used. The front door opened straight into the "sitting-room," which led directly into the front bedroom. The kitchen and Asia's room at the back had yet to be boarded in and lined. Then there was to be a lean-to to contain a scullery and a small porch.

The house stood well off the ground on wooden blocks through which the wind could blow what tune it pleased. There was no question of painting it or finishing it in any way. Of course the boss had visions of something more later on. But this would have to do, perhaps for years. It was to be a makeshift, something in the nature of a picnic. Tom Roland, who had lived most of his life in the open air, had acquired the picnic spirit. It had never occurred to him that it had to be acquired. He expected his wife to produce it immediately.

Alice dropped on to a box, realizing nothing but the cross baby in her arms and Betty crying miserably over her knee.

"Oh, Mother," began Asia consolingly, "look at that lovely fire, all that wood, and that funny kettle."

Alice looked into the glowing log fire in the crude brick fireplace, and at the iron kettle hung from some invisible bar up the chimney. The comfort of it did mean a good deal in that tragic moment. She remembered it afterwards as one of the few inspiring memories of that first day. It steeled her to look round the room.

She saw that it had but one window to its three doors, which cut up its space and shrank it till its walls seemed to be closing in upon her. It was lined, but unpapered. Bags of sugar, oatmeal and flour, and boxes of tinned groceries were piled up in one corner of it. There was nothing but a sack on the bare floor. It all looked just about as hopeless and as near the end of everything as it could.

"Here, cheer up," said Tom Roland briskly. "It will be all right when it's fixed up. Kettle's boiling. We'll have some tea."

He produced the thick cups he had been using, a tin of condensed milk, sugar and tea, and in a manner that was meant to be helpful and reassuring he made it and poured it out.

Forcing back tears, Alice drank it, while Asia reduced Betty to good humour by rolling about a tin of meat.

A shadow darkened the doorway.

"Oh, come and have a cup of tea," called the boss to Bruce.

"No, thanks," he answered promptly, dropping inside the door the baskets he had carried up. He did not wait to be urged, but hurried down the slope.

For the rest of the afternoon Alice had no time to feel sorry for herself. There was too much to do.

By six o'clock the furniture was all placed and the beds set up. Then Alice put the two tired children to sleep while Asia laid the tea. Alice was deeply grateful to Mrs. Harding for a stock of cooked food, enough to last for a day or two. When she came out of her room she found Asia dancing round a table neatly spread with cold chicken and home-made bread and butter and honey and cake.

It amazed Alice to see how the child responded to this new and strange environment.

"Oh, Mother, I love this place!" she cried.

The sight of the table in the glow of the fire, and her piano in the corner, and the sun setting upon the river, and the lights upon the forest wall opposite, and the great silence everywhere made up a mass of impressions so arresting that Alice stood still for a few minutes to try to realize it all. Then she called her husband, who with Bruce was taking the last load off the sledge.

"Come along and have a snack," he said at once to Bruce.

"Thanks, but I don't think I will. They're having dinner at the camp."

"That don't matter. Come along."

"I'm not presentable," protested Bruce. "I would have to change my clothes."

"Very well, we'll wait."

Bruce knew the boss loathed waiting for anything. He felt uncomfortable, but he had no adequate excuse. He and the boss had eaten together all along. He hurried to the camp at the head of the bay, shaved, and flung himself into a suit that still bore the stamp of a tailored past. It was the beginning of a new self-respect. Never under any circumstances did Alice Roland see him unshaved again.

Alice spent the minutes waiting for him in absurd unhappiness. She was exasperated at her husband for asking him to the meal, and she felt Bruce ought not to have accepted the invitation. She knew it would be all she could do to get through without some exhibition of feeling. She thought at first of pleading, as well she might, a headache or fatigue, but she felt that would only be delaying the evil moment. She saw she would have to meet Bruce again and again, and the sooner she got used to it the better. She could not get away from him or any other people the boss might have about. In those two little rooms there would be no privacy for her. Lack of it would be one of the worst things she would have to face.

When Bruce walked into the front room at the boss's answer to his knock he was in nowise conscious of the magnitude of the transformation in himself. After his long day in the open his eyes were clearer, his nerves more steady. The minute Alice looked at him she realized the enormity of her mistake. But it seemed just then only one misery more added to a day of horrors. She dare not let herself think about it.

"Oh, you do look nice; doesn't he, Mother?" cried Asia, jumping up from a chair beside the fire and beaming upon him.

Bruce's sad eyes lit up delightfully as he looked down at her, and then he shot a swift glance at Alice, hoping to see some glimmer of response. But the day had been too much for her. She did not look at him, and he knew by the change in Asia's face that she had been sobered by one look from her mother. But he understood.

The boss saved the situation by laughing. Asia's impulsiveness, a source of woe to her mother, was to him a constant stimulus to huge amusement.

"So, youngster," he said, "you've got an eye for a man already. Sit down, Bruce," indicating a chair by the table.

They all sat down, and the boss began to carve the chicken as if he were charging an enemy. All through the meal he dispensed what hospitality there was with a flourish, showed himself absolutely ignorant of the subtleties of social intercourse, excluded Alice from the conversation by talking fast to Bruce of timber measurements, sucked chicken bones with audible approval, whistled when he was not talking, and generally destroyed the slightest chance for moments of reflection.

At any other time Alice would have been humiliated by his behaviour, but now she was grateful to him for saving her from any obligation to say a word. All she did was to ask Bruce if his tea was right and if he would have any more. He had turned to her more than once trying as naturally as he could to include her in the conversation. But when he saw that she could not or would not respond he gave it up.

Immediately after the meal, to Alice's dismay, they started to weather-board the kitchen. But the tired children slept on. Asia, too, worn out at last, fell half dressed upon her mattress and so remained.

Craving to get away from the hammering and from them, Alice slipped out through the front door. She dared not go far away lest she be wanted, and for the same reason she determined not to cry. But when she had walked a few yards over the shaving-littered grass she broke down suddenly. She sank to her feet beside a bush at the top of the rise, and burst into drenching tears.

How long she had cried she did not know when something in the night arrested her. She dried her eyes, and, sobbing at intervals, looked around her.

At her feet the tide crept lazily up the little bay which rounded off the angle of the river. At low tide it was merely a circular mud flat, swarming with little crabs, and with a few small channels like ditches branched across it, and dotted with shallow pools that reflected the sunlight or the moon and stars. To her left, three miles down the river, steep ploughshare cliffs on either side of it made a gap that seemed to cleave the fore ground from something always misty that lay beyond. The river turned again on the far side of it to run on between low hills to the Kaipara harbour. That harbour, Alice knew, opened into the Tasman Sea, and through it came many a timber ship from Australia and the world far away.

To the east of her, a mile from the curve of the bay, and towering into the stars, a double-coned mountain stretched forth its velvety shadow to meet the tide. Alice had been only vaguely aware of it that afternoon, but now she stopped sobbing as she looked at its sombre dominance. The rising moon made silver-trellised bowers upon its crest while yet the river below lay plunged in gloom. The Maoris called it Pukekaroro, the seabird's hill, because before the storms great flocks of the friendly gulls, gathering inland, wheeled for days about it, screaming into the peace of its deep ravines.

Immediately to the left of it there was another wonderful gap, like a colossal doorway, opening into a veiled vista beyond. Through it one bright star, defying extinction by the moon, still twinkled. Tom Roland had told her that behind that gap, in the biggest kauri forest of the north, lay his dreams of wealth and future glory.

Alice looked from it into the wall of bush opposite her, listening to the strange cries of the morepork and the melancholy shrieks of the wekas. From a swamp somewhere down the river came the low weird boom of a sort of bittern. All round her there was a stimulating tang in the air, and now and again a salt whiff from the open sea.

Something she had never suspected in herself rose up to respond to it all. She had nothing of the gipsy in her, but she loved beauty, more especially the beauty that was created—as she would have put it—by the hand of God. And it was the hand of God that she saw in that night, in that mountain, that bush and that river. For the moment she forgot the world that lay so far away, the familiar ways of living, the things she knew and wanted, the kinds of people who mattered to her. She looked up at the stars, and she felt that God was there, and that his protecting arm was about her.

She turned her head quickly, hearing steps beside the house. She saw Bruce coming along the beginnings of a path that had been worn in her direction. She was instantly a prey to conflicting emotions. She had not the faintest notion how to bring ease into a situation in which she had been the first to put embarrassment. All she could see was the hideous mistake and no way out of it. Never simple and direct, she could not apologize, or see that frankness might undo the tangle.

As she was partly hidden by the shrub Bruce did not see her till he was almost up to her. He made no attempt to stop, but raised his cap, said good night, and passed on. Alice looked after him as he walked on towards the camp.

Then the front door opened, and Tom Roland looked out. "Alice, where are you?" he called. "Come to bed."

She clenched her hands. She had been away from him for a month. She knew he had been thinking all the afternoon of this hour. She knew that he would not consider the fact that she was tired to death. She knew he would simply feel injured because her vitality was not equal to his own. And she knew that if, later on, the children woke up and cried she would have to get up and look after them, and that he would blame her for the disturbance. In his eyes she would not be equal to her job.

She gave one hopeless look, like that of a trapped creature, round the mountain, the bush and the river.

Then she went in.

CHAPTER II

THE carpenter and Sonny Shoreman were working on the back shed, and Asia was amusing herself, and incidentally Betty and the baby, by playing with the shavings and chips, when she saw an astonishing figure making its way among the rushes and cuttigrass bushes that dotted the slope of the green hill that rose like an overturned basin a few chains away from the back of the boss's house. She sprang to her feet and called upon the carpenter to look.

"It's a lady," she exclaimed.

He grunted assent.

"A real *lady!*" repeated Asia. Her first impulse was to rush to tell Alice. Then she remembered.

The astonishing figure came on. Every detail of its appearance was a never-to-be-forgotten fact by the time it paused beside the shed. And surely only magic could have produced that small grand old lady, in a stiff shot silk dress of green and gold, with lovely old lace folded round her shoulders, a funny little old hat of lace and velvet upon her fine grey hair, distinction radiating from every inch of her.

In her hands she carried a card-case of tortoise-shell and gold, two books, and a magnificent bunch of violets.

Her bright blue eyes rested approvingly upon Asia's golden hair, and stared with frank pleasure into the questioning depths of those dilated young eyes.

"It seems to be a case of mutual surprise, my dear," she began. "I suppose you are Asia Roland."

"And you must be the fairy godmother," was the sharp reply.

The old lady laughed.

"That is just what I shall be," she said.

As she spoke Asia's eyes fell upon the violets. The visitor noticed the gasp of delight.

"Ah, you love violets?" she said.

Asia nodded.

"I brought them for your mother. Are you not going to ask me to come in?"

"Oh, yes, please. But my mother, she's asleep. She was so tired. She said I wasn't to disturb her whatever happened. She didn't expect you, you see. Would you mind if we sat in the kitchen? It's just finished, and it's quite clean. And I couldn't wake Mother for *anything*." It all came out with a rush.

The old eyes glowed.

"Indeed, you shall not wake your mother. I shall be very pleased to talk to you."

Asia glanced at Betty and the baby, who were playing amicably.

"They will be quite good with you," she said sweetly to the carpenter, who remained quiet as to his doubts. Then she proudly led the way inside, talking quickly and with guarded softness. "I can make tea quite well. I know how—I often make it for Mother. Have you come from those pine trees? We saw them from the river. Mother wondered who lived there. You see, we feel so lonely—at least Mother does. I like it here, but Mother hasn't been used to a place like this. She doesn't like it. She doesn't say so, but I know—I always know when she doesn't like things. No, you can't sit in that chair; it isn't comfortable—I'll bring you Mother's chair."

She disappeared into the front room, leaving the old lady standing in the middle of the kitchen. She reappeared, staggering, with an ancient mahogany rocker, which she cleverly steered without bumping through the door. The fairy godmother moved swiftly to help, but was waved airily aside. Asia placed the chair in front of the window.

"Now, sit there. You will look lovely with the light on

you. Mother does. This is a special chair, very special. It was once my granny's. It came from England. Mother loves everything that comes from England. Now, you look just right."

The child's eyes, glowing with admiration, looked the old lady up and down. The fairy godmother felt a very human lump in her throat.

"Now I must put the violets into water," continued Asia. She went to the cupboard and selected a plain white enamel basin. She loosened the flowers and arranged the leaves round them. Then she buried her face in them for a minute, and sniffed energetically. Finally, she placed the basin carefully in the middle of the bare, kauri slab table.

"You must have a garden," said the old lady, who had watched her with increasing interest. "I will give you plants."

Asia whisked round.

"Oh, thank you. That will be lovely. We would just love a garden." Then, with a grand manner, "Now I will get you some tea."

The fairy godmother rocked slowly while the child turned to the open fire place, where the kettle hung singing over glowing coals. All the while she prepared the simple tea Asia chatted on with delightful importance. It was clear she felt to the last degree the exaltation of entertaining so grand a personage.

"We have no biscuits," she said regretfully, "but you won't mind, will you? I can cut bread and butter. We have a cow, so I can give you cream. Mother says it's a luxury, and we haven't many luxuries. You see, we are very poor, and you are very rich, aren't you?" with another survey of the silk and lace. "But you won't mind our plain things, will you? Mother says it doesn't matter what we have, it's what we are. And Mr. Bruce says plain things are beautiful. Do you know Mr. Bruce? I think he is lovely, don't you?"

The old lady seized this chance with alacrity.

"I do know Mr. Bruce, and I do like him. It was he who told me you had arrived. Thank you, I take sugar, one teaspoon. Mr. Bruce told me your mother has a piano. That's another luxury. Does she play much?"

"Oh, yes, it makes me feel—oh!" she clenched her hands.

"Ah, you love music too. Tell me, where were you born—in England, I suppose?"

"No, I wasn't. But Mother was. She is English"—very proudly—"I was born somewhere in Australia, Mother told me once. I think it was Sydney. I don't really remember. I wish I could remember more. It's horrid to forget things, isn't it?"

The old lady choked on a mouthful of tea.

Asia jumped up in alarm.

"Shall I slap your back?" she asked. "I always do Mother's."

But the visitor waved her back, struggling with a fresh attack. Finally, righting herself, she laughed heartily.

"You amuse me so much that I can't help laughing," she explained.

"I hope your tea is as you like it," said Asia gravely, repeating her mother's formula.

"It is indeed. It is delicious tea."

The smiling old eyes noted the composed satisfaction on the child's face.

For another half-hour Asia fired questions at her enchanted visitor, who continued to rock slowly in the warm band of window light.

Suddenly a figure appeared in the middle doorway.

"Oh, Mother?" Asia sprang up. "Here is a lady who has come to see us. She is a real fairy godmother. I have made her tea."

For a second Alice stood dumbfounded by that vision in the sunglow. Then, recognizing the type of her amazing guest, she crimsoned with humiliation to think that such an elegant person sat within full view of a bucket of dirty water, a box of saucepans, and an untidy corner of groceries, still waiting for promised shelves.

The visitor stared frankly at her tall and graceful figure, simply dressed in dark blue gingham, and at her fine head wreathed with thick plaits of copper-tinged hair. She knew instantly what was disturbing her. She rose up out of the rocker, her blue eyes full of mischief.

"Yes, I'm in the kitchen, and do you know why?"

Alice stared at her.

"Because you were tired and asleep, and must not be disturbed, *whatever happened.* And to avoid disturbing you Asia brought me here, and told me to talk in whispers. And I have not enjoyed anything so much for years. Now you know you do not have to apologize." She held out her hand.

Still too astonished to speak, Alice took it and looked at her.

"Ah, I would know anywhere that you were English," said the old lady with undisguised satisfaction.

"Yes," murmured Alice.

"Thank God for that. These awful colonials get on my nerves. They think and act as if England didn't exist. It will be delightful to have an Englishwoman to talk to again. I am Mrs. Brayton. I live at the back of that hill," indicating it with a nod, as she sat down.

"In the pines?"

"Yes, in the pines."

"Oh!" gasped Alice, unable to realize all at once this good fortune. Then she saw the violets. Tears rushed to her eyes.

"I know just how you feel," cried Mrs. Brayton impulsively. "You've been here one week, and you think it's the end of everything, and that you'll die, and that there's no God. I know. I felt that way. But I've been here nearly fifteen years, and I have grown to love it. I wouldn't live anywhere else now. You'll feel the same by and by. I have my son, and my old English servants, and my garden and my library, and all my own things about me. And I get the London papers, and the reviews and magazines. And I have a magnificent view. I tell you I love it. And you can be happy here if you want to."

Alice struggled with her amazement.

"I can see you are tragic, my dear. You must be cured of that. You must think of the compensations. You must have a garden. I will send you plants. I find there is nothing like a garden for soothing the nerves and giving one a good opinion of God's ways. And the country is the place for children and books. Nothing like it. I know the first week is paralyzing, but you have got over it now, and soon you will begin to realize the bush, and that mountain and the river. And they will mean more to you than you think. No place can bury you, my dear. We bury ourselves. I'm an old woman, so I can lecture you. And if I have stood it you can. You are young, and you have children to help you out."

Her eyes rested on Asia, who sat leaning forward, listening feverishly. Alice flushed, and for a moment there was an eloquent silence.

Then Betty and the baby tumbled in from the yard, laughable objects of dirt and crossness. Seeing that Alice was ashamed of them, Mrs. Brayton took her in hand.

"Now don't be cross with them. Children ought to be dirty and hungry. It's their natural condition. Mine always were. And what does it matter whether I see them or not? What does anything matter in a place like this except that we be human? You can't bring drawing-room conventions here, my dear. This life is real. Artificial things are ridiculous in it."

While Alice struggled with a discomposure that she could not immediately control, Asia lured the children outside with diplomatic promises of refreshment.

"Will you come into the front room?" Alice tried to smile.

The old lady wondered how any one as good-looking as she could have remained such an iceberg.

They walked into the front room, Alice carrying the rocker.

"Ah, a Brinsmead!" said Mrs. Brayton, her eyes on the piano.

"Yes," said Alice, glad that she had something good to show. By the time they sat down she had recovered some of her self-possession.

Mrs. Brayton took in at a glance the tasteless and poverty-stricken appearance of the little room. Apart from the piano there was not a thing in it to interest her. She saw that as yet there were no pictures, no books, no ornaments. She knew that the wooden sofa and the cane chairs were the cheapest things of their kind that could be bought. And she guessed that the girl before her had somewhere in the past known a very different setting. She noticed her shapely hands, the poise of her head, the unmistakable signs of generations of culture.

"Do play to me," she said, looking at a pile of music on the top of the piano.

"I'm badly out of practice," Alice began nervously. She hated to play before strangers.

"Oh. everybody says that. But you will have to begin to play to **me** some time, so why not face the evil moment now?" The old lady smiled mischievously at her.

Facing the evil moment was not one of Alice's strong points, but she could not resist that smile. Uncertainly she moved to the piano, and chose a volume of Chopin. Through nervousness she made one or two mistakes, but in spite of that she played a nocturne and a prelude with great feeling and brilliant technique.

Mrs. Brayton was amazed and delighted.

"My dear," she exclaimed frankly, "I need hardly say I didn't expect to find *you* when I set out to call on Tom Roland's wife. Now, I don't mean anything against him. He's one of the few colonials I thoroughly admire. But how could one expect that he would have an accomplished musician for a wife. Oh, what your music will mean to me!

My playing days are done, but my old Broadwood is still fairly good. You must come and play to me often. And you can play with David Bruce. Have you heard him play the violin?"

Alice's look of confusion and astonishment was not unexpected.

"No," she stammered, flushing furiously.

"You haven't?" went on the old lady remorselessly. "Well, he plays beautifully, and has kept up his practice. You have met him, of course?"

"Yes," answered Alice most uncomfortably.

Mrs. Brayton pounced upon her.

"My dear, I hope you have not been putting on airs with poor David. Let me tell you he is a gentleman. They don't breed anything like him out of England. He is one of the few people I invite to dinner. He is one of the most interesting men I have ever met. And when we English people find ourselves away in places like this we can't afford to snub each other because of a difference in the work we do. We drop all that when we leave England. When I met David Bruce first he was digging gum, but when I found out he read Voltaire and played the violin I could have fallen on his neck and wept for sheer delight. All work is the same here whether you are paid or not and whether you work for yourself or not. My dear, you are very young, and you have been here only a week, and you are feeling very badly about everything. But you will learn that there are no class distinctions here, and you must take down your barricades. I was like you. I had to. You must forgive me. I am a chattering old woman." Mrs. Brayton stood up, and put her hand on Alice's shoulder. "Don't be offended," she said.

Alice fought to keep back tears.

"I'm not offended." She tried to smile. She knew she could not resent anything this elegant old lady might say. Nothing but gratitude for the sound of that cultured voice filled her heart. But she foresaw horrible complications arising out of her reception of David Bruce.

Mrs. Brayton sat down again.

"How many children have you?" she asked abruptly.

"Three," answered Alice, grateful for the change.

"And you were a widow. You must have been married very young the first time. I don't approve such early marriages. I think English parents make a great mistake to allow them. One thing I like about this country is that the women work, and learn something about life and men before they marry."

"Yes?" said Alice, not in answer to anything.

Mrs. Brayton detected the coldness in her tone.

"How far away do you live?"

Her abruptness was almost rude, but Mrs. Brayton ignored it. She saw she had ventured on a forbidden topic.

"Our property borders yours, but we are more than two miles apart by hill and gully. Do you ride?"

"No, I do not."

"Well, you can learn. It is not hard. And then we shall seem much nearer."

"Whatever brought you to this place?" asked Alice, unable to resist the question.

"Harold came up here land hunting soon after we arrived in New Zealand. He came out purposely to farm. And as he is the only human I possess I had to come too. I wept and protested, and declared I'd die. And he said I didn't have to come if I didn't want to. And he took no notice of me. There comes a time, you know, when our children do what they want to do. And I don't blame them. It's their right, and it makes them more interesting. Of course, I wanted most to be with him, or I would have done something else myself. So I settled down to it, and we made a house and garden. Then we planted an orchard, and got cows and fowls and bees, and soon had no time for introspection. It's five years since I went to Auckland. They call it a city, that little village! I don't care if I never see it again. No. Give me my garden and my view of the river, and the smell of burnt fern, and my English papers."

Alice listened humbly to this spirited chatter. Thinking herself the only white woman of her type who could ever have met so awful a fate, she had inwardly raged all through the week, anticipating her own degeneration. And here before her, after fifteen years of it, there had stepped, as if straight out of an English drawing-room, this silk-begowned old aristocrat, fragrant with the scent of violets. In a burst of gratitude for her presence in such a place she unbent.

"Oh, I am so glad to find you here," she said.

Mrs. Brayton smiled.

"Well, you're something of a discovery yourself. We must do all we can for each other. You must have a garden and fowls. Nobody can be despondent with fowls about. I have grown to love animals, even pigs. You must make Roland put up a fence and fix up a fowl run. Haven't you any books?"

"Only a few. I have not unpacked them yet."

"What a mistake. It might have done you good to look at them. I have quite a library. You can have as many books as you want. I have brought you Mrs. Humphry Ward's latest, and a wonderful new novel called *The Story of an African Farm,* by an Olive Schreiner, new writer to me. But perhaps you have seen them?"

"I have not, and I shall be very glad to read them," said Alice gratefully. "It was very kind of you to bring them."

"Do you read French?" asked Mrs. Brayton, laying the books on the table.

"Yes."

"That's good. Do you know Voltaire?"

"No."

"Now, don't say you're a Puritan," said the old lady, who had guessed she was.

"I'm afraid I am, rather," answered Alice doubtfully.

"Then you must be cured. Puritanism is an awful disease. You must read Voltaire. I consider him as valuable as the Bible. I shouldn't like to face the world without him. Are you a churchwoman?" To Mrs. Brayton there was only one "Church."

"No, I am not," replied Alice uncomfortably.

"Not a Wesleyan, I hope," in obvious alarm.

Alice laughed suddenly, her whole face lighting up. Mrs. Brayton thought it was a pity she did not laugh oftener.

"No, I am a Presbyterian."

"Oh, that's all right," with great relief. "It's a state church anyway, and they do educate their parsons. We have a nice young curate in this diocese. He will be coming to see you. I hope you will come to the Kaiwaka church sometimes. There is no Presbyterian church anywhere about."

"Thank you, I will come."

"Dear me,"—Mrs. Brayton rose—"I shall be left out in the dark if I stay any longer. I want you and your husband to come to have dinner with me some day next week, say Friday."

"Oh, thank you," as they walked towards the door, "but I can't leave the children."

"That's true. Well, I'll get Eliza King. She's a good, reliable girl. She lives at Kaiwaka, and often works for me. I'll send her down to look after them. They will be quite safe. She's excellent with children. And she will ride, and can go home at any hour. She is not afraid."

"But, please, I can't allow——"

"You will just allow me to do as I please, my dear. You can't come without some one to look after your children. I want you to come. I'm pining to know how the world looks nowadays. I'm just as glad to discover you as you may be to find me. I shall send Eliza King on Friday. And come early in the afternoon so that you can see my garden. Oh, and bring Asia—yes, now, I won't forgive you if you don't. And don't say you haven't any clothes, or any nonsense of that kind. As you have told your child, it isn't what we have, it's what we are that counts. If you talk philosophy to your child, live up to it."

They had walked out of the front door and round the house. At Mrs. Brayton's last words Alice laughed again, meeting the old lady's eyes.

"What a joy to have such a child," said Mrs. Brayton.

Before Alice could reply they came in sight of the back door and David Bruce, who had some fresh fish in his hand. He put them down on the doorstep, and turned.

"Oh, David, how are you?" cried the old lady. "I've expected you up for your violin."

"I can't shake hands, I'm fishy," he said, raising his cap to them.

"Well, if you are not busy you can walk up to the fence with me, and see me through. I nearly tore my dress coming down."

"With pleasure."

"Good-bye, my dear," said Mrs. Brayton, turning to Alice. "I shall see you next week, and remember when you are inclined to feel blue that, whatever happens, you will have an Englishwoman, and"—with a nod at Bruce—"an Englishman to see you through." The gloved hand rested for a moment on Alice's arm.

Alice mumbled something, but could not keep a tremble from her lips. She turned away hurriedly, went inside, locked herself into her room, and wept.

After saying good-bye to Asia, who had rushed at her from the kitchen, Mrs. Brayton stepped out with Bruce up the field.

"I've invited the Rolands to dinner next Friday. Can you come too?" She looked quizzically at him.

He smiled back at her.

"Not with them just yet, please."

"I see. She hasn't discovered you."

"That's nicely put. She is very young and uncertain."

"And very proud and conservative. But very attractive,

isn't she? What the devil made her marry a man like Tom Roland?"

"Hanged if I can guess. He has great qualities, but I doubt if they appeal to her."

"She won't like his skirmishes with other women."

"Well, my dear lady, what woman would?"

Mrs. Brayton laughed.

"Oh, some of them don't worry. They go and do likewise."

"I dare say. Should you think of suggesting it to Mrs. Roland?"

"Don't be absurd, David. Heavens! But she is armor-plated, isn't she? If I had a husband like that and a child like that I should find it rather a strain keeping up the family dignity."

"I should say she does."

"We must educate her out of it."

"Yes? I think you'd better go gently."

"Oh, I have won her now, David. It's you who have the work to do," laughed the old lady. "It is rather a dramatic thing, isn't it, that a group like that should have landed up here?" She looked round at the mountain, the river and the bush.

"It's just as dramatic that you should have landed here," he smiled. "I should like to see her face when she meets your house and garden."

He held the wires of the fence apart for her, stood a moment as she walked on, and then returned to the bay.

CHAPTER III

HAND in hand, Alice and Asia paused at the wooden gate outside the double wall of pines.

"Oh, Mother," whispered the child breathlessly, clutching her hand.

Through the trees they saw hot masses of colour. They heard the deep hum of a billion bees. They sniffed a sensuous air heavy with known and unknown scents. Trembling with anticipation, they opened the gate and stole in a yard or two, only to stand again.

Some gardens, like great masses of complex machinery, arrest and fascinate the intellect, and satisfy one's sense of arrangement, of clockwork management. They have no mysteries, however, no nestling places, no dream-compelling nooks. But inside that phalanx of pines above the river there grew a wonderful garden with all these things; a garden of dreams, a garden riotous with life; a garden of brilliant sunlights and deep shades; a garden of trees that hid the stars and of shy flowers barely peeping from the ground; a whispering garden full of secrets and suggestion; a garden where there was always something more to know.

Trees from England, trees from the semi-tropical islands, and trees from the native forest grew there side by side. There were creamy magnolias, pink and salmon lasiandras, sweet laburnum, banana palms, white trailing clematis, the scarlet kowhai and bowers of tree ferns. Azaleas and jasmine and lilac and mock orange bushes were dotted about at random on the lawns. There were beds and beds of stocks and geraniums, and roses and sweet-williams, and snapdragons and larkspurs, and lupins and lilies, and late narcissi and anemones, and early gladioli. There were jonquils in the grass, and violets and primroses filling up odd spaces everywhere. There were honeysuckled summer-houses and ivy-wreathed stumps, and marble bowls on rough stone pedestals overflowing with creepers. Climbing roses arched the pathways; damp thatched pavilions sheltered fragile ferns. A natural spring bubbled up to form a trickling stream that flowed, hidden by ferns, through a corner and on down the hill in a little gully of its own making to the river.

Everywhere in that garden trees and plants and shrubs leapt at you from the earth, with a wild joy in living, in spreading, in grasping sunward.

In the midst of it, half smothered in creepers, stood a bungalow house, surrounded by broad verandas, every one of them a sweet-scented arbour calling one to pause and stay awhile.

Alice stood still, fighting back tears. She could not then or ever after put into words what that revelation had meant to her.

"Mother, don't cry," said Asia pitifully. "Are you afraid?"

"Sh!" she answered harshly.

Just then a piercing scream curdled their blood. But before they could move there stepped into the sunlight on the lawn a few feet away a peacock, with his tail outspread. He stood still as he saw them, proudly displaying his glory to their astonished eyes. A peahen who had followed, stopped too, regarding them curiously.

Asia felt queer. She was certain now that by some invisible magic they had been spirited off to Fairyland.

The creaking of a wheelbarrow on the path broke the spell. Mrs. Brayton came into view and saw them.

"Oh, there you are," she called, dropping the barrow. "What is it? Oh, the birds. They won't hurt you. Come on."

She wore an old and grimy Holland dress, short to immodesty, her son declared, showing in full her frayed elastic-side boots and thin legs. Her little hands were lost in thick leather gloves, her head hidden in a straw hat tied under her chin. Anything more unlike the fairy godmother of the week before could not be imagined.

"I'm afraid we have come too soon," began Alice.

"Indeed, you have not. I have expected you for an hour. Did you think to find me dressed up, and sitting in my drawing-room with my hands folded, wasting time waiting for you? Well, you were wrong, you see. Now, will you like to see my flowers?"

"Yes, please," said Alice warmly.

The old lady saw they were overcome. It was one of the delights of her life to spring her house and garden upon the unwary. Many an unsuspecting curate, fresh from England, and sore at his exile into the northern wilds, had landed at that garden gate to be astounded, and humbled, and grateful, and stimulated and educated by turns. Many a derelict from a titled English home, driven by degeneration to the gum-fields, had strayed there, to get once more a glimpse of what he had left behind, to have self-respect for an hour again, and to learn what was happening in England from the lips of an Englishwoman, whose voice stirred up a horde of good intentions, destined only to pave hell as of yore, as well she knew. But none the less her house and her news and her time were for every one who, passing by, came in to beg a share of them.

"You must have flowers to take home," said Mrs. Brayton, "all you can carry, and you can pick them yourselves, anything in the garden." Detaching a pair of scissors from her belt, she handed them to Asia. "There, my dear, you cut them off, nice long stalks, but don't pull at them to disturb the roots."

"Oh, she won't——"

"Yes, she will do it quite rightly. She can't hurt anything. My garden belongs to everybody. I am particular about my conservatory. I don't give things out of it, and I notice that it's always getting blights and insects. I suppose that's a judgment on my selfishness. You are not picking anything."

"I can't believe that I can. It doesn't seem real," said Alice nervously.

"Oh, nonsense! This isn't a public park. Help yourself. Asia, show your mother how to pick flowers."

The child got the spirit of it first. She rushed about in ecstasy, pointing at things she wanted, and looking at Mrs. Brayton for approval. The approval never failing, she began to believe it was all true, and helped herself. Alice followed more timidly, not taking the biggest and best things, as Asia did, till her arms, too, were full.

"Oh, Mother, isn't this lovely?" Asia ran up to her with as many kinds of flowers as her arms would hold.

Mrs. Brayton's eyes grew misty as she looked at them. It was obvious to her that life for them had lacked many simple joys.

"What can we do with them all? We have nothing to put them in."

"You have bath-tins and buckets," said the old lady. "Use them."

Alice smiled into a cluster of tea roses.

Mrs. Brayton led the way to the front veranda.

"Asia, rub your boots well," said her mother fearfully.

"You can take them right off, my dear, and keep them off till you go, if you won't catch cold. I love children in their bare feet."

This was another shock to Alice, who began to realize that her notions of propriety would never be any use here. Asia took her boots off on the veranda mat, and then fearfully, reverently, as men tread before the shrines of their gods, they entered by a wide-open French door a large library and music room, which opened through an archway upon a rose red drawing-room.

Before they had time to get more than a first blurred vision, Mrs. Brayton rang a little bell, and there appeared in the doorway a prim and aged maid in a black dress, with a spotless cap and apron.

"Tea, please, Mary. And will you help me to carry out these flowers and put them into water."

"Yes, ma'am."

Instantly Alice felt as if she were back in London. It could not be a dream. She must be there. That particular kind of "Yes, ma'am" in the wilds of New Zealand was absurd, a figment of the imagination. She did not know that many a man from the gum-fields, that even Bruce, had felt as she did about it.

"Sit down," said Mrs. Brayton, "and excuse me for a few minutes. I must clean myself."

Left alone, Alice and Asia stared in wonderment about them. Facing them, on a pedestal in a corner by the archway, stood a cast of "The Winged Victory" of Samothrace. Round the walls, above the rows and rows of books, hung engravings of the great cathedrals of Europe. An open fireplace in plain brick took up a quarter of the wall opposite the drawing-room. On the mantelpiece was a row of old brass candlesticks, and on the hearth heavy old brass irons. Set straight before it was a deep faded lounge, on which a whole family could doze and dream. A grand piano filled in one corner. Bowls of flowers, and bronzes, and busts of great musicians stood upon the top shelves above the books. There were well-worn Persian rugs upon the dark, polished floor.

The drawing-room was an old-fashioned, over-crowded treasure house of things dear to the searcher after the choice and the antique. Rare engravings and quaint water-colours, in tarnished gilt frames, hung on the faded pink walls. There were cabinets full of china and glass, of old silver and jewellery, of enamelled and metal snuff-boxes, of fans and curios. Valuable Chinese and Japanese porcelain vases stood in corners and against the walls. Elaborate beadwork fire-screens hung from the white marble mantelpiece, upon which stood four great silver candelabra.

An alcove made a little gallery for a group of Apollos and Venuses and Muses. There were polished inlaid tables, with slender legs, and graceful chairs covered with silk and tapestry. Two spider-legged lounges looked comfortable with an abundance of cushions. The floor was completely covered with a crimson carpet. Three French windows, hung with rose silk curtains, opened out on to the veranda and a gorgeous bed of stocks.

Everything glowed with the voluptuous light that filtered through those hangings. The white Venuses were toned to a delicate pink, there were luminous splashes on the Oriental vases, and deep red lights waved over the beaded screens.

It was not a room to talk in. It was too swamping, too luxurious. If you sat in it for long you wanted to get back into the library, where you got the fascinating suggestion of it. It was an enervating room. It affected you like an overhot bath. It made you want to lie down and doze and dream among the cushions. But, seen from the cool, severe library, with its restrained tones of cream and brown, the red room was stimulating and alluring, like a Mephistophelian vision of a forbidden feast.

Alice sat half dazed. It was too incredible to be at once believed.

Thinking her mother absorbed, Asia gradually wriggled off her chair, stood up, and stole cautiously towards the drawing-room.

Alice came back to reality with a start. Her nervousness made her unusually sharp.

"Asia, come back at once. You must not move, or touch anything, or make a remark about anything. You hear me?"

"Yes, Mother," said the child, sitting down sadly. She was craving to explore and ask questions about everything she saw.

In a few minutes Mrs. Brayton returned, the fairy godmother again, in black velvet and lace. She was followed by the maid with the tea.

"You did not expect to get a real English tea within a fortnight of your arrival, I'm sure," she smiled. "Do you know Oscar Wilde? Now don't look horrified. He writes awfully clever things, and people will all be talking of them in ten years' time. He says that to expect the unexpected shows a modern intellect. Now if you had had a modern intellect, you would not have suffered half as much as you have about coming to these wilds, for you would have known that something surprising would turn up. I'm always preaching. You will get used to it."

The maid handed Alice and Asia their cups of tea, and then retired.

"You have been living in Auckland boarding-houses for some time, I believe?"

"Yes," answered Alice, wondering how much of their private life Roland had told her.

"Ah, a sort of fifth-rate Bloomsbury atmosphere, with everything, from your soul to your washing, under the eyes of the landlady. I know. Demoralizing! It would take the sense of adventure out of anybody. And I should imagine that a New Zealand boarding-house without English service would be like a bed without a mattress."

Alice laughed.

"I cannot say that I enjoyed the life. But it was convenient. And as my husband did not decide for some time where he would buy bush, we could not settle down in a house."

"No, of course not. How long have you been in New Zealand?"

"A little over five years."

"And before that you were in Australia?"

"Yes."

"That's where I was born, wasn't it, Mother?" broke in Asia. Then she knew by the look in her mother's eye that she had broken one of the commandments.

"Yes," replied Alice forbiddingly.

Mrs. Brayton saw that Alice froze at the approach of

personal questions. To divert attention from the subject she turned to Asia.

"My dear, you needn't sit up like a statue all the time. Give me your cup. You may get up and look at my things."

Asia looked at her mother, obviously perplexed.

"Oh, I see," went on the old lady, "you have been instructed not to. Well, your mother only meant till I gave you permission. I know you won't touch anything. And be careful not to bump against things."

Wild with delight, and with her hands carefully folded behind her, Asia trod as if she were in a room full of people with headaches. She was too overcome to speak. She stole about, standing, rapt, in front of things that attracted her. Once she put out her hand to pat a luxurious chair, but drew it back fearfully, and looked to see if she had been observed. Mrs. Brayton, who had been conscious of her impulse, gave no sign.

Soon afterwards, forgetting the laws of behaviour and all the accumulated "don'ts" of her past experience, Asia whirled round, bursting with excitement.

"Mother," she whispered loudly and feverishly, "come and look."

Mrs. Brayton was quicker than Alice.

"You go and look," she commanded almost fiercely. "Don't you ever refuse that request in my house."

Alice was too astonished to be offended. She felt that something personal and tremendous lay behind the old lady's tone and flashing eye. Without a word she rose and walked to the archway, and took the impulsive hand that Asia thrust at her.

"I couldn't help it, Mother," said the child sadly, suddenly remembering.

"Never mind," said Alice gently. "What is it?"

Asia pointed through one of the French windows at the peacock, who stood there looking as if he were about to walk in.

Mrs. Brayton, following, shook her fist at him.

"Will he come in?" asked Asia excitedly.

"Quite likely. I found him gazing at the piano one day last week."

Asia gave a little shriek.

"Oh, do let him," she said.

"I don't know, my dear. I don't want him to develop the habit. He will knock things over. You can shoo him away gently. And then you can run about the garden for a while. But don't go near the bees."

Alice returned with her to the library.

"Don't try to dominate that child. Reactions from domination are inevitable. And they are very painful things. And think less of behaviour and more of being human." Mrs. Brayton squeezed Alice's arm.

With a sick feeling of inadequacy, and hating to feel she was in the wrong, Alice sat down. It had never occurred to her to doubt her method of training her children. No one had ever dared to criticise her management of them. But she could not resent Mrs. Brayton's words. She only felt hurt to think she fell short in the eyes of the old lady, who had already gained a strong foothold in her affections.

Mrs. Brayton ignored her change of manner.

"Now, I want you to play to me," she said.

Emotionally charged, and determined to make the most of her one accomplishment, Alice went to the piano. Her delight at the beautiful tones of the old instrument helped to kill her nervousness. After a few bars she felt herself alone. As she played the Appassionata and the Pathétique it seemed to Mrs. Brayton that the spirit of Beethoven walked about that lonely house set in the pines, that the music in his soul mingled with the hum of bees in the garden and the sigh of the winds in the trees.

Asia stole in from the garden and stood silent by a doorway.

Alice played to a world of her own, to something in herself that had no other means of expression. She played with delicacy and with passion, with unerring feeling for balance, for light and shade. Mrs. Brayton felt that her music was the result of more than natural gifts.

When she had finished Alice sat looking helplessly at the keys. She knew she had revealed capacity for feeling, and she wondered why she hated having people know how she felt.

"Oh, my dear, what a treat!" said the old lady hoarsely.

Alice turned, and was overjoyed to see what her playing had meant.

Just then they heard whistling in the garden.

"That is your husband." Mrs. Brayton rose to meet him.

Alice was annoyed that he should arrive at that moment. Then she realized that he had been asked there to dinner several times, on his own merits, before he could possibly have gained any glory by exhibiting her as his wife. And he had dared to whistle familiarly to announce his approach through that garden.

Tom Roland entered boisterously, a hurricane of vitality. The Venuses and the Apollos seemed to sway as he passed.

"Well," said Mrs. Brayton gaily, "how's the bush?"

"Oh, pretty good. Tramway's begun. Soon you'll see the logs coming like greased lightning down that slope to the bay. Things'll hum, I tell you."

"I'm sure they will," she laughed, sitting down quickly, lest he should do so first, and be a fresh cause of humiliation to his too-observant wife.

In his rough tweed suit, hardly clean, he dropped into a tapestry chair, his reddish head against a background of "The Winged Victory." He stretched out his legs, and beat a tattoo on the chair arms, his green eyes roving.

"My dear," said Mrs. Brayton to Alice, with a twinkle in her eye, "your husband has turned us all upside down. Men from the gum-fields and boys from the farms are all flocking to his standard. He's a born leader. But he is wasted here. He should have been in the army."

Tom Roland laughed shortly.

"Oh, she don't appreciate me. She ain't interested in the bush."

"Well, she has never seen one. I was not interested till you took me through those wonderful trees that day. And you know I think you are a vile Vandal for cutting them down."

"Pooh! If you thought of things like that you'd never do anything."

"Quite true. The race is not to the delicate. It's to the ruthless and the strong."

"Don't know anything about that. But I do know that if you are a ninny you never get anywhere, and you never get anything done." He poked a finger into one ear, and tapped with his feet upon the carpet.

Mrs. Brayton laughed.

Alice, who had moved into a low chair, sat back, watching them. In that incredible afternoon this seemed the most incredible thing of all.

Ever since her marriage to Tom Roland she had avoided bringing him near the few friends she had made. She saved herself the pain of contrasts. His long absences had made this easy. Now she was face to face with the most vivid contrast she could have imagined. And it was not working altogether as she had expected it would work. She could not help seeing that the fastidious English lady tremendously admired the unpolished colonial.

She was glad when Harold Brayton came in. He represented things she was familiar with, manners she expected, responses she wanted. And he knew what she stood for in life, and appreciated her. She did not mind that he was a mild person who would never get anywhere, that he was not an empire builder. He was an English gentleman. That was his password to her esteem.

But she saw her husband in rather a different light before the evening was over, and as they walked home, with their arms full of flowers, she told him she would like to see the bush.

CHAPTER IV

"THERE, now, we begin to see them," said Mrs. Brayton.

She stood with Alice, Asia and Roland on a cleared track in the gap beside Mt. Pukekaroro. They had come up through the fern and the scrub and the outer fringe of bush by way of the cleared line cut for the tramway. They had passed one gang of men laying rails, and they now stood at the place where the low bush ended and the real forest began, with an open avenue before them, cut as far as they could see down a slight incline through a glorious tangle of undergrowth. The sunlight, sneaking through the tree-tops, picked out spots upon the mauled and trampled ground, and on the trunks of trees, and in the vivid heads of giant ferns.

With a catch of her breath, Alice saw, towering up out of the green depths on either side of that open way, row upon row of colossal grey pillars, seemingly as eternal as the hills, losing themselves above in a roof of impenetrable green. The pungent smell of their innumerable little cones mingled with the heavy smell of banks of moss about their roots. A faint sound of the morning breeze stirring in their topmost fringe of leaves leaked downwards.

"There!" Roland put down the luncheon baskets he was carrying, and waved his hand airily at them. "Best bit of bush in the colony. Nothing to beat it outside of California. Those trees have stood there thousands of years. Might have stood there thousands more."

"And you are going to cut them down!" exclaimed Alice, as if it were sacrilege.

"You bet I am. Great job too. Takes some tackling." He was proud that he had dared to stake everything he possessed on this great adventure. He knew that he was being discussed in Auckland business circles as a bold spirit and as a coming man.

"I've told you what I think about it," said Mrs. Brayton.

"Rot!" laughed Tom Roland. "What would you have people live in in this country? Timber is cheaper than bricks. Those trees make houses for the poor. Somebody has to cut 'em down. Look at the people who can own their own houses in New Zealand. Why? Cheap land, cheap timber. Something you don't have in England. And you talk sentiment to me! Pooh! Come on." He took up the baskets.

After they had moved on a little way they heard the reverberating sounds of axes swung by a gang of men working on ahead.

Alice walked silently, Asia as usual holding her hand, and gasping and pointing at intervals at things that thrilled her.

They had now been three weeks at the bay, and Alice had learned that there was a village at Kaiwaka, two miles past Mrs. Brayton, where six houses, a church and a store stood within sight of each other. She had learned that there was a fortnightly mail. She had learned also that there were possibilities in Tom Roland's scheme, that there would soon be a village at the bay, with its store, and some day even its school.

She had learned, too, that she might be able to live on by the river without having daily visions of premature decay and death. She was twenty-eight, and healthy, and she knew she would take some killing. She had begun to see the sense of trying to fit in, of readjusting her sense of values, of learning the language that belonged to the mountain and the river.

On two afternoons in the last week she had taken the children to the top of the green hill behind the house, and had sat under the straggly cabbage trees. She had looked across the gully at the block of pines, and had pictured the old lady in the garden within, and the peacocks strutting on the lawn. And she had looked down the river through the gap at the low hills, indigoed in the vista beyond, and at the walls of forest to the north, and at the mountain cutting a great wedge out of the eastern sky.

Then her thoughts came back to the babies pulling grass beside her, and to Asia making daisy chains. She saw how they loved it, and because it was going to be good for them it had to be good for her. She was determined that, outwardly, at least, she would be cheerful about it. She knew that Mrs. Brayton was the chief factor in this effort at reconstruction. Already she loved the old lady with a passion born of years of longing for some kindred spirit.

As she walked, crumbling twigs and chips underfoot, Alice felt around her the stirring beginnings of things. No one could have realized that invaded silence of ages, have seen those violent assaults upon eternal peace, without feeling that it was a big thing to break in. She heard Tom Roland talking of tramways, of engines and trucks racing along the slopes, of dams and waterways, of mills and ships, as he outlined once more his plans for future greatness. And there was something powerfully arousing about it all. It had fired Mrs. Brayton. It began to fire her.

The ringing thud of axes, the crackle of disturbed undergrowth, the sounds of voices and the clanging of iron tools grew louder. At the end of the avenue they came out upon a clearing beside the rocky bed of a shallow creek. It was here they were to see felled one of the kauri trees.

Roland explained that this was to be the site of a camp and tool and truck depot. Four tents stood to one side. Near them a group of men were putting up the framework of a wooden building. Great piles of rough hewn sleepers were stacked up here and there. Logs had been jacked to one side, and the earth flattened by their rolling over it. The ground was covered with chips and small branches crushed into the loose soil. Men in all kinds of singlets and dungarees were sawing logs, squaring sleepers, clearing away the wrecks of tree heads, and making ready to dynamite a large stump.

"There's our tree," said Roland, pointing straight across the clearing at a grey pillar, exposed against the forest background. "Biggest we've tackled yet. It's right in the way of the tramway."

They saw men at its base blocking an unsightly gash upon its farther side. Roland laid down his baskets.

"They'll be ready soon," he said, moving forward to a group of men, whom he hailed with a free and easy air.

With varying degrees of accuracy of aim and thoroughness, they all sent a hand to their heads or caps as they caught sight of the women of the party.

Alice saw David Bruce standing some distance away, guarding the dynamite. Her eyes rested on him for some seconds. Asia saw him too.

"Mother, there's Mr. Bruce," she said, as if she were claiming an old friend.

"I see," said Alice frigidly.

"My dear," broke in Mrs. Brayton, "do you see that thin, fair man talking to your husband? He's the son of an earl. There are some queer mixtures in this bush. Just look at this face nearest us. Roland says he is the most reckless blackguard he has ever known. They call him Shiny. They must be a sweet family to manage. My God! What has he done?"

The man named Shiny had suddenly dropped his axe, and doubled up with a violent volley of oaths.

"Oh, he's hurt," cried Alice, and to the astonishment of Mrs. Brayton, she ran towards him. She saw blood gushing from his thick boot. "Tom," she called. But already two men had reached his side, and Alice heard Bruce's name shouted sharply.

Shiny stopped blaspheming as he saw her.

"Pardon, ma'am," he said gruffly, as he began to undo his boot.

As Alice stood helpless, with no notion as to what to do

first, but with an instinctive feeling that she ought to help, David Bruce ran up. She saw the men gathered round make way for him, and she saw that he was the man for that emergency.

"Rags," he commanded.

"And salt," added Shiny.

Two men started for the tents. Bruce knelt down, and as he pulled off Shiny's boot a jet of blood shot out from the gashed foot. Alice turned her head away. Then she forced herself to look back.

"I have clean towels," she said to Bruce.

"Yes, please," he answered, looking up at her, as he closed the wound with his hands.

As she hurried to the luncheon baskets she wondered if the look in his eyes had been meant for approval, and she knew she hoped it had been.

By the time she reached him the men from the tent ran up with a bundle of rags and the kitchen bag of salt. The wounded man, who had sat up throughout, reached for the latter, and dived his dirty hand into it.

"Lord! man," exclaimed Bruce.

"Best thing to stop bleedin'," answered Shiny defiantly.

"Yes, if you can stand it."

Bruce took off his sock, and Shiny rammed the handful of clean salt into his gaping, squirting wound. They saw him clench his hands, but he never made a sound. Even the boss looked at him with admiration.

Alice leaned down with her towels.

"Thank you," said Bruce, looking up again into her face. He made a pad of one towel, cut the other into strips, and rapidly bandaged the foot and doubled up the leg.

Alice walked back to the place where Mrs. Brayton stood holding Asia's hand. Somehow the accident had affected her feeling for the place, had put a touch of kinship into it that was not there before.

"That man put a handful of salt in that cut, and never groaned," she said hoarsely.

Mrs. Brayton smiled.

"Why not? They have marvellous nerve, some of these men."

"Are there often accidents?" gasped Alice, anticipating fresh horrors. "What will they do here without a doctor?"

"Why, there is a doctor. David Bruce is a doctor. Didn't you know that?"

Alice looked at her, too amazed to speak.

"Yes, my dear. He isn't registered in New Zealand, and can't practise for money, but he is a fully qualified English surgeon. He could get registered any time he chose. He's the only doctor this place is likely to have. And it's lucky to have him, considering Dr. Mount, of Maungaturoto, is eighteen miles away."

Alice looked down, overwhelmed by the thought that had entered her mind.

The group about Shiny had broken up, and now Bruce and the boss and one of the men were carrying him to the camp. The women waited where they were till Roland returned.

"Nasty cut," he said. "Good man, too. No use for a week or two now. Always the way when you're in a hurry. Now, they're about ready over there."

He set off towards the creek, and called to the men who were working at the base of the tree. It was to fall across the stream, and a little to one side. Roland selected a safe spot in the clearing, some sixty yards from it.

A sharp whistle rang out. Some of the men laid down their tools to watch. There were cries of "Ready," and answering calls from those in the danger zone. Then the little group of fellers put in the last wedges and drew away from the base of the doomed tree.

"Now, then," said Roland.

The little party stood tense, their faces turned upwards to the magnificent head of spreading branches stretched into the deep morning blue. There was not yet a quiver in all the dark mass of foliage, no sign of capitulation to the wanton needs of man. Straight as the course of a falling stone the slaty grey trunk shot up seventy feet without a knot. Nothing could seem more triumphantly secure.

Suddenly there was a suggestion of quiver. The sky line wavered.

"She's coming," said Roland.

The whole world seemed to lurch, slowly, slowly; then the top branches shook, the great trunk swayed, the foundations cracked. The whole tree gave one gigantic shiver, poised for an instant, suspended, hesitating, and then, realizing as it were, the remorselessness of fate, it plunged forward, filling the whole visible world, and cracking horribly, till its longest branches caught the ground with a series of tearing, ripping sounds, preliminary to the resounding roar as the massive trunk struck and rebounded and rolled upon the earth.

The air was filled with dust and flying twigs, the whole clearing shook, and from the sides of Pukekaroro the echoes came rolling back. There followed a short extraordinary silence, into which there returned by degrees the familiar sounds of the axes and the revolving handles of the jacks.

"There, that's over," said the boss cheerfully. "I guess we can have lunch now. You stay here. This is a good place by the creek."

He could not understand why Alice had tears in her eyes, or why she looked at him as if he had committed a crime. He set off for the luncheon baskets, swinging his arms and whistling gaily.

Mrs. Brayton, Alice, and even Asia stood silent till Bruce came up to them.

"I'm afraid you will have to move," he said. "We are going to dynamite a stump, and things will fly about a bit. Will you go to the edge of the forest there, by the creek?" He led the way. "This is safe," he said finally, selecting a spot, where he left them.

"There are times when I hate being a woman," said Mrs. Brayton with disgust. "This is where you and I are nobody." Folding her heavy tweed skirt under her, she sat down upon a rock. "This is why men dominate us, my dear," she waved her hand at the clearing. "Sheer brute strength."

Alice, who had always been a drawing-room woman, took her words too seriously. She looked round the clearing at the various evidences of that brute strength, and felt herself trapped into submission by it. Never in her life before had she been face to face with such an exhibition of physical power. It overwhelmed her with a sense of her own helplessness.

"Mother, look!" cried Asia, pointing to the stump.

With a loud explosion, the earth about its roots heaved up, and the stump itself was lifted several feet into the air. Then it settled down, the torn roots obtruding.

Asia danced about, shrieking with delight. Killing her impulse to subdue her, Alice sat down beside Mrs. Brayton.

"No wonder women have to submit to men," she said dejectedly.

"Goodness! Don't say that! I've never submitted to them. My dear, you don't know how to manage them. They're more afraid of our tongues than we are of their muscles. Cultivate a tongue."

Alice smiled doubtfully at her. But she said nothing, for she did not want to convey the impression that she did not know how to manage Roland. Asia rushed up to her.

"Mother, is Mr. Bruce coming to our picnic?"

They saw him coming towards them with the boss.

"Very likely." Alice tried to speak naturally.

Mrs. Brayton was amused at the sudden change in her. Asia ran to meet the men.

"You are coming to our picnic?" she cried to Bruce.

"I have been invited," he answered solemnly. He had not had a meal with them since the day of their arrival, though it had sometimes been difficult to dodge Roland's peremptory invitations.

"Oh, how nice," said the child.

Alice bowed with restrained courtesy as Bruce raised his hat to her. The boss examined the ground around them.

"Yes, this isn't a bad spot. We can make a fire there. Did you bring a billy?"

"Dear me, no," said Mrs. Brayton.

"Plenty at the camp," said Bruce promptly. "I'll get one."

"Oh, may I go too, Mother?" asked Asia.

But Alice silenced her by a look.

"Good heavens!" burst out her husband. "Nothing will harm her. The men won't eat her. She's got to get used to them, anyway."

"Oh, very well." Alice flushed with anger as she turned to unpack the baskets. She hated interference between herself and Asia, and this incident was enough to spoil the day for her.

Bruce and Asia returned immediately, the child swinging the tin can. She was allowed to fill it with water from the creek, and then the boss fixed it cunningly on cleft sticks above his fire, while Alice spread out the lunch on a clean table-cloth. Mrs. Brayton had supplied most of the food. There were two chickens, ham sandwiches, home-made bread and butter, and honey.

The fire blazed merrily beside them and the stream trickled slowly along its shallow stony bed. The clearing had grown strangely quiet as one by one the men had thrown down their tools and gathered in the kitchen tent. Intermittent sounds of gruff laughter drifted over to them. The sun shone out above the clearing in a cloudless sky. They smelt the earth, and the sweet chips, and the moss and the fern on the banks of the stream. Black and white fantails flew about them inquisitively, to Asia's delight. The breeze murmured in the forest behind.

"Now, what's wrong with this?" demanded Roland, looking at his wife, as he set down the boiling billy. "Don't this beat your drawing-room teas?"

Alice determined to be pleasant.

"I think it is very enjoyable," she said.

They arranged themselves around the table-cloth. Asia sat herself next to Bruce, and during a lull she fired one of those bombshells that had made Alice decide a dozen times never to go out with her again.

"Mother," she said, looking very puzzled and serious, "I wish you would like Mr. Bruce. I think he's lovely." Then she choked on her sandwich as she saw the swift gleam that flashed across her mother's eye.

For an instant there was one of those awful silences when a group of people are struck dumb, self-conscious, helpless, before the open expression of things they are not accustomed to express.

David Bruce did not lose his presence of mind. His profession had taught him to deal with people as children. He had found that simpleness and naturalness could take the wind out of the sails of the most persistent convention.

He turned his sad eyes upon Asia, who was looking as if she were on the verge of tears.

"I'm glad you like me," he said gravely. "But that is no reason why everybody should, or why they should show that they do in the way you show it. Don't you know that everybody is different? Don't you know that we all like different things and different people, and that we all have different ways of showing that we like the same thing? When you see something you like you jump into the air, and shriek, and clap your hands. Now, I like lots of things you like, but I don't jump and shriek at them. I did when I was a boy, but we alter as we grow up." He took a deliberate bite out of his sandwich and went on. "You think that because your mother doesn't call me David, as Mrs. Brayton does, or rush at me and take my hand, as you do"—here Roland broke into a loud guffaw—"that she doesn't like me. But all people treat me differently, even all the people who like me, and why shouldn't they?"

Asia was now looking up at him with great interest. He had been determined to restore her peace of mind. He could never bear the unhappiness of children. He had a very different feeling towards adults who manufactured and perpetuated so much of their own embarrassment.

"Why are people different?" she asked.

"We don't know. But don't you think it's a good thing they are?" He smiled.

"I don't know," she said, very puzzled. "I think grown-up people are very queer."

"Yes, my dear," he said gravely, "we are often very queer and very stupid, and I'm sure I don't know why we are." There was a note of weariness in his voice.

"Shall I be queer?" she asked. She had now forgotten the origin of the conversation.

"Very, I should say," he replied with emphasis.

And at that Mrs. Brayton and Roland laughed loudly.

"Oh, dear," said Asia.

"Oh, never mind," smiled Bruce, his eyes lighting up. "Everybody else will be queerer than you."

During this time Alice had sat forcing herself to eat and drink. She had not dared to look at anybody. For the first moment she had been too sick to think. She had always felt embarrassment as positive pain. She had never been able to cope with a difficult situation. And she was one of those who always make the situation worse for everybody else. The worst thing about this was that her attitude to Bruce had been put into words. She felt now as if a net had been drawn round her from which she could never escape. The thing said was so much worse than unsaid. She would hear it when she looked at Mrs. Brayton. She was afraid Roland might speak about it to her.

But, as Bruce had talked on, another element had entered into her feeling. She was amazed at his simpleness and naturalness, and at the power of personality that lay behind his management of the situation. He had done so easily what to her was an impossible thing. In spite of herself she had to admire him and be grateful to him.

She could not recover her self-possession during that

meal, but she managed to get through it without attracting attention, or she thought she did.

Mrs. Brayton got a chance after lunch to speak to Bruce.

"David, what an awful moment! How could you manage it like that?"

"Good Lord! When you have stood by as many death-beds as I have, and have seen the backyard side of people as I have, you don't get upset by trifles."

"It was awful for her."

"It didn't have to be. But some women enjoy misery. When she has had enough of it she will decide to enjoy something else."

"She is beginning to like you, David."

He laughed.

"She is progressing that way. Three weeks ago I was a piece of machinery. To-day I am at least a human being."

"Good," laughed the old lady. "I shall expect to hear next week that you are practising the Kreutzer Sonata together."

He smiled.

"If she's considering that in a year's time she will be very smart."

"Well, David, if you can't do better than that——" Her eyes gleamed with mischief.

He raised his eyebrows at her. But he knew there was no serious significance in her words. Smiling at her, he turned back to his work.

Mrs. Brayton, Alice and Asia walked back to the bay together in the middle of the afternoon.

The conversation consisted mostly of Asia's questions and observations, and of Mrs. Brayton's answers. Alice made painful efforts to appear natural, and to make casual remarks. Mrs. Brayton helped her by providing all the diversion she could. They stopped to pick ferns and moss, and the old lady explained how they could be kept fresh by careful treatment. She told Asia the names of the trees and the creepers. She told them the strange history of the rata vine, the powerful forest parasite, and by good luck found one of the chrysalis worms from which it is said to grow. In spite of herself Alice wás interested in this story. She was astonished at Mrs. Brayton's fund of information, and envied her her lively interest in everything.

That night, soon after they had finished dinner, Bruce knocked at the boss's back door. He had in his hands the luncheon baskets that Roland had forgotten to bring down from the bush. Alice was just walking out to shake the table-cloth when his figure loomed up in the doorway. The light of the kitchen candle fell upon his face. Bruce ignored the fact that she started and flushed.

"I've just brought your baskets, Mrs. Roland," he said.

"Oh, thank you," she stammered, not daring to look at him. Then nervousness drove her to ask after the injured man.

"He's getting on all right, thank you. He isn't worrying. They rather like accidents, some of those chaps. It gives them a rest."

He was turning away when Roland, who had heard his voice, called from the front room.

"Oh, Bruce, is that you? Come in and give me a hand with these calculations."

While Alice and Asia washed up, the voices of the two men checking figures formed a low accompaniment.

"Asia," said her mother, as she hung up the damp towels, "I am going outside for a while. You go to the children if they cry."

Wrapping a shawl round her head and shoulders, she walked out into the spring night, along the cliffs to a spot where a huge solitary totara tree grew precariously upon the edge. She sat down upon one of the uncovered roots, and with her head in her hands gazed down upon the river, running still under the stars. There was not a sound of lapping against the white beach at her feet.

Alice and Roland had been married four years. They had met in Christchurch soon after her arrival in New Zealand. In a tragic moment, when she was almost penniless, and sick with dread of the future, he had been kind and helpful. Something told her that he was honest with her, but she had not borrowed money from him without much prayerful consideration. When he suggested that she should come north to Auckland where he lived and knew many people, and where he promised to get her the music pupils she needed, it seemed too much like the finger of the Lord for her to refuse. After many appeals to God to help her, she finally accepted his offer because there was absolutely nothing else between her and starvation.

Roland had done all that he promised, and more. He found her music pupils, and he financed her beginnings. He took her to a quiet boarding-house kept by a friend of his, where she was comfortable and decently fed. He managed her all along by his frankness, his general decency and his vitality.

He had proposed marriage to her almost without any previous signs of affection. He had been rather blunt about it, but she thought that was due to nervousness. She had taken a week to think about it. Every time she was in danger of refusing she had looked at Asia. Every time she was in danger of accepting she had looked into her own heart. Finally, with her eye on Asia, she had accepted him, but not entirely without feeling for him. She saw that people liked him, and she guessed that he would get on. And she was attracted by his impulsive kindness, and by his sweeping energy.

And so she had married him, determined to do her duty, and hoping to get some happiness by the way. But very soon after the marriage the incompatibilities began to assume those undreamt of proportions that are the despair of those who would do their duty. Before a year was over Alice felt that a good deal of her had died.

Roland's reasons for marrying her had been a curious mixture of impulsive need of affection, and business acumen, and a satisfaction in being benevolent. He saw in her a poor, but beautiful young widow, who would very well fit in with his schemes for future greatness and social recognition. He would never have admitted his class inferiority, but in his secret heart he knew he valued her largely because she belonged to the class that ruled the world. Naturally, he expected a return for his money, and he looked for that when he proposed to her. But at the same time he had a comforting sense of his own goodness in rescuing her from the necessity of making her way slowly by teaching the piano.

There was more heart in it, however, than either he or she suspected. And it was this unsatisfied heart in him that drove him to the other women. To them he went for the stimulus and affection that she could not or would not give, and back to her he came for the logical conclusion that she never refused, because she had contracted to give it.

They had never openly quarrelled. Once or twice, when he had become blustering, she had risen and left the room, afterwards ignoring the breaks. There were times when her calmness nearly drove him mad. But he had extraordinary common sense, and he knew it was useless to rage at her. Within a year he, too, had begun to see that something he had hoped for had gone out of their union, if, indeed, it had ever been in it. The thing that annoyed him most was that he could not make her love him. He felt that something tumultuous lay beneath her calm. It piqued his curiosity. He tried to be good to her. And he wondered why the devil he was always wrong. He was just as determined as she was to do his duty.

Thus far they had drifted when they came to the bay. Ever since learning of the isolation of the bush life, Alice had looked forward, with alternating moments of resolute calm and wild despair, to a future of self-suppression save in so far as she could grow again in her children. The possibility of any other man in her life had never occurred to her.

On this day of the picnic it entered her consciousness for

the first time. She had felt before this that something about David Bruce challenged her. Her thoughts had turned to him many times in those three weeks. Now the knowledge that he was a doctor forced her to think of the possibilities arising from his position. If her children met with sudden illness or accident she would have to send for him. Intimacy seemed to be inevitable. And then she had always surrounded doctors with the halo that most women put upon them and curates, and bishops, and reformers, believing them to be the props of mankind.

Seized with a premonition of evil, she stared up at the stars and then at their reflection in the river. She now saw in Bruce the unconscious breaker of her fine scheme of life-long martyrdom. This meant that he was another thing to fight. She must kill her impulses even to think of him. She tried to feel that she had thought of him only because she had treated him badly, that it would be quite easy not to think of him any more. Because of her behaviour to him she knew he would make no advance, and the best thing would be just to go on as she had begun, and let him think her cold and distant. She could be courteous, of course.

But she was secretly afraid of her impulses. She could not understand why any one who hated them as much as she did should have them so violently. She had been taught and she still believed that impulses were monstrous inventions of evil to be fought and suppressed. Her own experience had already taught her their terrible results. The assurance that "Whom the Lord loveth He chasteneth" had never filled her with the satisfaction said to be enjoyed by those who believe that God uses them to demonstrate eternal laws.

For years she had lived so apart that she did not realize how in the world about her the impulses and instincts had begun their innings, backed up by biology and the Individualists, as powers to be discussed, lauded, developed, and allowed to run their riotous course unchecked. She did not know that the instincts had now accumulated a cult, along with the eugenists, the feminists, the cremationists, and Bernard Shaw.

New Zealand, even more than any other part of the world, seethed with the atmosphere of social and moral experiments. But, in its boarding-houses, the last stronghold of organized prudery and artificial and anæmic chastity, no wandering vibrations of the Zeitgeist had ever reached her. No thought of having any fun with any other man had ever entered her mind. She did not see any human relation as fun. And the mere thought that she might come to care for David Bruce filled her with alarm.

But, she reflected as she sat there, if nothing ever began there would be nothing to fight. All she had to do was to prevent the beginnings. She began calmly to think of ways and means. Her treatment of David Bruce now seemed like a blessing in disguise. She would go on as she had begun; that is, she would keep him at the distance she had already made inevitable. In any case there was nothing else for her to do. There was no reason for her to like him if she did not wish to. There was no reason why she should openly accept him as anything but a mere acquaintance.

After all, it was simple. Duty always was when you faced it clearly. She realized that above all things she wanted peace. She thought of her compensations. She had Mrs. Brayton and her children; she had her music and her books. She had a home, such as it was. And there was her husband. She knew now that he was a power in the land. He would make money, and perhaps he really meant to do his best for her and the children. She determined that she would try to think better of him. With tears dropping from her cheeks she bowed her head under the stars and prayed to God to help her.

Then she got up and walked calmly and serenely home.

CHAPTER V

ALICE started back from the kitchen fireplace. The dusk was closing a late autumn day. When the sounds outside became more clearly defined she turned towards the door with a breath of relief. She knew the footsteps very well.

"You sent for me, Mrs. Roland?" Bruce's form filled up the small doorway.

"Yes."

Alice stood back in the shadow. It was apparent that in a month or two she would have another child, and, as the attitude of mind that had been imposed upon her demanded that women be ashamed of motherhood or of its signs before the event, and blissfully idiotic about it immediately afterwards, she blushed whenever a man came near enough to see her. Bruce, who had seen previous blushes, guessed that she was blushing now.

"There were two men here this afternoon, looking for my husband," she went on. "I didn't tell them how long he would be away. Did you see them?"

Bruce felt that she was frightened. He knew something unusual had driven her to send for him. It was the first time she had ever done so.

"Yes, I did," he replied. "They went off some time ago. That's all right."

Just then his eye rested on a heavy iron camp oven set on the hearth. When he had seen it that morning it had stood in the woodshed.

"Mrs. Roland," he said sharply, "are you lifting that oven about?"

Alice was so amazed at his tone that she answered meekly "Yes."

Bruce took a step into the kitchen, anger in his eyes.

"Mrs. Roland, do I have to tell you that you are committing a crime against yourself; a most unnecessary crime? I came here this morning to know what I could do for you, and you could have asked me to bring it in."

She felt condemned.

"I'm used to lifting it," she said weakly, in justification of herself, and without thinking what her words implied.

"Used to lifting it!" repeated Bruce.

"I mean, when my husband is away," with a return to dignity. But that was a lie, and she knew that he knew it.

"Then in future, Mrs. Roland, when your husband is away, you will please let me know when you want it moved. You will not lift that oven again. Your doing so is an insult to any decent man on the place. Do you want it put out now?"

"Yes, please," she said helplessly. She stood as void of volition as a straining post as he swung to the fireplace, and grasped the oven by its semi-circular handle.

"The woodshed?" he asked.

"Yes, please."

Hot and cold by turns she watched him swing it out. Then he came back to the door.

"Is there anything else I can do for you, Mrs. Roland?"

"No, I'm sure, thank you."

"You have enough cut wood?"

"Yes, plenty for a day or two."

He turned.

"Oh, do you know where Asia is?" she asked.

"I haven't seen her since she brought me your message, but I'll hunt her up."

"Thank you," she answered.

Bruce got as far as the kitchen window when he turned and retraced his steps.

But he was no longer the doctor. He had become the foreman again.

"Mrs. Roland, if that money is worrying you, perhaps you

would like me to take charge of it till Bob Jones comes for it. He mayn't be here for a week, and it's a big responsibility. It would be quite safe with me."

"Oh, I don't think that is necessary," she said nervously, but striving to be calm. "It ought to be quite safe with me. And besides, my husband left it in my charge."

He saw it was hopeless. She was too proud to show how frightened she really was. Knowing the likely effect upon her of fear and responsibility, he was angry at her stupidity. There was nothing to do, however, but to accept her decision. He turned away again, leaving her more wrought up than ever.

He guessed that she imagined that every man about the place knew of the plant of money at the boss's cottage, awaiting the arrival of the bush contractor. He knew she would think that the desperate-looking tramps who had applied for work that day had come to take stock of the house with a view to robbery. He was sure her nights were one long agony of fear. But against her impenetrable barrier of reserve he was as impotent as a jellyfish. It made him furious.

Bruce had gone warily with her in the past eight months. He had never forced a moment with her, but he had given her chances, not too obvious, which she never took. He knew that she avoided him, and he could not understand why. She had become courteous. She had managed to smooth down the bald uneasiness of her beginning into a routine of indifferent pleasantness. But she never sat in the front room while he and Roland worked if she could possibly avoid it.

In the last two months, since the completion of the store and the arrival of Bob Hargraves, who was to be bookkeeper and storeman, they had done most of their night work in the store, and Bruce had been only rarely to the boss's house. He knew Alice had employed Sonny Shoreman to milk the cow, to cut wood, and to run what errands there were. But Sonny had now gone to work in the bush.

and so, since Roland's departure three days before, Bruce had called morning and evening, as a matter of course, to ask Alice what he could do. He found that the boss had arranged with Bob Hargraves, who was a cheerful and obliging soul, to milk the cow. Of his own accord Bob had also seen to the wood, so that it did not leave Bruce much of an excuse to call.

He was the more surprised, therefore, when Alice sent for him. And as he walked away from her he wondered exactly what she had wanted of him. He felt it was more than the assurance that the tramps had gone.

At times he felt badly about her attitude towards him. She attracted him, and he could see no reason why he should appear disagreeable to her. He could not believe that pride alone was responsible for her continued aloofness. He did not ask that she should treat him as an intimate friend. He knew that sort of thing was not to be had for the asking. But he felt that he had a right to demand that she should get off the defensive with him, that she at least should treat him as if he were the decent man he knew himself to be. And this last he was determined to make her do.

He thought savagely now, as he strode on down the slope towards the sandspit, of his one lapse in that eight months, when he had ridden away to Hakaru, the place that boasted the best public house for miles around, where he had whiskied himself dead to the world for a week. For two weeks after his return he had not gone to the boss's house, and when he did, and had first met Alice's eye, he had felt, with terrible sensitiveness, that he saw in it, veiled with Christian pity, a deep condemnation and disgust. It made him hot to think of it.

He paused on the path. Just below him, set in the low rushes on the bank, loomed the framework of the new blacksmith's shop, with a corner of the store projecting beyond. Down from the head of the bay, across the mud flat, over the spit in front of the store, ran the elevation for the tramway to deep water, still in process of construction.

A shapeless black cloud curled over the northern range, bringing premature darkness upon the river. An erratic wind, now wheezy, now snorting, rustled and clicked through the cuttigrass bushes. Bruce stood awhile, enjoying the sadness in the moaning of the wind and the gloom in the shades about him. He was mostly too busy to enjoy such luxuries as reactions to the atmosphere, but when he did take time to respond to the voice of nature he got something that he remembered.

He heard footsteps crunching on the shells. Asia came running round the end of the cliffs, a chain or so away. She panted towards him. When she reached him he saw by her eyes that she, too, had been caught by something in the night.

"What do you think?" she began mysteriously. "There are two men round in the old boatshed. They came to the house this afternoon and frightened Mother. Now they're there. I saw them. I played Red Indian, and followed them. They shouldn't be there, should they?" Her eyes were alight with the spirit of adventure.

"They should not. But I'll settle them. Now, don't tell your mother about it, will you? Let her think they went away this afternoon." He put his hands on her shoulders.

She looked up puzzled.

"That's lies," she said.

"You needn't tell any lies," he smiled. "Don't say anything at all."

She still looked puzzled.

"Why is Mother so frightened?" she asked.

"Is she frightened?"

"Yes, she's often frightened, and yet she says God takes care of us. And she's been worse lately, and it makes me afraid too." She looked up at him with a worried expression in her eyes.

"Oh, don't you worry about it," he said reassuringly.

"Your mother is not very well, that is why she is nervous. But she will be better soon."

"Do you believe we are quite safe? Do you know God takes care of us?" she asked abruptly.

"Yes, I know that you are quite safe," he answered firmly.

"Then, why have you been up the last three nights sitting in our woodshed?"

Startled, he looked down into her face.

"You saw me?" he demanded.

"Yes."

"Did your mother see me?"

"I don't know. But I didn't tell her, because I thought you did not want us to know."

"Thank God for that!" he exclaimed, forgetting he was talking to a child. "Do not tell her that, either, will you?"

"What were you doing? Were you taking care of us?" she asked.

"Yes," he said frankly.

"Then God doesn't take care of us?" she cried, startled.

Bruce hesitated.

"We have to take care of ourselves as well," he began, "and not do foolish things. Now, listen while I explain to you. Your father left a lot of money in your house when he went away. That was foolish, because somebody might try to steal it. Your mother knows that, and so she is frightened. And that is why I came to take care of you."

But she was not satisfied.

"Then why didn't you come in and stay with us?" she demanded.

Bruce groaned inwardly.

"But your mother would not like us to know she is afraid," he replied.

"That is silly!" She stamped her foot. "When I tell her you sat out in the cold she won't mind, I am sure she won't——"

"You must not tell her," said Bruce firmly. "Now,

please, remember. There is a reason why I do not want her to know. And I am all right outside. And I will take care of you. Don't be afraid any more. Nothing can hurt you or come near you. Now, to please me, you just keep it all a secret."

Her eyes glowed with importance. She felt it was wonderful to have a real secret with him. She seized his hands.

"Oh, Mr. Bruce, you are lovely," she cried. "I just love you, lots."

He laughed, ignoring her fervour.

"Go home, Red Indian," he said, "and think it is all a story, and don't be afraid."

She ran joyously up the hill. Bruce stood for a moment watching her; then he walked on towards the kitchen.

The big zinc building near the head of the bay was now the scene of its second daily scrimmage. Some forty men, in all stages of crude cleaning up, stood about outside, washing at basins set on boxes, rubbing down soapy faces, or diving into boxes underneath their bunks for garments that seemed no cleaner than the ones they were discarding.

There were old men and young men; men of finished and unassuming blackguardism, and crude youngsters swaggering with first knowledge. There were men who had decency still healthy, but not obtruded upon an unsympathetic world; men who remembered their mothers. There were men who did not know what decency was, and who, to use the current phrase, would have robbed their mother's coffins.

There were strange social inequalities in that gang. English university men bunked next to the colonial born sons of pioneer traders. The men who still got literary reviews and scented letters read side by side with those who revelled in Deadwood Dicks and got no letters at all.

Individual eccentricities were lightly taken and sometimes curiously respected, provided they were not paraded as a virtue. The one thing the motley group would not stand, individually or collectively, the one thing its members could detect instantly was "side," and any man who arrived with affectations soon had them as effectually knocked out of him as he would in a big public school. The nomad of the bushes is a grim realist. He has no use for the trimmings.

But he does cherish a secret admiration for those men who, being superior, do not parade the fact. Every man in that crowd liked the boss. He worked with them. He ate with them. He swore with them. He was extraordinarily fair with them. He had a way all his own of being familiar, and yet, at the same time, commanding their respect.

And every man liked David Bruce for quite different reasons. They would have found it much harder to say why. The fact that he was a doctor had a good deal to do with a never-mentioned sentimental regard that entered into the feeling of many of them. But they would have liked him whatever he had been. His fine physique and athletic training were assets to be reckoned with, but it was his simplicity and straightness in all his dealings with them that commanded their attention most.

As he strode into the kitchen now, men near his bunk made way for him.

"Going to shoot somebody, doctor?" asked Shiny, catching the expression on his face.

"Probably," replied Bruce calmly, hauling, to their surprise, a revolver out of the box beneath his bunk. "I want a volunteer," he added.

"Me," snapped Shiny.

"Come on, then. Bring your rifle."

Bruce turned to the cook, who was putting what he called the finishing touches to the long, bare table, laden with tin basins of potatoes and cabbage, and dishes of tinned meat. The steam rising off them dimmed the glasses of the kerosene lamps hanging from the beams above.

"I'm after those tramps, Jim. They've been hanging round all day. Did they come here?"

"No," replied the cook.

"All right. We'll give them a meal. Then they'll have to get out. We'll be back in about half an hour."

Bruce lit a lantern, and was followed out by Shiny, who was as jolly as a boy at the prospect of a diversion.

When they heard the cautious steps upon the sand, the two tramps drew back into a corner of the boatshed. But the light of a lantern turned suddenly upon them revealed them clearly to their captors, and showed them Shiny's rifle pointed inconveniently straight in their direction.

"Hands up!" he roared.

As they knew they had no hope in a fight they obeyed.

"Come here," commanded Bruce. "I ordered you off hours ago. I told you you could go to the kitchen and get some food. And I told you you hadn't a chance of getting work with us. You couldn't last a day at our job. And the trouble with you is that you don't look as if you wanted work. I don't wonder the farms turned you down. Now, before we do anything for you we'll see what you've got. Go through them, Shiny."

Bruce covered them with his revolver while Shiny turned out their pockets, and overhauled them carefully. A few pence and a couple of knives was all he found. The wretched wasters, sick, hungry and desperate, made no attempt at protest. They had honestly tried to get work, but for weeks every man's hand had been against them. They had heard two men say the night before at the Hakuru public house that Tom Roland was a fool to leave money where it could so easily be got at, and they had been drawn as by a magnet to the bay that day to see if there was any chance for them. Under the guise of asking for work they had taken stock of distances, and their short interview with Alice had shown them that she might easily be frightened into silence. They had not had anything so desperate as murder in their minds. All they wanted was money.

"Hm!" grunted Bruce, as he saw all that they possessed. "That looks pretty hopeless. Come on. We'll feed you first."

Bruce could not show how badly he felt about the wretchedness of life for such as they. But he showed more sympathy than they expected as he asked them where they had tried to get work.

Back at the kitchen the tramps were seated at the end of the table, where they ate silently, their heads down, and refused to be drawn into conversation. When they did not answer the more friendly questions the crowd began to bait them mercilessly, to ask them about their love affairs, and what hotels they preferred, and the brands of wine they would recommend. David Bruce listened for some time in silence. Then he stood up.

"Here, shut up, you fellows," he said good-humouredly, "and pay for your fun. These poor devils haven't a bob between them. Now you wouldn't find starvation interesting, even as a new experience. Come on, you've all got something you'll waste in the course of the next week or two." He put half a sovereign on the table.

After every man had found something he could spare Bruce handed nearly six pounds over to the tramps, who became obsequiously and pitifully grateful.

"Now, I'll see you down the road to Point Curtis," said Bruce.

He lit the lantern, and they followed him out to the accompaniment of a bombardment of coarse suggestions as to how not to waste the windfall. As they went round the head of the bay Bruce told them they could get a gum outfit at the Point Curtis pub, three and a half miles down the river, and that they would be shown the way to the gum-field where they could easily make a living digging gum. When they had gone half a mile down the Great North road he stopped. The moon was just coming over the top of Pukekaroro behind them.

"Now, listen to me," began Bruce, peering into their faces, "don't you come back here. We have done all we'll do for the present, and if you make yourself a nuisance look out! British law hasn't arrived here yet, and some of us aren't particular how we do up corpses for the Almighty. But if you go on that gum-field and keep straight, and get some strength up, you can apply for a job later on. Go on, no thanks necessary."

He stood looking after them till the sound of their footsteps died away on the road. He knew they were pretty hopeless, but he had to give them the chance. He heard two weeks later that one of them was drowned while drunk in the river by Point Curtis. He never heard of the other again.

Returning to the kitchen, he sat down outside and smoked till some one came out to ask him to play.

Bruce always enjoyed the incongruity of music in that kitchen, walled with its rows of narrow bunks, with its bright nickel lamps hung from the central beams, its colossal fires in the open zinc chimney, and the limp figures of the men smoking or reading on their beds, or playing poker at the corners of the table. Later on, Bruce and many other men built shanties and houses for themselves, but at present the whole force of workers about the bay was crammed into that one building, with as little room as the sailors have in the fo'c'sle of a battle-ship.

Bruce didn't play down to his audience unless they asked him to. Sometimes the crowd would hum to an air they knew, but mostly they listened in silence. When he was in the mood—as he was this night—some men would drop books, and with their hands over their eyes be carried back to something they had valued. Bruce's music was the one thing they were not ashamed to show feeling about.

When he had played for an hour, he put away his violin, and went out, not to meditate on his past, as some of them supposed, but to play watch-dog to the boss's wife.

CHAPTER VI

"ASIA, it's time you went to bed." ¶ Alice did not say it convincingly, for she dreaded being alone.

"Yes, Mother," said the child, understanding that it was not an order, and making no attempt to move. She sat in a tangled attitude on the narrow sofa, her head bent low over a dilapidated *Boys' Own Annual* that Roland had bought for her at an auction sale in Auckland, her brains on fire with the adventures of a party of explorers in *The Silver Canyon.*

The glow of the open fire, rivalling that of the kerosene lamp, played on the bare walls of the front room. It had been lined, but was still unpapered. A plain, oblong table, with a flowered cover, stood in the centre. The floor was now covered with a new linoleum of much too large a pattern—Roland's choice—but there were no rugs. On the narrow mantelpiece was a row of Alice's books, Tennyson, Browning, Charlotte Brontë, Cowper's poems, Drummond's *Ascent of Man,* Butler's *Analogy,* Paley's *Evidences, The Pilgrim's Progress,* and some children's books—*Line Upon Line, Peep of Day,* and more modern ones issued by the Religious Tract Society. There were no knickknacks anywhere, and no pictures. Alice's piano, which seemed to fill up half the room, suggested magic rather than plain fact.

Alice sat with a heap of mending beside her, but she was so restless that she could hardly sew. She had been getting more and more wrought up each day since her husband had left for Auckland. On his previous absences she had been nervous enough, but she thought that as time went on she would get used to it. Now the responsibility of the money imposed upon her nervous condition was driving her fast toward hysteria. The appearance of the tramps that day was the last straw. After they had gone she worked herself into a fever fighting her desire to send for Bruce. The mere sight of him, she felt, would steady her nerves, and she wanted to be sure that he was about. But she did not want him to know that she was frightened, she did not want him to offer to do anything. She only wanted to be sure that he was there, within reach.

For over an hour she had kept going to the window to look for him, but not once had she caught a glimpse of him. Finally, unable to resist the impulse, she had sent Asia after him, and had then dreaded his appearance, not knowing what she could say. His words about the tramps had somewhat reassured her, but his words about the camp oven had charged her with another kind of excitement. It seemed to her to be such an intimate incident. He had assumed the right to take her in hand, and she knew she had been helpless to resist him. After he had gone she sat down, sick and trembling, her nervousness increased. She thought of sending to ask Mrs. Brayton to come down to stay with her. But she felt this would be an appalling confession of cowardice. She knew she would have to be alone again and again, and she told herself she had to get used to it. But, as the evening wore on, she wondered how she could possibly get through another sleepless night.

She jumped up suddenly, walked to the front door, opened it and looked down upon the starlit river, and up at Pukekaroro, looming dark against the moon. Then she heard the sound of Bruce's violin. She stood there listening till the music stopped. Then she found that she was very cold. She shut the door and put more wood on the fire.

She tried the experiment of repeating hymns and religious poetry. But she was terrified to find that the thought of God failed to help her. It grew late, but she said nothing more about Asia's going to bed. When it was nearly eleven, however, the child got up of her own accord, kissed her mother good night, lit her candle, and went out through the kitchen to her little room, which opened off it. The one window opened towards the back with a view of the bare hill.

Asia did not undress. Instead, she put on an old astrakhan jacket, and knelt down to pray that her mother would cease to be afraid. Then she took a dark blanket off her bed, wrapped it round her legs, and sat down by her open window, gently pushing it open further till the lower sash was up as far as it would go. She meant to watch for David Bruce. Since she had begun to read the *Boys' Own,* her mind had been a ferment of adventure and romance. Men were wonderful beings, she thought. She was full of exaggerated notions of their strength, their beauty, their tenderness, their care for women. Precocious beyond her mother's imagining, she knew also that there was something else, something mysterious, that made them creatures to be looked up to, feared and obeyed.

She had known the first night that she had seen David Bruce in the back yard that he was there to do something for them, and she instinctively felt that he was in some way taking the place of Roland. She knew he must be cold and uncomfortable, and she immediately made of him a hero. With his big body, and his kind eyes, and his gentle ways, and his unafraidness, he seemed to her the very incarnation of all the heroisms of her favorite heroes in the *Boys' Own.* And because he was a hero she had to be the heroine. And she would rescue him from the cold. This night she meant to make him come in to her bed, while she indulged in a riot of sacrifice by sleeping on the mat. So she sat watching for him.

Bruce crept cautiously by way of the cliffs to the paling fence at the back of the yard, and sat down on a low stump. From the store he had seen the light still burning in the front room, and he was afraid lest Alice should look out. He was not at all easy in his own mind about the money. There was more than one man in the boss's employ to whom £400 would be a formidable magnet. It would be easy for any one of them to get away to one of the great northern gum-fields, lie low for a time, and then ship by way of a timber vessel to Australia. So Bruce had let the impression gain ground among the men that he was staying at night in the boss's house on guard. They all knew he was armed.

This night Bruce was very weary, and he wondered how he was going to keep awake. He sat on till he was sure Alice must have gone to bed. Then he made his way slowly round the fence to the side gate and got safely into the yard without having made a sound. He started as he caught sight of Asia at the window, and shook his fist at her. He could see her mouth opening and shutting silently, and her fingers beckoning, but he waved her back.

Just then, as she sat in a frenzy of fear over the dying coals in the front room, Alice felt there was somebody about. With a courage born of sheer desperation, and to save herself from screaming she jumped up, moved to the front window and pushed aside the blind. But there was nothing to be seen in the moonlight but the things that were there by day. Then she walked quietly out into the kitchen. Asia, hearing her, gasped and gesticulated wildly at Bruce, who did not see her as he turned to pick up his rug.

Alice went straight to the kitchen window, and pulled aside the blind. She saw the figure of a man crouching in the yard. She gave one frenzied shriek, and fell in a heap on the floor.

Sick and trembling, Asia rushed to unlock the back door. Bruce almost fell over her.

"Light a candle," he cried, as he dashed into the kitchen. By the light of it he gathered up Alice's contorted body, carried her into her room, and laid her on her bed. "Get me a pencil and paper."

Asia ran to get her own candle, found her pencil and a piece of a paper bag, and hit her big toe badly as she ran back to him. He almost snatched the things from her and dashed off a note.

"Take that to the kitchen, give it to Bob Hargraves, and tell him not to lose a minute. And, child," he was now aware of her scared face, "don't be afraid, be brave. I shall want you badly to-night. Come back as fast as you can." He gripped her shoulders with hands unaware of their strength, and put more into her than he dreamed.

Primed with those words and that grip she flew to the kitchen, hammered on the door, and gasped her message to the first man who spoke. Bob was one of the few men in camp who owned pyjamas, which he stuck to in spite of much chaffing. He did not wait to change after reading Bruce's note, but snatched up a case of instruments from Bruce's chest, and yelling "Get a horse, somebody," he bounded out of the door, and got to the boss's house with Asia chains behind him. Back at the kitchen, he slipped on his lightest boots, and rode off as he was, bareheaded, for the only maternity nurse Kaiwaka possessed.

When Asia got back she found that Bruce had already made up the front room fire. Directly he heard her come to the bedroom door, he said:

"I must get the children into your room."

As he carried them out they woke and fretted, but she soothed them to sleep again. She had only just got them quiet when she heard Bruce calling her.

With a fierce excitement burning her from head to foot she hurried to and fro getting the things he had ordered. Action kept her thoughts busy. She did not feel the finger she scalded or the toe bleeding inside her woollen slipper. She felt that she was important, and that she had a fine opportunity to show Bruce how useful she could be.

It was not until she sat down with everything ready that she began to wonder what it was all about. She could not bear the inaction. She felt that something strange and terrifying was going on in that closed room, and she wanted to go in and help. She knew she would not be so frightened if she could see. She went desperately to her mother's door.

"Mr. Bruce, the water is all ready," she cried miserably.

"All right. Don't come in. Go back to the kitchen," he called curtly.

Before she had been back there long Bruce was calling for hot and cold water.

Action helped her again. She hurried with two jugs to the bedroom door. He took them without looking at her, and quickly closed the door, shutting her out from that horrible unknown. She wanted to scream, to beat her hands upon the door and beg to be let in. She felt that whatever it was if she could only stand beside Bruce she would feel better. Then she remembered that he had told her to be brave. She went back to the kitchen, and made up the fire there to keep herself warm.

In spite of her efforts tears poured down her cheeks, but she was careful not to be heard.

As she shook and sobbed the bedroom door opened, and Bruce called her again.

"Bring me a little hot milk; don't boil it."

That helped her. Hot milk was such a plain everyday fact. She prepared it carefully, and called from the front room when it was ready.

This time he saw her face.

"Oh, child." Again his hand gripped her shoulder. "Don't be frightened. She is going to get better now. Be brave."

Tears of relief rushed to her eyes. But he had no more time to spare for her. Once again he turned and shut the door.

Asia walked back to the kitchen fire sufficiently relieved to begin to be conscious of her burn and her bruised toe. She looked at the blister on her hand, and wondered if she had better put some vinegar on it. But she was now almost too tired to bother. She sank down on the sack in front of the fire, and believing that her mother was really better, she fell asleep.

She was partly roused by the sounds of a horse's hoofs

galloping up the slope to the cottage. As in a dream she heard Bruce walk through the kitchen to meet Mrs. King at the back door.

"'Ope I'm in time. I was away with Eliza at the Hakaru dance," puffed the steaming countrywoman.

"It's over," Bruce said. "Child born dead. She's very low. She will have to have very careful nursing. I gave a little chloroform. I'll send for Mount. There may be complications——" Their voices died away in the front room.

At last Bruce came into the kitchen. Asia rose stiffly from the floor half dazed and rubbing her eyes.

"Poor child," he said, holding her tight against him.

She sat up in his arms, feeling better and safe now that he was there.

"Why, look at your hand," he said.

"Oh, I scalded it," she said in a tired voice. "And my toe hurts too."

"Dear me, we must doctor you now," he said lightly. He was distressed to see how exhausted she looked. So he made a great fuss over her burn and her badly bruised toe, and bandaged them both carefully with rags, and was glad to see that he had successfully taken some of the shock out of her. Then they heated some hot milk, and drank it together, and then he ordered her to bed.

"Will you come and tuck me in?" For the first time since the accident she resembled her old self.

"I will," he smiled.

He went into her little room when she called to say she was ready. Her red and swollen eyes glowed at him from the pillow. The babies slept peacefully on their mattress on the floor. As he tucked her in, Asia flung her arms round his neck.

"I think you're just—just beautiful," she choked, looking into his tired, lined face.

He understood.

"Now, don't think I'm a hero out of a story book. I'm

just a mere mortal. And you've been a fine brave girl. Now go to sleep, because there will be a lot for you to do to-morrow. Good night." He kissed her on the forehead.

He was relieved to see five minutes afterwards that she was already asleep.

Feeling pretty much of a wreck, he went to consult with Mrs. King. When he saw that the patient was resting safely, he threw himself down on the inadequate sofa in the front room to get a little rest before daybreak.

CHAPTER VII

FOR a week Alice hovered between life and death, knowing nothing. In that time there was a hush upon the bay. Bruce had stopped punt building on the beach, and hammering and clanging in the blacksmith's shop and on the tramway. The men were careful not to call or shout within hearing of the house on the cliffs.

Alice learned by degrees afterwards how everybody had rallied round her, and how well she had been cared for. Mrs. Brayton had sent Eliza King for Betty and Mabel, prepared to keep them all with her indefinitely. Dorrie Harding came at once with the messenger Bruce had sent by the river, and she and Mrs. Brayton together made broths and jellies equal to anything a city hospital could have produced.

It was well in the second week before Alice dimly realized that Bruce was one of the people who moved about her in that misty world of fact that encompassed her bed. She was not surprised to see him, or annoyed to see him, or glad to see him. She accepted him as she did the others as part of that reality that her mind struggled at intervals to catch, but always failed to grasp with any degree of clearness. She was a body only. She felt merely pillows moved about her, warmth put to her feet, aches and pains soothed, wetness and dryness upon her skin, an interminable succession of teaspoons put into her mouth.

At the end of two weeks she had her first lucid moment. She clearly saw Dorrie Harding in the chair beside her bed.

"You here," she whispered faintly.

Dorrie leaned forward, smiling.

"You mustn't talk," she said softly.

"Have I been ill?" Alice disobeyed.

"Yes, but you are getting better. Now be good."

Alice's eyes closed and her mind grew foggy again. An hour later she recognized Mrs. King as somebody she had never seen before, but she was too weak to speculate about her. As her moments of consciousness increased she began to watch them moving about the room. In a day or two she seemed to be looking for something. Her eyes often wandered to the door. Her head turned at sounds. She missed something, but she did not know what it was she missed.

"Asia," said Bruce, when they told him. "Let her go in and hold her hand. But she mustn't talk."

But Alice continued to look for something. One night she remembered what it was. She had not seen Bruce for days. He had been in her room, but only when she was asleep. She could not yet remember what lay behind her illness, what the cause of it was, or about the baby, or anything of her former relation to Bruce. She only knew that she wanted him, that it was as uncomfortable not to have him as it was to be cold or faint.

"Hasn't somebody else been here?" she asked Mrs. Harding the next morning.

"When?" asked Dorrie.

"Last week when I was very ill—— I thought there was some one."

"Oh, no, dear, just Mrs. King and I; we are taking care of you."

Dorrie lied according to agreement. In the first week she and Mrs. Brayton and David Bruce had held a cabinet meeting on the situation, all deciding that it would be best for the present that Alice should not know the details of her accident, or that Bruce had been alone with her when the baby was born. They all felt that would be rather too large a dose of life for her to swallow without some preparation. They agreed to let her think for as long as possible that Mrs. King had been at once available, and that Dr. Mount had come when he was sent for. Mrs. King, Asia, and Roland, when he returned, were all duly drilled in the story to be told.

But Alice crept back to convalescence haunted by that memory in the shadows. And as her questions were answered, and as she began to remember, she felt more and more hurt that David Bruce, a doctor, had never been near her. Though she would have been startled had he actually appeared, the thought that he did not come began to obsess her. Once or twice she felt a little suspicious about those two blank weeks, and wondered if they were telling her the truth.

Asia had been allowed to look in at her mother early in the illness. Bruce saw that it would help her to see that she was really there, still looking like herself except that she was very white.

The illness had intensified her feeling for her mother. She was consumed with a passion of sacrifice for her because she had suffered. She formed resolutions of patience and usefulness that would have amazed her elders. But, as she stood beside the bed looking at Alice, Asia felt fearfully that in some way the accident had taken her mother away from her, and set her apart. It was her first conception of the infinite loneliness of human beings.

But she had exaltations as well as sorrows. She learned what a wonderful thing it was to have Bruce and Dorrie Harding praise her, and to see their eyes smile at her resourcefulness. There were days when she floated on air, dizzy with the passion of sacrifice. In those two weeks she experienced emotions that aged her by years.

Roland had returned in the second week. The telegrams that Bruce had sent after him had failed to reach him for days. When he got them he rode furiously from Auckland in an almost impossible time, ruining a good horse in the process, to find he was only a cipher in the crisis. He had to live in the men's kitchen, and was not allowed to see Alice till the third week. He behaved perfectly, and made no trouble for anybody. In a situation where he knew he was no use he was surprisingly tractable.

In telling him of the accident Bruce spoke plainly:

"Your wife ought never to be left alone. She is far too highly strung."

"Well, she doesn't have to be. I didn't know she was nervous. She never said anything. In future you'd better look after her when I'm away."

Bruce had not expected this. He had thought of Eliza King. He could not help smiling at Roland's simple and natural suggestion.

"Mrs. Roland might object to that," he said.

"Oh, pooh! She's got to get used to it."

"Well, Bob Hargraves or somebody would always be available. And there's another thing. You won't mind my saying it. No woman ought to do heavy lifting. We men are damned thoughtless about those things. I found Mrs. Roland lifting that camp oven the very day of her illness. That alone might be enough to injure her for life."

"I see," said the boss gratefully, "she doesn't have to lift it. If she'd only told me——"

"I know," said Bruce.

Roland had this conversation in mind the first time he was allowed to talk to Alice. As she sat propped up in bed he sat affectionately beside her, holding her hand. The fact that he had missed the telegrams because he was having a honeymoon with an adventurous widow drove him to an excessive demonstration of care. He was always beginning afresh, seeing very clearly himself that he was about to improve. His way was paved with good intentions. But he forgot that when other people looked behind they saw not even the ghost of a good intention, but only the substantial footprints of ill-considered deeds. He was now in a mood to make all sorts of amends.

"Why didn't you tell me you were nervous?" he plunged. "You don't have to be alone. Whenever I'm away you can have Bruce here. I've told him."

Wildly startled, Alice stared at him.

"But you know that can't be," she exclaimed.

"Can't be! Fiddlesticks! Why?"

"Why!" She did not know what she meant. "Think how people would talk," she added lamely.

"People! Bunkum! Where are they? The men, do you mean? I'd shoot any damned one of 'em who ever mentioned the subject. But they won't mention it. They've got some sense. And even if they don't know you they know Bruce. There's nothing to worry about in that." And that was all he saw in it.

Alice lay back gasping.

"And look here," he went on, "for God's sake tell me when you want that camp oven moved. You can't expect me to think of everything, and I don't know when you want things done unless you tell me. You don't have to lift it, or anything else. And when I'm away there are plenty of men about. You can trust 'em. They're not savages."

He thought he was doing quite well, and he could not understand why she lay back white and cold. He began to tap his feet nervously. With a glimmer of understanding Alice began to ask him questions about people they knew in Auckland, and in return he tried to be newsy. But when Mrs. King told him it was time for him to go he got up with a sense of relief, and whistling cheerfully to hide his conviction of failure, he went out, resolved to go to the new cottage of Bob Jones, his head contractor, to see if he could assist the newly arrived bride, a buxom and cheerful girl, to get settled.

Later in the evening Dorrie reported to Bruce that Alice had some fever.

"Lord! I hope he didn't tell her anything. If she is wakeful give her a powder," he advised.

Alice needed the powder. After her husband left her, her thoughts began to whirl in circles round her brain. She could not think a sentence to the end. Bruce had talked about the camp oven. Every one knew she was nervous.

Bruce had never been near her—had he been? Why didn't he come? She didn't want him to come. What had he said about the camp oven? Why had he said it? Who had found her that night? It must have been Bruce—was it Bruce? Who sent for Mrs. King? Had Dr. Mount really come? Who was the man in the shadows—had there been a man? Who buried her baby? Who was the man in the yard? What made her ill—was it the camp oven? Why didn't Bruce come to see her—just as a doctor? And so on; a maddening medley, without beginning and without end.

CHAPTER VIII

ONE afternoon, a fortnight later, Alice sat in her rocker by the sitting-room fire, with Asia reading the inevitable *Boys' Own* on the sacking mat beside her. She was now able to be up most of the day, and was so much better that Mrs. King had left to go to another case. Mrs. Harding had gone this evening to have dinner with Mrs. Brayton, leaving Asia in charge of her mother. Roland had been all day in the bush, but was expected back for tea, which Dorrie had left prepared in the kitchen.

Alice had not recuperated as well as Bruce thought she ought to, considering the great care and attention she had received, and he wondered what it was that was holding her back. He knew that she had asked many questions about her illness, but he gathered that Mrs. Harding had successfully kept the real facts from her. He thought it hardly likely that she was grieving over the baby to the extent that her nerves indicated.

With that inconvenient insight that so many introspective women possess, Alice suspected that she had not been given the true facts of her illness. As she grew better she began to wonder what they were hiding from her. She knew now that David Bruce had been at the house a good deal, even though she had no clear memory of him. She knew that he still came, for she heard his voice in the kitchen in the evenings. But she had never seen him, and she was appalled to find out how much she wanted to see him.

In those two weeks, as she sat at the sitting-room window, she had looked for him about the spit and the tramway. Once when she had seen him near the store, she had felt the quick fever in her veins painting itself upon her face and neck. She sternly fought these relapses. She told herself she must not allow any sentimental feeling about his connection with her illness to drive her into thinking of him. Again and again she repeated her little formula about not beginning. Then she would get angry with him for ignoring her now that she was well. As a matter of common courtesy, she argued, if not as a doctor, he should have come to see her. Her illness should have brought about a natural acquaintance between them. He should have seen that, and should not have held her to her mistake. It was his opportunity to ignore it. The natural antagonism between these two views wore on her nerves.

As she sat by the fire with Asia, it occurred to her that she had not had an opportunity of talking to her. The more she thought of it the more she saw significance in the fact that she had been alone very little with her. Of course the child had been very useful, and had worked unceasingly. Emotion stirred her as she looked down at her. Was she imagining, or did Asia look different? Had she been able to enter into the atmosphere of serious illness to any degree? Alice remembered the curious expression on her face as she had stood beside her bed. Suspicion entered her mind. She determined to find out what she knew.

"Asia, how long was Dr. Mount here when I was ill?" she asked suddenly.

She saw the child hesitate, and answer without looking up:

"I don't know, Mother; I didn't see him come."

"Did you see him at all?" demanded Alice.

"No—I—they didn't let me in." Asia began to feel uncomfortable. She did hope her mother was not going to ask her any questions. She was not quite sure now what they had told her to say. And it was one thing to be told to say it, and another to look into her mother's eyes and lie to her.

"Were you asleep when I got ill?" pursued her mother.

"I heard you fall, Mother, and I ran for Mr. Bruce." That was both safe and true.

"Go on," said Alice.

"Oh, Mother, don't ask me questions. I don't remember," she burst out, torn between the desire to keep the secret faithfully, and not to deceive her mother.

Alice drew herself up, an unreasoning rage taking possession of her.

"Asia," and she charged the word with ominous solemnity, "you must tell me all you know. Who has dared to tell you that you were not to talk to your own mother? Tell me that."

Asia sprang to her feet in dire distress.

"Mother, you will be ill again. Nobody told me," she lied bravely, "but every one says you mustn't be worried, and now you are getting worried."

Alice saw her advantage. She calmed herself.

"I am not worried. I am quite well now, and you must answer my questions. It will worry me if you don't. Now don't be afraid. You are my child, and nobody has any right to tell you what to do with me. Would you let anything come between you and your mother?" Alice felt this was perfectly fair, but she was inwardly furious to see that Asia did not seem convinced. It was the first time in her life that any influence had worked against her own with regard to her. She deliberately ignored the possibility that it had been done to save her. The fact that it had been done was enough to make her blind. "Answer my questions. After you got Mr. Bruce you took a message to Bob Hargraves, and he went for Mrs. King."

"Yes, Mother."

"Did you go back to bed then?"

"I got some hot water for Mr. Bruce, and then I went to bed."

"Asia," cried her mother furiously, "you are telling me lies. You did not go back to bed. Who told you to tell this story to me?"

The child drew away frightened and miserable, feeling herself trapped in a tangle of things she could say and things she must not say. And she did not know now what her mother had been told, or what she knew.

"Oh, dear!" she said pitifully, half to herself.

That convinced Alice.

"Did Mr. Bruce tell you that you were not to say anything?" Her voice hardened, and in that moment she believed she hated him.

"Oh, Mother," Asia was trembling, "don't be angry with us. I don't understand it a bit, but it was all to make you well. I will tell you if you are well—I was awake."

Alice tried once more to calm herself.

"Yes, and you helped Mr. Bruce. Now go on, tell me about it. When did Mrs. King come?"

"Well, it seemed a long time: I'd got everything ready. Oh, Mother, I can't tell you anything if you look like that. What is the matter with you? Are you ill?"

Alice realized that Asia was afraid of her, but she was not in a mood to think of her. She was fast getting to the borderland where accumulated anger becomes blind passion.

"Come here," she cried furiously. But Asia hardly moved. "Do you hear me?"

"Oh, Mother, do sit down or I shall run away. I don't like you when you look like that. You are not like my mother." Asia continued to sob.

Alice stood still, wondering if she heard her aright. What had happened to her worshipping, obedient child? The thought that something had come between them drove her to a frenzy of rage.

"You won't obey me! Oh, this is outrageous! I forbid you ever to talk to Mr. Bruce again. You are never to go near him again. You are never to speak to him again, never for any reason at all. Do you hear me?"

Asia stared at her, fierce rebellion choking her. Passionately as she reverenced her mother she knew she could not yield to her in this. She had rarely defied her even in a small way, and she had never before flatly disobeyed her, but as she stood there distracted by the inexplicableness of it all, something in her rose up to fight.

"I will talk to Mr. Bruce," she cried, and then, turning from her mother's terrible eyes, she fled outside. But even in that volcanic moment she remembered that she was supposed to be taking care of Alice. She stopped sobbing by the cliffs. She was sick with fright and bewilderment. It was horrible that things could be so sudden and so stupid. What had she done, what had Mr. Bruce done to cause her mother to act like that? She saw only one explanation. Her mother must still be ill, and now she had made her worse again. As she stood there she saw Bruce leave the store. Impulsively she rushed down to him.

"What's the matter?" he asked sharply, as she ran towards him.

"Mother is so angry with us," she gasped, tears dripping from her cheeks. "She says I'm never to talk to you again."

Bruce looked sternly at her.

"What has happened? What have you been telling her?"

"I didn't tell her. I mean I tried not to, but she would ask me questions. And she seemed to know—she said she knew I was not in bed. I didn't know what to say, and she said I must tell her."

"Oh, Lord!" exclaimed Bruce.

Asia burst into fresh tears.

"Oh, I couldn't help it. Don't you be angry——"

"Sh! child." He put his hands on her shoulders. "Don't worry any more. It can't be helped. Mrs. Harding was going to tell her all about it in a day or two. I understand why she is angry. But never mind, she will understand when she is told. It will come out all right."

"But she looked so awful. She will be ill again—she is ill, isn't she?"

"Yes," he said gently, "she is still ill, and sick people

often get angry at what seems to be nothing. But don't worry about her. Who is with her now?"

"Nobody. Mrs. Harding went up to Mrs. Brayton for dinner. We thought Mother was well enough."

"I see. Well, I'm going to talk to her. You stay outside till I go." He turned up the bank.

Alice stood frozen for some minutes after Asia ran out. Then she sank choking into her rocker, those last defiant words ringing like a death knell in her ears.

Asia had been one of her eternal verities. She had never allowed herself to think of a day when the child might combat her opinions, or question her beliefs, or dispute her commands. Much of her suppressed emotionalism had found vent in the affection between them. To her the bond had been more than human. She had been sure of her right and of her power to dominate her own child. In spite of Mrs. Brayton's hint she was still sure of her right, for her feelings died hard, fighting to the last ditch. But her sense of power had now received its first stunning shock. In that mad moment she did not stop to think or analyze. She saw only that Bruce was a rival influence.

As she sat lashing herself into a fever, the front door opened, and Bruce walked in and closed it behind him. For a moment she was so taken aback that she could not move. She felt a wave of helplessness closing down upon her. Then she remembered, her nerves snapped, and she sprang to her feet.

"How dare you enter my house like that? Leave it at once," she cried.

But he moved towards her. He saw she was in a white heat, and on the border of hysteria.

"Please sit down, Mrs. Roland. I want to talk to you."

His calm inattention made her want to scream at him. She had never been in such a state in her life.

"I will not sit down. Leave my house," she almost shouted.

He was vividly conscious of her dramatic appearance. At

last she had come to life. Her blue-grey eyes blazed with unsuspected passion. Her face, thin and whitened by her illness, was flushed to a deep crimson. Her tall and graceful figure was terribly alive with the fire of maternal rage. But Bruce looked anxiously at her, at a loss how to quieten her.

"Do sit down, Mrs. Roland. I can explain——"

"Explain—nothing could ever explain. You talked to my child—you told her not to tell me. You took advantage of a situation. I don't care what happened. It could have been avoided—it was outrageous. You presumed disgracefully. You had no business in this house in my husband's absence—you should have got a doctor to stay. Nothing can explain—there could be no excuse. To teach a child to lie—to lie to her mother. Will you go out of this house?" She gasped for breath.

Bruce kept his eyes steady against hers, hoping to dominate her.

"You will understand when you hear——" he began quietly.

But she was beyond reason.

"I shall tell my husband that I ordered you out of this house, and that you refused to go," she choked, and sweeping past him, she entered her room and locked the door behind her.

Even though he knew that she did not know what she was saying Bruce was hurt, and he was annoyed to think that he could not manage her. He understood her anger, and he was sure that when the inevitable explanation was fully made she would be ashamed of her outburst. But he knew that her shame would not improve the strained relations between them, that, in fact, it would only make them more difficult. And it hurt him to be at variance with any human being.

He stood for a few minutes outside to think how it could now be straightened out.

Spun from a gold and crimson sunset a wavering fringe

of colour undulated upon the cold ripple of the river. The chill of winter put a sting into the evening air. Down below him, along the tramway and on the spit, the men were gathering up their tools. He saw Roland riding along the edge of the bay. He had a curious feeling of being utterly apart from this nest of people whose affairs dovetailed, and whose motives and reactions, often inexplicable to themselves, were an open book to him. He went down to tell Roland what it was advisable for him to know of the incident just past, and to tell Asia how to treat her mother.

For some time after she fell upon her bed Alice lay sobbing weakly, conscious only of the physical results of her outburst. If she moved she felt dizzy. Her head ached abominably, her feet grew cold. She lay in a delirium of misery till Asia tapped at her door.

"I'm bringing your tea, Mother," she called, in matter-of-fact tones.

Alice remembered that her door was locked.

"Put it down," she called thickly.

She forced herself to get up, bring in the tray, and drink a little of the hot milk. Then she undressed and got into bed. She drew the sheet half over her face as she heard some one come to the door. But Asia did not speak to her as she put two hot water bottles into the bed, and drew the blinds, and left the front window open at the bottom. Somehow Alice knew that David Bruce had been telling her just what to do.

If she could possibly have grown any more miserable as the evening advanced she would have, but even her capacity for misery was limited. She tried to still her uncomfortable questions by telling herself that her anger was justified, that what she had said was true, that nothing could ever excuse Bruce. Then she remembered that she did not yet know whether the lies that they had told her might not hide a situation that had not before occurred to her because it was so unthinkable—a situation that she shrank from now, and refused to think about.

She was still refusing to think about it when Dorrie Harding stole into her room. Alice pretended to be asleep. Dorrie renewed the hot water bottles, put milk and biscuits on the table beside her, raised the window a little, and went out. Nobody came near her again. But she heard voices in the kitchen till midnight. She knew they were discussing her. She knew they were excusing her because she was ill. She remembered the anxiety in Bruce's eyes that evening while she was raving at him. But this conspiracy of carefulness and understanding only threw into greater relief her own ignominious position as the person to be excused. She spent a wretched night, wondering how she was ever to look any of them in the face again, and craving to get away from every one of them.

"It's going to be damned difficult," Bruce had said to Mrs. Harding and Mrs. Brayton, "but it ought to be done now as soon as possible, to-morrow, if you can."

He had gone up to bring Mrs. Harding home because he wanted to talk to her apart from Roland. They sat in the library before a comforting fire.

"Oh, I can't do it," groaned Mrs. Harding. "She's an awful person to tell anything to. What is the matter with her?"

"Pride and Puritanism, those monumental bulwarks of the British character," growled Bruce.

The two women laughed.

"Your explanations are simple, but they don't help," said Mrs. Harding. "Can't you imagine her face when she is told that you were alone with her when the baby was born?"

"Poor thing," he said gently, "yes, that will be an awful dose, and she will never be able to endure the sight of me again. Really, it's a devil of a situation, and yet it is so human and natural. Oh, Lord!"

"I'll tell her," broke in Mrs. Brayton. "I'll go down in

the morning. I'm not belittling your talents"—she smiled at Dorrie—"but I think she will take it better from me."

"Oh, you are a brick!" cried Dorrie, "I've never dreaded anything so much in my life. And I'm afraid I'd lose patience with her. She is so stupid."

"My dear, think of her upbringing. Father a Presbyterian minister of the old school, wouldn't even allow Scott's novels in the house. Mother died when she was a child. One brother a missionary. A daily round of prayer meetings. No wonder she ran off and got married. And, then, I'm sure there was something funny about the marriage too."

"Oh, I know there are excuses for her. But lots of us have had a Puritan upbringing and we are not as bad as she is."

"The great trouble with her is that she can't be inconsistent," said Bruce gloomily. "She can't forget this week what she felt like last week. She began wrong with me, and she can't forget it. Ten years hence she will remember that she was rude to me this afternoon, and she will want to apologize for it all over again."

They laughed.

"Come on, Mrs. Harding. We must get back. I told Roland not to go near her, he's a blunderer, but there's no telling what he may do. And that poor child. She will have brain fever if anything more happens."

"I'll be down about ten," Mrs. Brayton called from the veranda as they went through the garden.

It was with some misgivings that the old lady walked into Alice's room the next morning. She saw at once that Alice knew why she had come, and so she began without any preliminaries.

"My dear," she said as she sat down beside her, "perhaps we have all made a mistake, but we did it for the best, and you must forgive us."

Then Alice saw that whatever the conspiracy had been they were all in it. Not that that added to her peace of mind. She knew that she was going to hear something dreadful, and she braced herself to get it over without any exhibition of feeling. Her head was aching badly, for she had hardly slept, but she was glad of it, because it distracted her attention, and helped her to keep aloof.

Mrs. Brayton found it very difficult to talk to her because she asked no questions, and only twice repeated a word or two, as if she had not heard aright. Mrs. Brayton was careful to put no emphasis on the things she knew Alice would emphasize; she lightened the details and she treated the whole situation as a thing common in that environment; and, by assuming that Alice would see it in a certain light once she was told, she planted a seed that after something of a struggle vitalized into a plant, a feeble one, indeed, but still a plant.

Mrs. Harding dropped in twice to break up the impression that this was a solemn conclave. She brought in chicken jelly and biscuits and refilled the hot water bottle. She, too, took the attitude that they were the people who had blundered.

"We did it for the best," she said, echoing Mrs. Brayton.

The whole story beat upon Alice's brain as a string of words that merely added to her misery without helping her to think. She wondered if she would ever be able to think again. When it was over, and Mrs. Brayton had gone softly out, after squeezing her hand, and telling her she must get well, she lay stupidly holding her head. She felt as if the sap had been bled out of her, leaving only a physical shell that ached because of the void inside it.

As she lay with her eyes closed Asia brought in her lunch.

"Mother, dear, you will get well quick now, won't you?" The child beamed at her. But a look of disappointment killed her smile as she saw her mother's eyes. "Oh, Mother, have you a headache?"

Alice nodded. She could not trust herself to speak.

"Let me bathe it."

Alice nodded again.

That headache was one of the worst she had ever had. At nine o'clock that night Bruce told Mrs. Harding to give her morphine. She was stupid the next day from the effects of the drug and dozed uneasily, taking little notice of anybody.

"How has she been to-day?" Bruce asked on the second evening.

"Awfully listless," answered Dorrie. "She wouldn't get up. Poor thing, she has tried dreadfully hard all day to be pleasant. But she has hardly looked at any of us."

"Hm! I'll see what I can do with her." He smiled.

Dorrie wondered what would happen as she saw him disappear into the front bedroom.

Alice lay with her eyes closed, her face shaded from the one candlelight by two empty cannisters that had been placed round it. Her masses of chestnut hair tumbled about her head. Her cheeks were tinged with colour.

Her eyes opened, dilated and blazed as Bruce without any announcement walked in, closed the door behind him, and drew a chair beside her. As he sat down he was conscious that he had electrified her. She was looking at him like a bird fascinated by a snake. He realized, too, that when she looked alive she was beautiful. But it was merely as a doctor, a psychologist, that he leaned over her.

"Mrs. Roland," he began gravely, "do you enjoy being ill?"

She looked helplessly into his steady eyes, feeling that they knew everything about her. She made no attempt to reply.

"There is nothing wrong with you now but your mind, and you have made it sick, and you are keeping it sick. You can get well as soon as you please. Now, why don't you? What good do you think you are doing yourself or your children, or anybody else? You are thinking only of yourself."

She was startled by this unexpected plainness. He was making no excuses for her. He was speaking with the dispassionateness of a stranger, making no effort to be soft or kind.

"Do you know what you are doing? You are making a luxury of misery. It's a common disease, but you ought to be above it. Now exert your will power. You can get well at once. Health is too fine a thing to be fooled as you are fooling it. If you don't like the past, forget it. Forget everything you don't like." He stood up. "You get up to-morrow, and walk round the house twice every hour if it is fine, and breathe all the fresh air you can, and above all things," with slow emphasis, "give that inconvenient memory of yours a rest. Good night."

Before she knew what she was doing she had put her hot weak hand into his cool firm one that closed round it with a grip she felt for hours, and then he was gone, leaving her aflame from head to foot.

"She is afraid of me! Now why the devil——" he said to himself as he went out.

Bruce's words did not help Alice to get to sleep. But before she began to think of them she held in her memory the picture of his face as it had looked down at her, the patience, the tiredness, the tragedy of his eyes. And she admitted that it was to her one of the most beautiful faces she had ever seen. She wondered why it did not seem to matter that he had done for her supremely intimate things, even that she had been rude to him. He seemed remote from such personal matters, so much bigger than any of the things she worried about. His presence had blotted out the past, his words carried her into the future.

His curt sentences came back one by one into her mind, and one by one she said them over to herself until she had them all set out in a row, as it were, for inspection. The mere repetition of them fired her with energy and determination. She saw that though life had beaten her into the dust she had to get up and face it again. Though she hardly slept, she got up after she had had her breakfast and began the walks. Through the morning she still lived on his mentality, but as the day wore on she began to get back to her own.

She craved to be alone to think, for she knew that when the excitement died down in her she would begin to think. She wished Dorrie Harding would go home. It was so hard to meet her eyes impersonally. The only person she could bear to see was Asia, Asia who was so easily diverted from the unpleasant, who so soon forgot the yesterdays, who did not look at her with eyes that veiled remembrance.

When she was not walking round the house she sat at the sitting-room window. She told herself that she needed all the sunlight she could get. And it was not the sun's fault that she was disappointed when the evening came. She had to admit to herself that the afternoon had been a failure because she had not caught a glimpse of David Bruce. As she went to bed she knew she wanted him to come to see her again.

But, hearing from Mrs. Harding that she was much better, Bruce did not enter the house. Instead, Alice had a short visit from her husband, who said that now that she was well he would come home the next day, and the following morning he mentioned that instead of going away himself on business he was sending Bruce.

All day Alice wondered when he was going and if he would come to see her before he left. She was hurt and then angry that he did not. When she heard Roland tell some one at the front door that he would be away a month she was frightened to find that it was a shock to her. She saw again what she was coming to, and that she must discipline her mind in order to fight her impulses.

In the course of the following weeks, free from the excitement of possible visits by Bruce, increasingly occupied with the return to her normal life, the departure of Mrs. Harding and the return of the children, Alice fought out once more the disagreeably active waywardness of her feelings, and defined again her duty as a Christian wife and mother. She realized that the situation was a complicated one. Instead of feeling embarrassed that Bruce had been her doctor, she was now particularly drawn to him on that account. Instead of hating him and disliking to see him because she had shamefully misunderstood him, she longed to humiliate herself in an orgy of submission to him. Instead of blaming him, she now felt Asia's love for him to be a further bond.

She admitted to herself that if she did not actually love him, she was on the borderland. And she knew that she would have to go on seeing him, that he might have to doctor her again, that there was no question of his going away. She knew that she could not be rude to him any longer. She knew that Mrs. Brayton and Dorrie Harding had made allowance for her up to the present, but that they would condemn her for any further stupidity. And she knew that she could not bear their condemnation. At the same time she dreaded to think what might be the outcome of intimacy between her and David Bruce. She still believed in the inviolability of the marriage bond, even in thought, as the first plank of morality.

It was a week or more before it occurred to her to wonder if Bruce cared, or might care for her. She went over all that he had done for her. She thought long over the exciting fact that he, unknown to her, had guarded her and her children those nights before her accident. She thought over everything he had said and done, but nowhere could she find the sign that she both hoped and feared to find. She knew that if he ever grew to care for her and told her so she would be helpless against any advances he might make. It was bad enough, she told herself, that she be in danger of loving him. She must prevent by every means in her power his caring for her. In a clear-sighted moment she admitted that, owing to her past behaviour, the latter might be the least difficult of her tasks.

She decided that it rested entirely with herself. But this decision was not as comforting as she felt it should have been. She prayed long and earnestly that God would reinforce her feeble will with some of that mysterious strength she had been taught to believe was available for those who desired truly to help themselves. She wavered between strong moments when she knew Providence was on her side and weak moments when she saw no evidence that He was.

David Bruce was away five weeks, first up the Wairoa, arranging for future timber shipments, and then in Auckland hunting up men for bush work, and buying machinery. In a weak moment he had succumbed to drinking whisky with the secretary of the Kauri Timber Company, and had been dead to the world for days afterwards. He bore little outward sign of this relapse on his return to the bay, but it was the reason why he did not go near the boss's house for a fortnight.

Then, on a wet Sunday afternoon, he appeared at the back door with a brace of pheasants. Alice was in the kitchen getting the tea when she heard the knock. As she had not heard any footsteps, she opened the door quite unprepared. Bruce ignored her start and her flush.

"I bagged these this morning, Mrs. Roland. The first I've had time to shoot this season. I would like you to have them." He held out the birds.

"Oh, thank you—I—it's very kind——" she stammered, taking them mechanically.

"Don't mention it. I had fun getting them. I am glad to see you are better." And lifting his cap, he turned away, seeing that she was uncomfortable at the sight of him. But he made up his mind that she should get used to the sight of him, and that he would find some excuse for calling two or three times a week.

CHAPTER IX

ALICE sat on a box in the back garden looking down the river. The sun had set, but opaline ghosts of clouds still trailed their "ravelled fleeces" across the pale lemon of the western sky. The cliffs of the river gap were fast merging into the wall of haze that deepened and spread from the horizon. The river ran silently undisturbed by leaping fish. The wekas were just beginning to shriek from the forest.

Alice drew her heavy cape around her, for the tang of winter was still in the air. She had seen that day the glow of a yellow kowhai in the bush, and had heard the croaky call of a tui trying out his throat in readiness for his flute song on the first real spring day. Bees had buzzed about their new garden, and Asia had declared that morning that she had found the first daffodil bud in her own little flower-bed. But the promise of spring had failed to inspire Alice. There was no response in her as she sat there looking down upon the river. She had spent a winter of glorious discontent.

The more she had tried to prop herself against her gods, the more she had tried to console herself with fixed principles, the more inadequate she had found them. They had not kept her from looking through the windows to watch for David Bruce as he came and went along the paths about the bay. They had not kept her from listening to his violin. They had not kept her from flushing when she met him unexpectedly.

The biggest cause of her uneasiness was that she had begun to question the verities. If you live beside a river sooner or later you have to. You can't help sitting beside it, and listening to it, and watching the water go by. And then you wonder idly where all the water comes from and where it goes, and when it began to run and why, and if it will ever end and why. And your thoughts run with it and change with it. And you go out at night to look at the stars reflected in the dark depths of it, and then you look up at the stars themselves, and you ask when and why again. And little by little you wonder if all that men have said about them is true, and who the first man was who said it. And you would like to be quite sure that he was inspired by God.

And that brings you to God. Is he up there, and what does he look like? And when you begin to wonder what God looks like you have reached the half-way house to the heights of scepticism. He must look like something or somebody, but whom and what? And does he really hear your prayers, and does he really care? And if he does not hear your prayers, what then? And if he does not care, what then?

Alice had reached a stage of mental convulsions when she no longer clearly saw God in His heaven and all right with the world.

Other fears, too, had been closing in upon her, fears that she could not crush or sweep aside. She had never been really well since her illness in the autumn. Lately the conviction had grown upon her that the first blow had been struck at her fine health. She was getting nerves. She became more and more nauseated by the terrible vitality of her husband. It was being stimulated this very day, she knew, by the sportive widow who had recently bought the Hakaru pub. Roland had not disguised the fact that he was going to see her. She was a good sensible woman, he said, and he wanted her to pick out likely men among her customers, and send them to him for jobs. Alice had not remarked aloud that it took a good many visits to arrange this simple matter.

Then, for two weeks now, she had feared that she was going to have another child. She had not expected to feel so badly about it. She had married knowing she would have children, that it was her duty to have them, that God approved of large families, that she ought to love and welcome all her children, and that she ought to feel a renewed exaltation in the knowledge that another was to come. But now she did not feel any of these things. She felt only a dumb rage, a sick helplessness, a fierce rebellion. And she had wondered more than once if it really was as wicked as she had been told to rebel against the word of God.

Everything immediately around her this Sunday conspired to drive her to distraction. The children had been unusually exasperating, and Asia, who could have helped her, had been away, Alice did not know where, the whole afternoon. She had merely asked her mother if she could go for a walk along the beach. For some time Alice had not been alarmed about her, thinking she might have gone to Mrs. Brayton. But now it was dark, and she knew the old lady would not have allowed her to stay so late. She fidgeted on her box, straining her ears for the sound of returning footsteps. Her fear soon got the best of her. She began to walk round the house listening and looking, and feeling worse every minute.

On her second round she stopped, her eyes turned towards a new shanty standing by itself at the foot of the green hill, well away from the back of the men's kitchen. Bruce had moved into it only a few days before. Alice had learned from Asia, whom she had allowed to go to see it, that he had a "carpet," a stretcher bed, books, tables, a cupboard for his clothes, and a special box for his violin. She had looked so often in its direction that she hoped no one had noticed. She could not tell now whether he was home or not, for she knew that his western window had a thick green blind.

As she looked she felt a sudden desire to go to him, and then an equally strong determination to fight this desire. She looked upon her attitude to Bruce that winter as her one great achievement. Although it still upset her inwardly to meet him, she felt that outwardly she had gained in poise. She had met his naturalness with what she thought was naturalness in return. She had been pleasant, but she never relaxed her vigilance as to the beginning. She had never asked him in. She never let conversation linger. She always assumed that he had urgent business with her husband. She knew that he must think it extraordinary that she had never referred to her illness, that she had never thanked him for what he had done for her. She had never sent for him. She had never stayed in the sitting-room on the evenings when he had worked with her husband. It tortured her to think that he must despise her, but she saw no other way of going on.

Now, however, the temptation to send for him grew more irresistible every minute. The better to fight it she went inside. She paced restlessly from the kitchen to the front room and back again, torn between her fear that something had happened to Asia and her craving to go for the man who could best help her. She looked into her room to see that Betty and Mabel were safely asleep, and had turned into the kitchen again, distracted, when Asia rushed in, bursting with excitement, her eyes aflame with adventure, far too preoccupied to notice the state of her mother's nerves.

"Oh, Mother," she panted, "we've found a cave, and Maori shells and bones, and this beautiful bit of greenstone."

But there was no response to her enthusiasm. Alice's reaction was swift and overwhelming.

"We!" she said sternly.

Asia felt a sudden chill. "It was only Reggie Broad, Mother. I met him on the beach. We explored some bush, just like a real party. It——" But the words froze on her lips. She could no longer face her mother's eyes.

"Reggie Broad went with you into the bush!"

With a sinking feeling Asia felt that it was an awful accusation. Reggie Broad was a coarse, rough boy, the son of the Kaiwaka storeman, who had recently come up from

Auckland. Alice realized his type, but to Asia he was a mine of information and amusement. They had had a thrilling and innocently joyous afternoon. That was all she knew. She faced her mother squarely.

"We didn't hurt anything," she said.

Alice moved a step towards her. She was now thoroughly unstrung.

"How long were you with him?"

"Oh, I don't know, Mother," she stammered, "since dinner—I—we didn't do anything wrong."

"You've been for hours in the bush with that boy!"

Asia choked as her mother seized her by the shoulder, and hurried her into her own room. Then she left her, shutting the door behind her, only to return a moment later with a strap. As the child saw the horrible thing that was about to happen she became faint.

"You wicked girl," cried Alice, grasping her arm. "How could you go away like that with that boy? You should have come to ask me—I don't know what's come over you lately—you must not do things unless you ask me. You must never speak to him again. Do you hear me—you are never to talk to boys or go anywhere with them. I must make you remember it——"

The suddenness and the inexplicableness of this first beating turned Asia into a raving little demon.

"I hate you! I hate you!" she shouted at her mother. "I hate God! I don't believe there is any. I like Mr. Bruce better than you—he wouldn't beat me for nothing. What have I done? Go away! I hate you! You'll never be my mother again. I won't live with you! I hate you!" And then howls and shrieks of rage.

"Oh, you wicked girl!" gasped Alice, astonished and frightened by this outburst.

Asia did not realize for some minutes afterwards that she was alone. She screamed and howled, goading herself to frenzy. When she had exhausted herself she staggered to her window, cautiously pushed it up, and dropped out.

She shot off in the dusk to the cliff where she scrambled and slid down by the roots of the big totara to the sand, and with nothing in her mind but the desire to get away alone she ran sobbing and whimpering along the beach to a little wooded dell, a fern-bowered spot, beloved of yellow-hammers and moreporks and tuis, and enlivened by the cheerfullest of streams that trickled over polished stones into the tide below.

The dell was Asia's Bible. If the babies had been very cross she stole off to it to calm her fretted nerves. If she failed to reach Alice's standard of patience in looking for the cow or in keeping the fowls out of the vegetables, it was to the dell she went to have it out with her turbulent soul.

She reached it now breathless, falling down in the grass on a small headland that stretched out into the mangroves. There she lay dazed for over an hour. Then her lips began to twitch, and with a rush came the scalding tears.

"She beat me!" she choked at intervals, broken-hearted. "She beat me."

She drew up her aching body, and sat with her chin on her knees, trying to find a reason for it, trying to believe it all a hideous dream, trying to think of the mother she had known that morning, the mother she now felt was gone for ever. She turned her swollen face up to the stars.

"Oh, why did she beat me?" she moaned. "I can't understand it a bit." She kept her face strained upwards to the stars, hard as crystal in the cold sky. But they did not comfort her, or divert her from the tragedy of her wrecked world. She looked wildly round the dell, and on to the still river, both things she had grown to love, but there was no comfort there either, no voice to reassure her, or tell her it was all a mistake. As she sat on anger began to take the place of bewilderment and sorrow. She felt the beating had been unjust. It had fallen upon her out of a clear sky. She had not known it was wrong to go away with Reggie. And why was it wrong?

She puzzled over this till she realized suddenly that it must be very late, later than she had ever been out before. She sprang to her feet, and turned mechanically homewards. Then she remembered that her mother might be angry again and beat her again. It never occurred to her that Alice might be anxious about her. Suddenly she felt she could not go home. She did not love her mother any more. She could not bear to face her. She wondered if she could not sleep in the monkey-house she had made for herself in a ti-tree in the dell. But it was cold, and she was shivering. She began to weep pitifully, like a lost child. Then she remembered Mrs. Brayton.

It was eleven o'clock, and the old lady was undressing when she heard a step on her veranda and a knock on her window-pane.

"Who is it?" she called.

"Asia," in a voice hardly recognizable.

"Good gracious!" Mrs. Brayton hurried with her candle to the front door. "Child," she cried, "what has happened?"

Poor Asia stumbled in with a fresh rush of tears.

"She beat me," she sobbed, clinging to the amazed old lady.

It was some time before anything else could be got from her, but bit by bit Mrs. Brayton pieced together the story.

After closing the door upon Asia, Alice went into her room, and fell into her rocking chair, crushing her hands into her temples. Paralyzing reactions always followed her rare outbursts. It was some minutes before she could think. Then a wave of remorse swept over her. She knew she had been cruelly unjust, that she had done the child a wrong she could never right, and that it would haunt her for years. The sight of Asia's agonized and bewildered face, distorted out of all recognition, danced before her, and the things the child had said rang in her ears. Was it possible that her own lack of control had so affected Asia that she raged blindly, or was she saying what she believed?

The thought appalled her. She pressed her fingers into her eyeballs to blot out the sight. She closed her hands over her ears to shut out the sound of those defiant cries.

Then she began to cry, and all the pent up feelings of that day and the weeks before it found an outlet in her drenching tears. She told herself she was a wicked woman, and that she deserved to suffer. At last, weak and pulverized, she got up, bathed her face, and went to make up the kitchen fire which had burned low. The tea that she had prepared stood untouched, the two chairs ready for herself and Asia. Alice was faint with hunger, but she could not eat alone. She knew that before she did anything else she must apologize. An apology was to her an absurdly momentous affair. An apology to her own child was entirely outside her experience. It was the first time she had ever felt called upon to make one. Nobody could ever know what it meant to her to walk to Asia's door, open it and go in. It meant so much that it was a minute or two before she realized that the room was empty.

"Asia," she muttered stupidly, staring at the open window.

As she was sure the child must be somewhere near she went outside and round the house, calling softly. She looked in the woodshed, she walked to the back fence, and she called up into the field and over towards the cliffs. Then she wondered if Asia had gone to David Bruce. The thought that she might have told him the story filled her cup of humiliation to overflowing. But when she went inside and saw that it was long after nine o'clock she knew this had not happened, for Bruce would not have kept her so late. For some time she fought the suspicion that kept coming to her mind. She walked from room to room with the restlessness of a wolf in a cage, getting more worked up with every step she took. At ten o'clock, as she stood desperate in the kitchen, resolved finally to go for Bruce, she heard steps. For the minute she thought they were his, but it was Roland who opened the back door.

"Hullo!" he began gaily. "What's up?" His face was flushed.

"I can't find Asia. She has been away for hours. I'm sure something has happened to her."

"Oh, nonsense!" he replied, failing to gauge her state of mind. "You're always alarmed about nothing. She'll turn up presently." And moving forward with some show of affection, he put his arm round her and tried to kiss her.

She sprang from him, her eyes blazing.

"What do you mean?" she cried furiously. "Do you realize that my child may be lying drowned in the river? She has been away since midday"—the lie was deliberate—"will you go out at once and get men to look for her, or must I go myself?"

He stared at her for a few seconds, too astonished by her outbreak to speak. She was something totally different from anything he had thought her to be. He was startled by the hate and disgust in her eyes. But he put that down to the frenzied state that he now saw she was in.

"Heavens, yes! Don't get excited. I'll get them," he said impatiently.

It was not till he got outside that he realized what a business it would be trying to find any one at that time of night. But he went to the kitchen, where the men were nearly all in bed, and asked for volunteers.

Every man got up, and started out with what lanterns there were to search the bay and the bush around it, the boss leading.

A little after eleven o'clock Bruce rode up to the stable near the kitchen, and unsaddled and fed his horse. He had been away all day at Kaiwaka at a bad case, and was tired and hungry. As he saw a dim light through the kitchen window he decided he would get something to eat before going to his shanty. When he opened the door he rubbed his eyes to see if he were awake or dreaming. One nickel lamp, burning low and smelling vilely, intensified the unusualness of the scene. The place was silent with the uncanny silence of a schoolroom at night. Not a man was visible. The dark blankets and night shirts of all kinds trailed over the sides of the beds and on the floor, telling of unexpected haste and confusion. The green eyes of the kitchen cat surveyed him suspiciously from a deserted bunk.

"What the devil!" exclaimed Bruce, backing suddenly, and running to the corner of the building. He looked at once in the direction of the boss's house, and saw that it was lit up. He caught a glimmer of two lights in the bush across the bay, and heard what he took to be a distant call and an answer. Without waiting to encourage his presentiment he began to sprint for the cottage. As he neared it he saw that a figure standing by the front gate turned swiftly and moved towards him.

Bruce was not prepared for his reception. Rushing up to him, Alice clutched his arm with both her hands, her hot eyes boring the darkness.

"Oh, have you found her?" she cried.

Startled though he was, the healer in him came automatically to the surface. He caught and held her hands, and looked down into her face.

"What is it, Mrs. Roland? I've been away all day; just got back. What's happened?"

"Asia—she's lost——"

"Lost! How? Where?"

"I don't know. She ran away—she may be drowned. For God's sake do something——"

He still held her hands, and she looked as if she was about to fall against him. She had never consciously been so near to him before. He saw that her reserves had melted. But, as that was not the time to speculate, he gripped her hands a little harder and spoke quickly.

"I can do nothing till you tell me more. When did she run away, and why?"

"It's my fault," she choked, the confession bursting from her, her pride gone. "I—I whipped her. She was away all the afternoon with that boy—Reggie Broad. She came home about six and I was so nervous—I didn't think what I was doing—I beat her. It was all wrong. And when I went to look for her she was gone. She may be drowned——"

"She is not drowned or lost," he interrupted firmly. "It would never occur to the child to drown herself. She has gone out and cried herself to sleep somewhere, that's all. Are they looking for her?"

His conviction and his presence steadied her, and she was conscious that he was still holding her hands.

"Yes," she answered, dropping her eyes.

"Where?"

"Oh, all about, I think, but they haven't found her——" Her voice broke again.

"Has any one gone to that little dell along the beach?"

"I don't know."

"Or Mrs. Brayton? Did you think of that? She might go there?"

"But she would have sent to say."

"Yes, but it would take time. Mrs. Roland, go in and get hold of yourself, and stop worrying. I'll get my horse. I know she is somewhere about. She is neither dead nor lost. She will be found soon." He gripped her hands intentionally.

And, believing him, Alice felt the fever go out of her as she watched him run back to the kitchen. She stood listening to the sound of his galloping horse as it pounded along the path to the store, and on round the beach. Another kind of excitement welled up in her as she realized the significance of this meeting. She knew it had done something to her, snapped some restraint. At that moment she did not care what the results might be. Worn out, but calmer, she went inside and lay down in Asia's room, confident now that Bruce would bring her back.

Before he mounted Bruce had looked into his shanty, as it occurred to him that Asia might have gone to him for comfort. As he rode along the beach he guessed many of the reasons for this tragic blunder. Although he had not looked for signs he knew Alice might at any time find out that she was going to have another child, and that the knowledge of it and the fear of it would spell disaster to her nerves. He knew, also, that Roland had paid several visits to the Hakaru pub, not to drink, for he was almost a total abstainer, but because he found the florid Mrs. Lyman a very amusing and flattering person. He did not blame Roland. He understood why he went to Mrs. Lyman.

Bruce had speculated with more or less chagrin that winter why it was that Alice continued to remain aloof from him. At times it amused him. But always it vaguely annoyed him. She was his first real failure in his management of human relations. He knew that more than one thing was responsible for her attitude. He refused to believe that embarrassment alone kept her from acknowledging adequately his service to her. He was not looking for thanks, but he knew she owed them to him. He had wondered lately if she behaved as she did because she could not bear to meet one who must know how her husband was acting, because she could not meet eyes that saw too much. But then, she obviously loved Mrs. Brayton, who knew and saw as much as he did.

David Bruce knew that he attracted women, though he never traded on the fact. But it had not occurred to him that he had attracted Alice Roland, because he did not see sufficient opportunity. Now, however, as she had stood near to him in the starlight, he had seen something in her eyes that was not the frenzy of fear, had felt something about her yielding hands, had sensed something about her that arrested him. But he did not take it very seriously. He was more concerned just then with finding Asia.

He passed two men returning from the dell, and heard that, as far as they knew, no one had been to Mrs. Brayton. To be sure, he searched the place thoroughly himself. He was afraid the child had fallen asleep somewhere, and the nights were still much too cold and damp for that to happen without dangerous results. When he had gone over every bit of the dell on foot, he led his horse through the barred gate in the beach fence that divided the boss's property from that of Mrs. Brayton, and then rode at a fast canter up the hill to the pines.

The front door opened as he ran along the shelled path.

"She's here," called the old lady, guessing the errand of the midnight runner.

"Thank God! I'll go right back——"

"Oh, David, wait a moment. I've just sent Harold—as soon as he got back from his meeting. He went ten minutes ago." Mrs. Brayton lowered her voice as he came up to her. "And you had better take her with you, hadn't you? She wouldn't go with Harold."

Bruce looked into the eyes of the old lady, who was still half dressed. She did not realize what a quaint picture she made.

"Poor child! Is she very upset?"

"Oh, she's been heart-broken. I've never seen anything more pitiful in my life. She hasn't the faintest idea why she was beaten. And she says she won't go home. David, what is the matter with her mother?"

"More than one thing, I should say, and I suspect another child. She was a wreck herself."

"Oh, dear! And Harold says he heard Roland was out riding with Mrs. Lyman this afternoon."

"Hm! Quite likely."

"David! You don't seem disturbed. Do you expect people to go on like that?"

He smiled at her.

"It's not a matter of expecting. I've noticed that they do. Now, where's Asia?"

He followed her into her kitchen, where the child sat worn out with her head upon her arm on the table, the remains of a chicken sandwich and a glass of hot milk beside her. She roused herself as they came in, and when she saw Bruce she jerked herself up defiantly.

"I won't go home," she said fiercely.

Bruce drew a chair beside her, and put his arm round her.

"Would you be glad to know that your mother is dead?" he asked gravely.

She drew away from him, stiffening, while every drop of colour faded from her face.

"My mother dead, my mother!" she choked, her hate suddenly gone, her lips quivering.

With a swift gesture he threw both arms round her and put his face into her hair as if she had been his own child.

"No," he said quickly, "she is not dead, but she has been very ill to-day, and she was worried about you, and she really did not know what she was doing when she beat you. We will all have to be very good to her for a while, and you must not do anything without telling her. She won't beat you again. Don't be afraid of that. And you must forgive her, for she is very sorry."

She raised her face, her eyes now shining. Her tangled hair fell about her grimy cheeks and tired shoulders.

"Poor mother. I didn't know she was ill again, or I would not have run away. I will go home." Mechanically she straightened her torn and tumbled brown wincey dress. Then she looked up at him again, and impulsively threw her arms about his neck and clung to him.

"Come on," he said after a minute. "We must get back as fast as we can. She is waiting for you."

Mrs. Brayton walked out to the pines with them.

"Tell your mother I will come to see her very soon. And take very good care of her, my dear," as she kissed the child.

"Yes, I'll tell her," answered Asia gratefully.

Bruce hoisted her on to the front of the saddle, jumped up himself, and with one arm round her, started off.

She was too tired to enjoy the ride, which at any other time would have been a great adventure. Before they had gone far she was sound asleep.

As soon as he got within speaking distance of Alice, who was waiting at the front gate, Bruce told her all was well.

Then he dismounted and lifted Asia down into her arms. As he did so he saw that, perhaps, at last she was prepared to take down her barricades as far as he was concerned. She said not a word, nor did he as he turned away to lead his horse back to the kitchen.

But he had gone only a few yards along the path when he heard steps behind him. Alice stood alone, Asia having tumbled sound asleep onto the front steps.

He saw that she had rushed after him on a sudden impulse, and that she didn't know what to say, as she stood trembling. He had no theory to account for the state of emotion he saw she was in. But he felt extraordinarily near to her as she stood there, and he knew that she needed him very badly. Quite deliberately he held out his hand and took one of hers that was holding her cape together.

Just as he was about to speak her reserve gave way.

"Oh, forgive me——" she choked.

"I do," he said simply, not pretending that there was nothing to forgive.

"I—I——"

"That's enough," he smiled, interrupting her. "You don't have to say it twice, or vary it. I am acquainted with the synonyms. I know all you want to say. I do not understand why you have been afraid of me, or why you have misunderstood me, but all you owe me now is a fresh beginning. And don't talk about it. Just begin. I think I can help you, and we'll talk about it some day, but not tonight. You have had a bad day, and you get to sleep just as soon as you can. Tell me"—he was still holding her hand, and she was staring into his face—"did any one give a signal that Asia was found?"

She was startled by this transition.

"No—at least Mr. Brayton—yes, I think he told some one."

"Did anybody blow a horn or anything?"

"Oh, yes, a whistle."

"Are they all back?"

"I don't think so. My husband isn't."

"All right. Now, please go in and forget everything unpleasant. You can, you know." He knew she couldn't, but he knew this would make her try to. He did not know that she wanted to throw her arms round him, but as she turned quickly away he felt as if he had rescued a child from the dark.

He continued his way along the path to the kitchen till he heard voices on the spit. Then he turned suddenly, as if he had remembered something, and led his horse down to the store where he met the boss. Roland was hot and irritable.

"Where the devil was she?" he demanded.

Bruce guessed Alice had not told him the whole story, so he took chances on what he might say.

"She was at Mrs. Brayton's. She'd gone to sleep in the afternoon, woke up in the dark, and lost her way."

"Holy Moses! What a fuss about nothing!" he exclaimed, taking up a lantern put down by one of the men who had walked on.

"Well, it looked bad," said Bruce rather indifferently. "By the way, as your wife was very badly unnerved, I gave her a sleeping powder. She ought not to be disturbed till she is thoroughly rested."

Roland shot a quick look at him, wondering if he meant anything by this. But he could make nothing of that noncommittal face, on which the weak lantern light cast shadows that brought out the lines. He noticed instead that his foreman drooped as if he were very tired. He knew where Bruce had been all day. He could not help wondering if Bruce knew where he had been. At first he told himself he did not care a damn if he did. Then he hoped he didn't.

"Is there a spare bunk in the kitchen?" he asked abruptly.

"Several. But take my shanty for the night." Bruce answered as if there were nothing unusual in the boss's question.

"No, no, thanks. I'll go to the kitchen."

They turned together along the path.

"Your wife's going to have another child." Bruce still used his weary voice.

"What! Damnation!" blurted out the boss.

"Well, they have a habit of coming," drawled Bruce.

Roland laughed uneasily.

"I suppose they have," he grunted, kicking at a tuft of grass in the path.

They walked on some yards in silence.

"Walker told me to-day," said Bruce in the same level tones, "that that boy of his who's had some engineering would be glad to have a job with you. He might be worth trying."

Roland was instantly diverted.

"That so? All right. I'll try him."

And business details occupied them till they separated.

CHAPTER X

WHEN Alice began to make peace with Asia the next morning she was prepared neither for the easy forgiveness and forgetfulness of the tragedy of the day before nor for the torrent of questions that was the result of the emotional intimacy of that reconciliation.

She was conscious that day that something was wrong with her method, and for the first time she longed to talk it over with somebody, and she knew the somebody meant David Bruce. She had awakened that morning thinking of him, and of his words to her the night before. She knew now that she had to see him and talk to him, that he could help her to straighten out some of the perplexities of her thinking that winter, and she wondered why it suddenly seemed to be all right. But as the day wore on, and the possibility of her seeing him that evening became more insistent, excitement welled up in her again, and her pet bogy, the beginning, arose to frighten her. She knew that if she longed to see him so much it was not right to see him at all.

But temptation kindly removed itself from her for a few days. When Roland returned from the bush that evening he made a fuss about some important paper he had forgotten to get from Bruce. And Alice learned that as the latter would not be down for some days her husband would have to make a special trip back to get it.

This left her alone to deal with Asia and her questions as best she might. And in the course of those few days she was appalled at the distance the child's mind had travelled, and hurt to find out that she had talked freely to others. In a moment of illumination she saw that this was the result of her own actions. Whenever Asia had begun to be inconveniently inquisitive, she had declared she had a headache, that she mustn't be worried, and she had thought by this means to stifle or divert that lively imagination and that vigorous curiosity.

Asia was indeed a revelation to her mother. She had been quick to turn from Alice's headaches to David Bruce, who never seemed to have headaches when she wanted to talk to him, and to Bob Hargraves, who had no scruples whatever about churning up her young mind, and to other men about the bay, who were amused at her naïve questions. She had pestered them all as to their views on God and the angels. She had collected their opinions on the subjects of what people ate in heaven, whether they wore clothes or not, whether they slept in beds, whether they were so strong that their legs and arms would not break, whether God really heard your prayers, what he really did to the wicked, and so on. And she had puzzled herself into a fever over the variety of their answers.

It was from the Socialist carpenter working on the beach that she first learned that there was no God, that nobody really believed in him, and that it did not matter whether there was a God or not, because people had to live just the same, and be nice and kind to one another, that the greatest thing in the world was to be liked, and that if you were kind you were liked, and if you were nasty you were not. As for hell, he successfully convinced her that no god of love could ever have thought of such a place for a minute.

It was when she asked him if she was to believe him instead of her mother that the carpenter saw he might get into trouble for talking to her. So he tried to explain that people had different opinions, but that some people did not like to hear about anything but their own, and so he asked her not to tell her mother what he had said. This troubled her so much that she had asked Bruce about it. He gave the carpenter and Bob Hargraves and others a hint that they had better leave her education to the people appointed to educate her. But he had difficulties with her himself.

"Do you believe God lives up in the sky?" she had asked him.

"I haven't seen Him, but lots of people think He is there," he replied.

But she was not to be put off.

"Do you believe He is there?" she persisted.

"I don't know," he answered truthfully.

"Do you say your prayers?" she asked.

"I pray in a different way," he evaded.

But this only started more questions.

And so it was that when she got this chance to begin on her mother she was a questioner experienced by considerable practice, mystified by the variety of opinion, and stimulated by something that was almost a conspiracy to keep her from the things she wanted to know.

God seemed a safe and simple topic, but they had not proceeded far with Him before Alice found herself in a hopeless mess.

"Mother, do you really believe God lives up in the sky?"

They were all out in the garden the second afternoon, Betty and Mabel playing in a big box, and Alice and Asia trying to dig a plot for vegetables.

"My dear, you know I do. Why do you ask? I've always taught you that God lives in the sky."

"Does He see us now?"

"Yes, He always sees us. I've told you all this before."

"Does He know we want to have a nice lot of vegetables?"

"Of course He does."

"Then why does He let the worms eat the seeds? That isn't kind."

"Well, they won't eat them all, and they have to live on something."

Alice thought this was satisfactory, but she saw that Asia

was turning it over in her mind. She could not understand why the child no longer believed her.

"You are not digging very well. You must go deeper than that," she said, hoping to divert her attention.

She had discovered that action and a new occupation were fine antidotes to Asia's mental restlessness. She had also learned that they might be a good thing for her own, and for that reason she had been glad to learn to garden. When she heard that Mrs. Brayton did a good deal of her digging Alice decided that she could dig a little too, and as soon as her husband had got her and Asia light spades and other garden tools they had begun to work out of doors whenever the days were fine, and now they had a few spring plants and rows of sprouting vegetables.

But along with these joys they had discovered the sorrow of worms, and Asia had developed an extraordinary vindictiveness for the predatory insects that destroyed the seeds and buds. Her mother had been amazed once to see her stamp with exalted fury upon a snail, which she called a villain and a thief, telling it that now she had got it she would show it no mercy, and giving a sigh of satisfaction when she saw its pulpy remains mixed with the earth. Indeed, snails and worms had had a good deal to do with Asia's speculations about God.

"Mother," she said, leaning upon her little spade, "if I was God, and could make nice things, I'd never make nasty ones. I wouldn't make snails and worms to eat up the flowers."

"But they do good in other ways," said Alice.

"But why should they do any bad things? God could have made them all good."

"My dear"—Alice tried to be patient—"we do not know His reasons. I do not know them any more than you do. But I believe that it will be all right, and we shall know some day."

"But I want to know now. It won't be any use to know when we are dead."

Alice stared at her, startled by this truth. She wondered if the child understood what she was saying, or whether she was repeating something she had heard. This thought had occurred to her several times lately.

But just then she caught sight of Mrs. Brayton coming down the field, and Asia flew to meet her.

The old lady had her arms full of spring flowers and two books of short stories by W. W. Jacobs. She greeted Alice with a spontaneity that hid no secret reference to any tragedy in the past, and they immediately began a discussion of the garden. Mrs. Brayton praised Asia's plot for which she had brought a parcel of young plants, and she gave Alice hints as to the care of seeds, and the best way to rake and hoe. Then they went in for tea and music.

The next evening, as Asia threw out the tea leaves, something in the spring night caught her.

"Oh, Mother, the stars are so wonderful. Come out and look."

They stood some minutes looking up at them.

"Mother, do play Red Indians with me, just for a little while. It's such a long time since you had time to play."

"Very well," smiled Alice, "just for a few minutes. Get my cloak."

Roland sat over his everlasting figures in the sitting-room, beside a fire. Alice knew the babies were asleep, and that she could be out without being missed.

Asia got a board and a box for them to sit upon, and with an air of mystery and suppressed excitement that amazed Alice she led the way to a Maori pit that Bruce had told her was the remains of an old fortification. There were several of them along the top of the cliffs.

"Now, Mother, we'll be good Indians, and the bad ones will come up the river to burn our homes. We must lie down and watch for them. Quick! 'Cause Indians can see in the dark. And when the fish jump that's the sound of their canoes. They don't make any sound if they're careful, but to-night they'll be careless, 'cause they think we are away. Quick, now, Mother, or they'll see us."

Wildly excited she dropped down into the pit, almost pulling her mother off her feet.

"We are safe," she whispered. "Now listen, and be ready to shoot, like this, see," and up went her pointing hands in imitation.

Alice was astonished at the vividness of the child's imagination, at the seriousness of her play, at this transformation from her ordinary self, or what Alice took to be her ordinary self. When a fish jumped she fired with an assumption of nerve and bravery, then she heard the screams of sinking Indians, and, what was still more unlike herself, she exulted in their destruction. In ten minutes they had won a great battle single-handed against innumerable foes, and then, the thrill of the fight passed, and their safety secured, Asia dropped back, panting, beside her mother.

She lay still for a minute or two. Then she drew up her knees, pressing her chin into them. Her hair fell about her face so that Alice, looking at her sideways, could see only the tip of her nose. With a pang at her heart the mother felt that the child had come in the last few months to live in a world of her own, from which, if she did not take care, she would be soon shut out.

"Mother"—Asia turned suddenly—"we've killed hundreds of bad Indians. We have not really, but suppose we had, do you think they will all go to hell?"

"Bad Indians have to be punished, like bad white people," Alice answered, hoping the questions were not going to begin again.

"Mother, is there really any hell? Mr. Bruce doesn't believe there is any."

For a moment Alice felt the resentment she had felt before that any one but herself should direct the thought of her child.

"There are people who don't believe in hell. But there

must be a place where bad people are punished," she replied uncomfortably.

Asia peered through the starlight at her mother,

"I can understand why bad people should be punished, but I don't understand why they have to go on being punished. Nobody goes on beating all the time down here. If Betty is naughty in the morning, you don't slap her all day and all night and on for ever. And I don't believe a good God would either. Mr. Bruce wouldn't. He told me. He's kinder than God."

Startled afresh, Alice looked away from her and down upon the star-spotted river sheen below. It was bad enough to be thinking something of this kind herself, but to have her doubts put into the hard form of words by her child was worse. At Asia's age she herself had been a clod to be moulded as her elders pleased. She had never doubted the things she had been told. She had never heard any other point of view; she had been too carefully sheltered.

"Asia," she said sadly, determined not to be angry with her, "you have been talking about things that only I should tell you, and so you are getting mixed up. You must not ask other people questions."

"But I want to know things, Mother. I must know."

"Then you can ask me."

Asia waited a minute or two.

"Are you sure you know, Mother?" she asked.

Alice began to get impatient.

"I know just as well as anybody else, and it is the duty of children to believe what their parents tell them. You are forgetting all the things I have taught you."

Asia thought a few minutes.

"You told me God answers our prayers, Mother."

"When we pray for what is right, yes."

"He does not answer mine."

"Then you have prayed for foolish things."

"No, I haven't. I have prayed a long, long time that you

wouldn't have any more babies, and now Mrs. Jones says you are going to have another——"

"What!" Alice sprang into a tense position.

"Oh, Mother, don't be angry. Why do you get angry——"

"Oh, oh!" Alice burst into helpless tears of shame and humiliation. For the moment she wished she were dead. There seemed to be no end to her sufferings.

"Mother, what have I done?" whimpered Asia. "I don't want you to have any more babies. I can't help it—I don't——"

"Oh, Asia!" Alice turned to her with a passionate burst of grief that hurt the child as much as anger. "You are going to make me ill. You will kill me if you go on like this. You must stop talking to anybody—anybody but Mr. Bruce. Do you hear me?" her voice rose. "I will not allow you to go anywhere. Where did you see that woman—Mrs. Jones? Tell me at once. Where did you see her?"

"She was in the store this morning. I heard her tell another woman——" Asia was sobbing now herself.

Alice clenched her hands to keep herself from screaming.

"Oh, how horrible!" she gasped, to herself. "How could she know? I haven't told any one. It must have been just suspicion. Vile creatures!" She wondered if her husband could possibly have guessed and told her. She knew he talked with what was to her disgusting familiarity.

"Mother, don't be angry," pleaded Asia.

"Asia, I don't know what I will do if you go on talking to people. You used to be so good. You did as I told you. Now you don't seem to care whether you make me unhappy or not——"

"Oh, I do, Mother."

"Then, listen to me. You stop listening to anybody or talking to anybody when I send you to the store. These people are not like us, and they have no business to know anything about us, or to talk about us. Now will you remember that?"

"All right, Mother. Can't I talk to Mr. Hargraves?"

"No," cried Alice furiously, "not to anybody."

Asia sobbed in perplexity.

"But I like him," she moaned.

"I can't help that. You must do as I tell you."

"All right, Mother," said the child with an air of resignation. "I won't talk to anybody any more. But how did Mrs. Jones know you were going to have a baby? Can't you stop it, Mother?"

"Oh, Asia"—Alice sprang to her feet—"go inside! I cannot talk to you any more to-night. Go inside. Don't be frightened. I am not angry with you. But I want to be alone. Go to bed." She burst into tears again.

Asia sobbed bitterly as she got to her feet.

"I don't understand why you are crying—I don't understand. Will you tell me, Mother?"

Alice looked helplessly at her. It never occurred to her to soothe her with the truth, and she was totally unprepared for such a situation with the sort of lies that might have been effective. What to do with a child who would think, and who wanted real reasons she did not know. She only felt that such precocity was most unhealthy. Asia was no longer merely her child. She had become a problem as well.

"I can't talk to you to-night," she repeated. "But go in and go to bed, and do stop thinking. You are not old enough to think for yourself. Now, kiss me good night. I am not angry with you now."

But the grief was just as inexplicable to Asia as the anger. She went sobbing inside, and sobbing she undressed and got into bed to puzzle about it for hours before she fell asleep. No sooner had she begun to develop a feeling for the world as a glorious plaything than this other sense of fearful things lurking just out of view began to oppress her. Along with the revelation of adventure in the *Boys' Own* had come the mystery of babies, and the still greater mystery of the things one must not say.

After Asia had left her Alice walked blindly down to the beach, and began to pace up and down the hard sand border between the pebbles and the mud bared by the low tide. She was too distracted to cry any more.

"Oh, God! What am I to do, what am I to do?" she groaned. She looked up at the stars. Was He there, that Comforter, that she had sought so often, and believed in so unquestioningly in the past, that prop she so badly needed? She felt she did not have to visualize Him, she only had to feel Him as a presence. If He was all round her she ought to be able to feel Him there when she needed Him as she did now, and if she could not feel Him what use was He?

"Oh, God, where are you? I want to know now," she said, and then she remembered she was echoing Asia's words.

She stood as if expecting that sign that all men look for in those desperate moments when doubt, gathering strength, gets its final throttling grip upon blind faith. But she saw nothing but the hard starlight, the black bush, the spotted leaden channel of the river. She felt nothing but the chill air, the pervading desolation of the swamp lands and the hills.

Struck by sudden fear she sat down on the gnarled root of a pohutukawa, which spread its knotty and grotesque shape like the clutch of a demon hand far out onto the beach. If there were no God to help her, who would, and what did her life mean? Could she go on living without God, without any knowledge of Him? Could she make the sacrifices? Suppose there were no heaven—no reward? What would keep her a decent person? What would guide her in her daily life? What had guided her but that hope of a future life, with its justice and rewards? How could she face life without that hope? What was she to tell her child? How did people live who did not believe in God? She knew there were those who did not. She had heard great names, Ingersoll, Bradlaugh, etc. But she had always vaguely thought that there was some special dispensation to deal with great geniuses and the heathen. She had given God credit for some powers of discrimination. But she had always believed that the average person had to have God in order to be decent. She didn't see how without Him people would be decent. The fact that belief in God had not improved the lives of many people she knew had never affected her belief in Him. Her father had taught her that one should not condemn good kerosene because it got dirty in a dirty lamp, and she had accepted the illustration as all-embracing. She supposed that everybody she knew believed in God. But as she sat there she began to wonder how many of them really did. She wondered if David Bruce did.

Her thoughts went back to Asia and the outrageous Mrs. Jones, and a fit of anger shook her again. She did not know how she was going to live in such a place with such people, and with such experiences. She could not bear to be talked about. Her reserve and sense of aloofness from anything she did not like amounted to a mania. She thought it was necessary to the preservation of her own personality that she should wall herself off from those who had not her own sense of taste. Platitudes such as "You can't touch pitch without getting soiled" had the force of gospel truth to her. She thought it dreadful that Asia should even see such a person as she supposed Mrs. Jones to be.

When her feeling had spent itself she began to think. She saw that if she continued to worry as she had done in the past months she would become a nervous wreck. She knew that even if there were no God, no heaven, no justice anywhere, she would still have to live on here by the river, feed and clothe her husband and her children, have more children, keep her house clean, do certain things and not do certain things. And it would not matter what she believed, the porridge must be well boiled, or her family would get indigestion.

This came to her with the strength and clearness of a pronouncement from the skies, but she realized that it did not come from the skies. Though she was far from believing that it did not matter what she believed, she now made the discovery that no matter what she believed there were certain ways in which she, being herself, must act. And she saw, too, that in order to act in those imperative ways she must learn to protect herself from the violence of her own feeling.

But like a child in the dark, she craved for the light. If it was not to come from heaven, she would have to look for it elsewhere. She felt that David Bruce could help her. She wanted something to justify her desire to know him. She told herself that it was part of his work as a doctor to advise his patients, and that she could without any disloyalty to her husband turn to Bruce for spiritual advice. She did not see that what she really wanted was emotional satisfaction, sex satisfaction by proxy. She would have indignantly denied any suggestion of that.

"I don't care if there is a God or not," she said at last, half fearfully, as she got up, "I have a right to have that man for my friend."

She was a little afraid as she looked up at the stars. But no thunderbolt or lightning shaft shot out of the sky upon her. The probable loss of God in His heaven might have disturbed her much more if her thoughts had not turned to the final comforter of all women, whether they spurn it intellectually or not, a son of man.

Uncertain still, but glad to know that David Bruce was something she really could see and hear, she walked home.

CHAPTER XI

IT will take me two weeks, perhaps three. I've told Bruce to look in. He will be down to-night. Now, there's no necessity for you to be nervous. He or Bob Hargraves can sleep here. Everybody will know why they're doing it, and nobody is going to gossip about you, and if they do they can't hurt you."

Roland sat on his horse prepared to start for Auckland. He had been called away by telegram the next afternoon. As he spoke he went through his leather satchel to see that he had not forgotten anything.

"Oh, my cheque-book; I must have left it in the brown coat pocket," he said, fidgeting.

Alice hurried in to get it. He was thinking of something else when she handed it to him, so he forgot to thank her.

"Well, bye-bye," he said lightly, stooping to kiss her perfunctorily; and waving his hand to Asia at the kitchen window, he rode off.

An hour later Alice stood in front of what she called her wardrobe, wondering which of two dresses she should put on. She flushed guiltily, knowing this hesitancy was due to the fact that she wanted to look as nice as she could. She knew she had no business to dress for any man but her husband. Then she told herself she was silly, and that there was no question of dressing up. She wore the navy blue cloth dress and the grey cashmere dress alternately. They were both plain, and they both suited her. But still, there was something to choose between them. There were times when she looked better in the grey—if she had a good colour, for example. And she had a good colour now, and she knew she was likely to have it all the evening.

She tried to quiet her rising excitement as she put on the

grey dress. It had long loose lines of the utmost simplicity, through which her figure showed soft and rounded. It had no collar, but there was only the suggestion of a V in the neck. After some hesitancy Alice arranged her best bit of old lace round her throat, and pinned it with a sapphire brooch, the finest bit of old jewellery that she possessed. Then she was afraid that Asia might ask her why she did not wear these things oftener. The thought worried her. She unpinned the brooch and removed the lace. But finally she put them on again, thinking that as the child knew nothing of Bruce's possible visit she would not connect the two events.

When she had finished, Alice looked at herself in the glass. She knew she was attractive, even beautiful, but for years now she had taken little comfort from the knowledge. Her fine grey eyes, whose expression had always been somewhat remote from the humanity at her feet, had grown harder, and still more unresponsive. She saw the suggestion of lines about her straight features, which the girls in the select school she had attended in her youth had called statuesque and Grecian. But her skin was as fine and as clear as ever, and her chestnut hair was full of dancing lights.

She drew back startled as she realized where her thoughts were leading her. The worst thing that could happen would be for David Bruce to see that she was beautiful, and to proceed as most men proceeded under the stress of that knowledge. She wanted his friendship, and she knew she needed it very badly, but if it were not forthcoming simply because she was a woman she must not bargain for it with her looks. Then she remembered that his helpfulness had not ceased because he had seen her in the most unbecoming of clothes and in the most unattractive of domestic settings. As a matter of fact, he had never given a sign that he was conscious of her looks. He had been exactly what she pretended she wanted. Then why was she dressing up for him now?

She was considering this when Asia called to tell her that the children's tea was ready.

After the babies were put to bed, Alice and Asia sat down to their own meal. They had had some further talk that morning, when Alice had told the child that she really did want a baby boy, and that that was the reason why she was going to have another baby, but that it was only their business and that other people ought not to talk about it, and she said Mrs. Jones could not know it, but that she had only guessed it. She was relieved to see that Asia was diverted by the idea of the baby's being a boy, and that she started at once to find names for him, and to plan out the fun she would have with him, oblivious of the fact that he would not be able to play in her fashion for a long time to come.

It was after eight o'clock, and they were both sitting by the front room fire, when Alice sat up suddenly, hearing steps outside.

"Asia, there's somebody coming. You stay here." She got up as she spoke, and as the knock sounded on the back door she went out to the kitchen, trying to calm the sudden leap of her heart into her throat.

"It's David Bruce, Mrs. Roland," he called at once.

"Please come in," she answered as she lit the candle. Her nervousness mysteriously left her as she looked at him. What it was about him that took charge of her and made her feel like a child she did not know.

Bruce had on his old tailored suit, a soft white shirt with a low collar, and a plain long navy tie. He looked easy and comfortable, and he entered the kitchen as if he had left it only the hour before.

"Well, how are your nerves?" he asked, smiling down upon her.

This simple question, so much to the point, surprised her. She did not know what she had expected him to say. She had wondered, reviewing the past, what he would say, and she had been afraid of the humiliation and embarrassment she was sure she would feel.

"I—I don't know," she confessed, wondering if he would just naturally stay, or whether she had to ask him to stay, and exactly what her husband had said to him.

"Well, are you starting at every sound, and looking for faces at the window?"

Alice found herself actually smiling back at him.

"Oh, no, I don't think—no, I'm not as bad as that."

Then she remembered that if she did not appear to be nervous he might not stay. That confused her. But she was saved by Asia, who bounded out from the sitting-room.

"It's only Mr. Bruce, Mother," she pleaded, catching Alice's forbidding look.

"And, of course, he's nobody to notice," he said mischievously, his eyes twinkling.

Alice could not help laughing nervously; and, laughing, her eyes met his. She knew she could not resist his boyish lightness. Asia seized his hand.

"Oh, you are cold," she said. "Can't he get warm, Mother?"

Bruce turned his dancing eyes upon Alice.

"You don't have to say 'yes' unless you want to."

But a quick light flashed across her eyes.

"Please come to the fire," she stammered awkwardly, not seeing how absurdly she was putting it.

Boisterously dragged by Asia, he followed Alice into the front room, and sat down opposite her in the glow of the logs.

"This is lovely," cried Ásia joyously, as she flopped on to the mat between them. "Now you tell us stories, Mr. Bruce. Tell us about Julius Cæsar. I love him."

"My dear," gasped Alice, "do be quiet. Mr. Bruce may not want to tell stories. And, besides, it's time you went to bed." Although Alice was growing excited now at the thought of being alone with him, she knew it had to come, and she wanted it over as soon as possible.

"Oh, no, Mother, it's quite early." Asia drooped to the verge of tears.

Alice did not wish to show that she wanted to be alone with him. She had hoped that would come about naturally.

"Can't I hear one story?" pleaded the child.

"Look here, young lady," broke in Bruce, "I have come here to see how your mother is getting along, and I can tell you stories some other time. I want to talk to her to-night."

"Oh, dear!" she said sadly. Then a gay thought struck her. "Are you going to stay all night? You can sleep in my bed. I won't mind."

She did not understand why he laughed suddenly or why her mother turned to look into the fire.

"Why should I stay all night?" he asked, returning to gravity.

"Why"—she thought a minute—"we must have a man to take care of us, and Father has gone away."

"Yes, but you know it might not be convenient to your mother to have me to stay. You should have found that out before you asked me. There might not be enough for breakfast."

"Oh, but I know there's plenty. There's porridge—and we can make lots—and there's bread and butter——" She stopped, for now Bruce had dropped his head in his hands, and her mother was laughing helplessly. "Why are you laughing?" she demanded.

Bruce raised his face. Alice looked at him and away again, leaving him to deal with the situation.

"Look here. You don't see that perhaps your mother does not want me to stay at all. There could be lots of reasons why she does not, but now that you have asked me you make it very hard for her not to ask me to stay because she would not want to hurt my feelings by showing me that she does not want me. And so, before you asked me you should have found out whether she would like me to stay or not. A strange man in a house is a lot of trouble; he's not like a member of the family. Your mother might want to stay in bed in the morning, but if I were here she would feel she would have to get up. Do you see?"

Though she kept her face turned to the fire, Alice listened breathlessly.

"I see," said Asia slowly. "But you are not a strange man. And I can look after you. And you get your own breakfast, and make your own bed, you told me."

At last Alice turned to speak, but Bruce waved his hand at her with a smile.

"Wait a bit," he said, just as if he had been assisting her to deal with Asia all his life. "I'm going to make her see it if I can."

"Listen," he took one of Asia's hands. "You want me to stay, and because you want me to stay you think your mother wants me to stay, and you also think I want to stay. But you are thinking only of yourself. You are not really being unselfish. And this is your mother's house, not yours. Now, don't you see that you can't decide for us. You don't really know what we want to do. And that is why children should wait for older people to say what they want to do."

"Oh, dear," she said pathetically, "mustn't I ever want you to do anything?"

"Oh, yes," he smiled, "but you had better whisper it in our ears first to see if it is all right."

She turned instantly to Alice to take him literally, and seeing it coming they both collapsed.

"Oh, Lord!" he groaned. "I congratulate you on having remained sane."

Whether it was because she had laughed little for months, or because the relief from strain was so relaxing, Alice laughed out as she had not done that winter. Feeling that they were making fun of her, Asia was deeply hurt.

"I think you are nasty," she choked.

Then her mother turned to her.

"My dear, I wish you would remember what Mr. Bruce

has said. But it is all right for him to stay to-night if he wants to—" she looked at him, blushing, and adding quickly —"and if he can spare the time to look after us."

"Certainly," interrupted Bruce promptly.

"But I wish you would remember that this is not your house, and that Father and I are the ones to ask people to come. She is always asking people to come and stay," she looked explainingly at Bruce.

"Naturally," he smiled. "Children are so interested in everybody and everything. And exclusiveness isn't an instinct; it's a cultivated precaution."

"Oh, but"—she wanted him to uphold her—"it's impossible to have them."

"Well, they all understand that, don't they? Did any of them ever come?"

She looked rather uncomfortably into his amused eyes, seeing that she was foolish.

"Asia, you must really go to bed now. Say good night to Mr. Bruce."

Piteously disappointed, the child held out her hand.

"May I kiss Mr. Bruce, mother?" she whispered, her face lighting up as this idea came to her.

"You certainly may," answered Alice hoarsely.

Asia fastened herself upon him as if she meant to stay there for ever, and he was about to disentangle her when she jumped up, struck by another idea.

"Mother, I haven't any uncle. Couldn't Mr. Bruce be my uncle?"

"My dear," Alice laughed suddenly, meeting his quizzical eyes, "perhaps Mr. Bruce would not like that."

"Oh, dear! There I am again," she exclaimed mournfully, seeing that she had forgotten the teaching of the evening. "I can't remember. It's too hard."

"Why would you like me to be your uncle?" he asked solemnly.

"Oh, it would be so nice. And then, you see, if you were my uncle, you would be a member of the family, and you could come often and stay, and you wouldn't be a bother. Oh, do, please."

Asia did not know that her simple proposal was to create an attitude of mind that would extend beyond the house on the cliffs, and be accepted as a matter of course in the years to come as a relation that went unquestioned. How far it affected the consciousness of either Bruce or Alice at that moment neither could have said; but they both had a "feeling" about it.

"Well," answered Bruce, as if he were considering a weighty proposition, "it's a responsibility, but perhaps I can live up to it. Uncle David—it sounds benevolent, domestic, respectable. By all means let me be Uncle David. It will be good for me. But"—he remembered Alice—"your mother?"

"Oh, please, yes," she interrupted him, half-way between laughter and tears.

"All right," he smiled at Asia, "I will be your Uncle David."

"Oh, how lovely!" And she fell upon him vigorously.

"To bed," he whispered, disengaging her arms.

Regretfully she went out, and for some time they heard her fussing about in the back before she returned to be waved abruptly by her mother into the front bedroom.

Erratic flames from the log fire spurted short-lived lights over Alice's piano, along the floor, and about the furniture. Apart from the sounds made by Asia there was nothing to break the silence of the night outside. It was a heavy silence threatening rain, and it brought the hills and the forest nearer, but it also added to the cheerfulness of the fire and the security of the little room.

Alice sat up a little straighter in her rocker, outwardly composed, and determined to behave naturally. Her anticipatory feelings now seemed absurd to her as she looked at David Bruce's face turning towards her.

He had come to her that evening with a knowledge of her difficulties that would have astonished her. Though he did not pretend to understand her or any woman in detail, he knew that to her inbred mental deviousness, the knots of the feminine mind, were added the deadly ramifications of Puritanism and the Scotch temperament.

Since seeing her the night of Asia's disappearance his thoughts had turned seriously to her, for he saw he would now have to deal with her in a more personal way. He had wandered about the bush one night considering the elements in the situation. He remembered the look of fear and fascination on her face the night he had walked into her room to put some kick into her, the fact that she never met him naturally even though he had ignored the inconvenient past, and he considered the something that had arrested him at their last meeting when her reserves had broken down.

Bruce knew without vanity that as a doctor he appealed to the emotional side of women. He knew that as a man he attracted them. He knew that in any situation where he had to deal intimately with a woman he had to reckon with these two possibilities. He was something of a sex psychologist, and he had learned how to minimise emotionalism in others, but he knew that in order to treat them successfully he had to remain dispassionate himself.

The unknown quantity in this situation he saw to be himself. He knew Alice attracted and interested him. But he felt sure he would know how to deal with any situation that was likely to arise. The fact that he had not been in love with any woman for ten years had rather dimmed his impressions of the devastations of that kind of fever.

But even while Asia dominated the scene between them, Bruce had been conscious of Alice's heightened colour, of her aliveness, of the softness and delicacy of her renewed maternity. He had noticed the lace and the brooch as things he had not seen her wear before, and he had wondered if they had any significance beyond that of the ordinary feminine desire to dress up for a man.

His eyes were smiling as they turned from Asia's retreating form to Alice.

"What a child!" he said lightly. "But she is a bit of a responsibility, isn't she?"

"Yes, indeed." She was grateful to him for this easy opening. "I'm afraid I don't quite know what to do with her"—she looked humbly into the fire—"she's grown so old, and she seems to me to be too precocious. Isn't it unhealthy?" She looked at him appealingly.

"Unhealthy!" His eyes twinkled at her. "Why, she's the healthiest child I ever saw. She actually thinks! I know that's often inconvenient and embarrassing; but it's perfectly healthy."

She could not help smiling. In spite of what she thought she ought to be feeling her spirits were rising to respond to the magnetism of his presence.

"Well, she may amuse other people, but at times she is a trial to me." This was a good deal of a confession, as he saw. "Perhaps you can help me," she added.

"I think I can." He leaned forward a little, talking half to the fire and half to her. "You know, if you will pardon my saying it, God and the angels are not enough for an intelligent child like that. They are too abstract, and they feed only the emotions. And then, they are rather troublesome when it comes to being exact, don't you think? And children demand exactness, things they can see and handle. Does she know anything about arithmetic?"

"But," she interrupted breathlessly, "wouldn't you teach children about God?"

"Why, certainly, more or less as a fairy tale. And I would give them arithmetic as an antidote. A child like Asia needs arithmetic and other things that are useful on this earth. Are you going to send her to school?"

"To Kaiwaka? Oh, no. It is too far, and"—she paused, ashamed to add what was in her mind about the country children not being good enough for her child to associate with—"I teach her a little. She can read very well, and she practises music an hour every day."

He looked at her as she sat up primly in her chair, and

wondered if she really thought that that was enough to fit Asia to grow up and meet the New Zealand world.

"What do you mean her to be?" he asked curiously.

"Why," she looked worried by this question, "I don't know. But it is too soon to think about it."

"You are wrong," he said quietly. "That's the mistake that has always been made about girls. But it won't do for this age, or this country. Do you really think that child can grow up to meet life on adventure stories false to life, on religious tract stories false to life, on the Bible, a collection of legends with no more revelation in them than those of the Maoris, compiled like every other story and rumour—that's true, you don't really live by them yourself—none of these things will teach your child to meet a real situation, any more than they have taught you. Blind faith does stimulate emotion, and there is a place for emotion," he smiled at his own preachiness, "but it has contributed nothing to self-preservation, which is the strongest law that rules this world."

He did not know that she was startled because he was putting into words the things that had disturbed her most that very week.

"I don't mean any disrespect to your faith," he went on, "but we need more than faith to deal with this world. We need knowledge. And we cannot begin too soon to give knowledge to our children. We have given it to our boys, but we have left our girls to traditional notions about religion and love with disastrous results." Seeing that these last words disturbed her, he went on, "I could teach Asia some things, if you will allow me—geography, arithmetic, history, perhaps some French. Mrs. Brayton has hosts of old books that would do, and it would not take much time to set the lessons. She would do the work with very little incentive, and she would soon cease to be a problem. I should like to do it."

Alice looked dumbly into his face, and in a minute emotion had her by the throat.

"But I can't trouble you," she stammered, "after all you've done——" Her voice broke and he saw her lips begin to quiver. Then she plunged. "Oh, Mr. Bruce, I don't know what to say to you, I can't explain, I have been all wrong, I don't know what you must think of me—it was a dreadful mistake." She paused, for in the face of his smile words seemed so foolish.

"Let's be thankful it was a mistake," he said cheerfully. "It would have been so much worse if I had really deserved all those things you were thinking of me."

She could only stare at him, amazed that the past could be eliminated because he laughed at it. She wondered what it was that gave him the power to dominate a situation, to take the difficult stuff of hard words and elusive human currents and make of them an atmosphere of ease and simplicity.

"Don't you mind that I was rude to you?" she asked, surprised into asking the thing she wanted most to know at that minute.

Bruce drew himself up, dropping his bantering manner. He knew quite well that they could not go on without a frank straightening out of the difficulties between them.

"If people are rude to me," he said gravely, "I ask myself some questions. First, do they know what rudeness is; second, are they deliberately rude; third, why are they rude to me in particular? Now I know that you know what rudeness is, therefore I can't excuse you on the score of ignorance or lack of sensibility"—he smiled, seeing she was listening in astonishment to this dispassionate analysis —"but I do not believe you were deliberately rude; that is, I believe you were trapped by an unfamiliar situation into a wrong beginning, and, unfortunately, wrong beginnings have a sad tendency to perpetuate themselves; their vitality is distressing. Behind you I saw British pride, with which I am familiar. I admit I was annoyed with you sometimes, especially when you brought needless suffering on yourself, but I was never really hurt by you."

She looked at him, unable to say anything. Nobody had

ever talked to her with this directness before. She did not know how to meet it. Bruce knew he had not offended her.

"Well?" he smiled.

She was fascinated by his leisurely manner.

"Mr. Bruce, I don't know what to say to you. I have never met any one like you before."

He liked this simple statement.

"In what way am I unique?" he asked mischievously.

"Why,"—she thought a moment—"you don't seem to notice anything. You don't seem to be hurt."

"Why should one be hurt? It's a great mistake to let people hurt us. We put a terrible power into their hands. Why should we give them that power? What right have they to it? And they would never have it if we did not give it to them."

She remembered these words as one of the philosophical landmarks of her life.

"Oh, if I could only feel that," she burst out. "Everything hurts me." Then she flushed at this confession.

"I know," he said gently, "and it's one of the first things I want to help you to get over."

He drew himself up in Tom Roland's arm chair again, for his body had a habit of sliding down and seeking comfort that was not to be had in that cushionless article. His informal movements arrested Alice.

"You are not comfortable," she said.

He smiled at her, hesitating between the truth and the polite lie.

"May I smoke?" he asked, realizing what it was he really wanted.

"Oh, certainly. Pardon me for not thinking of it."

She watched him take out his pipe and tobacco-pouch. There had been a time when she thought smoking disgusting, but she had become accustomed to the habit to the extent that she tolerated it. She had felt up to this moment, however, that no gentleman would smoke a pipe in her presence, but she realized, as she watched him take the tobacco out of his pouch and roll it, that she might have to reconstruct her ideas of what a gentleman might do.

Bruce had been so accustomed to smoking with Mrs. Brayton, who smoked with him, that he had his pipe filled before he remembered that Roland smoked only mild cigarettes, and that but seldom.

"Oh, pardon me"—he looked quickly at her—"I forgot for the moment that your husband does not smoke a pipe——"

"That does not matter. I don't mind; I wish you would, please."

But he felt the suggestion of concession in her manner.

"Now, now," he shook his finger at her as if she were a child, "are you speaking the truth?"

She blushed furiously.

"I thought not." His eyes twinkled again. "Now, look here"—Bruce had acquired many colonial informalities of speech—"now that I am Uncle David, and a member of the family, I'm going to scold you, so sit up and take it like a man. I shall smoke, since you are willing to allow me, for then I shall lecture you much more pleasantly."

She had to smile at him, though a little surge of excitement thrilled up in her.

Bruce lit his pipe and puffed for a few seconds, careful to keep the smoke away from her.

"Mrs. Roland," he began, with more gravity, "I wish you always to speak the truth to me. I don't allow people to lie to me."

"Why, Mr. Bruce," she exclaimed, astonished.

"Now, you are going to tell me that you always do speak the truth. And I am going to tell you that you don't. You lie every day of your life in manner, in thought, in action, if not in actual words. We all do. We deny the facts of life. We refuse to see them. to believe them if they are pointed out to us. And even if we see them, we say we don't. We say what we think is advisable, not what we suspect may be true. In fact, Mrs. Roland, you, and all women of your type, are the most frequent liars in the world, and I will prove it to you in the course of time. But all I want you to begin with is that you must not lie to me. It is unnecessary, because I know you are lying. I have heard just the same kind of lies over and over again. Every doctor has."

He saw that she was more startled than hurt by his words; that, in fact, she was not hurt at all.

"Well," he said, smiling again.

A spark of controversial fire flickered in her eyes.

"Will you always speak the truth to me?" she asked.

"Certainly not."

"Why?" she demanded.

"Because you could not bear it."

She drew herself up in her chair.

"What do you mean? She was stung into a determination to show that she could bear it.

But he continued to smile at her.

"Just what I say. You could not bear it. Few people can bear the truth. What they always take to be the truth is that which concerns other people, some remote abstraction. But bring the truth about themselves, their own families, their own friends, to their notice, and they will not believe it, or believing it, they will go to pieces, fall ill, become hysterical, go mad, commit suicide, deny their gods, and all the good in life."

"Mr. Bruce, in what way cannot I bear the truth? What is there you know?"

She broke off, flushing, thinking of Mrs. Lyman. He thought of her too, but he deliberately ignored it.

"Oh, now, don't be alarmed. But you see, you are alarmed. Now you don't like the truth that your child, Asia, doesn't believe the things you tell her to believe—there, wasn't I right?" He knew he had caught her. "You were taught that children must believe what they are told. You have never tried to find out if children really do believe what they are told, why they ought to believe what they are told, when they ought to leave off believing what they are told, or anything about it. You think that because your child thinks for herself she is unhealthy. You think that what is true for you must be true for her. How do you know it has to be?"

Alice stared at him, startled by the truth of his words and the revelation of his knowledge of her.

"I don't know," she answered helplessly, looking away from him into the fire. Then she looked back. "But there must be something true. I must teach her what I think true."

"Certainly. But don't be alarmed because she begins to find truth for herself." He puffed on contentedly.

"But," she persisted, "there's only one thing true about anything——"

"Ah, there we have it again," he interrupted. "The old bogy, the truth absolute. Of course it troubles you. But, you see, who is to decide what is true? A grey day is depressing to you and restful to me. What is a grey day? It is two things. It is one thing to you, another to me. There is no absolute truth about it."

He pulled himself up in his chair again.

"Then how can one decide about anything?"

"We decide as we feel." He smiled at her. "You think not? Perhaps not always at once, but finally, yes. And our feelings train our beliefs. We have a nice example to hand. Have you always approved of smoking?"

She could not help smiling.

"No," she replied.

"Do you approve it now?"

She hesitated.

"I don't mind it," she evaded.

"Do you like men to smoke a pipe in your presence?" he went on.

"I—I haven't thought——"

"Oh, yes, you have. You have had decided opinions about it. Now you can't deceive me. Out with it."

She looked into his laughing eyes, her submerged sense of humour rising to respond.

"I have thought that no gentleman would do it," she said.

Bruce threw up his head, laughing delightedly.

"Do you think so now?" he demanded She blushed, looking at him and away again. "Do you?" he repeated.

"No," she answered very low.

Bruce saw that she had suddenly plunged into emotion, but intent on conveying his idea, he ignored it for the moment.

"There," he exclaimed triumphantly. "In ten minutes you have modified, if not changed, a belief you have held for years. Why? Simply because your feeling suddenly told you to reject the old belief. You will allow me to smoke, you will actually begin to approve my smoking, you will insist on my smoking, because you like me, because you think you have been horrid to me, because you feel you have to be nice to me. And, because you feel these things about me, smoking will cease to be a sin or a bad habit to you. Now what is the truth about smoking? Is it what you used to feel, or what you feel now, or what you are going to feel?"

Again she brought her eyes back to his face. She had been carried on by his words from the emotional reason for her change to its intellectual significance. The revelation in his last words was something of a shock to her.

"Why, I never thought of it that way," she said slowly.

"It's a good thing to think of everything that way," he answered.

There was silence for some seconds while he smoked and she looked into the fire, which had begun to die down. Alice leaned down to take up a piece of wood.

"Don't make it up for me," said Bruce, leaning to take the block from her. "I must get to bed when I've finished my pipe. I'll have to start pretty early in the morning."

His sudden change to the affairs of daily life made her more conscious of their bodily nearness and their common isolation from the world outside.

"What time would you like breakfast?" she asked hurriedly.

"You needn't think about breakfast," he smiled, remembering Asia's words. "I'll go to the kitchen."

"You will do nothing of the kind."

"Pardon me, but I will. We will begin as we are likely to go on. This is a business arrangement, not a social pastime. If it is going to be any trouble to you it will defeat some of its own ends. I have to go up to the bush tomorrow, and I must leave here about five o'clock. Now, you know, I'm not going to have you get up at that hour to get my breakfast, especially when I can get it at the kitchen. You are not going to stand on ceremony with me, now that I am Uncle David."

Alice thought that she had never seen eyes that smiled as his did.

Bruce knocked the ashes out of his pipe, put it away in his pocket, and leaned towards her. He had to raise his face, as she was sitting up very straight.

"You are not going to be afraid of me any more, are you?" he asked simply.

She was instantly startled into lying.

"Why, Mr. Bruce, I——" But she stopped, seeing where she was going. Her face fell in confusion.

"See that," he said quietly. "Your first impulse is to lie. Now, you *have* been afraid of me. I don't quite know why, and you need not tell me why. But there is no reason why you should keep it up."

He sat up again, leaning back in his chair, while she sat nervously twitching her hands and looking into the coals.

"Mrs. Roland, I think that before anything else I am a doctor, and I see most people as children. I can't help it. I have looked so often into the helpless and frightened and appealing eyes of the sick and the dying that my whole attitude to people is coloured with the knowledge I have seen there—the general loneliness, the common fears, they are all the same. They differ only in degree. And when I see people I see first their troubles. I often ignore them, but I see them. And I have learned that troubles can be marvellously minimized by taking them out and looking at them. It's the first thing I set out to teach people. I want you to learn to talk to me. You won't do it easily at first, because you don't know how to. But you will learn. Here are you and I. We shall be much thrown together in this place. I shall have to be your doctor, because Mount won't come here now that I am here. Because I can help, I shall have to help you in many ways. It is inevitable in a place like this. It will be accepted by everybody without question. There is no reason why you should not accept it. I want you to know that you can send for me at any hour of the day or night, for any reason whatsoever, nervousness, loneliness, anything at all, and be sure that I shall understand, and that I shall never misunderstand."

Bruce knew that for some seconds she had been crying silently. He leaned down again, talking into the fire.

"Now I know that a good many things are troubling you, because a good many things trouble everybody. We are all worried about religion, about our children, about fears of poverty or illness, about the behaviour of the people we care about. But if we shut these things up within ourselves we add fuel to their fire, and in the end they burn us up. If we can compare notes with some one else, it is often a help. We find out that we have no monopoly over sorrow. You would be surprised if you knew the tragedies that there are here within a radius of twenty miles of you, while you think yourself the most ill-used person in the place."

He stopped. His voice had grown a little tired towards the end.

Alice turned towards him, not caring now whether he saw her cry.

"Oh," she choked, "I don't know what is the matter with me."

"Why, there is nothing the matter with you," he said lightly, "but your absurd tendency to make trouble for yourself. Nobody else wants to make it for you. There is no conspiracy of evil around you. Most people will do their best for you if you will let them. Their results may not always please you, but, at least, they will mean well. Nothing can hurt you but your own attitude of mind. You have good health, good looks, you can make people like you. What else matters? But if you don't take care you can wreck your health, you can poison your mind, you can make yourself everlastingly miserable quite easily. Now, you will have to choose sooner or later, as the evangelists say, why not now?"

He smiled at her, seeing that her eyes were shining with a mixture of emotions. He had deliberately ignored several elements in her situation, giving her what he thought most useful. He knew he had talked like a Christian Scientist, or an ism of some kind, but he knew she would depend for a long time to come on some ism or other.

"Well, will you think over what I've said to you?" he asked. "You'll find it useful." He stood up.

Mechanically Alice got to her feet, her eyes dry again.

"I will think about it—you have helped me more than I can say."

She looked into his face, and for a second all that she felt about him flashed from her eyes.

"That's good. And now, Mrs. Roland, you cease to worry about anything, even about the child that's coming—now don't blush, and don't look away from me. What is the matter with you women? You each act as if you were the only person who ever had a child, who knew how a child was born or why it was born. You each act as if no man could possibly know that children are born, or as if it were a disgraceful thing for them to know. You each act as if it really were a shameful thing to have a child, or as if nature were disgusting in her processes, neither of which things is true. It may be tragic to have a child, it may be unfortunate, it may be unwise, but it is never disgraceful.

And for you to blush about it to me, who have already nursed you—why, don't you see how silly it is?"

In spite of her confusion she had to look at him, and the real impatience in his eyes cured her. His look was so impersonal that she saw that she was to him in that moment only a "case," and that her emotionalism was ridiculous.

"Mr. Bruce, I will try, but I can't be different all at once," she said rather pathetically.

Instantly his face and manner changed, and his eyes lit up.

"It's too bad of me to scold you," he said in tones that were like a caress, "but I do want you to see that you cannot be foolish with me. I don't allow it. Now I shall be down about the same time to-morrow night, and if you want any help during the day send for Bob Hargraves. He's a decent chap; you can trust him."

He moved from the fireplace, Alice following him. She was less certain of herself when he was not talking to her, more vividly conscious of him the more she was aware of their being there alone. But she noticed that he seemed oblivious of it.

"I must get you a candle," she said. "And you would like some supper."

"I would like a glass of milk, thank you, if you have it to spare." He stood by the door while she found a candle in the kitchen and lit it. While she got a glass and poured out some milk for him his eyes roved round the room, but he was fully aware that she was making of the simple service something in the nature of a reverential ceremony. "Does the roof leak there?" he asked, his eyes on a corner.

"Yes." She looked up at it.

"Well, I'll fix that some evening. You remind me. You see, as Uncle David, I can be made use of in all sorts of ways."

Their eyes met, and for once hers responded spontaneously to the mischief in his. He, too, thought that if she only knew how attractive she looked when she smiled she would do so oftener.

"I shall certainly make use of you," she said.

"Do. That's what I'm for. And I'm presuming you'll stay nervous, Mrs. Roland. If you developed Amazonian courage my presence here would be superfluous."

He meant nothing by that observation, but it raised a quick excitement in her, and she thought more of it afterwards than of anything else he had said. But at the time she replied with a nervous little laugh, that she was only too likely to stay as she was.

He drank the milk and took the candle from her, looking as he did so to the fireplace.

"You have wood in. Is there anything I can do?"

"Nothing more, thank you," she said, with eloquent emphasis.

But he ignored her warmer manner.

"All right. Good night. I hope you will sleep well."

He held out his hand, gave hers a quick, strong grip, with no suggestion of lingering, and turned from her into Asia's room, where he was to sleep, and shut the door.

Alice closed the centre door behind her as she returned to the front room, leaving him shut off in the back of the house. She could not go to bed at once. She knew she would not sleep. She sat down to think over the things he had said, and of how he had looked as he said them. She knew it was the most extraordinary talk she had ever had with any one, and not at all what she had expected. She knew it had been managed by him, and that he had taken her in hand, and cut out her emotionalism. But the thing she wanted most to know was whether he understood the cause of her emotionalism. But she could not tell from his manner whether it meant anything special to him to sit there with her. She did not know if he had noticed what she had on or what she looked like. And yet she had been vividly aware of every line on his tanned face, of the thickness of the black brows over his deep set eyes that lit up and twinkled like those of a child, of his straight nose and mouth, his thin cheeks and chin, of his fine black hair, and of the droop of his head when at rest. She had been conscious, but less clearly so, of his movements, his easy strength, the sweep of his big limbs.

As she went over what he had said she found no disturbing suggestion in it, save in the one light remark about her Amazonian courage, but after turning that over for some time she decided there was no barb of innuendo in it. He had offered her the one thing she told herself she wanted, a prop. And it did not seem to matter to her whether she grew to love him in secret or not, if only they could go on like that. And she believed they could go on like that because he looked like it. She told herself that if she could just love him it would be a relief; she would want no return. It would be a delicious joy just to have him stand by her, to be always there, her friend, and yet—mingled with her new peace of mind was a curious regret, an insistent curiosity to know whether he thought of her at all. She finally went to bed and fell asleep thinking more of this than of his advice and philosophy.

When he had heard her close the centre door, Bruce noiselessly stole out to pick up the small bag he had left in the yard, and in again. He stopped in the course of undressing to stare at nothing on the floor.

"God! She's going to fall in love with me! Will that help her, or will it not? How the devil am I to know? Ought I to go away? She will have to have somebody. Might as well be me." Then he knew he did not want to go away.

He took up the whole of the next evening mending the kitchen ceiling, with Asia in a flurry of helpfulness handing him tools. He also fixed a loose handle on the cupboard door, and promised to put up another shelf in the porch when Asia said they needed it badly.

In a week's time Bruce had established several precedents and had reduced Alice to a simplicity that she would have thought incredible a month before. He ignored the way she looked at him, and treated her one or two expressions of feeling in such a matter-of-fact manner that she was well on the way to a calm acceptance of their friendship—outwardly, at least. He refused to be drawn into lengthy soul explorations, amazing her by his indifference to a future life, or to the great subject of right and wrong.

"Mr. Bruce, how do you get on without God?" she had asked him one night.

"Well, as you see," he said, stretching his feet comfortably towards the fire.

She looked into his amused eyes for some minutes, considering this answer.

By the time the boss returned David Bruce had given her a good deal to think about, but he realized that she had not got much further than an exchange of gods.

CHAPTER XII

OH, David, what is it? Have the booms broken?"

"No, no. Now do stop anticipating."

As the storm that had raged since early morning prevented Alice from hearing his steps, she had started at the sound of the porch door being slammed against the wind and rain. When Bruce stepped dripping on to the sack placed just inside the kitchen door, she could think of only one thing, the thing that had driven her wild with anxiety all day.

"They are all right?" she asked, still doubting.

"Yes, really. I've just come to have a look at you. I knew you would be worrying. And I want something hot for the boss."

As he spoke he took off his peaked oilskin cap, and undid the straps on his waterproof coat.

Alice put down the sewing she had in her hand, and came round the table to help him. But he waved her back, for he was too wet to touch.

"Do take it off, and have a cup of tea. I was just going to make some. Are you wet underneath?"

"No, I'm fairly dry. I won't harm. Yes, I can stay a few minutes."

She turned from him with an attempt at lightness, and got out the teapot and cups and saucers.

Bruce hung his coat on the door, and wiped down his face. Above the howling of the wind he could hear the voices of the children playing peaceably in Asia's room. Alice saw that he moved stiffly as he walked to the table and dropped into a chair.

Although it was not yet four o'clock night was beginning to close down upon the bay. After eight hours the storm showed no sign of a break. It was a healthy giant of a storm gone mad. In fierce gusts it lashed itself against the house, with now and then a lull more sinister than all the racket. With an incessant pelt and patter and swish and hiss it drove against the windows, through the sashes, and underneath the ledges, and spread damp splotches on the lining boards inside. The rain beat through weak places in the roof, and dripped with leaden drops into the tins Alice had placed to catch it. With each blast the linoleums heaved up on the roughly fitted floors, the doors strained on their hinges, the whole place rocked alarmingly on its wooden blocks, and the zinc roofing rasped against its heavy nails.

As Bruce sat down something shrieked in the wind with a sound that scraped the lining of the ears, and a piece of spouting, wrenched by a gust, carried away and beat a short tatoo against the wall, before breaking off to be blown against the fence.

He gave one glance round before looking at Alice's startled face.

"Spouting," he said reassuringly. "Don't be frightened. The house won't blow down."

"I hope it won't, David. That really would be the end of everything." Though she tried to smile he knew she was not far off tears.

This third winter had been the worst they were ever to know. Twice before, during storms, the booms had broken in critical moments, and the logs had been swept for miles up and down the river banks, to be recovered only after weeks of search and the patient manipulation of high tides. Also, a dam in the bush had been wrecked, and the tramways broken up. Roland had worked two shifts of men to repair the damage, and to try to keep pace with his orders. At the same time he had planned a mill of his own, to be begun with the spring. He now had shipments of machinery on the way from England and America, he had everything he possessed mortgaged, he had borrowed to his limit, and he owed a number of his men three months' wages.

The booms, which stretched from the beach below the house right across the river, were now packed with logs ready to fill the largest order the boss had ever had from the Wairoa, and the tug steamers were due to tow them away. Bruce knew how desperately the boss needed the money, and that if the booms broke again and the shipment was delayed it would be a crippling blow from which he might never recover. Bruce had watched him that day as he had recklessly jumped hour after hour from log to log, straining his eyes for signs of a break, and muttering at intervals, "If this damned thing busts, I'm done."

Bruce also knew that, though Roland had carried himself pluckily enough that winter in public, he had used to the full what he supposed was his right to work off steam on his family. There had been occasions when his inflamed nerves had snapped even in the presence of his foreman. There had been an anxious and hushed air about the house all the winter. Bruce saw that both Alice and Asia hailed his every appearance with looks of relief that were more eloquent than words, and as he knew Roland never resented his presence he had made the most of his privileges as Uncle David, and he had acted as a buffer between the opposing nerves of the strained household.

But he knew they had all reached almost the limit of endurance, and as he looked at Alice now, knowing, though she had not yet spoken of it, how it was with her again, he felt love and pity for her surge through him afresh.

Her face became less anxious as she made the tea. He saw she would try to be light so that he might have a diverting moment. When he rose to place a chair for her, she waved him down.

"Don't get up, please. You look too tired to move. I suppose you have not sat down all day."

He smiled.

"No. One doesn't, on those booms."

The anxiety came back to her face as she sat down. "David, do you think they'll hold?"

He realized as he looked into her eyes, hard with sleeplessness, how much it now hurt him to see her suffer.

"My dear girl"—as he took his cup from her—"they've held all day and we haven't found a weak spot. We've doubled every outside chain, and two men are standing by every post and wedge. We have half the bush force down to go on to-night, and not a man has balked on the job. They're good for the night if they are needed. Now I think we'll weather it. Try not to worry."

Impulsively he held out his hand across the table, and without a word she put hers into it. Though they had done this before in crises without too significant emotion they both now felt a sweep forward, something akin to the storm that revelled in its strength to toss the world about outside. After a minute he gave her a quick, strong grip, and then began to drink his tea.

"Where is Asia?" he asked, just missing her.

"Oh, she's milking."

"What! Why, Bob would have done that."

"I know. But she wanted to. She has been pining to get out all day. You know, she loves storms." She smiled grimly.

"The children good?" he questioned, as if he owned them.

"Yes, for a wonder."

He ate rapidly for a few minutes.

"Could you get me a couple of sandwiches for Tom and a hot bottle of tea? I must go."

While she got them ready he vulgarly stuffed bread and butter and cold meat as fast as he could into his mouth, making no apologies. Then walking to the back door he strapped himself into his oilskins.

With the bottle of tea and the package of sandwiches Alice walked over to him and put them into his big pockets. Then, as she looked up at him, he felt as if something swept out of her to clutch his soul.

"David, is it very dangerous on the booms?" There was no diffidence in her voice or in her eyes.

"Well, it's a risk if one is not very careful." He saw what was coming.

"Have you been there all day?"

"Yes."

"Promise me you won't go on them again." As she spoke she stretched out her hands to him.

As he seized them he saw her through a mist. He hesitated only a second.

"I promise," he said hoarsely; and then, taking up one of her hands, he kissed it, and crushed it against his cheek.

Swept off her feet, she swayed towards him, but in a flash of clear-sightedness Bruce saw that they must not lose their heads. He put an arm about her shoulders, and held her firmly, but made no attempt to move or kiss her. As they stood like that they could hear the beating of their own hearts above the roar of the storm. Bruce deliberately extended the time of his hold upon her, knowing that he was giving her a memory to help her through the night. When, at last, he drew away from her, he took her face between his hands and looked calmly into her eyes with all the understanding she craved to see, and with all the force of the declaration she had begun to want.

She stared back helplessly at him.

"You know I understand," he said simply. "That is all that I can say, isn't it?"

"Yes," she whispered, lowering her face.

His manner lightened.

"Now, to please me, you try to rest. And don't worry."

She looked up again, her eyes shining.

"It's all right, David. I can go on—with you to help me——" Her voice broke.

"Cheer up," he smiled. "You are not going to lose me. You'll find me as adhesive as a Spanish fly blister."

Before she could answer he stooped and kissed her hair with a touch so light that she felt only the thrilling suggestion of it, and then he was gone through the door into the rapidly gathering dusk.

She ran to the front room window, and he, seeing her, as he came round the corner, smiled and waved gaily at her, and again when he had passed through the gate.

Though he had tried to minimize its significance, Bruce knew that this was but the beginning of something whose end he could not see. He knew that to say "Stay there" to sex emotions once started would be as foolish as to say it to logs bursting through a tripped dam. He foresaw that the conflicts between the "dont's" and the "I musts" was likely to be long and troublesome.

As Alice watched him she, too, felt that what had just happened was inevitable. Though she told herself that her love for him was entirely spiritual, that she never wanted it to be anything else, she had craved to know whether he felt anything "special" for her. For the two years, during which, as Uncle David, he had outwardly preserved the manner of a favoured relative, he had given her no sign that he was in love with her. The friendship had been all that she could have dreamed of the ideal, all that was safe for a Christian wife and mother, and yet—she had wanted the sign, just the sign, she repeated to herself, of something more.

Now that she had the sign she knew she did not want it to alter anything. She just wanted Bruce's love as a beautiful secret to hug to her soul as compensation, as food for her starved emotionalism. She had ceased to argue about the right and wrong of it. So long as it was spiritual she knew she was entitled to it. It did not occur to her that David Bruce might not be able to keep his love for her on the same plane of exalted spiritualism where she expected hers to abide for ever.

As she watched him go down the slope in the driving sleet she felt that the terrors of the coming night had been mysteriously lessened; that, after all, even if the booms did burst, she could face Tom's ruin. For the moment the thought of the coming child ceased to trouble her.

As Alice looked back over that long nightmare of a winter, she felt she could never have come through sane without David Bruce. She had had the feared second miscarriage two springs before, and then a baby boy, now a ferocious little mass of vitality, almost a year old. One of the worst things she had had to endure that winter had been the eternal restlessness and screeching of this terrible infant, which Roland had resented as if it had been all planned to annoy him.

Then, even before the winter had begun, they had faced extreme poverty. Alice had taken much too seriously her husband's statement that they had only so much a week to live on, and that he couldn't go into debt for food. Thinking all women were naturally extravagant, he had given her quite unnecessary warnings about economy, and he never noticed the strained literalness with which she carried them out.

The winter had not progressed very far before Bob Hargraves put it to Bruce one night in the store.

"I say," he began, "it's none of my business, but I don't think they are getting fat up there. It's been pretty plain feeding this last month. And yet, at the men's kitchen, they are living on all the expensive tinned stuff we can get them."

Bruce, who had begun to have his suspicions, looked into Bob's kind eyes.

"What have they had?" he asked.

Bob read out so many pounds of oatmeal, barley, flour, sugar and salt.

"Is that all? No meat, no butter, no eggs?"

"That's all. I say, Bruce, hang it all, I'm willing to wait a month or two for my screw if they're as pushed as all that. And I guess some of the others would too."

"Thanks, Bob. That's decent of you. I'll find out."

And it was two or three evenings later that a deputation

of men had astonished the boss by telling him they could wait for their wages till the spring.

Then Bruce had gone to Mrs. Brayton.

"They're actually going hungry!" he declared wrathfully. "I've found out from Asia that she and her mother have been going for six weeks on two meals a day. They've had no meat except those fowls you sent. Their own fowls are being killed one by one for the boss, and the children have the bones when he's done with them. They get little more than enough butter from the cow for him. Their vegetables are nearly done. And that crazy girl would starve before she'd say a word, and she'd starve before Roland would see that she was starving! God! The stupidity of it!"

"And things wasting here!" exclaimed the old lady, as furious as he. "But how are we going to make her take them? You know she will think she is an object of charity, one step off the workhouse."

"I'll fix it with the boss. For God's sake send them down something to-morrow."

The next day, when Harold Brayton arrived at the house with a sledge, Alice stared into his non-committal face.

"You say Tom ordered them?" She looked down at the packages.

"Yes. Where shall I put them for you?"

Alice kept quiet while he carried in a sack of potatoes, a side of bacon, and a box containing a cheese, some pots of honey, a bag of dried apples, a salted ox tongue, a dozen eggs, some keg butter for cooking, some fresh butter, and a pair of fowls all ready to go into the oven. But as soon as he had gone she dropped into a chair by the table and burst into tears of humiliation. She did not believe her husband had ordered them.

Asia ran in from the back garden, looked at the sumptuous array, and then at her mother, whom she took to be weeping from happiness.

"Oh, Mother, don't cry any more. Let's eat some of it. Let's have a party. I know Granny sent it."

"You know!" Her mother sat up. "Did you tell her we were poor?"

"No, Mother——"

"Asia, you have told somebody—Uncle David—I see you have. I'm ashamed of you! You know we should keep our troubles to ourselves. Other people can't feed us."

But Asia was learning wisdom, and refused to be upset.

"If they want to, Mother, I don't see why they shouldn't. Do be sensible, and let's have a party."

But all the party spirit Asia was able to coax into her mother was destroyed when Roland came home.

"Yes, I ordered it," he said angrily, "and they'll send stuff every week. You didn't have to starve and make me ridiculous in the eyes of everybody. All I said was we had to be careful; but, of course, you couldn't get it right."

"You know I have always been careful," she replied, weeping afresh.

"Oh, of course, you're never wrong." And he stamped out of the room.

It took Bruce all his time during the next day or two to restore Alice to peace of mind.

"There's no charity in it," he protested, in answer to a remark of hers. "It's a business deal. Every one lives on a credit system. And between your husband and the Braytons the advantages are theirs. Tom's plans will make Brayton. The township here will mean better roads, a bigger local market, increased price of land, and by and by a weekly steamer and a quick route to Auckland—doubled and trebled prosperity for every one who lives here. And no one knows it better than the Braytons. If they could not wait for the money for a little dairy produce it would be a pity."

This view of it had comforted Alice. But Bruce had not ended with that.

"And even if it were charity, you have as much right to

live as any one else. For heaven's sake, my dear girl, bury that damned conscience of yours, and get up and kick something. Kick Tom; he needs it. Kick anybody who bothers you. Forget you're a lady. Get rid of your disgusting humility. Don't take everything lying down."

Alice had been able to smile at his shots, and much advice in the same strain had helped her to adopt various measures of mental self-defence. She was learning to care less how her husband spoke to her, learning to make more allowance for his nerves. She would have got on still better with her own attitude of mind had it not been that she could get no more sleep than he did, and sleeplessness was her most deadly foe. Bruce suspected much of what she had to put up with, but he did not know everything.

Alice turned from the window as she heard the children calling for her in the kitchen, and as she got their supper Asia came in dripping from head to foot.

"There won't be a thing left in the garden," she said sadly, putting down the milk pail.

"Never mind. We will manage."

Asia looked at her mother. This cheerful remark was unexpected.

Asia was growing lanky, and some of her childish gaiety had been submerged by the sense of responsibility she had developed in the last two years. The buoyancy of her naturally sane and eager temperament was to triumph later over her present riot of seriousness, but at twelve years old she was prematurely aged by two great emotions. Alice had no idea of the complexity of Asia's outwardly natural devotion to David Bruce, or of the depth of her understanding of her mother's tragedy. She never knew how many nights the child sat up in bed, wretched beyond description at the sounds of Roland's sleeplessness. She had no idea how much she saw and heard.

But she did see and rejoice in what she would have called the noble qualities of her child: the devotion, the sacrifice, the sense, the usefulness. She could not have managed without her any more than she could without Bruce. And, if it could have been possible for her pride in her to have become greater than it was before, it would have increased that winter.

Asia began to shed her wet clothes as she stood on the sack.

"Oh, dear," said Alice, looking into the pail, "is that all she gave?"

"That's all, Mother. She was in a bad mood. No wonder, poor thing, shut up all day in that little yard. I explained to her, but, of course, she couldn't understand. And I sang to her, but it was no use."

Alice could not help smiling.

"Well, it can't be helped. You and I will have to go without milk for tea and breakfast."

"All right." Asia picked up her wet clothes.

She wondered all the evening why her mother did not seem as anxious about the booms as she had been earlier in the day. As far as she could see, the storm was as bad as ever. They sat up late, Asia reading to her mother while she sewed.

After she had gone to bed Alice stood by the window for some time staring out into the night. She wished some one would come to tell her how things were going. She wondered more than once if Bruce were keeping his promise. Again she hated the feeble part of waiting that women had to play in a crisis of this kind. As she caught sight now and then of dim lights moving in the swirl down below her, she could imagine the men fighting for dear life to save the boss's logs with a loyalty that she had learned to value. She knew they would be swearing and laughing with a recklessness that fascinated her. To her it seemed superhuman that they could fight the gale for hour after hour in the cold and wet.

After a while she began to walk about the room restlessly, wondering what the future would bring, wondering if she and David Bruce could keep their beautiful friendship unspotted from the world, wondering if she could possibly go on living with Tom Roland and having his children, wondering what would happen if the booms burst.

At last, worn out, she threw herself down on the front room sofa, covered herself with a rug, and fell into a nervous sleep. There she still lay when the opening of the back door at three o'clock startled her into a sitting position. Dazed, she jumped up and walked to the kitchen door.

"The booms," she muttered, staring at her husband and David Bruce, who were helping each other out of their heavy coats.

"Safe," said Bruce quickly. "And the storm's gone."

All at once she realized the sharp stillness.

"Safe," she repeated stupidly.

"Yes, yes," exclaimed Roland impatiently. "And we're frozen. Can't you get us something hot?"

While the two men went into the sitting-room to strip and beat warmth back into each other's bodies, Alice revived the kitchen fire, where the night logs soon blazed up. Before the men were ready she had hot soup and a kettle of boiling water. She was wise enough to see that they were beyond answering questions as they staggered out and dropped into chairs. While they ate and drank she got hot water bottles, and made up a bed for Bruce on the sitting-room sofa. She had taken the precaution to put all the children into Asia's room, so that there would be no noise to wake her husband in the morning.

But Bruce decided he would go to his shanty, and, without a chance to look significantly at Alice, he took one of the hot bottles and went out, more tired than she had ever seen him.

Without a word Roland fell into bed to sleep for fourteen hours without a break.

Before Alice had cleaned up the mess of wet clothes the first glow of a golden sunrise was blazing a background for

Pukekaroro. With a queer, vacant feeling, now that the strain was over, she lay down on the bed she had prepared for Bruce, and slept lightly till she heard the sounds of the children awake, in the back room.

CHAPTER XIII

BRUCE was the only man who could not sleep long that morning. He had not fallen like the rest of them into a heavy slumber. He had merely dozed and tossed feverishly, his mind tormented by the vision of Alice's hard sleepless eyes, and by the struggle he knew was ahead of him, complicated for the time being by another of his periodical fits of fever and depression whose only cure seemed to be oblivion. He had hoped that the storm and the fatigue might help him to work off for this time at least that horrible urge towards a climax that swamped out his will. He had given up arguing with himself about it, but he had not given up, nor did he intend to give up the fight.

Twice in the last eighteen months he had gone under, after struggling to a point where something broke in him. He had ridden off, to return in a few days with the ghastly sensitiveness of the man who feels that lack of control is the unpardonable sin. He had kept away from Alice, who, he knew, condemned such lapses, and had no understanding of their mental or physiological bases, until he had lost all signs of the madness. But he always hated meeting her again with that brand upon his soul.

Though he knew it to be disease, it did not alter the fact that it was the tragedy of his life. And now, as he tossed in bed, he saw it was coming again.

Unable to rest, he got up, gave himself a sponge bath, and exercised for half an hour to try to take some of the stiffness out of his limbs, and to tire the hot aliveness of his mind. Then he stood for some minutes in his doorway, staring up at the cabbage trees, more scraggy than ever now that they had lost half their long leaves in the storm.

Looking at his watch, he saw that it was half-past eight, and he wondered if the cook would be ready with something to eat. He walked round to the front of his shanty. There he stopped short to look at the damage wrought by the storm.

Roofs had suffered everywhere, and not a fence had escaped. The one that Bob Hargraves had just put up round his section, the nearest to the boss's house, was nowhere to be seen. Catching the wind as it curled round the cliffs, it had been scattered in all directions.

Sheets of zinc, palings, boards, tins and cans of every description were littered about between the cottages, along the paths, among the bushes in the field. Two brick chimneys had collapsed into shapeless heaps, and the big zinc one at the kitchen had been twisted as if the demons of the gale had tried to wring its neck. Further along, boats that had been torn from their anchorage lay smashed on the spit, or were carried high and dry up the banks. Timber stacks were levelled, and a shed on the spit had been wrecked out of existence.

But the waters of an innocent and peaceful river lapped gently about the boundaries of the great booms. Every log was safe and sound.

An unnatural stillness hung heavy over the bay, where by day there was now always a constant flow of bustling activity. There was not a sound about the cottages or the kitchen, hardly a column of smoke from a chimney. Bruce guessed that every house would be still till the exhausted men awoke.

Looking towards the boss's cottage, he saw Alice in the yard. He knew that the sooner he faced her and continued their normal ways the better. With the half-formed thought that she might help him he went to her.

She took her cue from him and greeted him naturally. He looked from her round the devastated yard, and at the children, and at the baby, Bunty, as Asia had nicknamed him, tucked under her arm.

"Tom?" he asked.

"Asleep, thank God! He has not waked. I fed the children out here, and shall keep them out till he wakes."

They walked to the end of the wash-house, and looked at what was left of the garden and the fence.

"You didn't sleep long." Alice was thinking more of him than of the wreckage.

He did not look at her. He was afraid she might guess what he was coming to. And he knew she would understand it less than ever following on the incident of last night; that, like all women, she would think that caring for her ought to keep him out of all temptations, and revolutionize his natural tendencies.

"No, I was overtired. But I'll sleep presently. Where's the cow?" His eyes sought her in the field.

"She got out in the night. Asia has gone to look for her." She felt that he was shutting himself away from her, and she thought he meant to show her that they must not return to any significant expression of their feelings. It hurt her that he should think she might become weak and demand any change in their friendship. She registered a vow to show him that she could be just as strong as he could. "Have you had any breakfast?" she asked.

"No. They seemed to be asleep at the kitchen."

"I'll bring you out some." She smiled lightly up at him. "Will you hold Bunty? I daren't have him inside."

He took the baby, glad to be diverted by him, and while tossing him up and down he took stock of the damage in the yard. He was glad to see that the wash-house had held, and that beyond the fence and the spouting there was nothing that could not soon be mended.

Then he went into the shed, and sat down by the rough table on which Alice put her wash-tubs. Bunty, who chewed his thumb contentedly with unusual good humour, gazed up into his face in a way that amused and arrested Bruce, who began to speculate about his future and his unknown possibilities. As he did so, he heard piteous weeping in the yard. Startled, he jumped up, and as he reached the corner of the shed he met Asia, who raised a streaming, utterly hopeless face.

"Good God, child! What is it?" With his free arm he pulled her back into the wash-house.

"Something dreadful has happened," she choked, "worse than anything. I don't know what we will do."

"Tell me," he commanded. He was more upset than he could have believed possible at the sight of her break-down.

"The cow is drowned," she moaned. "Our dear Daisy drowned!"

"Drowned!" repeated Bruce.

"Yes, drowned. She got out in the night and she was so hungry she went down to eat the mangroves. And now she's drowned."

"Are you sure?" he asked, a lump now in his own throat.

"Yes, quite sure. She is stuck in the mud. I went out and poked her—she never moved. And her eyes are just awful. She's quite dead, I know." She was heart-broken. "Oh, what will we do?" she sobbed.

"Oh, child," Bruce soothed her, "don't cry any more. She isn't hurt now. And we will get another cow."

"But we have no money, not any at all."

"Never mind. Mr. Brayton will give us one."

"But it won't be Daisy. I loved her. Oh, why did she have to die?"

Just then Alice stood in the doorway with a tray.

"What is it now?" she cried.

"Sh!" Bruce held up his hand. "It's nothing. It's only the cow."

"The cow!" she exclaimed, putting down the tray, and staring at Asia's miserable face.

"Yes, she's drowned. Now don't——"

But it was no use. For Alice, Asia's break-down was the last straw. She dropped onto the bench beside her, crying helplessly.

"Oh, Mother," Asia threw her arms round her, "poor

Daisy! It must have hurt her so. Her eyes are awful."

Bruce looked at them for a minute, and then, swept by an impulse he could not and did not want to control, he dropped Bunty on the floor, and gathered them both into his arms.

He saw that Alice recovered almost immediately. He felt the short experimental pressure of her body against his, and then she sat still, but he could feel excitement working in her. He made his soothing gestures less significant, and then, as she grew calmer, he closed his hand upon her shoulder.

As he sat thus, with Asia clinging to him on the other side, he thought of Tom Roland, lying inside asleep, and beguiled himself for the minute with the bitter humour of the situation. Alice wondered at the change in his expression, and did not understand what there could be in it to amuse him. To her the incident was a milestone on the road of emotional experience. It would have hurt her badly to feel that it did not mean a great deal to him. But she knew that outwardly they must ignore it, and she thought the change in his manner was meant to remind her of that fact.

As she raised her face to his to give him the look she could not resist, her eyes fell on the tray, and his breakfast, fast becoming cold.

"Oh, David, we are selfish," returning to her normal manner. "Asia, get up, dear, and have some breakfast with Uncle David."

Then she and Bruce saw that Asia was more in need of comfort than they. Haunted by the dead Daisy's glazed eyes she could not eat, but kept sobbing at intervals in a way that wrung Bruce's and her mother's heart.

To help her they went out and began to clean up the yard and the garden, and there they all worked, keeping the children quiet and busy till it was time to have another picnic meal outside.

By the middle of the day the bay began to show signs of life. After lunch Bruce went to direct the men on odd jobs of straightening out the wreckage. Then he went up to the Braytons for another cow. When he got back at five o'clock he found Roland had just waked up, delighted to hear that one of the tug steamers was coming up the river for his precious logs.

Half an hour later the spit and the booms were alive with men preparing rafts to be ready for the morning's tide.

It was eleven o'clock when Roland and Bruce finally left the captain. When they reached the store, Bruce said he had to get something out of it. The boss turned from him, ignoring his manner.

"Hm!" he said to himself, as he went up the bank. "Poor devil! He's got it again."

But Roland wasted no time moralizing about his foreman, or judging him, or feeling sorry for him. He accepted his weakness as something that was there, and that was the end of it.

Bruce unlocked the store, meaning to get himself some food. As he picked out a tin of meat and some jam, he startled a mouse, and took up a stick to kill it, but was not quick enough. He moved boxes and bags, hunting for it, but continued to miss it. Then, forgetting what he had come in for, he went out, locking the door behind him, and walked along the bank to the beach below the cliffs.

He meant to pace that sand till he tired himself out, even if he walked all night. He was amazed afresh at his own vitality, at the heat of the liquid that flowed through his veins. He did not try to argue about the good or the bad of it, but set himself to fight it. But, as before, his mind grew frenzied in the hopeless struggle against his body.

The still river and the fresh night did not help him. The silence of the hills only mocked his fever. He craved for the only thing that could help him to break the weight of the accumulated suppression in him, the only thing that could still the beat in his brain. He could feel flames licking round the inside of his skull, eating up everything in his head. He felt them burning through his body, galling the nerves in his legs, stinging the soles of his feet.

But he fought on till he thought he was too tired to feel any more. Climbing round the base of the green hill, he picked his way among the rushes behind the boss's house. When he reached his shanty, however, something blazed up in his brain, and a hundred nerves snapped through his body. The thought of going in and getting calmly in to bed was too flat, too banal to be endured. He knew he would burst if he tried to force it on himself.

As if pursued, he strode to the place where his horse always stood tethered. He saddled it, mounted, and galloped off into the night.

He only meant to ride and ride, and let his horse take him anywhere it would.

But in less than half an hour it had landed him at the Point Curtis public house.

CHAPTER XIV

"YOU got my message," said Bob Hargraves, raising his face from his desk as Bruce walked into the store.

Sensing something wrong, he looked down quickly.

"Why, no, Bob. What is it?"

"I sent Dick after you. He must have missed you." He lowered his eyes uneasily. "The boss has been whiskying himself blind at Point Curtis all day."

"What!" Bruce fell back a pace, as if he had suddenly run into a wall. He stared back at Bob, who had made an effort to look up without recognition of the fact that Bruce himself had been back only a week since his own break. Every man about the place knew that Bruce's lapses were not a subject for comment or for joke. No one had ever hinted to him of any knowledge of them.

"Afraid it's true," said Bob, trying to speak lightly.

"What struck him?" exclaimed Bruce, looking for a reason. It was a well-known fact that Roland was almost a teetotaller. "Anything happened? I was in the bush last night."

"Yes. Some of the new machinery has been wrecked on the Three Kings. He got a telegram about it last night. He scared me. I thought he would go crazy." Bob saw that Bruce's thoughts had turned from the cause of the boss's outburst to the probable effect of it upon his family.

"I tried to calm him down before he went home," he went on, "but by the look of him this morning he had not had a restful night. He rode off about ten, I supposed to the bush, or I would have got word up to you. I knew nothing till Harold Brayton came along about four, and said he was down there and pretty mad. He had tried to get him away, but couldn't. He thought you had better get down there as soon as you could."

With a groan Bruce walked a step or two to the door, where he stood looking out unseeing upon the river. The knock-off horn had just sounded at the kitchen, and along the tramway and the spit and on the booms the men were gathering up their tools, and tidying up things for the night. Bruce was vaguely conscious of their movements as he tried to think how this last disaster was to be faced. This blow had fallen out of a clear sky, and there was more to think about than its effect upon Alice, though that had been his first concern. Bruce knew even better than she did how deeply the boss was involved, and what risks he had taken, and how many men would suffer if he broke down. He knew, also, how greatly he had been trusted because he was believed to be absolutely reliable. One of the first things to be done was to see if it could not be kept quiet.

Then, realizing the need for prompt action in various directions, he swung round.

"Do they know at the house, Bob?"

"I don't know. But Brayton would hardly tell them."

"We must keep it from them. Get round the men this evening, Bob, and tell them to keep it dark. I'll go up to the house before I go after him, and I'll think out something when I see what he's like. And hang around, in case Mrs. Roland wants you. And remember, you don't know anything." Without waiting for Bob to reply, he swung out and up the path.

Mingled with his anxiety for Roland and his concern for Alice was a numbing sense of humiliation. He wondered if the boss had flown to whisky because his own recent breakdown had pointed the way. He felt that if Alice got to know she would think so, and it made him feel like an accessory to the deed. It was impossible to think of Roland's orgy without thinking of his own. He dreaded now above all things that Alice should learn of it.

Bruce had seen Alice twice in the past week, but only for a few minutes at a time. Though Roland had always covered up his tracks by saying he was away on business somewhere, he was sure she knew, and he had been particularly sensitive this last time because he had a horrible conviction that he had failed her by going away as he had after their revelation of feeling, and he felt she thought so too, and that she did not in the least understand the nature of his problem. It made him sick to think that she grieved over him in secret, or that she condemned his weakness. It was the one thing about which he could not be humorous. And he knew, as he went up the slope, that her attitude of mind would be much more uncompromising toward her husband, not only because she both feared and loathed drunkenness, but because she would resent it fiercely as something she had not bargained for in her relations with him.

As he approached the front gate the door opened, and he knew she had been watching for him. Before he reached her he saw what the night had done to her, that she had had no sleep, and that her eyes burned with fear. In her relief at seeing him she forgot all about his recent absence or the cause for it.

"Oh, David, where is Tom?"

He took the hands she held out to him.

"God!" he groaned. "Was he as bad as that?"

She moved her head, unable to speak. He closed the door behind them. He could hear Asia giving the children their tea in the kitchen. Alice motioned him into the bedroom so that they could talk without being heard.

"Where is he?" she asked again.

He saw from the mixed expression in her eyes that she sensed something, and he wondered what it was. But he lied quickly.

"In the bush. I've drugged him. We will look after him up there."

He thought he detected a flicker of suspicion in her eyes,

but it was instantly swamped out by relief. She sank into her chair, pressing her closed hands into her eyeballs in a dazed sort of way.

"I couldn't have stood another night," she said wildly.

For a moment he wanted to tell her that she didn't have to stand that, he wanted to tell her many things he had looked for opportunity to say, but he knew she could hear nothing then, so he merely took her hands and gripped them. Then he remembered Roland.

"There is something I have to do," he said. "But I expect to be back by nine o'clock. Now lie down, and stop thinking. Send for Bob if you want anything. I will stay with you to-night. There is nothing more to worry about. Leave the future alone." He knew that his short sentences, shot at her, had a curious hypnotic effect upon her, but he was anxious about her as he looked down at her. He was afraid she could not stand more without a break-down herself. And all this was a very bad beginning for another child. But he had no time to stay longer, and with another grip of her hands he left her.

When he got to Point Curtis he found Roland raging like a wild beast. He had laid out two men, and it had taken four of them to get him tied down. He tried to spring at Bruce, thinking he was a log about to fall upon him. The public house was full of men who had taken a hand at trying to calm him. Curiously enough, nobody seemed to regard it as a joke.

When Bruce heard how much whisky Roland was said to have consumed he treated the proprietor to much language unbecoming to an English gentleman, and scared him with the prospect of losing his license, and a period in gaol. After drugging the boss and leaving careful instructions to cover any emergency, he rode back to the bay, and sent down Shiny and another man to help with the nursing, and to bring him up in the morning if he was well enough. Then he went round the cottages, reassuring the men, and asking them to keep the story in the place.

He found Alice lying on the front room sofa, with Asia bathing her head. She asked him no questions, and made no attempt to talk. He was a bit perplexed by her indifference to her husband's state, for he knew she must guess that he was really ill. It showed, he thought, how bad was her reaction from her own fear and suffering.

From Asia, after her mother was asleep, he heard the story of the night before, when Roland had paced the floor hour after hour, muttering and delirious, declaring at intervals that he was done, and that he would kill himself. He gathered that Alice had been unable to do anything with him, but that she had probably made him worse by suggesting things that inflamed him to irritable rage.

"It was dreadful, Uncle David." Asia shuddered at the memory of it. "And we did not know where to find you in the bush, and Mother said you were wanted up there anyway. But it was awful! I have never been so frightened. And I did wish you were here. I am never frightened when you are near."

As she looked up into his face he felt he was indeed the *deus ex machina* of their troubled lives. To distract her attention from his god-like qualities, which he knew absorbed too much of her thoughts, he turned to lessons, which had been lately neglected. He found that she was well ahead of all that he had set her, and after an hour's fresh work he was glad to see that her mind was diverted from personal problems by the insistent vagaries of French verbs.

When he told her to go to bed she was too tired to make any protest, or to linger as she usually tried to do.

Bruce sat on for some time smoking by the kitchen fire before turning in on the stretcher bed that had been prepared for him. Exactly how they were all going to emerge from the present mess he could not see, but the first thing to be done was to get Roland restored to health and sanity. He thought curiously about him as he sat there, wondering if he realized how much of an outsider he was in his own house. But it was impossible to guess what the boss saw, or suspected, or thought. He had never given a sign to show that he recognized the possibility of more than met the eye in his home. Bruce had little clue to the processes of his mind except in relation to business transactions and to men in connection with work.

In certain ways Roland seemed to have come into the world ready made; in others it looked as if he would never learn and never grow. It had always interested Bruce that he should accept people without question as he found them; that, with the one exception of his wife, he tolerated with good humour all sorts of idiosyncrasies, all kinds of manners, all varieties of moods, all species of sins. The only kind of criticism Bruce had ever seen him pass had been a shrug of the shoulders or an amused twinkle of the eye. Still pondering over his unique power over men and his curious inconsistencies, Bruce went to bed.

The household was asleep in the morning when he went out, leaving a note to say he would be back later. When he got to Point Curtis, Shiny, who had been up with Roland all night, told him they had had a lurid time, but Bruce found the boss a whining, nauseated wreck, as feeble as a baby, his delirium gone, his mind in a stupor of depression. They carried him to a boat on a mattress, and rowed him up to the bay, where he was landed by the men's kitchen, and taken to Bruce's shanty, to be carefully nursed under his directions.

When he called later in the morning at the boss's house, Bruce was relieved to see that neither Alice nor Asia disputed his story that Roland was getting better, but would have to stay in the bush another day or two. He could see they were only too glad to shelve the responsibility of looking after him. This made him feel a great pity for the sick man, though he understood well enough the reason for Alice's relief.

That evening his story fell to pieces.

As he sat down by the sitting-room fire with Asia, who had worn an air of suppressed worry during tea, he saw she had something to say. Alice had hardly left the room for a minute before she burst out with it.

"Is he really drunk?" she asked anxiously.

"Sh! What do you mean?" Bruce looked quickly over his shoulder in the direction of the kitchen door.

"I heard the men talking about it down by the store." She looked fearfully at him, seeing he was angry.

"You'd no business to listen," he said sternly. "Have you said anything about it? Have you told your mother?"

"No." She felt her heart jump with fright.

"Then don't speak of it, to her or to any one."

"Then it's true," she said, unconsciously raising her voice, "he was drunk."

"Sh!" commanded Bruce harshly.

But it was too late. Alice stood in the doorway staring at them with hard and startled eyes.

"Drunk!" she repeated. "So that's the matter with him!"

As he rose to his feet he was gripped by a resentment of her attitude, the blind superiority of a "good woman" for weaknesses that were not her weaknesses.

"I think I'll go and get drunk now," she said slowly. "It is certainly my turn."

For a second he looked into her passionately scornful face as if he had not understood her, while the bitter truth of her words burned into his brain, and the hard contempt of her tone stunned his ears.

As she did not consciously mean her words to apply to him, and did not for the moment see that she had included him in her condemnation, she was surprised to see him shrink and then turn from her without a word toward the front door. As he closed it after him, she started forward.

"David," she called hoarsely.

Then she remembered Asia, who now stood up sick with the realization that another dreadful thing was about to happen.

"Don't you move from this room," cried Alice, as she rushed out of the front door.

Bruce was turning the corner, going towards the back gate.

"David," she called again.

As he neither stopped nor turned, she began to run after him. Stumbling, though the night was clear with brilliant stars, she followed, her mind blistered by the scalding thought that she had hurt him in a way he would never forget. All that she had recently suffered, all the fears of the immediate present, even the shock she had just received, vanished as she ran and called after the man who would not turn or answer.

When she seized his arm she had forgotten that she was a Christian wife and mother, forgotten that she was a lady.

"David, you shall not go. Forgive me—I didn't see what I was saying. I didn't, David. I can't bear to think I hurt you. I don't care what you do—you know I don't. Oh, say you forgive me and forget that I said it. I can't have you misunderstand me—I'd rather die. Forgive me——"

Her voice broke as she flung herself upon him.

Coming out of his nightmare of pain, he found her arms gripped round his neck, her eyes wild with a fear that startled him. Mechanically he clutched at her to keep himself and her from falling. That fierce precipitated embrace had not lasted a minute before they were both infected by the fever of it. He could not look into her eyes and see what he saw there and remain unmoved. The fence against which they leaned, and the stars, and the night, and all sense of time and place were blotted out by the mist that covered his sight, a mist wherein he saw only her lips as they inevitably drew his own to them.

But the very intensity of the abandonment contained the seeds of its rapid disintegration. Only a few hot minutes had raced by when Bruce raised his head and looked over her shoulder into the night. He felt her eyes fixed for some seconds upon his face, then her head nestling into his neck. He felt her body, hot and trembling, against his, moving, how consciously he could not tell, with a seductive ebb and flow of pressure. Even while he was inflamed by her unmasking of her feelings, he realized that he could not encourage her, because she lacked the courage of her emotions.

Partly realizing his growing detachment, and partly seeing independently the madness of this, she drew herself up a little, prepared to excuse her emotion or minimize it, as his attitude might require.

When he turned his face to her she could not read the complex mystery of his expression, but she did see that there was no dominant light of fierce joy or conquest in his eyes, but more than anything else a troubled questioning. She looked back at him helplessly, leaving him to take the initiative. As he did not take it, she nervously stammered a question that had nothing to do with the real thoughts of either of them at that moment.

"Do you forgive me?"

"Forgive——" he repeated absently. "Oh, yes. Please don't mention that again."

He still had his arms about her, and he made no attempt to remove them. As he spoke, he drew her even a little closer, but held her steadily and dispassionately. She tried to realize every second of this contact, knowing that it could not last. As he continued to be silent and to look away from her, it dawned upon her that her lack of control had only added to his problems. Suddenly demoralized by this thought, she staggered blindly away from him, beginning to sob.

Divining the reason for her movement and her tears, he caught her back to him, and held her more firmly than before, stroking her head, and pressing it into his neck, but still saying nothing. It was not long before he had comforted her back to control.

Still forgetting everything but their own immediate problem, she looked up at him.

"David, I am sorry for this," she began with a tragic calmness that was comic.

She was surprised to see that his eyes smiled at her in the starlight.

"Why should you be?" he asked. As he saw she did not know what to say he went on, "Are you really sorry?"

When she turned her face away he took it between his hands, looked calmly into it, and repeated his question.

"You are not sorry," he answered himself, "and neither am I."

As her eyes flashed at him he leaned down and kissed her deliberately on the forehead, on her hair, and then on her mouth.

"You know that I love you," he said quietly, saying the words he knew she craved to hear. "And now that we have come to this, there is a great deal more to say."

Again he looked past her into the night, marvelling at the psychology of women, in whom love could swamp out so much more thoroughly than in man all other considerations. He knew she was saying to herself that nothing mattered now that he had told her he loved her, while to him everything mattered just the same.

As a background to his feeling for her there was the picture of Tom Roland lying ill in his shanty, the picture of a fine enterprise on the point of wreckage, the picture of a number of dependent people loyally trusting the man who had made them promises.

"Let's go in," he said simply.

It was not till they opened the front door that they remembered Asia, who was sitting where her mother had left her, half crazed by misery. Bruce groaned when he saw her. Nothing hurt him so much as the overwhelming sorrows of children. He turned from Alice to restoring her to peace of mind, and for half an hour he devoted himself to putting her to bed, and to comforting her so that she would sleep.

And while he did this Alice sat by the sitting-room fire, waiting for him, and coming back by degrees to a realization of the hard cold facts of life that faced them both. At first she was stunned by the complexity of them, but she attempted no solution of them. Her mind balked at what seemed to her the impossibility of fitting them in to any scheme of life that she could face. She was proceeding on the assumption that the scene she had just gone through would alter everything, not outwardly, but in her own mind.

When Bruce came in and closed the door behind him she saw that he was thinking of something else.

"Look here, my dear, we shall really have to keep our troubles away from that child."

Then he saw that she had expected something very different from him. He stood on the mat looking down at her, the enigma of her strength and her weakness puzzling him afresh. Even though her face was pinched for lack of sleep it had lost none of its power to attract him. Now, as she looked back at him, her cheeks were flushed and her eyes brilliant. He knew she was waiting for a lead. He wondered if she knew what she really wanted, whether she had faced any other kind of future, and actually how far he dominated her.

Without attempting to kiss or caress her, he dropped into the chair opposite. Then, drawing it nearer to her, he leaned forward and took one of her hands.

"What are we to do now?" he asked, his eyes upon hers.

"Why, David, we can't do anything."

In her tone he read finality and renunciation. He knew perfectly well she wanted no scandal, no exposure, that she would never consider running away with him, but he wondered if she had thought about it or faced it, and he was curious to know.

"You have not thought of going away with me," he asked lightly.

Even as the startled light flashed across her face she saw he was not serious.

"Don't be alarmed," he smiled back. "I am not going to ask you to. I never shall. But just what have you thought about it? You knew we were coming to this, didn't you?"

"I—I—yes—I thought, perhaps——"

To her surprise he laughed.

"Oh, woman," he said, shaking his head at her. How he could laugh with all that volume of a situation hanging about their ears she did not know. "My dear, you hoped we were coming to this, you meant us to come to this. Yes, you did—you are just like every other woman. And I did, too, just like every other man. And now that we are here the question is, do we stay as we have been, or do we go on? Because we have to do one thing or the other." He gripped her hand more firmly as he went on. "There's one thing I must tell you. I cannot go on making love to you in any form here in Tom Roland's house while I take Tom Roland's money. It was inevitable, I think, that we should come to a confession of our feeling for each other"—he carefully ignored the fact that she had made the advances—"but now we have to make a decision as to action. I can only go on making love to you on one of two conditions. Either I tell your husband and have his consent to go on, which he is hardly likely to give, or we go away. I will not deceive Tom Roland. Even if I don't go round recruiting for the front ranks in heaven I do have a standard of decency for this earth."

He felt her stiffen as she drew herself up.

"David, I have never thought that I could leave Tom. I—you misunderstand me—I did want to know that you loved me, but I know it can't alter anything——" Her voice broke.

"I know, my dear," he said gently, "but we have to be very clear as to exactly what we can do without being disloyal to Tom. Now, I'm no saint, but I cannot go on kissing you as we kissed to-night, I cannot go on telling you I love you, except in a light and dispassionate way, we cannot go on having emotional scenes—all these things will have a physical effect on me—I am not made of ether. If we are to go on safely, we must shut down at once on all thought of drifting. Now the Lord knows how we are going to do it. I don't. But we have to. If we can't, I shall go away."

"Go away!" He saw how her face whitened at the mere suggestion of it. "David, you would go away!"

"Oh, my dear." He dropped forward onto his knees, putting his hands into her lap. "I do not want to go away. Will you understand me? Will you help me to keep the friendship what it was a year ago? Later, when we have beaten the fever out of it, we can be more expressive. Will you understand that I love you, even if I can't go on telling you so as long as you live with Tom? Will you understand that I am like every other man, that your loving me does not turn me into an ascetic, that I can't stand sex provocation any more than other men can, and that, because I love you, you will stimulate me if you are not careful? I have to be frank, my dear. Women like you don't see these things, or won't admit them till they are thrown at them. Now, are you going to help me?"

Though he had purposely turned his words into an appeal for assistance, as if he were one of the weaker brethren, she was stung by the implied indictment of herself, at the same time that she was moved to heights of renunciation as she looked down into his questioning face.

"David, I can go on," she answered proudly. "I shall never ask you to be any different. I don't want you to be any different. I only want to know you love me. I understand quite well that we can only be the friends we have been. You will never need to appeal to me again." Unconsciously her attitude was one of self-defence.

He did not dare to smile at her, but took her assurance soberly as he drew himself up and sat back in his chair. Then his manner changed.

"I want to talk to you about Tom," he began gravely, knowing that he was treading on thin ice.

She looked away from him into the fire, realizing with some surprise how completely her husband's last offence had been blotted from her mind, and that now that it was brought back to her consciousness the force of the shock was broken. She was even ready to suspend judgment until Bruce had spoken.

So far David Bruce had ignored phases of her married life about which he knew she had tremendous reserves, even when, as her doctor, he might have spoken without presumption. Though he had nursed her on several occasions, he had never entered her room save as a professional man, with a manner the more impersonal because he was so privileged. Only once or twice, and that very lightly, had he advised her as to how to deal with her husband. Many times he had wanted to speak, but had not found the occasion right. Now he saw that Alice did not resent the fact that he was likely to speak plainly.

"You needn't be afraid about Tom's taking to drink," wincing as he used the phrase and not looking at her. "He may never do it again. He was temporarily crazed. It's a pity you did not send for Bob that night."

"Why, David! I can't let outsiders know how he behaves——"

"Behaves! Good Lord, my dear girl!" He sat up suddenly, his eyes alight with a rare impatience. "Do you suppose he went on like that for fun, or to annoy you, or what? He was facing ruin. He was temporarily maddened, and really there are excuses for him. Do get out of your head the idea that he meant to be a brute to you. Don't be any more hostile to him because he was ill. You know you don't help yourself or him by that attitude."

She merely looked helplessly at him and back into the fire. He wanted to get up and shake her out of her extraordinary dumb control.

"My dear, I'm going to be very frank with you now. You

judge Tom too harshly. Your life with him would be more bearable if you realized better the difficulties he has with life. I know he is a trial, and that one has to learn how not to be hurt by a man of his irritable type. You can only learn that by realizing his difficulties. Now you know less about Tom than any one else. All you can see about him is that he makes you suffer. You think he does it purposely, and for that you almost hate him. He is not rude to you on purpose at all. His irritation is a reaction from strain. He has no idea how much you suffer from it. He would be astonished to find out. If you could grasp that fact you'd feel less badly about him."

He leaned down to put more wood on the fire.

"And, my dear, he has his troubles like the rest of us, and, like the rest of us, his worst trouble is himself. A man driven by his fever of vitality is a victim of his inheritance. But you could resist his pressure if you tried. You don't have to produce his slippers in two seconds when he demands them. Make him wait your time, or go and get them himself occasionally. The whole house doesn't have to hold its breath when he comes in. What do you suppose he could do to you if it didn't? Why, if you turned on him he would be just as helpless with you as you apparently are with him. You would ruin the best man in the world on the treatment you've given Tom the last two years. It will be hard work to undo it, but it is what you have to do if you are ever to be at peace with him. And he isn't enjoying the present state of things. He would like it to be different, only he doesn't know how."

As he saw she was crying silently he went down on to his knees again, this time putting his arms round her.

"My dear, you must stop being hostile to him. That is not fair. If your marriage was a mistake, it is just as hard on him as it is on you. And, if you mean to go on with it, you might as well try to make some adjustments. Tom is not rough on purpose. Few people are. You feel so badly about Tom's manners that you are apt to overlook his great qualities. You know, we British are too damned superior about our culture and our refinement, too intolerant of differences. We forget that the pioneers and the sons of pioneers made the world possible for us. If you could get away from Tom a little, and see him as other people see him, and get some independent estimate of him as a character, it might help you."

Alice made no attempt to reply to him, but cried on quietly while he soothed her by stroking her hands and putting them against his cheek.

After some time she recovered her control.

"Where is he, David?" she asked tragically.

"In my shanty. We brought him up from Point Curtis this morning."

"You will bring him home to-morrow, please."

"He may not be well enough. He is likely to be pretty sick for some days."

She looked down questioningly, he thought.

"Well, just as soon as he is well enough, will you bring him home?"

"I will."

They sat on for some time without another word. With his arms still about her, David Bruce put his head down on her lap, and she put one hand on his hair, and kept it there steady. She knew it might be a long while before they would allow themselves the luxury of this amount of intimacy again, so she concentrated her attention upon it that she might carry the memory forward to help her to ward off the menace of the future.

At last Bruce moved and looked at his watch, remembering Roland. Getting up, he drew her with him, and holding her face near to his looked steadily into her eyes. Still silent, he kissed her on the forehead and then firmly on her lips, before he stood up away from her.

"I must go and look after him for an hour or two. It will be late when I get back. You go to bed. And remember that you need only live one minute at a time."

With the smile that always warmed her and eliminated the fear of evil moments, he turned and left her to piece together for herself once more the puzzle of a fresh beginning.

CHAPTER XV

THE next morning Alice sent Asia for Eliza King who came at once and took the children home with her. It was late in the afternoon before the boss was carried up on a stretcher. He was still too ill to know where he was or what had happened to him. It was Alice's first experience of him as a sick man, and she felt the new sensation of pity for him as she leaned over his white, strangely silent face. For the next three days, while she nursed him, she revolved over and over in her mind Bruce's words, wondering if she could ever become sufficiently indifferent to him to be able to live comfortably, in spite of the incompatibilities.

On the fourth morning, as Roland appeared to be much better, Bruce said he would go to the bush for the day.

"I think he is all right now. He may sleep a good deal. Don't wake him on any account. If you want anything, send for Bob. I might not get down before eight or nine."

As Alice watched him go, she marvelled that they could have ignored as they had done in the last three days the great moments of that night, and it brought home to her the fact that life was possible after all, that one did not sit down and die so easily, and that the will to live had a useful friend in compromise.

An hour after he had left she went softly to the bedroom door, which was propped open for a few inches. The blinds had been drawn, leaving the room almost dark. Alice listened carefully, but heard no sounds of tossing or moaning. When she came again later she heard the low sounds of the heavy sleeper. With a sigh of thankfulness she returned to the kitchen.

At intervals during the day she listened at the door, always with the same result. When, about five o'clock, she stood once more, something, she never knew what, arrested her, and made her catch her breath and turn sick.

Tom Roland had always slept heavily and noisily, usually snoring and moaning by turns. But Alice detected something entirely new about this breathing, and with a sudden presentiment she rushed to the windows and drew up the blinds. The setting sun, shining straight in and reflected on the river, coloured the inside walls and lit up every corner. She turned to the bed where her husband lay on his back with his mouth open. His face was bluish grey, and strangely loose and withered.

Hardly knowing why, she snatched at the blankets, uncovering an empty laudanum bottle. She recoiled, as if it had been a revolver aimed at herself. Then she stared at it, and from it to him. For some minutes she was utterly unable to think. She stood like a graven image, with sightless eyes turned upon him.

Then by degrees came the questions. How much had he taken, and when had he taken it? Was he dying? Would anything save him? If he died—what then?

And then her cheeks blanched, her eyes hardened, her lips set.

Why not let him die?

She did not know what to do to save him. David Bruce might not be back for hours. Would that time make all the difference? She need not have discovered the laudanum, or suspected the nature of his breathing. She was obeying Bruce's instructions by leaving him alone. Who would ever know if she walked out of that room, leaving things as they had been, and said nothing?

She staggered to the window that looked down the river, and threw up the lower sash, which had been closed to keep the blind from flapping. She saw nothing but the blurred blaze of the sinking sun like a great fringed splotch of crimson upon a grey sea.

Was he dying? Did even the minutes matter?

She drew her hand over her eyes.

"Oh, God!" she groaned. But she was not thinking of God. The vision in the mist that swept over her eyes held the sad, tired, accusing face of David Bruce. She rushed to the door. "Asia!" she called sharply.

"Yes, Mother," from the kitchen.

"Go down to the store and ask Mr. Hargraves to come here at once."

As the child ran out, Alice dropped onto the sitting-room sofa, feeling that she would faint, but she pulled herself together as she heard Bob scrambling up the path, and, though white, she was calm as she met him at the door.

"Could you find Mr. Bruce in the bush for me?" she asked.

"Yes, certainly."

"Then please go at once and get him here as soon as you can, and do not say a word to any one about it."

"You may trust me, Mrs. Roland," he answered anxiously, realizing from her face that it was a desperate business, and without waiting for further information he rushed off for the kitchen and a horse.

"What is it, Mother?" gasped Asia, who panted back as Bob raced off. "Is Father worse?"

"He seems to be. But don't say anything about it. Uncle David will be here presently. You go on getting the tea."

Alice's voice sounded strange to herself, and in a daze she walked back into the bedroom, wondering if there was anything else she ought to do. She tried to think of some one at the bay who would know what to do, and then she remembered that she dare not tell them. She felt instinctively that it must not get out. The Braytons? She could trust them.

She wrote a hurried note asking for advice, and asking Mrs. Brayton to keep Asia if she could send Harold Brayton back.

She felt terribly alone as she watched the child running up the green hill. Every little sound about the house made her jump. When she found herself looking back over her shoulder with swift fear she knew it was time to set her teeth against a possible collapse. As she stood in the kitchen again she realized that she could not stay alone in any room wondering what was happening, that she would have to go in and face it.

Once she began to walk to her room she felt better, and when she stood beside her bed she was amazed to find she could look calmly, even coldly, upon the man who lay dying there.

For the first time since her marriage she felt herself entirely detached from him. Up to this time she had been unable to see him to any extent as others saw him. The others had not had to feed him or sleep with him; while, for almost the whole of their married life, she had known him only as an irritable and irregular eater, a restless sleeper, and a man who had made their intimate relations merely a continuous performance of abruptly passionate acts.

They had never read a book together. He did not like music. Once or twice when she had pointed out a sunset to him he had said, "Humph! Not bad," and had jerked on to something else. His presence had always meant irritation, tenseness, uncertainty; his absence a blessed relief.

And yet she had always known that men trusted him and admired him. She knew that the world saw in him a great driving force, a reliable friend, a generous enemy, the soul of business honour. And she had grown almost to hate him.

She knew, as Bruce had said, that it was because he had made her suffer, because he had dominated her, because she had been afraid of him—that poor thing that lay there dying. She had come in the last three days to see that perhaps, after all, he did not realize how she suffered, that it was, indeed, largely her own fault. And, as she looked at him, she wondered how she could ever have been afraid of him, he looked so pitifully harmless.

And then there was the hard cold fact that she had seen before Bruce had put it into words, the fact that he was not happy, either. What had she ever done for him that could not have been done by a housekeeper or another? And he had certainly expected something more of her. Though this was not the first time she had met this question, it came to her now with the force of a revelation. She had wronged him in marrying him more than he had wronged her because she had doubted from the beginning the results in which he believed and hoped.

But it was more than anything else the fact that he was dying that killed her hostility to him, and the fact that he had meant to die brought home to her the misery he must have faced. Had he been afraid? Had life seemed impossible to him? He had always seemed like life incarnate. She had never thought of death in connection with him, or of fear.

When she turned from him to go out into the dusk her battle with him was more than half won. She knew that if he lived he could never again hurt her as he had hurt her in the past.

As she opened the front door and looked towards the mountain there was enough light for her to see a horseman come out of the bush at a headlong gallop down the road beside the tramway. Something about that mad race against time stirred her out of the coma into which she had fallen, and lifted her spirits. She was ready for action, ready for anything when Bruce dashed up to the gate.

"It's Tom," as he leapt from the steaming horse. "He's taken laudanum. I didn't know what to do."

With one eloquent look at her he sprang up the steps, leaving her to fasten his horse.

Pulling the bed-clothes off the boss's body, Bruce put his ear to his heart. He soon saw that he was nearly gone, so nearly that it was doubtful if anything could save him.

As he realized it he pulled himself up, and as he looked down upon Roland his teeth set, his hands clenched, and the veins stood out on his face. Only he could save the boss, and he did not know that he could. And nobody would ever know if he did not.

For a moment, while temptation strangled his will, he stood stiff. Then he swept his hands across his eyes as if to ward off some unseen terror, and, the power of decision returned, he raised his head quickly to see Alice standing in the doorway with her eyes glued upon him.

He had only to look at her to see that she knew what he had just been through, and that she had been through it first. But he dare lose no minutes then.

"When did he take it?" he asked hoarsely.

"I don't know, David."

"When did you find it out?" She knew why he asked.

"About five o'clock." He knew that was true, and he saw that her fight, too, had been short.

"An emetic—mustard and warm water—at once—I'll get that—you find me a big cork——" He jerked the words out as she followed him into the kitchen.

"We must get Brayton here—we can trust him."

"I've sent Asia—there is some one coming now."

"It's he. Good." He looked through the window. "Bob's following. We can trust him. We'll need them both."

He found what he wanted as he talked, and he was ready when Harold Brayton's horse stopped snorting at the back gate.

Alice's lips trembled as she met him. "Thank you," she mumbled.

With a sympathetic gesture he gripped her hand, and looked from her to Bruce.

"God! I'm glad to see you, Brayton. Hope you can stay all night? That's good. Come and help me now. Mrs. Roland, when Bob comes, please tell him to fix up Harold's horse in the yard here, and give him a feed, and take his own and mine to the stalls, and then come back."

Alice sat down dazed, feeling as if she were in a dream. She did hope there would be something for her to do. Then she remembered that the men would have to eat, and she began mechanically to prepare a more substantial meal than the one Asia had set on the kitchen table.

In the bedroom Bruce looked anxiously at Roland's blue face.

"I don't think he has much of a chance, Brayton. But his extraordinary vitality may die hard. We'll make him sick with mustard and water, if possible, and then we'll have to walk him up and down till he wakes, if it takes all night. We'll get him outside. It's warm enough."

By the time Bob returned from seeing to the horses they were ready to drag Roland's inert body out of doors.

As he entered the kitchen Bob held out a telegram.

"This has just come from Kaiwaka, Mrs. Roland. It was given to me at the stable."

Alice opened it indifferently as she looked at her husband's name on the outside. Bob, who stood waiting for instructions, was upset to see that she dropped into a chair on the verge of tears. Hearing Bruce's voice, he went into the sitting-room, still unaware of the cause of this summons. He stopped, startled, when he saw Roland propped up between the two men.

"Bob, you can be trusted, I know," said Bruce quietly. "The boss has taken laudanum. We mayn't be able to save him, but if we do, and it got out, it would lower his credit pretty badly, shake confidence in him in the future, you understand. So it must never be hinted at."

"I understand."

"Just help us out with him, and then Mrs. Roland will give you a meal. We shall have to take it in turns to eat and rest."

When they got outside, Bob told him of the telegram.

"I'll go in for a minute," he answered.

Alice, who was crying with her head on the table, pushed the yellow paper towards him without a word.

Taking it up, he saw that it was signed by the secretary of the Kauri Timber Company. When he had read it through he understood why she cried. It told Roland that the company would stand by him in his recent loss, that it would advance payments on its new contracts with him, and finance him further, if necessary, and that he was to go ahead with confidence with the work on his mill.

Saying nothing, he merely put his hand on her shoulder before going outside.

Bob waited for half an hour before going in again. Rather nervously he told Alice that Bruce had sent him for something to eat, and he was almost alarmed when she asked him to sit down with her, for she was not famous for her approachableness. But she began at once with a simplicity and directness that surprised herself.

"Let us talk about something cheerful, Bob. Tell me about the girl you are going to marry."

She surprised him into shyness, but when he saw after a few questions that she was really interested, he produced a photo from his vest pocket.

Alice looked into the sweet, fresh, girlish face with a sudden swelling in her throat.

"She's far too good for me," said Bob humbly. "And I hate to bring her to a far-off place like this. But I told her about you. And she said she guessed if you could stand it she could."

She looked through misty eyes at Bob's young decent face, seeing him afresh.

"I shall be very glad to have her here, Bob. When does she come?"

"Well, I don't know exactly, Mrs. Roland. As soon as I can get the house built, anyway."

As she handed him a cup of tea across the table she remembered that he was one of the men who were waiting for wages, wages that now he might never get. But at her first reference to it he brushed it aside, and seeing that he was helping her, he continued to talk of his plans for his future home.

As she sat alone after he had gone out Alice wondered

why she had ever been afraid of a strange place and human beings. In a little while Harold Brayton came in, anxiously sympathetic.

"Still a hope," he said gravely, as he sat down. He did not offer useless sympathy, and being without a cheerful topic that he could suitably introduce, he sat and ate with an awkward silence. He was much more vividly conscious of the tragedy in the house than Bob had been, and less able to be diverted from it. Alice had to exert herself in order to save them both from embarrassment.

After he had gone she began to listen for David Bruce. She heard the slow dragging steps from the front to the back, the pause while they turned, the same shuffling to the front, the pause again. There was something indescribably weird about the low monotony of it, about that desperate tramp to cheat death hovering overhead.

When, at last, she heard Bruce's steps at the back door, she rose to meet him with a curious apathy. But he read the question in her eyes in spite of it.

"I can't say yet. He will not be out of danger for hours."

As he dropped into the chair opposite her he felt her unusual detachment, and guessed that her mind was so satiated with adversity that she could not suffer any more. In silence she poured him out a cup of strong coffee, and he noticed that she did not look at him as he commenced to eat and drink. After some minutes he felt her eyes fixed upon him with a look that was so insistent that he had to raise his face even though he made an effort not to.

"David, why couldn't we let him die?"

He was startled by her matter-of-fact tone as much as by the frankness of her question. He stopped eating, and looked thoughtfully at the fire for a minute before answering.

"Yes, indeed, why couldn't we? That is an interesting question," he answered slowly. "You could have done it, and I should never have known. I could do it still, and no one would ever know. And we both want him to die."

They looked at each other across the table. They were

both dulled by weariness and the recent rapid march of domestic events to a point where they could make no further demonstration of feeling, and yet they felt at that moment, as they had never felt before, that they were united for all time, bound by bonds immeasurably stronger than the kisses of passion, or the vows of emotional moments.

"Well," smiled Bruce.

She did not try to answer.

"What stopped you?" he asked lightly. "Did you think of God?"

"No. I thought of you."

"Oh, much the same thing," he said, with a wicked little chuckle.

She could not help smiling.

"What stopped you, David?" she asked after a minute. She wondered why his face became suddenly grave. "Did you think of me, David?"

He drank two mouthfuls of coffee before replying:

"No. I dare not." Then looking into the fire, he went on slowly, "I thought of the men who have trusted him, and I thought"—he turned his eyes to hers with a tragic appeal—"I remembered that once, years ago, I let a man die in much the same way."

Alice did not start, nor did the expression in her eyes change as she returned his look.

The abnormal stillness deepened round them till the sound of the dragging steps outside shuffled back into their consciousness again.

"For a woman, David?" Her tone held no hint of judgment.

"Yes."

"How old were you?"

"Twenty-four—and I had been drinking."

"Did she ever know?"

"Yes. She never told any one—but—she sent me flying."

"It was her husband?"

"Yes."

"How old was she?"

"About thirty-five."

"Thirty-five—and you were twenty-four."

In her tone he read a damning indictment, but not for him. A flash of flame swept her eyes as she got up. Moving swiftly round the table she dropped on to her knees beside him, and put her head on his lap.

He set his teeth against a swirl of emotion.

"Oh, get up, dear, please."

Alice raised a quiet and tearless face, and without a word she went back to her chair, and looked into the fire. David Bruce knew that henceforth her love for him would be rounded out with fuller understanding.

With difficulty he ate a few more mouthfuls and then he stood up. She rose at once and came and stood opposite him. He thought that pale though she was he had never seen her look as beautiful as she did then with her eyes shining at him.

Seizing her hands, he raised them to his lips.

"God! dear. It is good to be understood and forgiven one's sins."

Her eyes filled, but she did not try to speak, and he left her, standing thus, her face a beacon for the night.

She sat still by the fire for half an hour before she cleared and reset the table, and made up the fire, knowing it would be her task to wait on the men during the night. When Bob Hargraves came in she sent him to lie down in Asia's room. Later she dozed at intervals on the sitting-room sofa, sleeping more than she could have supposed possible. Once or twice changes were made in the night without arousing her. She felt no excitement, no suspense. She knew long before they brought Tom Roland in at the dawn that he was saved.

BOOK III

CHAPTER XVI

ASIA was eighteen.

For months the inevitable fact that she would be eighteen had dominated her thoughts, and her mother, watching her, sensed with her uncanny aptitude for presentiment that something was in the air. What that something was she feared so much that she refused to think about it.

Now Asia's birthday was two weeks behind her, and Alice had seen for days that the dread something was fast approaching. As she paced the beach below the cliffs one evening, with the river running silently beside her under the cool spring stars, she knew she was only indulging in her old habit of putting off the evil hour. As she walked, she hated the thought that old habits could still dominate her. She hated her own exhaustless capacity for suffering. She hated her terrible dependence on the people she loved. She hated her inability to be just where she suffered.

At last, shivering, but not with cold, she set her face homewards. Ahead of her, across the river, she saw the moving lantern of the mill watchman going his rounds, and the red lamps on the ends of the wharves, and the head lights of a big Australian barque that lay moored to one of them.

Tom Roland's dream was coming true. He had built his mill and enlarged it, and was considering enlarging it again. Almost as fast as the logs could be run down from the bush they were sawn and loaded into the timber vessels that now came from all parts of the world in a continuous procession up the river.

By day the whole bay vibrated with the whistle and screech of the circular saws, the tear of the breakdowns, the rasp of the drags, the rattling of chains on the skids, the hum of the belting, the scream and clank of the donkey engines as they loaded flitches into the voracious holds of the ships, and, as a running accompaniment to all these, the triumphant roar of the great engines that drove every wheel and chain and belt.

The shutting off of all this fuss and buzz now intensified the silence of the nights. Even Alice was conscious as she walked home of the absence of the throb of the engines, of the vacant stillness of the hushed machinery. The intermittent sounds of the night were dwarfed by the memory of the day's loud speech. She heard, as it were, from a long way off, snatches of song from the barque, and the sounds of an accordion played somewhere at the head of the bay.

She turned wearily round the cliffs, and proceeded to climb steps now cut in the clay up the bank to a path above which joined at the boss's front gate with the old path leading directly down to the store. She paused several times, trying to fortify herself with the freshness of the night. Once she lingered, listening to the cry of the new baby, the second, at Bob Hargraves' house, a chain or two on the other side of the store path. As she stood, sweet scents floated down to her from the shrubs and flowers that now hid the foundations of her home.

Roland's picnicking days were over, and with the prospect of prosperity he had been willing to make of his house something more of a setting for his increasing success. The year before he had practically rebuilt the whole structure. A narrow central hall now ran from the front door to a large lean-to containing a porch, a scullery and a bathroom with a fitted tin tub, the latter creating a precedent for the entire northern end of the Auckland province. The distinction it gave his house in the eyes of passing travellers was a source of great satisfaction to the boss. Two bedrooms had also been inserted into the middle of the cottage, just behind the enlarged front rooms.

Alice would have appreciated the changes much more if she had been consulted, or any notice taken of her wishes. But the only people whose advice Roland had deigned to consider were Mrs. Brayton, Bruce, and Asia. It was Asia who had had most to do with the scheme of interior decoration. Each stage in the furnishing of the rooms represented a stage in her artistic development, and each stage was the result of a visit to the Hardings, now removed to Auckland, and of explorations into the latest fads from America, which country largely influenced the evolution of household art in New Zealand.

As Roland was not as susceptible to the progressive nature of art, or as inclined to take it seriously as Asia was, he could be persuaded each time to impose only a little of the new upon the old, with the result that the patterns of the wall papers and the linoleum did not always agree, nor did the furniture balance properly in the room space, nor did the colours always harmonize. But Asia had high hopes of some day seeing it as a perfect whole.

At first Alice had been enthusiastic about the changes, but later she resented them. She could not see why it should be good to have a flowered wall paper admired at one time, only to have it scorned and discarded for a tinted one three years later. If it was beautiful once why was it not beautiful for ever? Mrs. Brayton's wonderful rooms had not been changed since the day they had first seen them. But in spite of her, and it was this that hurt, the evolution of art in the house on the cliffs had proceeded.

From the beginning she had been so thankful herself for every hard-won addition to mere comfort and convenience that the claims of art seemed ridiculous. For a person who had a passion for one great art she was singularly indifferent to others. Also, it seemed hard to her that Asia should be given money to make a show, when she had had to fight for every inch of comfort she had ever gained.

It was not that she was jealous of Asia; it was rather that Asia's success at managing people, and particularly

Roland, brought home to her her own continued failure in this direction. It was true that she now got on much better with her husband. With success he was less irritable, and in ways he had become more considerate, particularly, she had noticed, during the last year. But she knew that her victories had been mostly Asia's victories. One instance came again to her memory, as she stopped for the last time before entering, outside the fence, at the corner by the cliffs.

It had been their first fight to get help in the house, help that was badly needed, as Alice grew less able to do her share. Asia was fourteen when she first began to question whether washing Roland's heavy flannels was part of the fixed duty of woman. Alice, though physically and temperamently unfit for housework, had never protested against anything, realizing that it was all in her marriage contract, and she told Asia it was no use to resent it. But Asia was a young rebel, fast developing a fierce hostility to anything that savoured of a law or an order, and she finally drove her mother into asking Roland for the extra money to pay for help.

"Good heavens! What are the girls doing?" he had demanded. "If they want luxuries of that kind where will it end?"

And Alice had succumbed immediately, and had wept about it in secret.

Asia stood it for a few weeks longer, and then one morning, when the flannels were heavier and dirtier than usual, she had burst in a white heat upon Tom Roland, who happened to be lying late in bed, and had told him that his flannels and his boots would stay dirty in future unless he got some one in to clean them.

He had stared back in amazement at her raging face, and then a flicker of amusement crossed his eyes.

"Holy Moses," he snorted, "if it's as bad as all that, get two washerwomen."

"You don't know how to manage him, Mother," said Asia wisely, later in the day.

That stung Alice to make a stand that night when her husband tried to get even with her. He had said only a few words when she turned on him.

"You stop annoying me about nothing," she commanded, and turning half dressed, she walked out of the room and left him alone for the night, to digest his astonishment as best he could.

No one was more surprised than she was at the happy results of this incident. Asia calmly requisitioned one of the men's wives for all the washing and heavy cleaning, sending for her sometimes two days a week, and never again was a word said.

There was one thing for which Alice was supremely grateful to her husband. Never had he given a sign to show that he misunderstood her friendship with David Bruce. Though she knew they gave him no real cause for jealousy, she was none the less surprised at his apparent indifference to the amount of time they saw each other. She rightly took this to be a tribute more to Bruce than to herself, and it was one thing that was independent of Asia's influence.

For three years now Alice had felt something growing between herself and the child she idolized. It had begun with Asia's first visit to the Hardings in Auckland, and it had been increased by later visits, and especially by the theatre going that had risen up like a bogy to affright Alice. In vain Bruce told her that every girl got stage mad and got over it. In vain Asia told her mother that she was not going to the dogs because she loved plays. The unforgettable fact was that Asia continued to go to plays even though she knew it hurt her mother. Alice knew she had slipped into some other world of thought, and was shaping herself by a philosophy that she herself feared. And it was the end of all this that she feared. And somehow, in her mind, the beginning of the end had become associated with Asia's eighteenth birthday.

It was because she had felt it coming nearer that she had gone out this spring night to try to bring herself to face it.

After closing the front door behind her Alice stood in the hall listening. The stillness of the house seemed ominous. She moved to the sitting-room door, and when she saw Asia sitting alone by the fire she had the feeling of a creature trapped by something that has lain in wait for it.

Hearing her there, Asia raised a pale and uneasy face towards her.

"Mother, I want to talk to you." She tried to make her voice casual, but it sounded strained.

Throwing off her cape, Alice walked slowly to her chair on the other side of the hearth, her face growing whiter.

"Where are the girls?" she asked weakly, feeling that she wanted no interruptions.

Betty and Mabel, who were now thirteen and eleven, were no longer referred to as the "children."

"They've gone to bed." Asia leaned down to put more wood on the fire.

"Is Tom home?"

"No. He won't be back to-night. He has sent word."

Alice sat down, seeing Asia through a mist. The worst thing of all about this to her was the sense of her own utter helplessness to prevent, or postpone, or alter by one fraction the purpose of the clear, fearless, arrogantly youthful eyes that looked up at her with a tragic pity.

Asia was beautiful with a radiant vitality that stung every one to life when she entered a room. Her features were not classic like her mother's, nor faultlessly regular like the ideal of the adolescent, for they were too strong. But she had a fine white skin, delicately tinted, eyes with the subtle draw of deep pools, and masses of soft gold hair that waved with a dozen tints as she moved. She was eager and hungry for life and beauty, voracious for adventure, tremendously sure of herself and her right to live as she pleased. She had no conception of the chasm that separated her at eighteen from her mother, either at the same age or now. But she knew only too well the likely effect of what she now had to say.

The attempts she had made to show her mother whither she was tending only convinced her it was best to wear a mask, and when the inevitable break came to make it as short as she could. For years she had lived more closely to Mrs. Brayton and to Bruce than she had lived to her mother. She realized the tragedy of it. She knew what she had meant in her home. She knew what a blank she would leave behind.

As she looked at her mother's head bowed to the fire, she saw afresh what the years had done to that drooping figure and that pale, proud face, mellowed and more gracious certainly, and in ways more beautiful than ever. She wondered if she would ever solve the everlasting enigma of strength and weakness behind those suffering eyes. She set her teeth on the thought that she was now going to add to the grey hairs, the lines and the droop.

As she braced herself to speak, her mother raised her face, with a manner suggestive of noble resignation.

"Well?" she said patiently.

"Oh, Mother," began Asia miserably, "I know I'm going to hurt you dreadfully, but, oh, please, do try to understand."

Alice resented the implication that she might not understand all the more because she knew it was deserved.

"What is it?" she asked coldly, inviting the worst.

"I want to go away. I want to earn my own living. I want to see the world."

"Yes?"

They were both looking into the fire. Those three sentences were what Alice had feared to hear, and she felt her heart set in her chest like a ball of plaster.

Asia had known beforehand that she would get no help,

but she had determined to say everything there was to be said as shortly as possible. She clenched her hands on her knees, for she knew the look in her mother's eyes was just as bad as she had expected it would be.

"It isn't a new thing, Mother. I've wanted it for years, but I made up my mind I would wait till I was eighteen. I've thought about it till I've been sick—I know what it will mean to you—but I cannot help it. I must go. I can't be a parasite—I just can't."

A flood of shame swept over Alice's face, and blinding tears rushed to her eyes, but Asia did not look at her as she forced herself on jerkily.

"And I want to see the world. It's all so wonderful to me, and I'm not afraid, and I know I can get on. You needn't worry about me, and, of course, I will come home to see you; but I can't stay here any longer. I have used this place up—I've breathed every breath there is to be got out of it. I would have gone two years ago but for you. I have thought of you. I've tried to tell you, but you wouldn't listen, and so I went on keeping it to myself till I couldn't any longer. I had to tell others—Uncle David and Mrs. Brayton."

Alice sat up stiffly.

"You've told them first!"

"I had to tell somebody, Mother."

The pain of this hardened Alice.

"And what do you think you can do?" she asked with a shade of scorn.

Asia winced, but kept anger out of her eyes and voice.

"I have music."

"Yes, so had I."

"Well, Mother, I've got to try, even if I fail, and I won't fail."

"Oh, you foolish child, what do you know of the world?"

If there ever was a question better designed to make youth hate age and fight it, it is not on record.

Asia bit back the words that leapt to her lips. If she

had not been so conscious of her mother's misery she would have said things that neither of them would have forgotten.

"If I don't know anything of the world," she replied quietly, "it's time I began to learn, considering I have to live in it."

"And may I ask how you are going to begin? Do you think you can capture the world in a week?"

"No, Mother. I am not quite mad. I am going to the Hardings; they will help me."

"Oh, I see. They know too." All trace of tears now left Alice. Henceforth she was frozen.

"Yes, I wrote to them. They think I can get on. The world is different from what it was when you tried. Mother, do see that. Do understand. Everybody helps women today. And it's nothing for a girl to earn her own living."

"Oh, isn't it? You don't know anything about life and men. You don't know what girls have to put up with, especially when they—they look like you. You don't know yourself, or how clever men can fool you, and lie to you."

"A good many women seem to survive it, Mother. I don't see why I shouldn't. I'm not afraid, and if I make mistakes I will learn. I'm not going to the devil."

Her proud self-confidence angered her mother.

"How little you know what you are talking about. You've lived a sheltered life here. You've had no chance to learn what men can be, or how you yourself can feel."

A curious smile flitted across Asia's eyes. Getting up suddenly, she walked to the window and looked out into the darkness. Her "sheltered life!" She smiled as she thought of it: of crude rapidly arrested scenes with Sonny Shoreman; of staggeringly sudden and unexpected caresses on the part of various men, a Kaiwaka curate, a surveyor, an English derelict working on the gum-fields, and others; and of her own adolescent passion for David Bruce, not yet out of her system.

All this Asia saw again as she stood by the window, and

she felt that if there was anything she did not know about men it could only be something unexpectedly agreeable.

As she turned back to the fire Alice saw in her face that arrogant cocksureness of youth that so irritates the wisdom of age.

"If I am ever to marry, Mother," she said, sitting down, "it seems to me I might as well know something about myself and men. Or perhaps you have me pigeon-holed as an old maid." She did not mean to be scornful, but her mother resented her tone.

"Oh, well, it's useless my saying anything, I know. But you will learn." She could not avoid superiority.

"That's what I'm going for, Mother. For God's sake, understand. You must have realized that I would go some day. Why do you put me in the wrong like this?"

But Alice was suffering too much now to unbend. All she wanted was the hard cold fact.

"How are you going to get the money to begin?"

"Uncle David is lending it to me."

This was the unkindest cut of all. It looked like treachery.

"I see. And when do you go?"

"By the next boat, Mother."

Alice rose abruptly, her face turned to stone. Ignoring Asia's appealing gesture, she walked proudly into her bedroom, and shut and locked the door. She never undressed or slept, or wept all night.

Asia sat on, slow tears dripping from her cheeks. After a while she stole out into the back garden, but as if powerless to move any further she leaned against the wash-house and sobbed helplessly.

As a late moon rose over Pukekaroro she walked to the side gate and leaned upon it looking at the mountain. He reminded her of the nights and early mornings, of the moonrises and the dawns when she and her mother, watching by sick or dying babies, had turned their faces together towards his inscrutable calm. She remembered the other things they had shared: how together they had looked for the spring's first golden glory on the kowhai trees; how together they had listened for the first tui's song, and rejoiced over the first violet; how together they had watched many red suns go down beyond the river gap; how together they had played and loved Beethoven.

And she knew that she more than any one else had always been there, like the impossible friend in the melodrama, always on the spot to share the good and the bad. And why could she not have kept on doing it for ever?

Why? Why?

CHAPTER XVII

MRS. BRAYTON sat back on the big lounge in front of her library fire, an open book on her lap, her reading spectacles—the only kind of artificial aid she deigned to use—on the end of her nose. For some time she had sat thus, listening for steps in the garden, the light from her reading-lamp rivalling that of the dancing flames upon her faded silk gown. The night outside was filled with the soft soughing of the wind in the pines, which to-night seemed to the old lady to be more melancholy than usual.

When at last she heard the crunching on the shells a look of animation shot into her eyes and she straightened herself up. When alone, she had to admit to herself that she was growing old, but she was determined that she would not yet be old in public. Her blue eye was almost as keen as ever, and her manner had kept its fire, and her body its poise.

"Come in," she said, rising at the tap on her window-pane.

Asia entered like a blast of river wind. She was hatless, as usual, her hair tossed about her face, her eyes feverish, her cheeks burning, her breath hurried from her fast walk. She took the old lady's hand, bent and kissed her lace and ribbon cap in a courtly fashion, looked for a moment into her eyes, and with a gesture that was both tragic and comical dropped beside her onto the lounge.

Mrs. Brayton, whom no storms could ever more ruffle, preserved her serene ease, and while waiting for Asia to get her breath, she rose again to put wood on the fire. After a second's abstraction Asia bounded to her feet, took the tongs from her, and fussed with the fire till there was a fine blaze. The action relieved her. Dropping back into one of her tangled and unlady-like attitudes, she drew her hand over her eyes.

"Thank God!" she exclaimed. "By to-morrow night it will all be over."

Mrs. Brayton turned to her, prepared to listen.

"I would have come down, my dear, but David said it was better not."

"Oh, Lord, yes! I've never known anything so awful as these last two days. I don't know what has come to Mother. The pater went to the bush yesterday, saying he would not be back for a week. He hates a gloomy atmosphere. Betty and Mabel are scared to death, and even Bunty is subdued. The house is like a *morgue,* and that foolish mother of mine like an avenging angel. All because I want to do a perfectly natural and rational thing. Oh, how is it that human beings can be so silly?" She drew herself up, trying to hide her own emotion under a veil of disgust.

Seeing the old lady's eyes fixed questioningly upon her, she went on.

"Oh, I've felt, Granny. But I've felt all I'm going to feel. There's a limit. If she had been different it would have broken me up to go. But she has made me hard. All I want now is to get the beastly business over. What is the matter with Mother, anyway?"

"It's being a mother; that's the trouble," replied Mrs. Brayton softly.

"Oh, nonsense! All mothers are not like that. I'm sure you never were." Asia saw a swift pain shoot into the eyes under the lace cap, and realizing that she had scored some never-mentioned wound, she pretended not to see, and raced on jerkily, "I know what I've meant to Mother. I know what she means to me, but I can't live buried in my mother, nor she in me. I want so much more than just one person. And I *have* waited, and I *have* suppressed myself. I'm not rushing off at the first impulse. I've done everything I could to please her, been a beastly hypocrite and lied—ugh! And I've managed her husband for her. And I'm not leaving her alone or in a hole of any kind. Things are better at home than they have ever been—the girls are growing up and Elsie is three and no more sign of babies. I've thought it all out, and I've waited. You don't think I'm a brute, do you?"

"No." The old lady had recovered her composure under this torrent.

"It can't have come as a shock to her. She must have seen it coming. And she's not going to be alone when she has you and Uncle David. Fancy any woman thinking herself ill-used when she has Uncle David!" She paused, and instantly the silence became significant. Then she turned to Mrs. Brayton with one of her characteristic whirls. "I want to ask you something," she said.

The old lady's eyes smiled a permission to proceed.

"Have you ever thought about them—wondered?"

"Why, what do you mean?" The keen eyes narrowed a little.

"About their friendship, I mean. I've often wanted to ask you. They're a mystery to me." She stared abstractedly into the fire.

"A mystery!" repeated Mrs. Brayton.

"Yes. They must love each other. I'm sure they do; but whether there's ever been anything I can't say. And it's been so easy for them—the pater away such a lot and when I have gone out in the evenings I've said where I was going and how long I'd be away."

"Child!" exclaimed the old lady, aghast.

"What—why—wasn't that sensible?"

"Sensible! Oh, ye gods! And this is the child! The unsophisticated country child!" Mrs. Brayton stared at her, too amazed to be shocked.

"It's the result of your teaching, yours and Uncle David's." There was a twinkle in Asia's eyes.

"Oh, child! How can you say that? You have moved, I think, a little faster than either of us suspected."

"Well, my home has been the sort of place that one would move in, if one could move at all," replied Asia grimly. "Isn't Mother enough to make you think? And is there anything slow about Tom Roland? Why don't our parents realize that we children have eyes to see and ears to hear? I slept for years with only a thin wall between my parents and me. Slept, did I say? I sat up for hours shivering, sick and faint. I cried, I prayed, I raged. I grew old listening to them. I grew to have a pity and then a contempt for them both, and then just a tolerance. I couldn't understand, and I don't understand now how human beings can be so stupid, and so cruel, and make so much unhappiness for each other. Why did Mother stand it? What good does it do to stand things? She never made him any better. Oh, she's a mystery to me."

Having nothing to say, Mrs. Brayton sat still.

"Mother has taught me one great lesson. I'm done with misery. I shall have nothing more to do with it as long as I live. I shall train my mind to ignore it. I won't cease to help people, or to be sympathetic, but I'm not going to suffer over anybody any more. I shall be like Uncle David. He never worries about anything."

"Well, if you can manage it as well as he does," smiled the old lady.

"Oh, I shall. He's a wonder. He has even improved Mother. She must love him! And if there hasn't been anything between them how—how could she resist him?"

She lowered her eyes, flushing suddenly.

"Child!" murmured Mrs. Brayton breathlessly, feeling as if she were getting out of her depth.

But no water was too deep for Asia, who had more than a nodding acquaintance with deep waters.

"I have loved him, you know," she went on, taking up one of the shrivelled hands. "Really loved him, I mean—not only the hero-*worship business*. He could have done anything with me he liked lots of times in the last year or two. I've been quite helpless—that's one reason why I wanted to go away before. I'm getting over it a little now and I know what it feels like, and if Mother feels the same about him and if he kisses her—well——"

Unconsciously she crushed Mrs. Brayton's hand till the rings cut her fingers.

The old lady was astounded by this revelation.

Feeling her silence, Asia turned from gazing at the fire. "Why are you surprised?" she demanded.

"Oh, child!"

"Didn't you know I loved him?"

"Why, yes, but not in that way."

"And why not in that way? Don't we all have feelings—passions?"

"Oh, my dear, passion is too strong a term for eighteen to use."

"But it's a biological necessity that eighteen feels," retorted Asia grimly. "And why did you lend me books on sex and biology, you two, if you didn't expect me to study the facts of life?"

She glared at the old lady.

"Oh, my dear, of course you may read books——"

"I see, but I must not apply their information rationally to life!"

"Well," with a suspicion of a twinkle in her eye, "a personal experience is a very different thing from scientific statements in books."

"Do you think I don't know that?" Asia drew herself up till she towered over the bent figure on the lounge. "But the statements in books are to prepare us for life. You prepare me for life, and then you are amazed that I begin to live. You grown-up people amuse me. You think you own a monopoly over experience, and that you ought to."

She drew her knees up to her chin without apology, balanced herself on the edge of the lounge, and stared into *the fire.*

"It's perfectly natural that I should have fallen in love with Uncle David. Anybody would fall in love with him. All the girls in the place are silly about him. They hang around watching for him—and some of the married women too—— Why, he's the only man in the place! But he never looks at anybody but Mother, and nobody knows how he looks at her."

"Asia, my dear"—Mrs. Brayton sat up very straight—"I think you are seeing things that do not exist. Your mother and David have a rare and beautiful friendship—a spiritual friendship. You have no right to think into it something that is not there just because you feel too deeply."

"Why, it's because I feel that I know how they could if they wanted to, and I don't see why they shouldn't want to."

"Oh, my dear."

"Look here, Granny"—Asia bounded to her feet, and stood with her back to the fire—"here you have been educating me for years to understand unusual situations, and to discriminate, and now, when I apply my knowledge to the facts under my nose, you try to put me in the wrong. You know Mother does not love her husband. You know he does not love her. You know how he lives. You know that Mother and Uncle David care for each other. You know they have all sorts of opportunities. And you profess to be amazed that I see it, that I understand it, just because I am only eighteen. I'm not morbid about it. I'm not curious. I'm only interested. I'm not jealous. He's the only thing worth while that poor Mother has ever had. I'm only too glad for her to have him. And that's why it's so hard to have her unkind to me——"

Her voice broke unexpectedly, and she dropped back on to the lounge, burying her face in her hands.

Mrs. Brayton put a sympathetic hand upon her knee.

Presently Asia recovered, and tossed back her crumpled hair.

"Granny," she said grimly, "I am no babe. You know I have told *you about some* of the men who have begun to make love to me, and I knew how to take care of myself. I know more about men than you think, more about all of us. The fact is, we human beings are not a lot of book heroes or devils, we are animals, more or less veneered, and the sooner we see it the better. As Uncle David says, Tom Roland is a victim of overmuch vitality. The pity is that he didn't marry Mrs. Lyman instead of Mother. That's just the matter. Good heavens! Why did she marry him? I have never dared ask her since I was a small child."

Mrs. Brayton had no astonishment left to spend upon this latest wisdom, and she turned helplessly away from the question.

"Can you imagine why she married him?" persisted Asia.

"Why—why do most people marry, my child?" she evaded.

"Do you believe she loved him?"

"I don't see why not. He is very attractive to many women."

"Oh, I think she was just lonely, and afraid, and he dominated her—poor Mother."

They sat silent for some minutes.

"You know," Asia began again, "I have often wondered what my father was like. He must have been a more joyous soul than Mother, perhaps an awful scamp, and that's why she would never speak about him."

"Perhaps."

Asia looked curiously at the old lady, feeling she knew more than she would say, and wondering idly what it was. But only idly, for she had been singularly incurious about her father. It had never occurred to her that it could possibly matter what her father had or had not been.

"I'm sure he was a sinner," she mused, "and Mother has never forgiven him. Sin—sin—the word that has hypnotized the world."

"My dear, what are you talking about?" Mrs. Brayton *turned lightly* to her.

"Treason, Granny. I don't believe in sin." Her eyes twinkled back.

"By what standard do you propose to live, then, out in the world?"

"I shall do what I want to do, and I won't do what I don't want to do."

"Hm! It sounds very convenient."

"That's quite safe, Granny, if you use your intelligence as well as your emotions."

The old lady laughed suddenly.

"I should call it a very dangerous doctrine, my dear."

"Well, that's all Uncle David believes."

"Indeed, are you quite sure?"

"Yes. But he is so nice that he never wants to do anything nasty."

"I see."

They sat still again.

"Oh, dear," began Asia, going back to the old theme, "I do wish Mother would let me go away in peace."

"Well, my child, she cannot help making this a personal matter. It's quite right for other people's daughters to want to go away, but when it's your own it hurts. There are times, unfortunately, when your intelligence and your emotions conflict. You may manage to escape that disagreeable situation."

"Oh, I don't expect to always," interrupted Asia, half laughing, "but I hope I shall always be able to make up my mind to face the inevitable cheerfully, and that's what Mother can never do."

"Have patience, child. She's learning. You young things are so intolerant."

"Intolerant!"

"Yes, almost as bad as we are."

They smiled together, and Asia drew nearer to the old lady, realizing that the evening was going, and that presently the good-byes she hated to think of would have to be said.

They talked jerkily at intervals, putting off any reference to the end. They were both conscious of the uncertainty of life, and that they might never meet again. As soon as the silence between them became strained, Asia turned.

"You'll go and see Mother soon, won't you?"

"Certainly, my dear."

Asia stood up, feeling a lump growing swiftly in her throat. Taking up the tongs, she poked viciously at the fire.

"Oh, dear! I am going to miss everybody horribly, and the place and everything."

"Yes," said the old lady gently. "I know you won't forget us."

Asia turned and looked down upon her.

"I can't tell you what you have been to me," she said nervously. "You have made me—you and Uncle David."

Mrs. Brayton's eyes were very bright.

"My dear, you know that in that hoary controversy I hold with heredity. David and I may have hurried you up a little—I see we have, but the final result will be almost as if we had never been."

"Oh, rot!" returned the wise child, stretching out her hands.

She drew the old lady up to her, and for some seconds she struggled for expression. Then she bent quickly with streaming eyes.

"Good-bye," she choked, kissing the lined forehead. "I will write." And moving away abruptly, she fled out by the French window, and along the garden path.

Mrs. Brayton stood still, a few unmanageable tears straggling down her cheeks. Then, afraid that her son might come in any minute and see them, she sat down and wiped them vigorously away. She readjusted her spectacles upon her nose and took up her book. But she saw no words upon the blurred pages. Her thoughts had not followed Asia. They zigzagged from a skeleton in her own cupboard to the picture of Alice sitting alone waiting for a feared to-morrow.

CHAPTER XVIII

THE next day, having purposely postponed her packing, Asia was busy till the last moment. Betty and Mabel went about the house all the morning with hushed voices and scared eyes. As this was the first domestic crisis into which they had entered it assumed the terrifying proportions of a world break-down. Bunty played outside, and the baby, Elsie, after being once severely slapped by Alice, retired to break her childish heart among the runner beans in a corner of the garden.

But there were no signs of emotional upheaval about Alice. There were dark rings of sleeplessness about her eyes, but she went about as usual, shirking none of the little things she did when she was well. And with her there moved an atmosphere that froze everybody who came near her.

Asia was to leave at one o'clock. She did not attempt to sit down to lunch. Instead, she choked over slices of bread and butter as she finished her packing. Alice and the children sat down to a sad meal, where the two girls sobbed at intervals, and held each other's hands under the table, and where Bunty was the only one who ate.

After lunch two men came to carry Asia's trunk down to the sailing boat where David Bruce stood waiting for her.

At last, with a flushed face, Asia came out of her room. Alice immediately left the kitchen and walked to the front of the house. Asia kissed Bunty and Elsie, telling them that if they were very good she would send them something nice. Betty and Mabel sobbed openly upon her shoulder, as she begged them to be kind and helpful.

"Take the children out and down to the boat," she whispered, as she turned out into the hall.

Alice stood by the door of her room.

"Good-bye, Mother." Asia looked straight at her, holding out her hand.

But Alice could not meet her eye and ignored the hand.

"Good-bye," she answered coldly.

They leaned towards each other, and with averted eyes their cheeks slid past each other. Each felt the other stiffen, hesitate, and harden again, and then Asia was gone out of the door, through the gate, and down the path.

Alice stood looking after her. She saw the children join her. She saw the blacksmith come out of the smithy, and Bob Hargraves out of the store. She saw men come from the tramway and the booms, and form a little circle about Asia as she stood on the beach. She saw them all shake her by the hand, and all the hats go off as some one pushed the stern of the boat away.

As Bruce hauled up the mainsail, Asia sat down by the rudder; then she turned homewards, and seeing the figure in the doorway, scrambled to her feet, and waved.

For the life of her Alice could not wave back. She tried to, but her frozen limbs refused to move. Her throat burned. Her eyes burned. She dimly saw the group on the beach wave with an energy that seemed purposeful to hide her own immobility. She saw the figure in the stern of the boat sit down.

As the sail, catching the wind, shot out of the little channel by the end of the spit into the river, Alice moved mechanically into her room, and to her western window.

She saw the boat head down stream, but she could not believe it would go on. She said to herself it must turn back. When it reached the first point she thought she saw it swing. Her hands clutched the side of the window, and her breath raced. But no, it went on. At the next headland she gasped again. It was turning now. But no, it went on. It reached the gap, and her heart stopped. She *saw it turn* in the channel. But no, it was only tacking.

It went on. It disappeared. Even then she waited, looking for it.

After eternal moments she grew dazed. The full truth had burst upon her at last and had stricken her soul. Asia had gone, not merely removed by distance, but gone out of her life and understanding, gone till she herself should bring her back, she who did not know how to bring her back. With an inarticulate cry she fell on her bed, and lay like a stone.

David Bruce did not look at Asia till they were well out into the channel. Then he sat down in the stern beside her, his right hand on the mainsail rope, and his left along the back of the seat behind her as she steered.

He said nothing, knowing she was beyond speech. Once or twice she looked back to see the children still waving from the cliffs, but not the figure at the window.

Presently he saw that tears were dripping off her cheeks.

"She might have waved," she choked, giving way suddenly.

He merely closed his hand upon her arm.

At the gap Asia looked back for the last time, seeing no one, but only the grey house with its black spots of windows, and the group of buildings clustered below, and the long streamers of smoke flying with the wind from the mill chimneys.

As everything was suddenly cut off by the cliffs at a turn in the river, Asia felt as if her old life was as suddenly cut off from the new. It was as if a wall had descended between them. And with the elasticity of youth her thoughts leapt to the future, and she told herself it was silly to suffer any more. But as she turned her face for the first time full upon David Bruce she remembered that she still had to say good-bye to him.

She had barely begun to mention it when he stopped her.

"For God's sake, child, have no tragic last moments with me. I am not going to retire to weep and pray, nor do I expect to die before you come back. For heaven's sake let's dilute the awful occasion with a little cheerfulness. I have to go back to your mother."

And Asia actually laughed, and saw that the sun was shining on a golden kowhai on the bank, and that the river was a shimmering thing of blue and silver beauty.

"That's better," said Bruce. "Your young life is not blighted, nor the world wrecked. And everything will go on just the same, and everybody will realize it in a week. Your mother will readjust herself, and will soon be revelling in your letters. She doesn't know it now, but she will."

"I know. All this has been so unnecessary, so stupid."

As there was nothing to be said, he said nothing.

"You will let me know at once if she is ever ill—seriously, I mean, won't you?"

"Certainly."

Silence fell between them, while Bruce watched for gusts from the gullies, and Asia listened to the swish of the spray against the boat. She had always passionately loved sailing, and she could not be unhappy long with the wind whistling past her ears and the spray tickling her cheeks. It was not till they came in sight of the Point Curtis wharf and the waiting steamer that she remembered what was happening to her.

There were things she had meant to say to David Bruce, things she had often imagined herself saying, but they were destined to remain unsaid. Bruce kept her busy for the last half-mile taking notes of things he wanted her to do for him in Auckland, and by the time the boat touched the landing steps the steamer was all ready to go, was, in fact, only waiting for her.

Two men ran forward for her trunk and bag, and before she realized it she was at the gangway with Bruce, and some one was yelling, "All aboard."

"Why, they are ready," she said vacantly.

"Yes." He smiled.

Putting her arms round his neck, she looked fervently

into his eyes, revealing something of what she had meant to put into words.

But he ignored it.

"Take care of yourself, little girl, and don't forget to come back," was all he said as he kissed her.

Blinded by tears and fighting for control, she hurried with her head lowered across the gangway, seeing no one. At the gunwale she stood looking back at him as the ropes were cast off and the steamer began to draw away. She knew that in the world to which she was going she would not look upon his like again.

But she was wise enough to know, even as she stood there, that she would get over her adolescent emotion for him, and keep unspoiled the hero-worship.

As Bruce looked after her, he hoped he would be there to greet her when she came back. He waved his hat, and was glad to see her smile in return. He stood till he could no longer distinguish her face upon the deck, and when he turned he found himself alone upon the wharf.

Fighting the shock of emptiness that the people left behind always have, he dismounted the slimy steps to the boat, hauled the sails, and started homewards with a heavy heart.

He knew that to him, also, the bay would never be quite the same again, and he understood why humanity all down the ages had feared and resented and hated change.

CHAPTER XIX

BEFORE Bruce reached the bay Alice had left for Mrs. Brayton's.

She did not go straight there, but stayed for over an hour in the dell, sitting on a little point above the mangroves. A tui sang in the gully behind her, shags occasionally flapped by on their way up stream, sparrows and fantails flew about her inquisitively. But she was dead to the sunlight and the call of the spring. She shed no tears. She scarcely moved.

When she finally reached the pines Mrs. Brayton was working on a bed for annuals. The old lady knew it was no occasion for flippancy, and even if it had been she could not have risen to it. For once she was at a loss as to how to proceed.

But Alice greeted her coolly, begged her to go on with her raking, and suggested that she should help her. The loveliness of the Spring day in that sheltered and seductive garden had an instant effect upon her.

So, avoiding carefully any reference to Asia's departure, they hoed and raked together, talking as they worked of plants, the last curate, the delay of the English mail, and of the topic that was then absorbing the attention of all English people in New Zealand—the declining health of Queen Victoria.

But even as they talked Alice felt that Mrs. Brayton must think her a fool, or worse. She knew the old lady could hardly avoid taking sides. She had been rather bitter during the last three days about the part she and Bruce had played in helping and perhaps encouraging Asia to go. The thought that her two best friends had helped to bring about the thing she had dreaded for years was not an easy one to dismiss, and only her urgent need of those friends helped her to forgive them. The thought that she herself was hopelessly in the wrong did not make it any easier for her to look either of them in the face. Less ashamed to meet Mrs. Brayton, she had come first to her, feeling blindly that until she was at peace with both of them she would be utterly alone in the world.

She hoped the old lady would not order tea. There was something about the sociability of that meal that made it impossible to bolster up reserves, and Alice hated to think that the moment would be fixed when she might have to begin the inevitable references to Asia's departure.

Fortunately, the new curate appeared, and he was welcomed with a warmth not always bestowed upon the usually well-timed visits of country curates at meal hours. He stayed to dinner, with no smallest notion of the situation into which he had precipitated himself. However, his ignorance was infinitely more helpful than his knowledge could have been.

He thought Mrs. Brayton charming, and Mrs. Roland an attractive-looking, but frigid and dull woman. As a non-member of his church, she was more or less removed from the social sphere he desired, even at Kaiwaka. He had not been in New Zealand long enough to realize that in that radical country church membership did not constitute an entrée to exclusiveness, and that in the remote districts of the northern bushes it was not regarded as important.

By the end of dinner even Mrs. Brayton's powers of endurance were approaching their limit. Ordering a fire in her own room—for the night had turned chilly—and leaving Harold to digest the curate as best he might, she drew Alice by the arm out of the library and along the hall.

"I must be going," began Alice weakly, realizing that once they were alone again she would have to unbend.

"You are not going," said Mrs. Brayton with determination, resolved now to manage the business herself.

They entered the old-fashioned room with the firelight

playing about the four-poster, on the much patterned wall paper, and on the deep chintz-covered chairs.

Alice felt like a child led out for a parental scolding. And like a child she sat down stonily, frozen again, and unable to help with the beginning.

Taking one of her hands, Mrs. Brayton sat down beside her on the low lounge. She began rather nervously, but as Alice gave no sign of hostility she continued with more assurance, till her voice deepened and broke as she went on with the personal confession.

"My dear, I know how you are feeling, and you can't help some of it. But, you know, we have no right to make the young unhappy. Asia has committed no crime save the crime of being able to get on without you. I know that hurts—it hurt me once. But we parents are all wrong. We think these children of ours are our property, that they must come when we say come, and go when we say go. We think we have a right to discourage them, to hamper them, to fill them with innumerable fears, just because they are young, and we think they don't know life. My dear, they know more about life than we have any idea of, and they hate our interference. They hate it. And if we persist in interfering they will hate us. They may not show it. They may tolerate us afterwards. They may keep up a brave show of affection. They may remember our birthdays and keep us out of draughts, and encourage our secret affection for sugar candy. But the great thing will be gone for ever. They will cease to speak to us of vital things, and they will talk to us only about flowers and the weather."

"My dear"—the old lady paused, her head lowered, her hands closing nervously on Alice's—"I had one daughter. I idolized her—never for years did I let her out of my sight. I swayed her, so I thought, body and soul, and I believed we were the greatest friends on earth. I did not think she could do a thing that would displease me, and I thought that was the right thing between mother and daughter. Then the man came—a man I did not think rich enough or good enough. I talked of my rights and my will, and my affection and my sacrifice, and my views, as if I had a monopoly over these things. She listened—she was very courteous, she never answered me back—and then she ran away with him. They had one year of happiness, except that she grieved because I never saw or wrote to them, and when the baby was born and she lay dying they sent for me. It was more than I deserved. I went. All she had time to say was, 'Oh, Mother,' and then she lay back dead. I have seen her as she lay there every hour of my life since——"

She stopped, for Alice had burst into a devastating passion of tears.

For nearly an hour Mrs. Brayton soothed her, saying little, and knowing that the tears were a relief.

Neither then nor ever afterwards did Alice make any reference to the story she had just heard, but it altered her whole attitude of mind towards Mrs. Brayton, and drew her to her as nothing else could have done, and killed her pride and her foolish aloofness.

"I do not know what is the matter with me," she choked, struggling for composure. "Feeling makes me blind. It does something to me—I don't know what. I have been cruel to her and it is all my fault. And to-day I couldn't wave to her. I couldn't—I wanted to, but I couldn't——"

"What!" Mrs. Brayton sat up. "You didn't say goodbye to her!"

"Oh, yes, in a way—at the house; but at the boat she waved, and I could not. And I wish I had." Her tears flowed afresh.

"Then you can send a telegram and say so." Mrs. Brayton realized the pathos of this little incident. "I'll write it out, and the curate can take it to the post office to-night, so that it will go first thing in the morning. Will you do that?"

"Yes," sobbed Alice.

The old lady filled in a telegraph form and wrote: "I am sorry I did not wave—Mother."

"There," she said, showing it.

"Yes, please send it."

When she returned from giving it to the curate she found Alice had recovered some composure. She sat down beside her again, and patted her hands.

"You will get along, my dear," she said gently. "We all do. We all get along somehow. And it is very foolish of us to think we cannot."

"Oh, I know; I am not going to die. But, oh, God, how I will miss her, and there is another child coming." Her voice ended harshly.

It was some seconds before Mrs. Brayton could trust herself to speak.

"I am sorry to hear that," she said gravely. "She didn't know."

Mrs. Brayton felt this was a case where something ought to be done, though what, she could not have put into words. Then her thoughts turned to helping Alice to face it.

"She might not have gone if she had known, but sooner or later, my dear, she had to go. Now you can get on without her. Make up your mind to it. The matter with you is that you don't adjust your mind beforehand to possible readjustments in your life. Everything is always a shock to you."

"I don't know how to help it."

"Oh, yes, you do. You know everything changes. Realize that it will. You knew perfectly well your child would grow up and go away from you, but you refused to face it. You said, 'She will not go,' instead of saying, 'She will.' You did not want her to go, and you tried to think she would live by your wants. I know why she means so much to you, but you don't own her. She is only yours if you understand her. You must love her less and understand her more. My dear, do you know a line of Oscar Wilde's—'For each *man kills* the thing he loves?' You don't. Well, take it home with you, and think about it. It's one of the most telling lines in the language."

Alice leaned back, repeating the words to herself. It hurt the old lady to see the lines on her face and the pallor of her cheeks and the twitching about her eyes.

"Cheer up, my dear. There's plenty to live for even yet."

"I will try," said Alice feebly, with the faint-hearted resolution of a person attempting what she knows to be an impossible task.

But before they went to bed Mrs. Brayton had succeeded in comforting her beyond her hopes.

As she walked home in the fresh morning air, and looked down upon the sun-specked river dancing its way to the sea, the natural vitality in Alice reasserted itself, and she realized once more that she could begin again, and that she would not make the same tragic blunder in the future.

She had not been home ten minutes before Bruce appeared to know if there was anything he could do. When he had gone she told herself that she was in danger of taking what life had left her too much for granted.

At midday he brought her a telegram.

"It isn't bad news," he said at once. "I've had one."

As Alice read it the tears sprang to her eyes. It was very short, and said simply: "Cheer up I am still your child."

She told him of the telegram she had sent.

"I'm glad you did, for it was a pity you did not wave. It hurt."

"Oh, David." Her lips trembled.

He put his arm round her a minute, saying no more.

Asia wrote every week. In the third letter was the news that she was off on a six months' tour of New Zealand as pianist to a concert company at the fabulous salary of six pounds a week. To Alice this meant going on the stage. It took her some weeks, with the assistance of Bruce and Mrs. Brayton, to adjust her mind to that, but they managed to keep her from writing, even cautiously, what she thought of the experiment.

At the end of the first month she was amazed to receive a present of four pounds from Asia. And possibly the regular receipt of that amount every month helped her to modify her views of concert companies.

At the end of six months Asia was prevented from accepting a second engagement by a telegram from Bruce:

"Your mother very ill baby a week ago born dead she forbade us tell you serious relapse your return work wonders."

Later in the day he received her reply. He broke gently to Alice the news that she was on the way home. She immediately showed signs of improvement, and four days later she was well enough to be propped up in bed to watch for the first sign of the sailing boat beyond the gap.

It was cold and wintry, and the river was a dull and angry grey, cut to intermittent foam by an irritable wind, but it seemed to Alice the friendliest river she had ever seen. She was not strong enough to sit up all the time. So Betty stood by the window to watch too.

"I do hope the steamer isn't late," said Alice, dropping down after half a dozen disappointments.

"Now, Mother, don't," pleaded Betty. "You must not get excited." Her eye caught something beyond the gap.

"Oh, is that it?" cried Alice.

"Mother, don't jump up like that. I'm not sure, but it looks like the boat." She picked up a small field-glass. "Yes, I think it is the boat—yes, I'm sure it is. Now lie still, Mother, for a while."

"Could she see if we waved?" asked Alice eagerly.

"No, Mother, not yet."

"I must see," said Alice perversely. She lay with her head to the foot of the bed. They had turned her round so that she could look out. Betty raised her till she could see the grey sail on the dull water. Then she sank back again, her long plaits of hair falling about her shoulders, her face flushed, her eyes brilliant.

"You must wave," she said imperatively, "something she can see. I am sure she could see a sheet. Hang it from the window."

"Oh, all right, Mother. But I'm sure she can't see it yet."

"Do as I tell you," said Alice, with sudden fierceness.

"What's this?" said Mrs. King, coming in. "You must keep calm, dearie."

"Mother wants a sheet waved from the window, and there is such a wind," said Betty.

"I don't mind the wind. It won't hurt me."

"All right, dearie." Mrs. King sensed the situation. "But you must lie down and be covered up."

"Very well," replied Alice meekly.

Mrs. King and Betty opened the window and held out a sheet that flapped furiously.

"This is silly," protested Betty. "I'm sure she can't see, and the children can wave from the cliffs; that would be better."

"Now, now," soothed Mrs. King. "Look, what's that? Isn't that something waving from the boat? That's not the sail. Don't you move," sternly to the bed.

"Is it really?" begged Alice from her mound of blankets.

"Yes, she sees. She's waving. Now just you keep calm."

Feeble tears of happiness ran down Alice's cheeks.

"Tell me where they are," she said.

They announced the progress of the boat bit by bit as it came scudding on, with the sails full reefed and the foam flying away in two wings behind it. It was just such a day as Asia loved best to sail upon the river. When it reached the mill, three low whistles rang out across the water.

"That's for her," cried Betty excitedly. "A salute. Uncle David said the engineer was going to."

Alice flushed again with pride.

"Wave from the front window now," she commanded.

"They're in the channel, Mother," went on Betty. "I can see her. She is standing up and looking this way. And she has on a dark dress, and a white thing round her neck—I wonder if it's fur. Oh, my! she's waving. Oh, Mother, I must go. Mabel and Bunty and Elsie are off down the hill——"

"Go on, then," said Alice.

"Sh! quietly," frowned Mrs. King, as she bounded forward.

"You needn't hold the sheet any more," said Alice hoarsely. "Tell me when she's coming. I hope they won't keep her."

"They're just by the spit now. Mr. Bruce is pulling down the sails. She's moving to the bow, now she's jumped out, and she's running. The children have got to her—she isn't stopping, bless her! They're all after her. Now she's got to the store; she's waving at somebody—it's Mr. Hargraves and Mr. Roland. She isn't stopping. Now, dearie, be calm, she will be here in a minute, and you must be quiet, or she can't stay with you."

"I will be quiet," said Alice peacefully. "Nothing matters now."

They heard the wild shrieks of the children following her, and then running steps and the click of the gate.

"Mother," called a ringing voice from the front step.

And then Mrs. King went out to take the children rotind to the back.

Alice saw nothing but a brilliant face that grew into the room till, leaning down to her own, it filled all space.

Mrs. King persuaded the children to go down to Bruce to help to carry up Asia's things. There were two trunks, and a travelling-bag, and a roll of umbrellas, and a rug. The girls gazed awed at this magnificence.

"Three umbrellas!" gasped Mabel.

"Do you suppose she brought anything for us?" questioned Betty.

The mere idea drove them all wild.

But Bruce told them they would have to wait. At the end of an hour, he said, Asia would have to leave her mother, and then it would be their turn. As they followed him up the hill, they all fought about carrying her umbrellas and the rug. When everything had been set down in the back porch they sat down fascinated upon it, lest by chance any of it should be spirited away.

"I hope she brought me a railway train," said Bunty. "I told her I wanted one."

"Greedy pig! That was just like you," retorted Elsie, who was secretly aggrieved that she had not possessed his forethought.

While they waited with burning impatience, Mrs. Bob Hargraves arrived with her babies. She was a fresh and charming young mother, who had won her way rapidly into the home life of the boss's house. Glad of a diversion, Betty and Mabel turned excitedly to her and her children.

Soon afterwards they heard a rustle of silks.

"Oh, here's Granny," said Mabel, and everybody made way for Mrs. Brayton, who was dressed almost as she had been when she first walked down the green hill to the house on the cliffs. Of all her ancient gowns the now much-darned green and gold was Asia's favourite.

"Get a chair, Bunty," commanded Betty.

"I couldn't wait, my dears," said the old lady, as she sat down. "I was watching for the boat, and I knew she couldn't stay very long with your mother."

A few minutes later the waiting party was joined by Tom Roland and David Bruce.

"Oh, Uncle David, isn't it an hour yet?" cried Mabel.

"Just about," he smiled, as he moved on into the hall.

Mrs. King then joined them, and after a few more minutes of waiting Bruce returned.

"She's coming," he said.

With her swift light step, and an exciting little jangle of keys, Asia swung down the hall, pausing for a moment to put her coat and hat, her white fur, and her small handbag into her own room, which like the rest of the house, had been gaily decked with flowers. Her face was flushed, and there were traces of tears in her eyes as she stepped into the porch.

Mrs. Brayton was the first person she saw. A thrill fired every one, even Roland, to stand up, as she bent over and kissed the trembling old lady. Then she turned more lightly to Mrs. Hargraves.

"Did you bring me a railway train?" exploded Bunty.

"Yes, I did." And Asia joined in the general laughter.

That unpacking was a wonderful adventure. Things that had already become necessities to Asia were still luxuries at the bay, so that to Betty and Mabel almost everything that came out of those trunks was like an item from *The Arabian Nights.*

But the best thing about it all was that Asia had forgotten nobody. She seemed to have divined correctly what each person would have chosen for himself. Bunty was soon hugging his railway train, Elsie, a fully dressed sleeping doll, while Betty and Mabel gushed over fine silks for new dresses.

With a surprised grunt Roland accepted a pocket-book, and Bruce and Mrs. Brayton smiled over new books and music. Asia's generosity had not stopped with the family, for there were gifts for Mrs. Hargraves and her children, and for every other child about the bay. And she had remembered all whose pronounced tastes had ever impressed her own groping progress towards finding out what she wanted. For a mystic working on the tramway she had brought a book on theosophy, and, for the carpenter, the latest word on socialism.

So it was no wonder that for weeks the whole bay revolved about her return, her clothes, and her new ideas. With the latter she had come back stocked with the latest novelties in everything from wall-papers to cremation. Before she had been home a fortnight everybody knew that she had got the boss to promise that the sitting-room should be entirely refurnished according to her own instructions, that the stove should be moved from the kitchen to the scullery, that the kitchen should be transformed into a dining-room, and that the house should have a veranda built round three sides.

But with all this everybody agreed that greatness had not spoiled her. She walked in by the back doors as she had always done, and not even the most critical could find a trace of anything that might be called an "air."

Alice, growing stronger from the moment she arrived, did not worry now about the prospects of more adjustments. The things she cared about were that Asia brought in all her meals, that Asia was the first person to kiss her in the morning, and the last to tuck h[illegible] in at night, that Asia noticed more quickly than any one else, excepting Bruce, if the light was in her eyes, that Asia kept the house quiet, and put fresh flowers in her room every day. All these things she saw even before she had got over admiring the velvet cloak with fur collar and cuffs that had been the gift chosen for her. And it really seemed more important to her that Asia should not shake the bed than that she should have a tailored suit and six evening dresses, even though the latter did rather take her breath away.

When by degrees she began to notice changes of manner and suggestions of worldliness, she told herself it was nothing to worry about; that the main thing was that in the fundamentals, her fundamentals, the world, as far as she could see, had not spoiled her child.

CHAPTER XX

"WE must be about there, Ross," said Barrie Lynne. Both men looked out of the Kaipara train upon a narrow tidal creek that wound a serpentine course about a great waste of mangrove flats. Beyond them a line of shining sandhills suggested beaches and the open sea. From the Kaipara harbour, as yet out of sight, came a pungent salty smell, pleasantly mingling with the freshness of the spring morning.

With spasmodic jerks that rattled the teeth in the jaws, the train slowed down to the Helensville station, where the long-suffering passengers, with an air of extreme thankfulness, gathered up their parcels and scrambled out.

The people who passed through Helensville belonged, with but few exceptions, to the desperate, the disappointed, the sanguine, and the disillusioned. The desperate headed for the northern gum-fields as a last resource; the disappointed were teachers, or members of the Civil Service ordered to such minor positions as third-grade post offices or inspectorships; the sanguine were farmers or fruit growers, confident that the soil only needed their special attention to yield up its share of riches; and the disillusioned were those who had passed that way before.

Nobody ever stayed in Helensville except the people who failed to make connections between the steamers and the trains. They constituted a floating population upon which three hotels and two boarding-houses flourished. Nobody ever lived in Helensville except the people who had failed to make a living anywhere else. Everybody who went through it was told the old gag that its name should have ended with the first syllable, but there was no evidence that in that event it would have rivalled its famous namesake for interesting company. It might have done better with regard to climate and to smells.

Allen Ross sniffed on the station platform.

"Let's see how soon we can get out of this," he said.

A chain or two away one of two small steamers, lying against a wharf that was merely an extension of the station grounds, now emitted columns of smoke and whistled ostentatiously.

The two men followed the passengers from the train, who all hurried towards it. On the way Ross singled out a tall, grey-haired man.

"Pardon, can you tell me where these steamers go?" he asked.

Taking his pipe from his mouth, Bruce looked curiously into the stranger's face and at that of his companion.

"Certainly," he replied; "one to the Wairoa, and one to the Otamatea."

"Which goes first?"

Bruce smiled, realizing some element of chance. But he had no presentiment of how much.

"The Otamatea boat, as soon as she can get away. That's in about a quarter of an hour."

"Thanks. Any settlements up there?"

"Yes."

"Could we camp, and get boating and fishing?"

"Yes, anywhere."

"That sounds as if it might suit." With an interested nod he turned to Lynne, and Bruce walked on.

"Shall we settle it that way, Barrie?"

"By all means."

They hurried back to the station to make the necessary arrangements about their luggage, and when the *Ethel*, delayed on their account, finally got away, the two men, with all their belongings, were on board.

The passengers, with the sense of selection peculiar to travellers by boat, soon arranged themselves according to *their* social and commercial grades. A government inspector, to whom all northern doors were open, began to talk to a landowner and his two daughters, who, to the envy of their own section, had just made their annual shopping tour to Auckland. Near them the commercial traveller, without whom no boat or train ever got anywhere in New Zealand, listened to their gushing with mingled feelings of boredom and amusement.

Five saddened teachers, who had vainly hoped for moves back to civilization, talked heatedly of the unfairness of the recent examinations, and confirmed each other's idea that the Board of Education needed to be tidied up.

Seated on a coil of rope, dressed in cheap new ready-made clothes and soft hats—the hall-mark of the comparatively prosperous searcher after work—sat two men, who had already, with native cunning, picked out Bruce and the landowner as possible employers of casual labour.

Down on the lower deck, by the toy hatchway, sat two seasoned gum-diggers, maudlin and nervous after a giddy week in Auckland, and near them, as if conscious of kinship, sat a curved and shrunken figure, with a brand new gum outfit beside him, who was heading for the gum-fields as a last resource. Those who knew the ropes gave him the benefit of a second glance, for, though drink and general misery had drained the individuality out of him, he might, as far as their previous experience went, have been anything from a bootblack to a university professor or the son of an earl. It was his horrible cough, rather than the pitifulness of his latest profession, that first attracted Bruce.

A pioneer family, munching blackballs and bananas, was huddled together, also on the lower deck. To the shy and awkward children the voyage was an adventure beyond their grasp. To their sanguine parents it was part of the hopefulness of the new beginning, and had in it, for that reason, as much of a pleasant thrill as they would ever know.

Completing the familiar elements of the human cargo, a many-coloured Maori group laughed and chattered in the bow with their native philosophic indifference to the turns of fortune that is the despair of the envious white man.

Allen Ross and Barrie Lynne both felt, as they leaned against the gunwale, the eyes of most of the *Ethel* world upon them, that they were the unknown quantity. A splendid isolation was forced upon them, for, apart from Bruce, there was no person of their quality aboard. As a matter of fact, their presence seemed so unusual as almost to demand an explanation.

Bruce himself had not been able to resist another scrutiny of them as he took a privileged stand beside the captain at the wheel. He wondered idly what had turned them northwards. It was not the shooting season, and there were no trout streams worth while north of Auckland, he reflected, but as the dark man looked cruelly used up he guessed that a desire merely for rest and an outdoor life explained their trip in that direction.

The little boat was now well under way, twisting and turning with the creek. Allen Ross looked over the mangrove flats at the western sandhills with the exhausted, but thankful air of one who knows he has finally outrun an enemy. His head, always carried high, was covered with thick black hair that slightly waved. His keen face, which was curiously eager for a man who even at thirty knew most of the crooked ways of men, was long and thin and lined. It was unusually tanned for a city dweller, as his whole bearing obviously proclaimed him to be. It was not easy to tell at first wherein his compelling attraction lay. But, tired though he was, his singular vitality travelled like an electric current round that little boat. Before they reached the open harbour every woman and many of the men could have given the details of his physiognomy and dress.

His friend Barrie Lynne was built on weaker lines. He was just as tall, and just as straight, and just as easy. He was more conventionally handsome. But when the two men were together the eyes of most people passed over him to Ross and stayed there. It was true that a larger number of women had passed their hands through Lynne's soft brown hair, but that was a matter of their opportunity rather than their desire. Lynne made a habit of succumbing to temptation. Ross made a luxury of it. Lynne could never ignore a hint. Many an eye had vainly flashed at Ross. Almost any attractive woman who signified her willingness was good enough to climb with Lynne to the Venus Mount. But Ross required special qualifications in the woman who should listen with him to the birds twittering in the dawn. To Lynne a feeling for the dawn was not important. To Ross it was.

This was not obvious to the unsophisticated passengers on the little boat. All they saw was two handsome men who, they instinctively knew, had got the better of the world, and to those more or less helpless people who see in the world only a series of enemy powers to fight, instead of a series of friendly powers to use, there is nothing more wonderful than the besting of them.

Lynne was interested in watching the passengers in return. He got the tragedies and comedies of the collection without much speculation. Ross was not so interested. He knew that there were few people on that boat who from his point of view had ever done anything worth while. And so for him the passengers, with one exception, did not exist.

The exception was David Bruce. When at dinner-time he appeared at the saloon table with the derelict, who had hitherto sat ignored and apart, Ross found his eyes wandering again and again back to that story-telling face.

"That man is stunning, Lynne," he said. "Look at the way he's handling that wreck. He has the manner of a doctor."

And many times during the rest of the voyage Bruce found the dark eyes of the tired stranger fixed upon his face.

When they came up from dinner they found the whole expanse of the Kaipara harbour spread out before them. As they neared the heads they saw billowing up into the sky the lines of the "comber, wind hounded," that heaved and thundered and broke upon the dangerous bar. The *Ethel* began her dreaded somersaults, and though the agony was brief it temporarily changed for many their views of life.

After skirting the mouth of the Wairoa, the *Ethel* turned into the wide mouth of the Otamatea. They passed several fish-canning factories, and an old missionary station, with its rows of poplars along the beach, a clump or two of pines, and the wooden fences buried between rows of huge geranium bushes running wild. Deserted many years previously, it wore an old-world air of unpruned maturity and uninterrupted peace.

At intervals along the banks, from small Maori settlements clustering by little sandy beaches, there came calls that were vigorously answered by the natives aboard. Three times the *Ethel* stopped at toy wharves from which roads led off into the wilds. After unloading cases and barrels whether there was any one to meet them or not, she snorted off as if she despised these menial tasks. Now and then some one pointed out a collection of buildings with its familiar pine clumps as the home of some big sheep man or orchard grower.

About four o'clock Lynne called attention to a small sailing-boat that came zigzagging down the river. Both men saw that Bruce was interested in it, and that he left his conversation with the captain to watch it, as, with reckless daring, it tacked across the steamer's bows, cut through the water on the left, and came round on the wind at her stern with a flourish, and so alongside.

"It's a girl!" exclaimed Lynne, in amazement.

Then the figure at the stern stood up, one hand on the tiller, and the other gripping the mainsail rope.

Asia was not unaware of the fact that she was the episode of the voyage. But she was so accustomed to striding her little world like a colossus that she knew it merely as a detached matter of fact, and not as a matter for self-congratulation.

"Hullo, Uncle David," she called, "where's Mother?"

"She is going to stay another fortnight."

They went on talking for a minute or two, while all the passengers flocked to the side to admire the way she handled her little boat. Many who knew her kept their eyes glued upon her, anticipating the coveted smile of recognition. The landowner's daughters were sure that if she would only look at them she would approve their new clothes and hats, and they felt a smile from her would now add to their standing for the rest of the trip. But Asia did not see them.

She was wearing a blue serge dress, short skirted and open at the throat. A fascinating sky-blue woolly cap perched jauntily upon her tangled golden hair. The breeze flapped her skirt about her bare legs. Her clear skin, painted by the swish of the wind, told of the simple life, strong nerves and beauty sleep, and in her eyes there glowed the joyous spirit of the wood nymph and the water sprite.

Neither Ross nor Lynne attempted to disguise his interest.

"I say, she's stunning," whispered the latter.

"Why not?" smiled Ross.

"Well, here," and Lynne included the whole landscape in a glance.

"Why not, if he is?" with a nod at Bruce. "She called him 'Uncle.'"

"She looks like city to me."

"Well, she sails that boat like one who belongs to the river."

"That's true. I wonder who they are." Lynne looked from her to Bruce again.

Ross followed his glance, and he was still looking at Bruce when Asia first caught sight of him. So he did not see the sudden blaze that leapt to her eyes, nor the swift stiffening of her loosely poised body. As it happened, only Bruce noticed.

After a short amazed stare at the two strangers Asia avoided looking squarely at them again, and soon, with a parting nod at the captain, and without a glance at the many who were waiting to be recognized, she close-hauled the sail, and shot away.

All the way up the river she sat still, once or twice forgetting to manage thè wind and narrowly missing an accident. In her eyes there now gleamed the vision of new adventures, a premonition of great things to come.

As she shot away from the *Ethel,* Ross and Lynne smiled at each other. Both wondered where, when, and how they would meet the presiding goddess of the place again.

Round the next bend there came into view the Point Curtis wharf, with its goods shed and trucks, its two-storied hotel and store.

When Lynne saw the little sailing-boat run in and tie up to the wharf, he walked over to the captain.

"What place is this, captain?" he asked.

"Point Curtis, Mister."

"Is there any more of it than that?" Lynne pointed to the hotel.

"There are farms, and the gum-fields, and then there's the bay."

"The bay?"

"Timber settlement up the river. Owned by Mr. Roland."

Lynne had heard Asia's name whispered several times among the passengers.

"How far is that?" he asked.

"Matter of three miles or so up the river," jerking his head to the right.

"Could we put up tents there, do you think?"

"Oh, yes, anywhere about."

"Thanks."

Lynne walked back to Ross under fire of a volley from many a wildly interested eye.

"Let's get off here, Ross. Captain says we can camp—what the devil are you grinning at?"

"We land here then," smiled back his friend.

As the *Ethel* drew near the wharf, an amazing number of human beings rose mushroomlike in the doorways of the buildings, and from boxes, sacks, and trucks upon the wharf itself, and all, as if worked by the same spring, moved for the same spot with the same object in view—that of being next the gangway when it was run ashore. If it had been possible to tell with precision exactly where the gangway would be run out, an ambitious few would have been found outlining that place to quiz the strangers from an unobstructed point of view, and to claim greetings from neighbours and acquaintances. There was in that little crowd one maiden lady of uncertain age and uncertain everything else, whose chief claim to local fame lay in the fact that ever since the *Ethel* began to make her regular trips she had been of those who had pressed the gangway railing to their bosoms, and who could have touched every passenger as he came ashore. She was there now, feverishly watching to see where the casting ropes would land, and who would pick them up, and where they would be tied.

Near waiting traps and sledges, thin patient horses stood tethered to stumps, where they had for hours hung their heads in mute unfed dejection. Sporting dogs of mongrel breeds fought and gambolled, and came near to causing accidents upon the narrow wharf. A number of children wheeled an empty truck along the primitive railroad, their harsh screams of excitement drawing upon them the wrath of their elders.

The women in the little group looked as if they had been stretched out and dried on crosses in the sun, and then dropped suddenly and left to curl up and contract. Their skins were like wizened russet apples at the end of a winter storing. Most of the men had grown permanently tired and warped fighting unexpected eccentricities in the seasons, unexpected diseases in the crops, and unexpected cussedness in the soil.

Both Ross and Lynne looked curiously at this unfamiliar crowd, seeking the face of the girl from the boat; and they finally saw her near the back, at the head of the steps. She met their eyes once with a look that neither of them could call even mildly interested, and then she waved her hand to Bruce.

As he had no luggage save a small handbag, Bruce was one of the first to step ashore. The men noticed that everybody seemed to know him, and that his hat was permanently raised as he made his way through the group to the steps.

Ross and Lynne stood still till all the passengers were embarked, watching the sailing-boat leave and continue its way up the Otamatea, then, having made arrangements for their things to be taken to the hotel, they got off leisurely, and with the eyes of most of the women about upon them they walked up the clay path to the hotel to engage rooms.

CHAPTER XXI

THE next morning the two men found their way up the road towards the bay, looking for a cottage they had been told might be to let. The hotel proprietor had advised them to have a house as well as their tents, and the lurid picture he gave them of the uncertainty of the weather in those parts had impressed them with the common sense of the suggestion.

At various places on the way they paused to look down through leafy gaps upon the river, which a fast-rising, angry wind was churning into clumps of froth. Every now and then a furious gust bore down branches in their faces, and sent showers of twigs scattering in all directions. There was an intoxication in the keen air that got them both by the throat.

Unexpectedly they came upon a well-trod path leading towards the river. They followed it a little way to find another branching from it, and after they had stood a moment speculating they followed this new one. It led into a small clearing, in the centre of which they saw what they rightly took to be the cottage they were searching. They picked their way over the logs, stumps and brushwood. There was a nice air of crudity about the small dwelling, bare and unpainted, and shut off from the world by its circular wall of bush. Ross liked it the minute he looked at it.

They walked round it, and looking through the windows, saw that it had three small rooms and an open fireplace. It was surrounded with its own wood supply in profusion, and for water there was a new zinc tank fed from spouting that ran round the corrugated iron roof.

"If this is it, I say we take it," said Ross.

"So do I."

"You ought to be able to write here, and it would suit me fine for study. I wonder how near we are to the mill."

"What's that?"

In a lull of the wind they heard a weird sound, new to them. It was the mournful shriek of one of the circular saws.

"Sounds like machinery," said Ross.

They retraced their steps to the well-trodden path. They had gone but a little way down it in the direction of the river when they felt rather than heard that some one was behind them. Swinging round, they came face to face with Asia, who was amused at their swiftly banished astonishment.

This time she did not hesitate to smile frankly into their eyes.

"Isn't it a wind?" she cried gaily. "We are going to have a storm. But our welcome to strangers is not always so ungracious."

Both men felt the fire of a new exhilaration course through their veins as they looked at her. She looked like the Greek spirit reincarnate. Her blue eyes laughed at them out of the freest body they had ever seen.

She was plainly dressed in a well-worn navy serge suit, a comfortable thing that had modified itself to her swinging limbs and swift motions. The pale-blue cap of the day before nestled into her hair as if it lived there. It had an impertinent air all its own. On her feet were tan boots stained with mud and dust. Her arms swung loosely and her hands were gloveless.

As her eyes passed over Lynne to Ross the expression in them changed.

"I've seen you often," she said to him, without waiting for either of them to answer her remark.

"Me?" For a moment Ross strained his memory in vain.

"Yes, in Sydney."

"Ah." And both men felt that much was explained.

"You know Sydney?" asked Lynne delightedly.

"Yes, a little. I was there two years. I came back eight months ago." She turned again to Ross. "I saw you first in the Domain. You were speaking to a howling jingoistic mob who yelled 'Pro-Boer' at you. But you kept on, and the police rescued you. I heard you speak for the labour movement many times. I know people who know you—the Gilbert Morgans. You were invited to meet me one evening, but you went to some meeting instead, and I don't think you ever sent a decent apology."

He did not attempt to apologize now as his eyes smiled gleefully back at hers, but after a minute he sobered, wondering uncomfortably how much she knew about him.

"The world continues to be small," said Lynne flippantly.

"Who are you?" she asked abruptly.

"Oh, my friend, Barrie Lynne," introduced Ross.

"The Barrie Lynne who writes?"

"The same," he bowed.

"Oh, then, I've read some of your stuff."

"I'm flattered."

"You needn't be. I came across it quite by accident."

He laughed into her mischievous eyes.

"May I hope that upon mature reflection you regard the accident as a happy one."

"Oh, yes."

Her tone was more casual than he liked, but he met it gaily.

"I'm sure you are a very discerning critic," he said gallantly.

"You're like that, are you?" she retorted. "Well, I may as well tell you I'm one of those awful people whom flattery does not flatter, nor deception deceive."

"Dear me," said Ross gravely. "What right have you to take the joy out of life that way?"

She flashed a delighted look at him.

"Don't you ever lie?" asked Lynne, aghast.

"Oh, of course. That's another thing."

She rose on her toes and caught a branch that was about to swish into their faces.

"What are you doing here?" she went on. "Are you looking for the mill?"

"Yes," answered Ross. "We want to find out who owns the cottage in there. We'd like to take it for the summer."

"Oh!"

She looked up into the trees, catching at another swaying branch.

"I can tell you that. It belongs to a Mr. King, a farmer who lives at Kaiwaka, about three miles along this main road." She waved in the direction. "I guess you will be able to get it. He built it for his daughter, who was to have married one of our men. But he was drowned six weeks ago."

"That so? Well, we will go after it at once, then."

The conversation came to an abrupt stop.

Asia plunged at swaying branches, not, as Lynne thought, because it showed off her supple figure to perfection, but because the joy of life in her had to express itself in motion of some sort. But after a minute or two she became aware that both men were looking to her for the initiative.

"Would you like to see the mill?" she asked Ross.

"We would very much."

"Come on, then."

As the path was not wide enough for three, Asia stepped out beside Ross, leaving Lynne to follow in a bad humour behind. Already the choice seemed significant. But he determined not to be put aside.

"I suppose we must explain ourselves, Ross," he began.

But Asia shot an arresting glance back at him.

"You needn't," she said curtly. "Nobody ever does here. We have 'Dukes' sons, cooks' sons, and sons of belted earls' scattered about the landscape, but none of them ever explained. Explanations stop behind at Auckland, though I believe they are going out of fashion there now. We don't care why you are here. This is the land of the lost, one of those happy spots where no questions are asked. Of course," she added mischievously, "the fact of a person's being here is usually all the explanation necessary."

Both men smiled.

"Oh, well," drawled Lynne, "if you are not a bit interested——"

"Well, if it interests you to tell me, of course, as a matter of courtesy——" she drawled back.

Ross could not resist laughing at his friend's bungling, and at his foolishness at being hurt by her indifference. Why the devil should she be craving to know why they were there? It was only too obvious they were not the first men she had seen.

But Asia had not meant to snub Barrie Lynne. So she turned to him sweetly.

"You are 'copy' hunting, of course," she said, "and you will find this place a storehouse of good yarns. I can put you on to several."

"Thanks, that will be fine," he answered gratefully.

They walked on some yards in silence. Asia was really curious to know why Ross was there, but she did not dream of asking. He rather hoped she was curious, but as he was not in the habit of explaining himself it did not occur to him to do so now. As they walked he threw his head back, sniffing the wind.

When they broke from the bush, to find themselves on a small rocky point about which the waves were lashing, Allen Ross stopped abruptly, and looked across the river at the desolate waste lands on the left bank below the turn.

"Good," he smiled, "I wanted to get away from the world, the flesh, and the devil——"

"Are you sure you have?" she interrupted him, with a wicked little smile.

His bright eyes met the challenge in hers with swift responsiveness, but he parried the stroke.

"I don't despair at the first sign of disappointment," he shot back.

Then she laughed merrily into the angry wind.

Swinging round, they saw ahead of them the ranges of waste timber and sawdust that spoiled the beauty of the banks for acres on the western side of the mill yards. Asia led the way along a maze of tramway lines into a narrow canyon walled up on either side by stacks of flitches and boards of regulation widths. When they reached the end of the first wharf, which was the scene of a tremendous bustle of men, trucks, clanking chains, and donkey engines, Tom Roland caught sight of them, and came briskly forward. He greeted the two men with his childish delight in a new audience, and when Asia had introduced them he proudly led the way into the mill.

"Single file," he advised, "and be careful."

They went past the goose and circular saws and the moving platform of the breakdowns to the skids, where the winch had just got to work upon a log that lay down in the booms.

To both men everything was new and absorbing. The great framework of the double mill, its solid log foundations, the huge beams that held up its iron sides, the big spaces overhead, the accumulated roar of machinery, the blurr of the circular saws whizzing at terrific speed, the monotonous singing of the complicated loops of belts, the tremendous thrill in the air—all these things got their imagination.

They looked curiously at the huge blackboards suspended from the cross beams, covered with figured hieroglyphics, intelligible only to the initiated, and at the men and boys who swung iron grips and levers in and out of the very jaws of death.

They watched the progress of a log from the booms up the skids to the side of the breakdown platform, where, with astonishing ease, it was jerked into position on the sliding floor. Halved and quartered, it was then levered with resounding thuds on to greased rollers and rushed towards the big circulars, which turned it into flitches. Then the small circulars, the drag, and the goose completed its metamorphosis into the regulation strips that were run on to various trucks and wheeled off, each kind to its appointed pile.

Roland then led the way to his engine room, where the two finest machines in the colony, as he was never tired of telling, lay carefully packed in brick, tended by a corps of perspiring stokers. The chief engineer came forward to be introduced, and to corroborate everything the boss said about the superlative qualities of his boilers, his driving capacity, and the excellence of all the appointments. After he had said all he usually said to impress visitors, the boss led the way again out into the timber yard, to a landing stage in the channel. There he showed the tramway, the booms, the position of the bush, and rapidly sketched the main details of the work.

The Australians enjoyed his enthusiasm. They realized a good deal of the difficulties he had overcome, and were amused at but not bored by his vanity. They noticed that Asia, who must have heard the tale many times before, heard it sympathetically, and inserted flattering details of her own occasionally.

The bay was now a township. It had its own post office, its little public school, its town hall, its football field. The store had grown till it was now a warehouse, ready to supply everything needed by the country-side for miles around. Bob Hargraves, risen to be its manager, was as proud of it as the engineer was of the engines.

Roland had reason to be proud of his success. The bay was now the biggest thing of its kind in the whole kauri milling industry. It had become a show place. The governors, when up that way shooting, always came along to see the big trees and the splendid dams back in the bush. Tourists from everywhere had visited it. The Government photographer had been sent to take numerous views of it, views that went into all the tourist publications, and hung enlarged in government offices all over the dominion. The boss could not help showing his pride in it. And he had a pleasant feeling that the world was a better place because he had made one corner of it.

When he had finished all he had to say, he asked the Australians what they were doing there. When they told him, he invited them to make themselves at home everywhere, he offered them a boat for nothing, he asked them to come to dinner any time they felt inclined, and made a date to take them into the bush the following week.

"It seems to be the sort of place we were looking for," smiled Allen Ross, as the two men walked back to Point Curtis for lunch.

"Yes," replied Lynne grumpily. "She liked you."

"Oh, don't be a damned fool, Lynne."

"Lord! Don't take me so seriously. What about the cottage?"

"I'll ride up this afternoon if I can get a horse at the pub, and if the rain keeps off. I shall enjoy a ride again."

CHAPTER XXII

SHIVERING with emotional excitement, Asia lifted her hands from the piano, after the final bar of the Kreutzer Sonata, and looked up into Bruce's face.

"Jove! You played that wonderfully." He smiled down at her. "You always do play well in a storm, you queer mortal. What's the matter?"

For she had turned her head suddenly to the window, which rattled viciously as blasts from the river drove against it.

"Oh, I don't know. But I feel as if there was somebody about."

Getting up, she went to the window, and pressed her face against the panes, peering into the blackness.

"Uncle David," she swung around, "did you hear some one call?"

"Why, no." He moved towards her. "Did you?"

"I thought I did. But I always do hear voices on nights like these. I hear the people who are being wrecked and the people who are being lost. And there are always some when a storm comes up as quickly as this one. I guess the pater stayed in the bush."

They moved back into the room. Asia closed the piano and put away the music. Then, abstractedly, she dropped into a chair by the fire.

Bruce noticed how unusually restless she was as he sat down opposite her and began to smoke.

"Oh, dear," she began, after a few minutes' silence, "Uncle David, I hate to disturb you, but would you go out and tie up that gate? I don't know what is the matter with me, but I can't stand that squeaking to-night. Do you mind?"

"Even if I did, I should go out and fix it. It is damned irritating."

She flashed a brilliant smile at him as he got up.

He went to the kitchen, took down his oilskin, found a piece of rope, and walked out by way of the back door to the front. Asia held the lamp for him at the sitting-room window.

As he wound the rope round the post, Bruce saw something dark on the ground a few yards away from the paling fence.

"What the devil!" he muttered.

But he pretended to finish the job before returning to the kitchen.

"Asia, come here," he called.

Asia closed as she passed it the door of the dining-room, where Betty and Mabel sat over their books.

"What is it?" she whispered. "Is there somebody out there?"

"You are uncanny to-night," he answered, looking at her curiously. "There is. I couldn't see who it was. But he lay in a helpless sort of heap."

"Bring him in," she said promptly.

As she held the lamp at the window again she tried vainly to catch a glimpse of the unknown man's face as Bruce carried him through the gate and round the veranda. As she hurried to the back door she travelled on the wings of a strange excitement.

But the minute she saw the thin face and the wet black hair she became curiously calm.

Bruce did not see who it was till he laid him on the floor. Then he raised his eyes to Asia.

"Well, I'll be damned!" he exclaimed.

She had told him before who Ross was, and of her interest in him in Sydney, and of her meeting with the two men that morning.

"And there be those who say that life is dull," he mused as he undid the sick man's collar.

Asia anxiously pointed out clots of blood in the thick hair.

"What has happened to him? Get him into my bed at once," she cried.

It was not until Bruce had got him undressed, washed and bandaged, that he could form any accurate opinion as to what had happened to him. Allen Ross was badly stunned and bruised, and for some time he resisted all their efforts to restore him to consciousness.

"Looks like a fall from a horse," said Bruce, as they sat over him. "And the bruises are an hour or two old. He's been struggling in the storm for some time, and I'm afraid he's got a beastly chill. He's getting darned feverish. I see where your room becomes a hospital. Blow the horn for Bob Hargraves. We'll have to let the other chap know."

CHAPTER XXIII

ALLEN ROSS stared spasmodically at the small pale blue object, wondering what it was. It had not hung on the door the night before, he would swear to that. He closed his hot tired eyes. But each time that he opened them it was still there. Presently he made out that it was round and woolly. But further effort to account for it became too wearying. Soon afterwards he made another discovery—somebody had taken the varnish off the door. He was glad, for he hated varnish.

After a short doze he once more studied the blue woolly object. He felt sure that somewhere, probably in some former reincarnation, he had been on familiar terms with it. It fascinated and perplexed him. He forced his eyes away from it.

Then he knew he was going mad. Yesterday the paper had been covered with enormous blue daisies attached to greeny-brown rose leaves on a yellow ground; to-day it was grey, with a frieze in pastel shades of blue and rose. Also, Daphne never fled from Apollo on the pub wall. Of that he was certain.

Once more he closed his eyes, trying to realize that he knew the facts of his personality and environment. He determined that, come what might, he would keep sane. He tried to go over what had happened the day before. He supposed it was the day before. They had walked up from the pub. They had seen the cottage. They had met——

His eyes opened and met again the woolly cap. Now he knew where he had seen it before. Now he knew where he had got to. But what had happened? It came back to him slowly—the ride to Kaiwaka on a cranky horse, the long wait for Mr. King, whom he had been determined to see, the setting out again in the dusk, the onslaught of the storm, the accident, the oblivion, the slow return to consciousness, the discovery that he was off the road, the sickening fight against stupor, the long desperate struggle to reach the river, the stimulus of the red mill lamps, the last drag along the beach below the cliffs, and up the slope towards a light, and, finally, wonderful music.

He was very tired by the time he had pieced it all together, and he realized that he was very ill. He found that he could not move without pain and faintness, so he lay still, trying not to think. But indistinct impressions of people, of faces, eyes, and low voices came and went in his sub-consciousness.

When he was able to open his eyes again they rested on rows and rows of books on plain shelves opposite the foot of his bed. By degrees he realized different things in the room: a Verestchagin print, the very incarnation of loneliness—one big palm tree, one vulture, one tiger, and one heap of a man in a jungle clearing. He saw Boeklin's "Isle of Death." He saw "Tivoli" and "Venice" and "The Fighting Temeraire" as Turner saw them. And he saw prints and etchings of old masters and cathedrals.

From a corner by the window "The Winged Victory" of Samothrace seemed to be leaping at him, and over the top of an old silver bowl of glorious roses that stood beside his bed he could see the head and shoulders of a small "Venus de Milo" and parts of brass candlesticks and bronze ornaments on a high mahogany bureau. It all seemed so unreal that he had to open his eyes upon it several times to be sure that it was really there beside that lonely river.

Feeling the strain of consciousness and enjoyment, he dropped off into an uneasy sleep just before Lynne stole in again to watch beside him.

Ross had already been ill four days. For the first two either Bruce or Asia had been beside his bed every moment, for his chill had turned to pneumonia. Lynne had been with him all the time, dozing fitfully on an improvised bed on the floor. He had faithfully obeyed all orders without fuss, and wisely saw that it was not the time to look significantly at Asia, or to take her kindness and hospitality for more than it was worth.

For the first two nights Ross had been delirious, and in his fever, as he tossed and turned, he had begged and implored something or somebody to leave him alone. Over and over again he had appealed with pitiful intensity to that invisible, implacable foe. His misery brought tears to Asia's eyes, and affected even Bruce.

"Poor devil! He has been terribly worried," he said to her as they watched.

On the sixth night, after Lynne and Asia had watched him fall asleep, the crisis well passed, he thought the situation was advanced sufficiently for him to tell her the story.

"I suppose you know he is married," he began.

"Oh, yes. I knew that in Sydney," she answered lightly.

Then, as she appeared interested, he went on to tell her of the wretched marriage to a pretty, heartless girl who thought she had brains and temperament, but who had instead the kind of hysteria that is the hardest in the world to deal with. She could be so charming to the people she hoped to get something out of that there were not many who knew what a hell she made of life for her husband. Finally, he had had to leave her, providing generously for her out of a small private income. But she had pursued him wherever she could, even into his law classes, and to his public meetings, where she had, on several occasions, made disgraceful scenes.

Worn out temporarily with work for his political party, wishing to study law in peace, and sick to death of her, Ross had stolen off to New Zealand, his departure known only to a few friends, who were to try to see in his absence if something could not be done with her.

Most of what Lynne told her Asia already knew, as she had had sidelights on Ross from various angles. She hid her amusement when Lynne tried to make it plain that when

Ross was rested he would return to his law exams, his politics and his career, and that, in future, women would be merely incidents by the way. She was much too discerning a person not to see why he thus casually disposed of his friend's plans. But she let him talk on.

At the end of another week Ross was well enough to take liberties with the situation. But he did not take them. He ignored, whether deliberately or not, Asia could not say, the privileges allowed to the sick. He was an admirable patient, pitifully grateful for all the attention paid him, and patient to a degree that surprised his nurses. He gave numerous signs of which he was unconscious of the trying experience through which he had passed.

While he was very ill he had been indifferent as to who sat with him, but as he grew better his eyes began to follow Asia wistfully about the room, and he kept looking at the door when she was out. But it was not until two nights before Alice returned that he attempted to take Asia's hand as she sat alone beside him.

CHAPTER XXIV

ASIA met her mother at Point Curtis with the launch, one of the new things that Alice had welcomed, for she had always been nervous in the sailing-boat.

The usual steamer-day crowd was waiting on the wharf as the *Ethel* was guided alongside with more fuss than if she had been an ocean liner.

"Dear me, your ma gets younger every year," said a farmer's wife, smiling as she spoke at Mrs. Roland, who had just recognized her as she stood near Asia.

"Yes," Asia looked curiously at her mother, seeing her afresh, and admiring her new tailored suit.

Alice had been in Auckland a month. She had gone mainly because the Brough Company was playing a series of modern plays which Asia said she must positively see, and because Asia had successfully educated Roland to face the fact that seeing plays was part of ordinary modern life for women whose husbands were in the position he was. Roland had become, as he had succeeded, more susceptible to the mandates of public opinion. He had been in the habit of taking women to the theatre if there was anything they wanted to see when he was in Auckland, but formerly the mere suggestion that his wife should take a trip to the city for the purpose of seeing plays would have met with a snort of scorn. However, Asia had taken full advantage of the fact that, at various times, passing travellers in for a meal had assumed that the wife of so prosperous a person as the boss naturally visited Auckland at intervals to keep up to date.

Though not a highly suggestible person where spending money on his wife was concerned, the boss had in the last year or two become more generous to her, and he was quick to see where anything in his treatment of her was likely to reflect upon himself. So that if she wished to go to Auckland she was now free to go, and she had on occasions accompanied her husband at his own request to attend some big function where the addition of a beautiful wife helped his social status.

This last time Alice had gone with Bruce as escort, a business trip for Roland happening to coincide with the arrival of the Brough Company. It had been the first they had ever taken together, and it had been the boss's suggestion. Alice had stayed with the Hardings, and Bruce had lived at an hotel. The morals of Auckland would have survived their staying under the same roof, and Mrs. Harding laughed at Alice's scruples, but could not cure them.

Frequent visits to the city were only a part of recent changes in Alice's life. Ever since the birth of her last dead baby she had lived alone in her room. She did not know that Bruce, in his capacity as doctor, had, after much deliberation, decided to talk seriously to her husband about her health, which had declined steadily after Elsie's birth. She had merely thought that at last he had come to feel that she was unattractive as a wife, and that he preferred to drop the pretence of caring for her in the only way she had supposed he cared. But she was puzzled over the fact that he had become, not less kind and friendly, as she would have expected, but more generous and more considerate.

Personally, she had no regrets for the change in their relations, but only an intense gratitude, mingled sometimes with the fear that as her health improved he might claim her as a wife again. He had never spoken to her on the subject of the change, which had come about naturally. Nobody had remarked on the fact that after her long illness he had continued to sleep in Bunty's room. Her children had not appeared to notice it. Asia had never hinted at any knowledge of it. And so the thing she had longed for, but could never have managed for herself, had happened without her knowing how.

Eight months before the arrival of the Australians Alice had had an operation which had been urged by David Bruce to save attacks of pain and debility from which she had long suffered. Asia returned from Sydney the day her mother went into hospital, and helped to nurse her back to what proved to be a second youth.

It was while they were both in a Rotorua sanatorium, where Alice was being massaged by the best masseur in the colony, that they got the news of Mrs. Brayton's sudden death.

As Alice had received a spirited letter from her only three days before, the news was a shock to both her and Asia, and the manner of the gallant old lady's passing, as it was told in the papers, upset them still more.

Mrs. Brayton had always declared that she would die standing, and she almost did. She had caught influenza, a disease she despised, and, in spite of David Bruce's protests as to its seriousness, she refused to go to bed. In the middle of one morning, after he had been up with her all night, and had told her she was not to get up, her heart-broken old maids found her gasping on the floor, partly dressed. Before they could even get her on to her lounge she was dead.

Asia kept the reports of the funeral from her mother as long as she could, but Alice evaded her and bought old papers giving accounts of it. It had taken on the size and importance in the public mind of a great event. Tom Roland had closed all his works, and the Kaiwaka and bay schools had a holiday. People from a radius of twenty miles had crowded round the grave in a corner of her garden, sobbing for something they had lost, even if it was only the oft-told tale of her open gate, and her home-brewed ale, and her pleasant chatter. To all who had seen her in her own domain she was to remain a vision, an ideal appropriately haloed by the grandeur of her material possessions.

The fact that she had left a good sum of money to local charities and to the school funds probably intensified somewhat the enthusiastic expressions of grief in some directions, more or less public, but she was privately enshrined for ever in the hearts of many to whom she had been a fairy godmother. As time went on she was more quoted than the Bible, and she became a sort of legend with the children growing up, a beautiful spirit of the river and the hills.

Her death changed the character of the bay for the three people who had been her real intimates. To Alice, Bruce and Asia some virtue had gone out of the place never to return. They all realized within a short time that its hold on them had loosened, that there was a vacancy about that garden in the pines that they were continually conscious of, that it was like a dull ache ever present.

The death of the old lady, combined with her mother's illness, had influenced Asia to subdue most of the effects of the city of Sydney upon herself. It was not until they had been back at the bay two months that Alice discovered that she had learned to smoke, and that she gave other signs of complete emancipation from the old-fashioned ways of her mother's generation. But Alice was not as shocked about it as Asia thought she was. She knew that Mrs. Brayton had smoked occasionally with Bruce.

Then Alice had seen, not without a secret amusement, in the last six months, that she was being educated by Asia in the direction of modernism. The process had really begun soon after Asia went to Sydney, with a positive avalanche of books that "Everybody is reading"—Shaw, Wells and Company. Alice suspected that both Bruce, who took with enthusiasm to "the intellectuals," and Dorrie Harding, who wrote continually of them, were in the plot to clear Puritanism finally out of her constitution. At first Shaw had shocked her—she took more kindly to Wells's sociological books—but by degrees Bruce got her to make the distinction between the "intellectual assent" and the personal deed with regard to actions she would not even have spoken about a few years before.

One result of her determination to interest herself in modern plays and books had been less introspection, and she had been surprised to see that her health had improved with her new interests. It had improved so much after she had got over Mrs. Brayton's death that she began to wonder what had happened to her, and more than once Asia had made scandalous remarks about her reaching the "dangerous age," remarks that at first amused and then vaguely disturbed her.

But the greatest joy of the past six months had been Alice's realization of her improved relations with Asia. Although the friendship between them had not included exactly the sort of confidences she felt she should have had, it had been something so much more than they had had for years that it was a source of emotional satisfaction that partly made up for the loss of Mrs. Brayton's sympathy. The only cloud upon it had been the knowledge that some day she would go away again.

There was one direction in which Alice's ignorance of Asia deceived her into thinking that there was yet nothing to know. Asia's adventures with men were entirely unknown to her mother. What personal experiences she had had in her concert tour in New Zealand and later in Sydney—nothing very disturbing to the stability of public morals, and no more illuminating to herself than those she had had before—she had kept entirely to herself, and, as far as her mother could see, she was much the same as she had been before she first went away. Alice firmly believed that however extravagantly she might talk, and however unconventional she might be in certain directions, she would be "moral" when it came to action.

Asia waited for the steamer with mingled feelings. Knowing herself, and thinking she knew her mother, she had a presentiment that their relationship was to be tested as it had never been.

But all thought of trouble was cleared from her mind by the sight of her mother in her new suit.

At forty-two Alice was now a more beautiful woman than she had ever been. And this time she came home flushed with what had been to her some social triumph. Dorrie Harding, who was more devoted to her than ever, had arranged a series of entertainments in her honour, and Alice had tasted something of a social homage that was more pleasant than she had ever imagined it could be. She had been a centre of attention, had felt that people listened when she spoke, and had known the delight of being well and suitably dressed among people who would approve her taste with critical intelligence.

She saw at once, with childish pleasure, that Asia was delighted with her new clothes.

"Why, mother, what have you been doing to yourself?" she whispered, as she kissed her.

"I feel better than I have for years," Alice smiled back. "Indeed, I don't know when I felt so well."

It was not until they were half-way home, after Alice had told with pride some details of the fine time she had had, that Asia attempted to give any local news.

"We've had a diversion too," she began carelessly, stooping to look at the engine.

"Yes?"

"Two men—Australians—on a holiday, and one of them met with an accident, and has been very ill. We've had him home. He's getting better. They're both very nice."

"Why, you did not tell me in your letters," said Alice, looking at her, and immediately sensing something significant in the omission.

"Well, I did not have much time. Mr. Ross had pneumonia and nearly died."

Asia again turned her attention to the machinery, but her mother was not deceived by her casualness. Instead, she felt one of her uncanny presentiments that there was more in this than met the eye.

Her presentiment crystallized into a conviction when she had been home half an hour. She had found Ross lying convalescent on the front room sofa, and Lynne, with his arms full of kites which he had made for Bunty and Elsie, waiting with them on the spit to meet her. Both men took her breath away by hailing her with boyish friendliness. She did not realise that her children had spoken of her in such a way that both men felt they knew her before they saw her. Nobody had hinted that she might not receive them in the same spirit that the boss and Bruce and Asia had shown. Allen Ross perceived the mistake immediately.

Usually, when Alice returned from Auckland, she was the centre of a pleasant fuss for a few hours at least; for, apart from the excitement of receiving the presents she now always brought for them, her children liked to know what she had seen and done, and they liked to rival each other in claims for her first attentions.

But this time her home-coming was robbed of almost all its importance by the fact that Asia was that night to give a dinner-party in the front room, partly to celebrate her return, but more, as she guessed later, to celebrate Ross's recovery. Alice felt the more hurt because she had looked forward to telling them more than ever what she had enjoyed while away.

Asia had no time to do more than unlock her mother's trunk before she said she must see about the dinner. Bunty seized upon the mechanical toy she had brought him, and rushed off to show it to Ross and Lynne. Betty, who now taught in the Kaiwaka school, and Mabel, who was a probationer in the school at the head of the bay, were not yet home. So that only Elsie was there to be impressed, and even she was obsessed by the coming festivity.

"It's to be a real dinner-party, Mother," she said, her eyes popping out of her head, "with all our silver, and candles, and just roses, Asia says, and I can sit up if I'm good. There, she's calling me."

And the child ran gaily off, leaving Alice alone with her

open trunk, and her things scattered over her bed. For a while she tried to go on with her unpacking, and to ignore the fact that she was feeling hurt. Then the air of fuss and importance about the house was too much for her. She went out to the kitchen after changing her suit for a house dress. Asia was putting the last touches to a pan full of fat spring chickens, with Barrie Lynne hovering about ready to hand her things.

"What can I do?" Alice asked.

"Oh, nothing, thank you, Mother," answered Asia briskly. "Everything's done now. We did most of it this morning. I've only got the flowers and the table. There's nothing else till dinner-time. You finish your unpacking, and then rest. Don't get overtired."

"I'm not tired," replied Alice with a sense of injury, as she turned away. There was no part for her to play, she saw, and for some reason she wanted to join in. She went back to her room annoyed with herself for feeling badly.

She took up a new brown silk dress, a lovely soft thing, shot with gold, that she had paid for with money given to her by David Bruce. She was half fearful that her husband, thinking his money had paid for it, would think it ridiculous extravagance, for there was nothing at the bay for her to wear it to, and she would have been still more afraid to have him know that he had not paid for it. She had always felt rather guilty about the presents of money Bruce had given her when she went to Auckland, and she had been careful to spend them in ways that were not conspicuous enough to attract Roland's attention. But the brown dress had been too much for her. She had bought it in company with Dorrie Harding and David Bruce, who both conspired to soothe her conscience as to her right to spend so much upon one garment. They had persuaded her to try it on, and once on it was fatal. Alice felt afterwards that much of her success was due to it, but as she looked at it now she thought she had been foolish to buy it, and that apart from Bruce no one would care whether she wore it or not.

As she stood holding it up Betty and Mabel walked in. They were now pretty, fresh girls, of no violently radical tendencies, and with no promise yet of the outstanding individuality of their father, or of the distinction of their mother. When Roland said they would have to earn their own living and be useful, whether he could afford to keep them or not, they decided to become teachers, and both had made satisfactory beginnings in the profession. To them Asia had always been something of an outsider, and they had grown up happy in their friendship for each other. They were just the attractive, normal, sentimental and conventional girls that organized society expects its young women to be.

"Oh, Mother," they cried together, kissing her, "what a lovely dress."

Alice was pleased that they liked it.

"You are going to wear it for our party," said Mabel.

"I don't know."

"Oh, yes, Mother. Do look nice. It's to be a swagger party. You must wear it."

"Well, I'll see."

Then Alice found the blouse lengths of silk that she had brought for them. They had barely thanked her when they heard Asia calling for them.

"She wants us," said Betty. "We must go. Oh, Mother, aren't Mr. Ross and Mr. Lynne *just lovely?*"

They ran out excitedly, leaving Alice once more robbed of her audience and shut out of the preparations for the dinner.

As she went on with her unpacking she heard the constant tramping up and down the hall, Asia's voice calling for this and that, sounds of furniture being moved, gay voices and laughter. She felt as if she had been away a long time, as if she did not belong there any more, as if *she* were an interloper in the house. Again she was angry with herself for being so stupid. Why should they not have a party, even if it were for the two men? Why should she not get into a party mood, and not act as if they had set her aside?

When she had put away all her clothes she went out into the garden. The children had finished gathering the roses, and were now busy inside. Alice strolled round the beds, rejoicing in new flowers, and planning where she would put the plants she had brought home with her. Then she sat down on a garden seat to watch a fine sunset that finally helped her to eliminate herself from her consciousness and sent her inside disposed to cast a more friendly eye upon the inevitable readjustments.

Soon afterwards Asia poked her head in through the doorway.

"Mother, do look nice to-night. You are the guest of honour, you know. Have you anything new to wear?"

"I have a brown dress," began Alice.

"Brown!" Asia sounded sceptical. "Well, if it suits you, do put it on." Then she vanished in the direction of the kitchen.

Then Alice decided that she would wear the brown dress, and that she would do her hair very carefully. After all, David Bruce would notice if no one else did. So she began one of the most painstaking toilets she had ever made. At the end, when she viewed herself in the glass, she felt she had not done badly. Her beautiful hair was only just beginning to show the grey. Her colour was better than it had been for years, and her eyes showed a vitality that she had thought would never return to them.

But her chief charm lay in something not to be pointed out in this feature or in that, not even in her graceful figure. It lay in something life had made of her, a capacity for being better than she knew.

She had no intention of making a dramatic entrance, but it so happened that when she walked into the front room Bruce, who had just entered, and Lynne and Asia, and the girls were all standing round the sofa where Ross sat propped up by cushions. The table was laid, the candles lit, the whole room bowered in roses. Everybody turned as she moved forward.

"Why, Mother, if you don't look stunning!" burst out Asia, in the manner of her early childhood. And the eyes of every one else reflected her opinion.

Alice paused, flushing, and obviously resenting this frank praise before men she did not know. Then, catching Bruce's eye, she was warned in time and smiled. But she saw that even that brief resentment had done something to the general enthusiasm, and that she must try to restore it. So, with the air of being very nice, she looked at Ross. She was not sure yet which of the two men Asia preferred.

"I hope this fuss is not tiring you," she began solicitously.

"Not at all, thank you," he replied warmly, his dark eyes glowing up at her, for he knew he wanted her to like him.

Bruce placed a chair for her, and sat down himself on the edge of the sofa.

"We still have to take care of him, though," he said, looking from Ross to Alice. "He has been a very sick man, Mrs. Roland."

This beginning restored the flow of talk that had been interrupted by Alice's entrance. Lynne and the girls chattered on among themselves, while Ross began, in answer to a question of hers, to tell Alice how he came to get ill. Before he was well begun the boss came in humming, as he did when there was anything unusual on to which he wished to appear quite accustomed. He had changed his suit and put on a clean collar at Asia's request.

"Well, how are things now?" he asked cheerfully, whisking up to the sofa party, with the air of inquiring after a business or a public movement, and not stopping for Ross to finish the sentence he had begun.

They all saw he was addressing the invalid.

"*I'm* improving fast, thanks." Ross smiled up at him

as if there was a secret understanding between them. He thoroughly enjoyed Tom Roland's idiosyncrasies.

As he turned to look for a chair, the boss got the full effect of his wife as she sat back in her rocker. He had barely seen her on the spit that day as she landed.

"Well," he grunted, oblivious of the fact that to her the Australians were still strangers, "you look as if you'd taken a new lease of life. Seeing plays must be healthy."

Alice was not yet equal to taking him lightly in such situations. Both Bruce and Asia saw the necessity for diplomacy.

"Get up and bow, Mother, and in future always wear brown dresses," laughed Asia.

"And keep on going to see plays," smiled Bruce.

"You see," Asia explained gaily to Ross, "we have at last got Mother to see that some contact with this wicked world need not interfere with the pursuit of higher things, so she has been seeing 'The Liars,' and 'The Gay Lord Quex,' and 'Niobe,' and 'Lady Windermere's Fan,' with the result that she has bought without my assistance that adorable dress, and looks younger than ever. I've always told her that too much pursuit of higher things was incompatible with a good complexion.

Everybody laughed, for Asia said it with delightful impertinence, mingled with her obvious affection for her mother. Even Alice laughed. But Ross, who was a sensitive person, knew that she thought the whole conversation in very bad taste. However, as Asia's remarks had been addressed to him, he felt he had to say something.

"Well, Mrs. Roland, if complexions are the test, you have preserved a very nice balance between God and mammon."

Alice could not help responding to the mischief in his eyes, or to the old-fashioned look of homage that followed it.

Then the conversation became normal again, and Asia and the girls went off to put the finishing touches to the sauces and the gravy.

The Australians knew that Asia had never imagined for

a moment that she would impress them by her little dinner. She had joked about using all the family silver, and so on, but there was no pretension about the function or the spirit in which it was given. But, all the same, there were things about it that were distinctive. Ross and Lynne had never seen so many roses in one room before, they had never eaten better chicken, they had never sat down with a man who interested them more than David Bruce, or with women who charmed them more than Asia and her mother.

And, to do him credit, the boss was at his best. It was his home and he had paid for everything. So, to him, the glory of the party was a reflection from his own generosity, and he was sure the two men understood this. It put him in most excellent spirits, and called forth, whenever he got the chance, his choicest collection of stories from his dramatic life.

Alice realized before the meal had gone very far, that she was, after all, really enjoying it, for everybody treated her as if she were, indeed, the guest of honour. Bruce's attitude she took, of course, for granted. It was too familiar a thing to be remarked. But she had not expected quite the amount or kind of attention that she received from Ross and Lynne. And it pleased her to feel that their homage was due to something more than her position as hostess. There was something especially flattering about the way Ross regarded her opinions of the plays she had seen. He did not have the superior air of kindly tolerance that Asia had been unable to hide. He looked and spoke as if he valued her judgment.

Alice had started the meal with reserves. She had meant to give the whole of her attention to Bruce in a manner that would convey to these young men the fact that, whatever Asia might think of them, her good opinion was something not to be easily won. But long before the meal was over she had succumbed to Ross's charm. And she did *not* remember till afterwards that Bruce had talked very little, and that he had given leads for the younger man to follow.

Several whispered conversations followed the dinner.

Lynne chose an unlucky moment, while helping Asia to put away the food in a dark corner of the scullery, to put his arms impulsively round her and kiss her.

"No, don't be a fool, boy," she said with a touch of contempt.

And though she talked on as if it had been the most negligible of incidents, the rest of the evening was saddened for him.

Soon after the table was finally cleared Bruce said Ross had to go to bed. Asia preceded him to her room, lit his candle, turned down the bed-clothes, and altered the windows. She lingered so that she would be there when he came in.

When he did he partly closed the door behind him.

"You are tired," she said softly, her eyes reaching out to him.

"A little, but no matter. It was a charming dinner, little girl." He stood easily before her, sure of his right to make a move if he wanted to, and, therefore, in no hurry to make it. "Why didn't you tell me your mother was such an interesting person?"

"Mother, why, of course, she's wonderful. I suppose I'm used to her. But she's really old-fashioned."

"Is she? It wasn't so obvious to me. She reminded me of an ivy-covered tower I saw somewhere in England that had weathered many storms. It had a beauty I shall never forget."

Asia looked at him. She knew he was not saying this to impress her, that, in fact, he had forgotten her for the moment.

"I'm glad you like her, and I hope she likes you," she went on. "But she is a very peculiar person to please."

"I prefer people who make careful selections. It is so much more flattering when they choose oneself." He smiled gleefully at her as he held out his hand. Then, moved by one of the few impulses he had let run away with him, he raised her hand to his face, held it a moment, rubbed it against his cheek, and kissed it lingeringly.

Raising his face, his eyes challenged hers with a look that asked many questions. Then he smiled as if the answers were satisfactory, and putting his hands on her shoulders, he turned her to the door without another word.

While Roland and Lynne smoked in the front room Bruce and Alice manœuvred themselves out into the dining-room, which was empty, for Betty and Mabel were washing up.

Bruce had talked with his eyes many times that evening, but he had to put it into words.

"My dear, you really are a miracle. I have never——"

"Oh, David, don't be foolish," she interrupted, half laughing. "It must be the dress."

"Partly. But mostly health."

"Yes, I do feel well. David, who are these men?"

He knew that was chiefly what she wanted to talk to him about.

"I don't know, any more than you do," he answered carelessly.

"Do you like them?"

"Why, yes, don't you?" He looked quizzically at her.

"I don't know," she began cautiously.

He chuckled.

"Are they going to be here long?"

"They've taken King's cottage below the mill for some months, I believe."

"They have!"

"Why do you say it like that?" He saw that she had already begun to anticipate.

"What are they doing here?" she evaded.

"Lynne writes, and is after 'copy.' Ross is studying for the law."

"*This* is a funny place to study for law."

"Not at all. It's a first-rate place. He brought a caseful of books."

Then they heard the boss saying good night to Lynne, who was returning to the cottage, and they rose to go back to the sitting-room.

Later Asia followed Bruce out of the back door to the side gate.

"I congratulate you," he began softly. "Your mother likes Ross. That was the object of the dinner, wasn't it?"

"Oh, Uncle David, you always deprive people of the pleasure of explaining their actions. It is unkind. But you were lovely at dinner, and didn't he talk well?"

"He did." He smiled at her over the gate. "You've certainly got something ahead of you to manage, haven't you?" he drawled. "I predict that your talents will not get rusty for a while."

She looked back at him, saying nothing.

"Didn't Mother look stunning?" she veered abruptly.

Bruce laughed outright.

"Don't you think you can snub me," he said, taking her by the shoulders.

"I didn't mean to, Uncle David," she answered seriously. She looked as if she wanted to say something more, but after a brief uncertainty she bobbed up on her toes and kissed him, and ran from him to the other side of the house.

Bruce pursued his way to his shanty speculating as to what the morrows would bring forth.

CHAPTER XXV

THE next day Alice saw that Ross was the preferred man. And she heard also, through one of the girls, whom Lynne had told, because they asked him, that he was married.

She knew that he possessed the same characteristics after she had received this information as he had before, but her opinion of them mysteriously changed. She did not mean to allow any sign of the change to appear in her manner until she had had more time to consider the possibilities that lay ahead. For two days she avoided danger by staying away from Asia and Ross, finding her excuse in the amount of work which she said had to be done in the garden.

On the third morning Ross told Asia that he felt well enough to move to his cottage. She knew that he was not strong enough to go, or to eat as he and Lynne would be likely to eat, and that he would not be ready for it for another week at least. And she guessed, also, why he spoke.

That afternoon, as Alice sat sewing and resting beside her western window, Asia opened her door after a short knock, and walked half-way across the room, where she stood with a rigidity unlike her usual ease and mobility.

Alice sensed trouble in her cool level tones.

"Mother, Mr. Ross talks of moving to-morrow. He isn't well enough to go, and he was to stay here another week. You must have made him feel he isn't wanted."

"I'm sure I've done nothing of the kind," said Alice warmly, as she looked up. "I've been perfectly courteous——"

"I didn't say you hadn't, Mother. You might be that, *and yet* not want him to stay. But he won't be any trouble to you, and you must let him think you do want him to stay."

Their eyes met for a moment, and Alice saw something new and defiant, and fiercely hostile at the back of Asia's, something she had never seen there before. It startled her.

"My dear, of course I've nothing against his staying. I had supposed he would. What do you want me to do?"

"Well, you will have to make it plain, Mother. Sick people are very sensitive."

"I don't know what I've done," went on Alice.

"It isn't what you've done, Mother, so much as something you're thinking. And you have a manner that would freeze hell." She saw her mother was hurt by this expression, but at that moment she did not care.

"What do you want me to do?" asked Alice with an air of resignation that taxed Asia's patience.

"Mother, you know very well. Don't pretend you don't. I know what you are thinking. But you might as well stop it, because that sort of thinking never does any good. Now I'm going to make tea. Will you have it with us? And will you act as if you were enjoying it?"

Though to Alice this resembled an invitation to put her head in the lion's mouth, she fought her feeling of hurt and resentment.

"Very well," she said quietly.

Turning, Asia swung out with an air suggestive of a final ultimatum.

Uncompromising candour was a thing Alice never could cope with in any one but Bruce, who knew how to temper it with humour and graciousness. Asia's cold words, sensible and straight though they were, left her sore and helpless.

She wondered how, after this interview, she could possibly go out and be pleasant and natural to Allen Ross. She wondered how she was to rid herself of the sense of fate that had hung over her for three days. She wondered how she could keep out of her manner the evidence of the thoughts that would crowd her mind. But she felt she must try. That something she had seen in Asia's eyes frightened her. She wanted passionately to keep something she did not know how to keep.

She stood up and looked out upon the sun-swept river and the drowsy western hills. All life seemed drugged in the enervating stillness of that soft spring day, all except that around the mills, which remained, as ever, oblivious of heat and cold, and sun and rain. She saw a clutch of flitches rise into the air between the masts of a vessel at one of the wharves. She watched it swing and drop and disappear into the hold. The hum and grind and scream of the machinery were deadened a little by the humidity in the air. But there was something in the vitality of that agglomeration of sounds that helped her.

She smoothed her hair, put in a new comb, inspected her hands, and taking up the garment she had been sewing, she walked into the front room. She did not know whether Ross knew that Asia had spoken to her.

"It must be tea-time," she began with a forced serenity.

Ross knew nothing of the recent interview, but he felt her restraint. Because she attracted him he was determined to overcome it. He raised himself off his cushions.

"I think Miss Roland is making it. Let me get you a chair."

"Oh, no, thank you," commanded Alice quickly. "Don't attempt to get up, please." She walked to her rocker near the fireplace. As she sat down she saw that he would have to turn round in order to face her and sit comfortably. He made a move to readjust himself.

"Don't move," she said, getting up again.

"Won't you come nearer, so that I can talk to you?" he asked.

She thought his voice sounded appealing as he looked at her across the top of the table, and unable to resist that friendliness, she dragged her chair to the foot of the sofa, and sat down facing him.

As he settled himself again one of his cushions slipped to the floor.

"I will get it," said Alice, as she saw him stoop.

The something curiously intimate about arranging cushions for a person, sick or well, affected her as she fixed them for him, and some of the hostility that had crept into her thoughts of him disappeared. He looked up gratefully at her, with the look of homage and genuine interest that had attracted her at the dinner. She felt that perhaps she had been misjudging him.

She took up her sewing.

"Have you been ill before?" she asked.

"I have never had to go to bed before," he replied.

"Then, it's a new experience."

"Quite."

"It is not a pleasant one."

"No, but I've found that it has its compensations." He smiled again at her.

She did not know whether he meant to include her company among these compensations. She would have been suspicious of any compliment, and she made no attempt to acknowledge it as such. She went on with her sewing, determined that he should do his share of making conversation.

Ross lay easily still for a minute or two, watching her. He liked the simplicity of her gingham dress and lace fichu, the grace of her bowed head, the delicate movements of her white nervous hands about the muslin and lace. Then the smallness and fineness of the garment interested him. He wondered if he dared ask what it was. Presently, when he had decided that it was not anything with an embarrassing name, he put out his hand.

"What is that?" he asked, touching it.

"It is a christening dress for a baby—the Hargraves'." Her tone implied that it could not possibly mean anything to him. But she held it up.

Ross looked at it, saying nothing. It was the first time

he had noticed anything belonging to a very little child, and he was amazed himself at the sudden effect it had upon him, at the things it suggested. He forgot all about Alice as he looked at it.

Feeling that his silence was significant, she stole a glance at him. She saw reverence, delicacy and sentiment in his eyes, and she felt that a man who could look like that could not be a villain.

"Can a child get into that?" he asked, taking hold of it.

"Oh, yes. They are very small at first, you know." She found herself actually smiling at him. His real interest in the little garment touched her.

At that moment Asia appeared in the doorway with the tea. She gave one look at Ross with the christening dress in his hands, and one at her mother leaning towards him, and then her eyes lit up with a wild amusement. But Ross barely looked at her as she walked in and put her tray on a small table.

"There's something very appealing about it, isn't there?" he said to Alice, as he handed her back the lace and muslin.

"Yes, I feel so," she answered, amazed that he should.

This little incident affected her opinion of him more than she was then aware of.

Asia came forward with cups of tea, her manner entirely innocent of any significance. After she had served cake she sat down on the end of the sofa, and led Ross to talk of his work and Sydney. He noticed while he talked, addressing himself almost entirely to Alice, that they both avoided looking at each other, and that Alice had lost the ease she was coming to when the tea was brought in.

He chose an appropriate place to say that it was time he stopped loafing and got to work.

"I have told Miss Roland I will get down to the cottage to-morrow. I have imposed on your kindness long enough," he said.

"I don't think you have imposed on my kindness at all," said Alice quickly, with a change of manner.

Asia rose to get more tea.

"Well, I must be an infernal bother," he went on, feeling something he could not define.

"If you are considering me," Alice achieved a pleasantness that surprised herself, "you must know that you are no bother to me. If Asia likes to make a trouble of you that is her affair." At this Asia wondered what had happened to her mother. "We are used to taking in strangers," went on Alice. "It is a habit we have acquired in this place, and we never make a trouble of it. You will please stay here till you are quite well."

Though still uncertain about it, he felt there was nothing for him to do but to thank her and stay.

That night Alice went out to walk up and down the beach to try to face what she was now sure was coming. She craved for Bruce, but he and Roland had gone that day to the bush to be away for days, leaving her more alone than she had ever felt before. Though she was by no means sure that he would see eye to eye with her in this situation, she felt he was now the only thing she really had. She had tried to take comfort from words spoken hurriedly by him the evening before when she had asked him if he knew that Ross was married. He had treated the matter lightly, had again begged her not to anticipate, and had assured her that Ross and Asia were as familiar with the conventions as she was, and that they could take care of themselves.

But now the look that had flashed across Asia's eyes that afternoon troubled her. It lit up the future for her. It opened out a panorama of disaster that now seemed to her to be inevitable.

Alice had faced more or less calmly for some time now the fact that Asia would probably marry some one she did not like. With the memory of Mrs. Brayton's story in her mind she had determined that whoever it was she would make the best of it. It was the one thing in her life she would have been ready for. She had prayed with but faint hopes that it would not be an actor, or a reformer of too pronounced a type, or a weakling of the kind that often attracted strong women, but she had prepared herself for the worst even in this direction. Her visions of a professional man and a "gentleman" were, she always knew, too good to be true.

But, as usual, the thing she had not prepared herself for was the thing that was going to happen. It had never occurred to her that Asia might fall in love with a married man. She had the familiar delusion that though other people's children did such things her own could not. And the bitter irony in the situation was that Allen Ross single would have been just the sort of husband she would have welcomed, while Allen Ross married was the least desirable thing in the world. She did not know yet whether there were any chances of a divorce, but even if she had known there were it would have made no difference to her just then.

The unkindest cut of all was that this situation came at a time when she had been about to rest upon her oars, when she had hoped that at last her life was to flow in the pleasant places, when at last her old haunting sense of failure had become less insistent, and the tragedies of her past had settled back into an undisturbed region of her sub-consciousness. It was this crowning cruelty that brought slow tears of self-pity to her eyes as she walked back and forth on the sand. She had so wanted peace. She had so wanted forgetfulness and some measure of happiness. It stunned her to think that there was design in this, the working out of some immutable law that would never leave her alone.

Then the old delusion that it must be stopped, that it could be stopped, and that she could stop it took possession of her. It was unthinkable that it should go on. She was sure they did not realize where they were drifting, sure they had not faced the facts, sure that even when they did begin to face them they would overlook something vital. But, she told herself, they were both fine and honourable, they did not mean to bring misery to each other, and they would listen to her. And she believed that what she had to say would open their eyes to the danger they were in.

She was anticipating the end before the beginning had well begun.

She felt calmer after she had made the decision to speak until she began to ask herself which of them she would talk to. The difficulty of it made her sick. She tortured herself with imaginary conversations, beginning now with Asia and now with Ross. But she knew facing them in theory on the beach was a very different thing from looking them in the face, and the suspicion that she might fail, and that they might go their own way in spite of her grew upon her. She began to cry helplessly. Then she raged against the man who had brought this upon her, then she cried again until she was too worn out to think about it any more. As she went to bed she decided that it might be wiser to wait and see how they went on.

When she met them at lunch the next day she wondered what she had been worrying about. Nothing could have been saner or calmer or more normal emotionally than the two people she had seen the evening before on the edge of the abyss of unbridled passions. There were no traces of nervousness about Asia, and as she watched Ross cut bread for the children she felt, as she had felt the day before, that he could not be a scoundrel. But it was only in their presence that she felt thus disarmed. Away from them her fatal intuition regained possession of her.

She tried to comfort herself with the knowledge that they belonged to a generation that had collected along with other ethical novelties the right to free and open friendships between the sexes. She knew Auckland was full of such friendships, but she had observed that, in spite of the freedom, they were commented on, and that people always wondered about them with a certain expression in the eye and a certain raising of the shoulders. It did not matter to her that the remarks were more often in the nature of amused speculation than judgment. The fact that they were remarked on at all proved to her they were not accepted naturally by society.

It was not till she had thought back and forth for three days that she remembered that her friendship with Bruce might have been questioned by the strictly orthodox. But she told herself at once that that was a very different thing from the friendship between Ross and Asia. She was so sure of it that she attempted no analysis of the difference. She shut her mind against any comparison.

She grew lonelier and lonelier each day. Her children were not rude to her, nor did they neglect her, but she saw that their attentions were a little forced. Hypnotized by the company of the two men they would forget her, and then, remembering, come ostentatiously to see if she wanted anything. She sat a good deal in her own room. The only time she really saw them all was at meals. She pretended to be busy gardening and sewing. She forced herself to be pleasant. One evening when Asia asked her if she did not want to join them all in a walk on the beach, she went, feeling it was a doubtful experiment, as it proved to be. She could not enter into their gaiety, seeing as she did the grim hand of fate above them all. She began to see treachery in Ross's careful attentions. She could not help it. She left them early with the conviction that she had spoilt their walk, and that they all knew it.

The next day, the day Ross was to leave for the cottage, Alice awoke with a headache. She did not mention it because it would look almost as if she had done it on purpose. All her children had planned to escort Ross to his home, and install him with a tea. Asia spent the morning cooking enough food to last the men for days. As it was Saturday, and they were all home, the house resounded with noise and laughter.

Alice felt miserably that she must make an effort to be pleasant at lunch. She drank hot water, took soda, bathed her face with eau-de-Cologne, and finally took brandy. But she looked so ill when she sat down to table that they all noticed it. She was sure she read in Asia's eyes a veiled impatience. After a few minutes she got up, and begging them to take no notice of her, but to go on with their fun just as they meant to, she left them, and went back to her own room.

As she was getting cold water and a towel to bathe her face Asia came in.

Alice turned on her desperately.

"Now what are you bothering about me for?" she demanded. "I can look after myself. It's just the heat."

"Why, Mother, it's no bother. You look very sick. You must stop gardening in the sun." Though Asia guessed that the sun was not the sole cause of the trouble, she ignored the other features in the case. She had made up her mind to manage her mother without emotional scenes as far as she could, and she was determined to be patient and to bear with her suspicions and premature judgments.

"I'm all right," persisted Alice. "I only want to lie down and be still."

"Very well, Mother."

"And I don't want any one to stay home with me this afternoon." Her tone implied that she knew she was a nuisance, but that she would not have any sacrifices made for her.

Taking her at her word, Asia said "All right" and left her.

Alice began to cry, but realizing that that would make her head worse, she controlled herself, and bathed her face and neck. Also, she meant to get up and see the party leave, and she knew she dare not show traces of tears.

When Asia came to the door to tell her they were going she got up, powdered her face—a performance she had taken to rather guiltily on her last visit to Auckland—and sniffed her smelling salts.

Faced with that smiling, eager group, she felt as if she were on trial. She felt she had no business to send them off with anything in their minds that would spoil their afternoon. She felt as if they were appealing to her to justify them in the enjoyment of their youth and good spirits.

"I'm better," she said, in answer to Ross's question. "I stayed out too long in the sun. I hope you will all have a lovely afternoon and a very nice tea-party."

"Don't you think you are well enough to come?" he asked.

Alice could detect no lack of sincerity in his tone.

"I won't come to-day, thank you," she succeeded in saying lightly, "but some time soon."

"May I stay till dark, Mother?" appealed Bunty, seeing she was in a gracious mood.

"If you have been asked to," she smiled.

And with that smile upon her face they left her. They did not forget, as they frolicked down the hill, to turn and wave to her, and something about that little attention, which none of her children ever forgot, touched and comforted her.

But before she had been alone long a sense of terrible loneliness overwhelmed her. Something like the stillness of death seemed to brood over the house. She felt she could not stay in it. So, as her head felt better, she went down to talk to Mrs. Hargraves, whom she saw sitting with her children on her back porch. With them she was forced to fight her own thoughts out of action, and the effort did her good. She stayed with them till she saw Roland and Bruce ride up to the stables by the men's kitchen. Then she hurried home to get a meal ready for them.

She had no chance to talk to Bruce that night, or for some time afterwards, for he went off on business to the Wairoa, and when he returned a government party had to be shown round and entertained for several days.

Asia did her full share of the management necessitated by this hospitality. She got Eliza King down from Kaiwaka to help, so that her absences would put no extra work on her mother. She did not try to get out of playing to the guests in the evening, and she went on one excursion to the bush.

But Alice, watching, saw that Ross and Lynne were included in all the hospitalities, and that somehow or other Asia was with them or with Ross every day.

When the visitors finally departed Asia told her mother that she was going to coach Ross with his French. She did not elaborate the statement to say when or where, but she began to disappear after dinner at night, and her hours for returning soon brought home to Alice the conviction that if she was ever to speak it must be soon.

CHAPTER XXVI

"NO French to-night!" repeated Ross.

He had risen from a stump to meet Asia as she crossed the clearing. He saw that she carried a kit stuffed with things done up in newspaper, and a lantern.

She had on an old print dress faded to whiteness, and wore no hat. A bit of the sunset came through the trees to gleam upon her hair.

"Where are you going?" he demanded, as she came up to him.

"Over on the gum-field. Somebody dying. I think he came up the day you did. Consumption. Uncle David was there last night. But he can't go to-night."

Allen Ross looked curiously at her. He saw she went to dying men as simply as she did other things belonging to the place. It did not occur to him to pay her any compliments about it.

"How far is it?" he asked.

"Between three and four miles."

"Why don't you ride?"

"The track's too bad at night."

"I want to come," he said, a light flashing across his eyes.

She caught her breath, but tried to answer lightly.

"You would be bored. I may read the Bible and pray."

But he did not smile, as she expected him to.

"Do you ever?" he asked gravely.

"Yes, often. Wouldn't you do anything a dying man wanted you to do?"

"Certainly, if I could."

They stood still, their eyes challenging back and forth. They both suspected that if they went together the night would hold more for them than the shadow of death.

"May I come?" he appealed.

She tried to keep her voice casual.

"Of course, if you want to. But it won't be pleasant. He may die."

Again he looked at her. "Die?" he thought. "Could anybody die with her about?"

But he felt he passionately wanted to go, that nothing could keep him from going. He answered her by reaching for her kit.

With a few remarks about the beauty of the evening they went out of the clearing, and a little way down the Great North Road before Asia turned into a track that led over the range on the northern side. It was wide enough for them to see their way in the sunset light. As it was a good deal of a climb they scrambled up silently, Ross a few paces behind her.

At the top, at a place where fire had cleared a space, she paused, and they both stood to recover their breath, and to watch the sunset and the view.

The river, right-angled in the hills below them, was veiled in places by the gathering haze. Above the mill it lay leaden in the shadow of the forest slopes, but about the gap it was alive under the opaline shades in the sky. Roofs and windows about the bay in the line of shafts of light flashed back copper suns of their own. Stalks of smoke, spreading into filmy heads in the still air, rose from the cottage chimneys. From the chained powers in the mill mysterious vibrations floated upwards, mingling with the night stirring in the forest trees. Intermittent sounds cut in upon the flow of the undertones—scraps of song and music, the barking of dogs, the deep singing tones of bullock bells, mellowed by distance.

Lights starting up about the hills below Point Curtis revealed the presence of farm-houses and Maori settlements.

East of them they could see only the bush wall that rose in tiers towards the gap beside Pukekaroro. To the north of them lay low land as far as they could see—the gumfield Ross and Lynne had heard so much about.

All Ross could see as he now looked at it for the first time was a wide area of what looked like nothingness in comparison with the view elsewhere. Its pigmy slopes and valleys, visible by day, now merged into the dead level of monotonous wastes. What vagrant trees it had were dwarfed to the level of the ti-tree and the fern, themselves the poorest of their kind, for the blood of the soil had gone centuries before into the life of a kauri forest, of which now the only trace was the gum, the hardened sap of the great trees that had once proudly whispered to the sun and the stars.

But as Ross looked at it there grew into it the colours he had heard Asia speak about. Such gullies as it had deepened into the strong barbaric blues that the modern artist has rediscovered for the world. Its burnt slopes sprang to life in patches of purple and brown that seemed lit from within. For five minutes its colours stayed hot and crude, like jewels glowing over a furnace, and then a film crept out of the night and dulled them, like clouds of grey tulle spread over a gay and many coloured robe. As they faded out they left the wastes they had glorified more desolate than ever.

Moved by the same impulse, Asia and Ross turned hungry eyes upon each other. Neither wanted to speak, but each wanted a swift assurance that the night had got them in the same way. Seeing that it had, they stood a moment, each trying to hide the exaltation of it.

Then Asia remembered the nature of their errand.

"Come on," she said, resting her hand for a minute on his arm.

The track down the ridge on this side ran through a section that had been swept by fire. A leafless, sapless company of trees, whitened by exposure, raised mutilated trunks and branches above an undergrowth of young fern. These forest ghosts, growing more wraith-like every minute in the twilight, formed a fitting gateway to that desolation whither they were bound.

When they reached the border of the gum-field at the foot of the ridge Asia paused to light her lantern.

Ross looked out over the gathering darkness where he could distinguish nothing that could act as a guide. Already he fancied he could smell the stench of stagnant swamps, the dust of dead men's bones.

"Do you know the way?" he asked. But he was not afraid. He would have followed her anywhere that night, for the great and glorious madness had got him, as it gets a man only once in life.

"Oh, yes." She looked up at him exultantly, knowing that in this, her domain, he would feel a feeble creature, and would the more appreciate her native cunning. "I know every inch of it. Our sick man is in the earl's hut—that is, we called him the earl. He had a title of some kind. He built it six years ago, and he died in it two years later—whisky. Then another Englishman had it. He was left money and went Home. Then a teacher, also an Englishman, drifted to it. He died there six months ago—whisky and pneumonia. Now this poor devil—whisky and consumption. I've read the Bible and prayed for them all in turn."

"You have!" he mumbled, looking at her as if he saw her afresh.

"Well, they want it. Funny, but they want it. But it's so pathetic, it makes me sick. These gum-fields are the saddest places in the world. They won't bear thinking about. Come on." And again she took up the lantern.

Some eight years before Roland had taken over from the government the right to lease this gum-field, which lay for miles beside his own bush, and since that time he and Bruce, and later Asia, had been more or less in touch with the strange company of down-and-outs who had applied for a licence to dig. In keeping with the usual custom, the diggers brought their gum to the boss's store for sale at the current rates, and were paid either in money or in kind, as they preferred. As Roland had never exploited the squeezing possibilities of the arrangement made by the field owners and leasers for their own benefit, he was besieged with applications, all of which he could not fill, because a field had a capacity for so many men and no more.

Ross had learned enough of the facts of the gum-digging life from Asia to be tremendously interested in its peculiar atmosphere.

In the early days of the colony's history fortunes had been quickly made by the men who had the chance to pick up in quantities, on the surface of the ground and in the beds of streams, the nuggets of amber gum that only the kauri tree produces. As the tree itself grows only in the northern half of the Auckland province, the fortune giving area was limited, and the day of speedy riches soon came to an end. Then men found that the most barren places of the "barbarous north" hid the treasure in unknown quantities in the ground; that where neither tree, nor shrub, nor plant could flourish there they would most likely find it in the decaying beds of long forgotten forests. And so they began to dig down for what before they had only to pick up.

Although, even in the palmy days, the actual digging of the gum was looked upon by the respectable as rather a shady profession, many a man got his start to commercial success that way, and so long as money could be made fairly easily the decent settler would sometimes be found on the fields along with the adventurer and the pariah. In the beginnings of the industry men were free to dig anywhere without licences, but, as the possibilities of the trade were recognized, the landowners, both state and private, began to demand their share of the pickings, and with capitalization a good deal of the romance went out of the life. As the years went on it became increasingly hard to make money. Grounds were gone over by succeeding droves of diggers who went deeper and deeper each time, and who left less hope and fewer chances to those who followed. When it came to the day that a bare existence was all that a man working for himself could expect to make, the fields became more and more merely a refuge for the worthless and the hopeless, and to say a man was a digger was to call him an outcast as well.

The simplicity of the outlay was one of the reasons why men of no resources took to the life. All the tools needed were a probing spear, a spade and a kit or sack. The market was the nearest store, unless a man was under contract to the owner of his field for his output. He scraped the dirt off his gum or not, as he pleased; the store would take it either way. But if he was thrifty, which he seldom was, he did his own scraping and got the higher price.

For living conditions he had the freest and cheapest thing in the world. The problem of unearned increment never troubled him. Those privileges that men acquire as the perquisites of propinquity made no claims upon his gratitude. He lived alone, and rarely looked for company. When he had staked out his claim on likely ground, he hunted for the stream or spring that nature seldom denied him, and chose the one as far away from anybody else as he could get. There, under skies often wet, but otherwise amiable, especially in the far north, he made a dwelling after the finest traditions of simplicity. Either he put up a tent, sometimes new, or made a hut of sacks and mud and ti-tree, or he built a nikau whare, an art learned from the Maoris, out of the broad-leafed native palm. For weeks, perhaps, he would not see a soul. Then driven by loneliness, or the need for a fresh lot of food, or the craving for whisky, he would carry off the gum he had ready, and "go on the razzle-dazzle" at the public house that every gum-store ran as a sure getter of substantial profits. If the owner was generous he did not let a digger drink all his money, but set aside for him some of his old food stock against the day he should go home. Then when the rest of his earnings had disappeared in doubtful whisky the thoughtful capitalist turned him out to sober him up again.

In the days when men worked mostly for themselves it might be a long time before a man who did not turn up as usual at a store was missed. He was likely to change his market once in a while, seeking a more generous buyer or better food. If he never turned up again, no one but a pal who had taken a special interest in him would try to find out whether he was dead, or had merely moved on to some other field. It was this freedom that attracted the characters that have made the gum-fields famous as a playground for the reckless and the damned.

Of all the English derelicts who have formed the majority of the floating population, the man who professed to be related to nobility has always been the most familiar type. The native born colonial, who affected to despise the ways of birth and breeding—with some reason, since he so often saw men of birth and breeding end their days in borrowed huts with no company but the wekas and the swamp rats—had a habit of sarcastically dubbing every Englishman who ever mentioned a title as "The Earl," uttered always with mock reverence. And it was a common saying that there were more titled Englishmen on the fields than ever came out of England.

The shades of suicide and murder have always stalked abroad upon the gum lands. Whisky and the loneliness have brought many a man to the jump into a swamp, or to a shot that no one heard, or to the rarer use of a razor, while the poaching of claims put the brand of Cain upon most of those who killed under the open sky. After a man had staked out a claim with the sticks that were often the only mark of occupation, no one could steal a march upon him and work his ground until he removed the signs. A break of this unwritten law was followed by swift vengeance.

Settlers who have tried to reclaim old fields for cultivation have come every now and then upon a skeleton out in the open in the fern, a skeleton nobody ever bothered to hide, because there were a thousand chances to one against its ever being found. And then, if it had been found, there was nobody interested enough to bother to suspect anybody of the deed. If a digger found a body in the fern he would look to see that it was really dead, and if so he left it, and said nothing.

Much of this Ross knew as he followed Asia, and the stories he had heard peopled the shades around him with a grim company of the lost men, and intensified his sense of the haunting melancholy of those open wastes that he felt rather than saw in the darkness around him. He wished he could see more as they went, but it took all his care to keep easily upon his feet as he dodged the treacherous remains of rotten stumps, jumped the pigmy ravines that split the track, and avoided other pitfalls of the narrow path that had been dangerously pocketed by the winter rains with holes that would break an unwary ankle.

On either side of the way he could see in the circle of light cast by the lantern that every inch of the ground had been turned by the spade, some of it recently; and Asia told him that a field was like the widow's oil, that men would poke about on much dug ground hoping that something had been missed by those who had gone before.

In places the pipe clay was so hard beneath their feet that the sound of their steps carried far into the night. They passed small clumps of scraggy ti-tree, and went over rises that had not seemed half so high from the range above. But the lack of real height and depth about them seemed to bring the glow of the milky way down about their ears. On the low horizons the stars seemed to spring up at their feet, and the zephyr that stirred the fern seemed to come clear from the heart of the universe.

They felt extraordinarily alone, for not a live thing moved round them till they came to a swamp. Then there was suddenly a ghostly movement in the rapoo and the reeds, and something they could not see rose up and filled the night with a mysterious fluttering.

Asia put the lantern under her dress, and when they got their sight they saw black specks against the stars.

"Swamp hens," she said briefly, as they watched.

As they went on again they smelt the rankness of the mud and the stagnant water, a rankness that stung their nostrils long after they had left the cause of it behind them.

At last, as they dipped down into a little gully, they saw a blackness looming out ahead of them, and soon afterwards the lantern showed the sacking walls of a hut made on a ti-tree frame. Before they got to the doorway a horrid sound that made Ross shudder was coughed out of the darkness at them.

"Good God!" he exclaimed. "What's that?"

"Consumption, the cough; have you never heard it before? Don't come in. If I want you I'll call you. There's no reason why you should see it. Uncle David said he was pretty bad."

She spoke softly, but he saw she was bracing herself to do what she had come to do.

As she went in he moved into the shaft of dim light that the lantern sent back into the heavy shadows.

The first thing he looked for inside was the figure on the low sacking stretcher over which Asia leaned. But he could see little of what lay beneath the dark blanket. As the sound of another wrenching cough burst from the sick man, Ross remembered with a pang of fear that Asia was breathing that poisoned air, and for a moment he felt she was taking risks no dying man was worth. Then he was ashamed of himself, but he was relieved to see that she took antiseptics out of her kit and used them liberally.

He looked curiously round the hut, searching for something to show what manner of man had lived in it. But for furniture there was only an empty box used as a table, with a tin mug and some plates, a pipe and tobacco, and some stale bread upon it. In the open zinc chimney there *hung* a suit of dungarees above the cold ashes of a fire that had not been lit for days. A gum spear and a spade leaned against the sack wall. There was a heap of clothes on the earth floor in one corner, with a dirty copy of *The Auckland Weekly News* near it. And the only other asset the sick man had was a small pile of unscraped gum, not enough to buy him food for a week.

Ross took it all in at a glance, and with the realization of its misery he felt his throat turn hard and dry.

Then he saw Asia take out a little billy she had brought and some matches, and with them in her hands she came out to him. He saw her lips were set against a show of feeling.

"Allen, there's a spring quite near, below us a little—there's the path. Get some water and make a fire and warm it. I must wash him."

"Wash him," he repeated, guessing what a revolting thing that would be.

"I can't let him die dirty," she said firmly. "Even if I knew he would go in an hour I should wash him."

Ross turned away from her, seeing her through a mist, and found his way by striking matches to the spring. As he looked about for sticks and lit the fire, which every colonial can make out of doors by instinct, he exaggerated the simple operation into something that seemed to stand out as a landmark in his life. As he sniffed the burning wood, and looked up through the smoke into the stars, he forgot the shadow of death hovering over the hut. For he was full of the thought of life, life and its wonders of love and romance.

When the water was warmed he carried it to the door. Asia had just finished feeding the sick man with sips of broth. Waving Ross back, she came forward to take the water.

"Let me wash him," he begged, feeling that he could not bear to see her do it.

She looked eloquently at him, but shook her head.

"No, you stay outside. He has bad bedsores—you wouldn't know how to do it. I can manage. I've done it before."

He went back to his little fire, sitting so that he could look in at her. He knew by the expression of her face as he watched her work, mostly underneath the blanket, that it was a sickening job, but he guessed she did not shirk one bit of it. She stopped twice to help the poor wretch over fits of coughing, and when she had finished washing him she worked an old sheet over him, and bathed his body again with alcohol.

Then, as he lay in comparative comfort for a few minutes, the digger's lips moved. Ross could not hear what he said, but he saw Asia move the things off the box, take something out of her kit, and sit down beside him. And then he heard the first words of the f[illegible]enth chapter of St. John. Sceptic and Socialist though he was he could not hear them without emotion. He had never tried to minimize their value to large numbers of the human race, but never since his childhood had they meant anything to him. But as Asia picked out the most comforting verses in the fourteenth and fifteenth chapters, and read them as he was sure they had never been read before, he felt that the spirit of them was the spirit that had saved and always would save humanity from itself, the spirit of the reformer, the dreamer and the idealist.

As Asia closed with the verse "I will not leave you comfortless, I will come to you," she seemed to Ross as she sat in her white dress, her golden head a little bowed, to be indeed the spirit of Christ come to cheer the dying man into the unknown future. A mist covered his eyes as he saw her kneel down, and heard her pray a simple little prayer that God would comfort the dying man, and forgive him, and give him rest. Setting his teeth, he got up, and walked away along the path.

He had always known that he could not play with her. He had never wanted to. So far he had not allowed himself to come to a full expression of his love for her, feeling that if he once began he would have to abide for ever by the choice, and realizing that divorce at the outset of a political career, even in the tolerant colonies, was something of a handicap. And then it was by no means certain that he could get the divorce. But whether or no, he cared not now as he looked up at the stars, for she was finally bound to his soul with hoops of steel.

He was so full of his own thoughts that he did not hear the further fits of coughing in the tent. He was in the grip of a sweep onward that had carried him away into the future, to visions of obstacles overcome and victories won. He started when he heard his own name come to him out of the night.

Walking back, he saw Asia poking something into the fire, and he saw that she had changed her dress for something dark. The lantern and the kit were on the ground near her.

"Yes?" he asked.

"He's dead," she said, her voice breaking.

"Dead," he repeated stupidly.

"Yes—that last fit of coughing. They often go like that. Poor thing, but, oh, it's a blessing—he might have lingered for weeks." Her voice ended in a sob.

Something twisted Ross's throat so that he could not speak. He saw mechanically that she was burning her white dress.

"What are you doing?" he asked hoarsely, because he could think of nothing else to say.

"I have to burn everything up that I can," she answered, forcing calmness into her voice.

Turning from her, he took up the lantern and walked into the hut to look upon the dead digger, who now lay wrapped in a sheet, his eyes closed. It was hard to tell what kind of a man he had been, for prolonged dying had taken all the distinctiveness out of him. There was no meaning in his grey face. He was simply skin and bone. Ross had never seen a dead thing that was so inexpressive of anything but naked misery.

He moved away from it with a groan. Just outside the hut door he saw a heap of the box, the blanket, the dead man's clothes. Asia had emptied all her antiseptics over them. With his foot Ross moved them down to the fire.

It was mostly in silence that they burned everything that could hold the fraction of a germ. When they had finished, there was not a thing left in the hut but the sheeted corpse on its stretcher, the tin vessels, the spade and the spear; and they had nothing to carry back with them but the lantern and the matches.

"What happens to him now?" asked Ross, when they had stamped out the fire.

"We report his death to Harold Brayton; he's the coroner. Uncle David will give the certificate. They may come to see the body or they may not. Our word is enough. And the pater will send men to bury him somewhere here in the fern. He never got any letters. No one knew who he was. He's lost. That's all." Her tone was a damning indictment of something and somebody.

Ross gripped her arm.

"Come away," he commanded. "We have done all we can. For God's sake let's get away from it."

Their tongues loosened as they walked, and the impatient anger of their youth and strength vented itself upon the institutions of ages. To them the pitiful end of the dead man was a synonym for the failure of civilization. It represented waste, cruelty and disorganization, stupidity and indifference. They talked of the awakening of humanity through the teachings of socialism, of the hopelessness of established systems, of the great future before the Labour Party of New South Wales. And that brought them to themselves and the part that Ross, and through him the part that she, too, would play in it. And the great thing now to both of them, as they retraced their steps, was that they were of the same mind as to how the world was to be remade.

By the time they had reached the ridge above the river

it was long after midnight. Their passion for the regeneration of mankind had worn itself out for the time being, and they stopped to look at a late moon of smoky gold that rose from the black shades of Pukekaroro. It was natural that looking together at her they should forget the failure of civilization.

They had not stood a minute before the realization of their own youth and nearness and common desires obliterated the troubles of the rest of the world from their minds.

They were caught by a conspiracy in themselves acting in concert with the time and the place.

Asia dropped the lantern, and it went out.

She did not stoop to pick it up because Ross's arm swept round her, pinning her helpless against him.

"God! I love you, you beautiful thing," he cried.

And so they, too, for a time under the midnight stars, forgot the dead man in the hut.

CHAPTER XXVII

TWO nights later, as David Bruce was walking alone towards his shanty from the store, he was arrested by a light shining from the dining-room of Tom Roland's house. He could not have told exactly why he stopped, for it was not unusual for a light to be there even at midnight. He speculated about it, knowing the boss was away, and that no one was ill. Suspecting why it still burned, he turned towards it with a sigh.

He walked in by the back door unannounced, and, as he expected, he found Alice sitting up alone. One glance at her face told him why she waited.

"You are sitting up for her," he said.

She resented the reproach in his tone.

"David, I cannot bear it any longer. I must speak. She stays out later and later every night."

He stood before her, making no attempt to sit down.

"Do you think speaking to her will stop that?" he asked wearily.

"Yes. She will have to listen to me. I have something to say that will make her listen."

For once he missed the significance of her positive tone.

"She will listen, my dear. She will listen courteously enough. She will tell you she understands your feeling and your point of view. And you know what she will do after that, don't you?"

She looked up at him and away again. He saw that her lips were set in an agony of determination, and that she was unmoved.

"She will do exactly what she wants to do," he went on quietly.

She dropped her face into her hands.

"She will not, David. Not after I have talked to her."

"Oh, my dear girl"—the impatience in his tone stung her—"don't you know yet that talking to people of her type does no good. It would be all right for Betty and Mabel. They would be scared off anything at the first breath of criticism. You would have to save them because in the end they would want to be saved. But do you think people like Asia and Ross are going to allow any one to regulate their feelings for them? For God's sake do see it before it is too late."

As he spoke her lips trembled, and tears welled up in her eyes. It hurt him to see that her recent colour was almost gone. It hurt him to know that she was still her own enemy. He determined to try once more to get her to see that she was not responsible for the sins of the world.

Leaning down, he pulled her up to face him.

"Come out with me," he said softly. "Get a cloak. And be quick. It would be a pity for her to find us here."

Mechanically she found a wrap and followed him outside. He led the way along the path towards his shanty.

"It's all right," he said, sensing her misgivings. "No one will see us, and no one will come."

She stood on the porch while he found and lit his lamp. Then he set his most comfortable chair so that the light would fall behind her. Nervous because she knew she was going to hear something unpleasant, she sat down stiffly, keeping her wrap about her shoulders.

The lamplight glowed dully upon metal things in the room, a tobacco jar, brass candlesticks, gilt picture frames. Bruce made no pretence of running elegant bachelor quarters. His shanty was a large unpapered room, lined with oiled boards, the ceiling showing the rafters. It had an open fireplace at one end, and rugs of no particular kind upon the floor. He had one bunk, rugged and cushioned like a lounge, several chairs, rough book and other shelves, a doctor's cabinet, and three tables. On two of the tables and on many of the shelves was spread a strange assortment of objects, good and bad. The good had been gifts from Alice, Asia and Mrs. Brayton; the bad, the sentimental offerings of numerous patients.

The room had an extraordinary atmosphere of comfort. Asia had always declared it was the friendliest room she had ever seen, that it had the peace of a confessional, and the welcome of a wayside inn. The only door, which faced the green hill and was shaded by a small porch, was always open, night and day, whatever the season or the weather, and the only things, as far as Bruce knew, that had entered with designs upon his property were dogs, cats and a calf.

Alice had long been familiar with every detail of it by day, but pursuing her policy of extreme discretion, she had never visited him alone at night. Her doing so now had a suggestion of adventure that affected her, making her still more nervous, and complicating the sources of her mental dislocation.

Bruce drew a chair near to her, putting his pipe and tobacco on a table within reach. The something about his leisureliness that had always fascinated her helped now to still the jump of her nerves.

The years had deepened the lines of suppression on Bruce's face, and had streaked his black hair with grey, but they had not dulled the humorous gleam of his brown eyes, or put even a suggestion of age into the easy movements of his limbs. Six years before this he had finally beaten out his periodical craving for whisky, and though that battle for the complete possession of his soul had not left him scatheless it had added to the power of his attractions and to his ability to make the most of them.

The triumph of his life had been his management of his friendship with Alice Roland. He knew she had never realized to what an extent he had controlled it. He had been amazed at the way in which she had finally settled down to it as something that would never change. He had wondered that she could go on living with Tom Roland as she had for years without open signs of revolt. He never had been quite able to understand her extraordinary acceptance of life as other people arranged it, her submission to her husband, her lack of fighting quality, of a sense of adventure. On the other hand he had never ceased to be astonished at her powers of endurance, her infinite capacity for silent suffering. He knew that her ill health had been the chief agent in cultivating her lack of initiative and her pitiful desire for peace, but there had always been something he could not get at in her. It had piqued his curiosity again and again.

He knew that though she had altered much in the last few years she was not half as broad-minded as she, with a pleasant vanity, had supposed herself to be, and he felt sadly, as he looked at her now, that in spite of all that he had tried to do for her, she was ill-prepared to meet the facts of life that were now about to descend upon her. Accustomed as he was to introducing the facts of life to unsuspecting people he could never do it without a full appreciation of the pain and disruption it caused.

With a short appealing look at her he dropped his head into his hands, and stared at a frayed piece near the corner of his rug. She looked apprehensively at him, fearing now that he was withholding some bad news.

"What is it, David? You are worrying about them too. I know it."

But she saw she was mistaken when he raised his face.

"I am not. I see no reason for worrying about them. It's you I'm thinking about."

"Me, David?" She returned his quiet look with one of grieved astonishment.

"Yes, you. I really don't know any one else that I should be worrying about at present."

She drew herself up a little, pushing back her cloak.

"Do you mean to say, David, that you don't believe those two are in any danger?"

"Even if they were I should not be worrying about them.

Why worry about people who will never worry about themselves? It's silly."

He turned to the table, and deliberately filled his pipe and lit it. Though she rarely criticized him, Alice thought his action seemed heartless. Her eyes hardened.

"David, I don't expect you to feel about this as I do, but I did think you would understand why I feel, and that you would help——"

Her voice broke in spite of her effort to keep it steady.

He melted at once, and, leaning forward, took her hands. Before he spoke he straightened out a piece of lace on her throat that had been crumpled under her cloak. He noticed for the first time that she was wearing a violet dress he liked, and that she had evidently expected him to dinner.

"You believe they are in danger," he began gently, "in danger of what?"

"You know, David."

"My dear, I don't know what you think the danger is. Do you mean that they may live together, or that they may be suspected, or found out? Just what do you mean by the danger?"

"David, if they do anything they will be found out."

He continued to look at her with solemn gentleness.

"Supposing you knew for certain they would not be found out, would you worry about what they did?"

Her eyes fell away from his.

"Would you?" he repeated.

"It's no use asking me that question," she said impatiently. "The two things go together. They cannot go on doing anything and not be found out."

"Do you know what they intend to do? Have they told you?"

He did not mean to hurt her by the question. It brought home to her the fact that she was probably the last person they would ever tell. As he saw her lips tremble he squeezed her hands.

"My dear. I did not mean that to hurt. But you know

you have nothing to go on but suspicions. Now, you may as well know what you really do have to face. I know, for they have told me."

She sat very still while he talked on, finding that in spite of what he said she was relieved to have it put plainly so that she could see what it meant.

"The thing they have to face is that Ross may never be able to get his divorce. Unless his wife applies for it he cannot at present. He left her. He keeps her. She is willing to live with him. Unless she goes mad, dies, or lives with some man, he will not be free. Ross and Asia are in love. He lives now as a single man. A useless, hysterical and selfish woman is the only thing between them and the conventions. They have a chance here that may never come to them again in life to love each other in freedom. Lynne, you and I will know. Tom will suspect. No one else will ever know unless we tell them, and none of us will ever tell them. In the autumn they will go to Sydney, not by the same boat, but she will go a month or so after him. They will not attempt to live openly together. They will work together. He plans to make her his secretary. They will not be reckless, or yell defiance at the world. They will know how to keep away from scandal. They both have fine and loyal friends who will cover up their tracks. As time goes on their friendship will be known and its possibilities suspected, but they will win the world to believe in their friendship, and to shut its eyes to what may happen between them in private. People like them can do that to-day. It can be done in every city. There are several cases in Auckland. You have met one pair often at the Hardings. Now I want you to see at once that you cannot stop one bit of all this. There are even people whom you like who would blame you if you tried to. Not that that would stop you. But if you will take my advice you will shut your eyes and see nothing until you are told, and then you will reserve your judgment."

He clasped his hands over hers as he stopped, and sitting up again, lit his pipe, and puffed slowly.

Alice sat very still looking away from him. She began to repeat to herself the things he had said, so that she would remember them all for consideration afterwards. She did not cry, now that she knew the worst, or feel like crying. She did not feel as wretched as she had expected to feel. She felt more than anything else a buzz and confusion of conflicting emotions and opinions that made her head spin. She sat clenching her hands in the effort to get some order into her thoughts. Things she wanted to know got mixed up with things she was trying to think.

At last something in the peace of the room and the stillness of the night, and the comfortable sight of David Bruce smoking soothed her brain. When she turned to him she was ready with the questions.

"Do you think they are right, David?"

The absence of hostility in her voice pleased him.

"I don't know that I have to decide that. They think they are right. If we judge them at all, we must judge them by that." He saw that for the time being she had forgotten her fears, and that something else was on her mind.

"You don't think she will be any different if she lives with him?"

He looked curiously into her questioning eyes in which there was more than a grain of unbelief.

"My dear, do you really believe that a girl is branded in some mysterious way if she has relations with a man on the prehistoric side of the marriage ceremony? Do you think the failure to repeat a few words alters cells?"

"It alters minds, David."

"Oh, no. It's the attitude of other people towards your action that affects your mind when it is affected. There is nothing in the action itself that does it."

"You would not think any differently of her, David? You *would* respect her just the same?"

"Oh, God!" He sat up suddenly. "You have known me for fifteen years, and you ask that question!"

But she continued her questions.

"You would marry a woman who had lived with a man?"

"Certainly, if I loved her. It would make no difference at all. I can't imagine why you ask. You know how I feel about these things."

"I know how you have talked when we have read books," she said slowly.

"I see, and you thought I was only talking." He leaned towards her again. "Well, I wasn't. And nothing that Asia could do with Ross could affect my opinion of her. Do you understand that now?"

He looked almost resentful. He could not understand her doubt.

"Yes," she answered, and looking down, she seemed to him to be facing some new difficulty.

He guessed rightly what it might be.

"Have you remembered that there may be a child, David?" She could not keep solemnity out of her tone for that.

Ready for her, he answered at once quietly.

"Of course. But that will be provided for. You know people of their type don't have children to-day unless they want them."

Although she had heard this hinted at before, it came to her with the force of a shock now that it was mentioned in connection with a child of hers.

"My dear girl, this comes as a shock to you because you don't know human beings. You have never really wanted to know them. You have shirked knowing them. You have divided them up into the good and the bad. You have put the people you liked with the good and the people you did not like with the bad. You have said to yourself there are certain things the good will never do, certain things the bad are likely to do. You have thought human beings were all of a piece. Because you have classed me with the good you would not believe I would do things you thought wrong.

As a matter of fact, I have done many things you would think infamous. You do not know Asia. You do not know how she thinks or what she would do, or what she knows. She knows more of life than you ever did or ever will. You can't tell her anything she doesn't know. It may be a stale joke to say the daughters of to-day could educate their mothers, but it is also a great truth. You do not know one-half of the things that have happened round you in this little place. You did not want to know, so we all formed a conspiracy to keep everything unpleasant away from you. You have had troubles enough of your own, God knows. But you have let them shut you up, my dear. That is the pity. Now, if you will only bear the truth, you have the chance to help. Give up judging where you don't know. It's so useless."

As she listened to him a conviction of failure, the most numbing and despairful she had ever known, swept over her. Remembering it afterwards, she wondered if it was under such stress of feeling that people committed suicide. When he saw tears of dumb misery coming to her eyes he pushed his chair beside hers, threw his arm round her shoulder, and began to comfort her, talking brokenly.

"Don't worry about it now, dear. Leave the past alone, and begin again. See Asia and Ross as they are—two fine young things who want to go through fire and water for each other. Let them. Whatever happens to them they won't whine or upset the world. They may be hurt—they are bound to be hurt whatever they do, courageous and thoughtful people are always hurt, no one can stop that, any sort of life hurts them—but they won't be broken. That is the great thing. I know it is hard to realize, but things have changed. You keep thinking of England as you and I knew it. You think they will be damned, but they will not out here. They will only be suspected—people will wonder, that's all."

She became amazed as he went on that he seemed to have no convictions about their action. There was nothing in his words to show that he had any regard for standards, that he recognized moral laws or the necessity for social safeguards. And yet she knew that his life had belied the lax philosophy that a chance listener would have inferred from his speech. She dare not listen to his heresy. It would have made of her whole life too ghastly a sacrifice to be contemplated.

"David," she burst out passionately, "I don't care what you say. There are laws—there ought to be laws. Where would we end? I believe we ought to make sacrifices to keep them. I believe the finest people do—you have yourself, you know you have—there are ideals. I must believe Asia right or wrong, wise or unwise. I can't let it go at just leaving them alone—I can't be indifferent. People may be more charitable—I suppose they are—but it can't alter my feeling."

"My dear, I know that." He turned and faced her. "I know you can't help feeling. I'm feeling about it myself. I think it is a pity they have to compromise with life that way. But I don't see that it is any worse a compromise than—than your marriage, for example."

Her eyes fell in swift confusion.

"You see, my dear," he went on gently, "there are things Asia could say to you if you began to talk to her. I can't believe that you don't see it. And what you ever thought you could say that would convince her I don't know."

As she threw her head up suddenly he saw that words had been stopped on the tip of her tongue, and that she was startled that she had nearly let them slip.

"What were you going to say?" he asked with curiosity. He saw fear and indecision in her eyes. He leaned forward, looking hard at her. "Do you mean to tell me that there is anything that you are afraid to say to me?"

"Oh, David," she threw out her hands to him. "There is something I have never told you—I don't know why—I have wanted to, but I was afraid it—it might make a difference. But now I know it won't, oh, David, it won't, will it?"

"Oh, do you have to ask me that?"

Even then she looked half fearfully at him as she answered.

"When I was eighteen I did as she is going to do, and she is the child."

"What!" he cried out. "That! that!" His voice broke off as if he had suddenly found himself alone. At the same time he looked at her as if she had just dropped through the ceiling. Searching his eyes for every shade of expression, she could see nothing but his incredulous amazement.

"You kept that from me," he stammered. "All those years you were afraid to tell me—that's what it was. And you were afraid to tell me. And it was that—God! now I see—it was that——"

He ended as if he were again talking to himself.

Curiously calm now that she had told him, Alice saw that her confession had been also an explanation, and that it seemed to answer some riddle that had long puzzled him. If there had been any thought in her mind of amazing him, any desire to give him the shock of his life, she would have had a sense of flattering success, but all she felt in the moment following his words was that his opinion of her was really not lowered, and then that he was hurt because she had never told him before.

"You were afraid to tell me——" he began again.

"Oh, David," she caught one of his hands, everything else swept out of her mind by that look of positive pain. "Don't think it was that. I—I often wanted to tell you, I know it would have helped me, but—but—oh, I don't know. But do understand—if you were a woman you would never tell that."

"Have you never told any one?"

"I—I did tell Mrs. Brayton—never any one else. Oh, David, don't look like that! It wasn't that I didn't trust you."

"Oh, yes, it was." He shook his head sadly. "And I confessed to you once."

"That was quite a different thing," she pleaded.

"Was it? Well, all right. But I have always prided myself on the fact that nobody would ever hide anything from me. I see it was a delusion, and I thought I hadn't any." His head dropped into his hands.

Alice stared at him. She could not believe that he was thinking more of that than of the thing she had told him. She sat tense in her chair, her hands clasped on her knee, unable to think, seeing as in a dream his stooping form before her and his hands pressed into his face.

But David Bruce's thoughts had swiftly turned from the discovery of the unsuspected delusion to the other aspects of the thing he had heard. In a flash he saw that her whole life had been a reaction from the pitiful mistake of her youth. He saw that the years had been one long penance, one determined sacrifice, one everlasting fear of being found out, one long support of the respectabilities, all the more fierce because she had suffered so much from her own failure to observe them.

He saw now why she had so carefully guarded her reserves, why she had been afraid to open out, why she had fought against the insinuating approach of confidences, why she had shut down again and again on discussions that might bring her near to an expression of opinion on moral lapses.

He guessed now that her marriage had been an escape to begin with, and afterwards a cross to be borne, a duty to be observed at any cost. Her early attitude to himself was now explained. It was all as clear to him as daylight.

He realized too, in those first minutes, that she would see this repeating of history with Asia as a Nemesis, an inevitable result of her own action.

And seesawing back and forth in these flashes of review and realization were moments of astonishment that he had not seen it before, and that she had been strong enough to keep it from him.

Because his natural responses were at first judicial it was a few minutes before the facts became emotionalized in his mind. Then the tragedy of the sacrifice and the waste sickened and enraged him. With a groan he sat up to find Alice's eyes devouring his face uneasily.

Impulsively he threw out his arms to her, and with a look that spread reverence about her like a soft and gracious garment he dropped on his knees, and buried his face in her lap. They sat like that for some time before he raised his face.

"Can you tell me about it, dear?" he asked gently.

"Yes, I can now, David." Her eyes shone at him.

Getting up again, he put his arms about her. At intervals while she talked his hands closed and relaxed upon her arms, but he said nothing. Though she hardly looked at him, she never for a moment found it difficult to go on with her story.

"I didn't know anything, David—no one had ever told me—my mother was dead. I had lived a lot to myself and I always felt so much, and I read silly romances till I longed for a husband. We were so shut up—my father wouldn't let us see men—and I don't know what was the matter with me, I suppose it was too much sex—but I craved to be engaged and married. I supposed it was wrong and I tried to fight it, but it was no use, and when I was eighteen I met the man. He was older than I—he was thirty—and he was the handsomest man who was ever seen in our town. Oh, it was the same old story, David. I attracted him and that made me infatuated, and when my father forbade him to call we met on the sly. He said we were engaged, and he promised to marry me—and so it happened. Only for two weeks, David, and then I got frightened. And one night he did not come—he went away and never came again. And then—then I found I was going to have a child."

She moved a little in her chair and went on.

"I nearly died of horror. I don't know now how I went through it. I couldn't commit suicide—I was religious. I felt I had to think of the child—that saved me. I took what money I had, and came out to Australia. My father did not even say good-bye to me—I never saw him after he found out. One brother helped me, but none of them ever wrote to me. Asia was born in Sydney, and I hadn't a ring or anything, so people guessed. But one woman, good kind soul, bought me a wedding ring and made me widow's clothes, and told me to go to New Zealand as a widow, and never to tell anybody—and to marry, if I got the chance, for the sake of the child."

As she thought she heard him groan she paused and turned her face, but he was staring ahead, and made no move to look at her.

"It was the wrong done to the child that obsessed me—it nearly drove me mad. I felt I had to save her. I would have told any lies to save her—I knew I was damned anyway—so I came to Christchurch with my piano and hardly any money. I couldn't stand the cold and I wasn't getting on, and one day, I remember every bit of it—it was snowing, and I was two miles from my room, with Asia—I had been in a shop and I lost my purse. I didn't find it out till I got outside. I went back, but no one had seen it. That was the last straw—it had nearly all my money. I just sat down on a chair and cried—you see what a coward I was—I felt I would die, and the child too, that nothing could save us——"

Her voice broke a little, but she recovered it and went on.

"Tom Roland was in that shop, and he saw me and came up. He looked so kind—and somehow I knew he was honest. He offered to lend me money, and he called a cab and took me home. I don't know how it was, but he got part of my story—he dominated me, I was so helpless. He told me he was to be there only a week, and he urged me to come north to Auckland where he knew people. He said he would get me pupils and he left fifty pounds with me—I couldn't stop him. I prayed about it till I was sick, but I couldn't see anything else to do. So I came, and he started me, and then he said he wanted to marry me—he had never touched me before—I didn't know that he cared——"

She paused again, and sat very still for a while. She felt Bruce's fingers grip into the flesh of her shoulder, but still he said nothing.

"He said he cared, David. He seemed to, but I—I did not love him. I told him I liked him. He said that was enough, that he could make me love him. And I knew he was liked—I knew he was the sort of man that would get on—and there was Asia. Oh, David, and I knew I would never get on—I had belonged to a family that made parasites of its women. No woman in it had ever earned her living. I could not face poverty. I had no commercial sense. I did not know how to manage people. I could not advertise myself—I thought that was vulgar—I could not stand alone. He dominated me, and I thought it was the best thing for the child, so I married him."

"He took me in good faith—I was the attractive and respectable woman he wanted for his wife. His belief in me made me more afraid than ever. I felt I had to be his slave because I had deceived him—and I did want peace. But there was no peace. I got so little sleep, he was irritable, he hated crying children—and he was so awfully alive. He always dominated me. I grew so afraid of him. I could never manage him—you know how I was—and it was just as bad as it could be when we came here. I did not see how I could live shut up with him—and then you——"

Turning, she saw that his face was set in lines of desperation.

"I saw that you would dominate me too, if I ever let you. It terrified me when I saw that I could love you. I don't know what was the matter with me. I could not stop myself caring. I tried, but I couldn't and I knew if you did anything—I was afraid of myself and I thought he would find out, and kill us, or make scenes. And so I was afraid of you, David, afraid of you——"

As she spoke he sprang out of his chair with a groan.

The cool detachment of her voice had maddened him to the point where he could not hear another word. The tragedy that had long since wreaked its worst upon her and was now only an ache in her memory had become to him, through her quiet telling of it, vivified into a present intolerable wrong. One of his rare sudden rages seized him. Shaking, he strode to his door.

"Hell and damnation! God in heaven, damn you!" The words, ground out, ended in an indescribable sound as he clenched his fists at something out in the night. Then he seemed to crumple up as he put out his hands to hold on to the door.

After a suspensive moment Alice saw what was the matter with him, and her one thought was to minimize it as a cause for suffering.

"Oh, David, it is all over now. It does not matter——"

"It does matter!" he shouted, swinging round. "It will always matter! That ghastly waste! That stupid sacrifice! God! It makes me sick to think of it—sick—sick——" Staggering forward as he spoke, he tumbled on to his bed, and lay face downwards.

Alice got up from her chair, and stood looking uncertainly at him. She had seen him impatient, even angry. She had seen him hurt. But never before had she seen his control really broken. When she saw his body shake and heard something that sounded like a sob she felt miserably helpless.

"Oh, David, don't cry," she choked, falling on to her knees beside him, and gathering his head into her arms.

But she could not stop him, and there had been nothing in that two weeks of anxiety, fear and impotent anger half so disrupting to her as his terrible sobbing, for he cried like a beaten man. It was hard for her to understand that he suffered more in the sorrows of others than he did in his own, that he hated cruelty and injustice in the abstract as most people hate insults and injuries to themselves. She could not understand why her story had moved him so.

He had known her life at the bay, she thought, and she had managed to live, often comfortably for periods in which she had gathered strength to go on. It had not all been intolerable, or she could never have lived.

She knew as well as he did that her life had been a sacrifice and a waste, but she had known it for so long that the thought of it had ceased to rouse in her more than a dull despair. Lately she had sought to forget it, to shut it out of her consciousness, and she had succeeded even better than she had hoped until the present blow had revived it all for her. But even then, and in the telling of it, it had seemed more like a dream than a reality.

Stupidly at first she tried to comfort Bruce, and then seeing that she could not, she broke down herself. They cried together like two heart-broken children, till, recovering himself, he drew himself up on his bunk, pulled her beside him, and sat still with his arms about her.

For some time they did not attempt to speak. Suffering a physical reaction, he did not even try to think. When, at last she turned to him, ready to talk, she woke him out of his rare apathy.

"Don't think about it any more, David. It's all over now. It doesn't hurt me now."

He stared stupidly at her, realizing she was trying to comfort him.

"You see now why I feel about Asia," she went on in a low voice.

He roused himself.

"Oh, my dear, don't talk about them any more to-night. Let them alone. Let them alone. I can't talk about them, or anything."

His head dropped upon her shoulder as if he were a tired child.

She soon realized her own weariness as she sat half propping him, watching moths crowd about his lamp. Mechanically she followed the agitated circles of one much larger *than the* rest till it dashed itself against the globe and fell blistered and maimed upon the table, where it plunged up and down in tortured throes.

The sound of its thuds attracted Bruce's attention. He could not bear the sight of its frantic agony. He got up and crushed it under his ash tray.

The action helped him. When he turned to Alice he saw her for the first time for half an hour. Something in his eyes as he looked down at her brought her to her feet. They stood for a minute looking at each other. Then he threw out his arms and drew her against him, and began to kiss her as he had not dared to kiss her for a long time. Although he did it quietly and deliberately something about it arrested her.

In his own time he stood away from her, and she saw how utterly worn out he looked.

"I'd better go home, David."

"Yes." He saw how white she was. "We can't talk any more to-night."

But there was something she felt she must say.

"David, I wish now I'd told you, but I did want you to go on loving me, and I was afraid. I couldn't be sure—there are so few people like you—and it makes no difference?"

As if to be doubly sure she searched his eyes again.

"No difference whatever," he answered gently.

The peace of that certainty was the peace of absolution.

It was not till they were out upon the path that she remembered how much the night had revealed.

As if he saw he spoke about it.

"Don't do anything, about Asia, I mean, till you've seen me again, will you?" he asked.

"All right, David."

At the front gate he put his arms round her again.

"I can't tell you what I feel about it—your story. I could never speak calmly about it. God! it won't bear thinking about—I've got to forget it. Good night. I'll be here all day to-morrow; I'll see you in the evening. Think about what I said, about Asia and Ross—because your life was spoiled you don't have to spoil theirs. Good night."

Kissing her on the forehead, he turned away at once and stumbled homewards.

CHAPTER XXVIII

REFUSING to think any more that night, Alice dropped into a heavy sleep from which she was startled only by Asia's knock and the usual question as to whether she would get up or have her breakfast in bed. As the door was not opened she merely roused herself sufficiently to say she would have it in her room, then she sank back to doze for some minutes before she remembered that something had happened. At first she could not think what it was. She puzzled over scraps of sentences that danced about in her memory like a spot of light reflected on a wall from a moving mirror.

Then her mind cleared suddenly, and she saw herself back in Bruce's room, and remembered that she had told him her story, and that it made no difference to him. She was not as surprised at this as she might have been. It seemed now as if she had always known that she would tell him, and that he would understand. It was other things in the evening that crowded upon her attention, that stung her to wide-awakeness. She knew she had not dreamt them. She knew they were true. She told herself she had to decide what she was going to do about them.

She stared at her wall as if she saw there in letters of fire that Asia was going away with Allen Ross, and that nothing could stop her, as if she saw there in burning words the reason why she, of all people, was the one least able to help or prevent them.

"Good morning, Mother; how do you feel?"

As the door opened wide Alice jumped, and stared at the familiar face and form that hid a mind so much a stranger to her. She could hardly believe that the greeting and the tone were the same ones that she had heard with little variation all down the years.

"Oh," she exclaimed stupidly, startled into temporization. "I must have dozed again." Her head dropped back, and she pretended to be very sleepy.

As in a dream she watched Asia fix the blinds, regulate the windows, and bring the breakfast table to her bedside. Nothing could have looked more innocent of defiance to the traditions than she did. She was dressed in the simplest of blue gingham frocks, her hair piled loosely on her head. If she felt uncertainty or anxiety she was clever enough not to show it. So far sleeplessness had left no telling marks upon her. She looked as fresh as the early morning, as sweet as an ocean wind, as sure of herself as a river running swiftly to the sea. Seeing her now in the light of her chosen future, her mother could only feel that she was too unreal to be true.

As she finished settling the breakfast table Asia smiled into her mother's eyes with a studied pleasantness. She knew her mother had not slept well, but she ignored the fact as one of those she had made up her mind to ignore. She thought she knew exactly what her mother's attitude was and would be, she felt words on either side would be utterly useless, she hoped they would get through the summer on the mutual understanding that there was nothing to be said, and she meant, if her mother went along without an open break, to talk to her some time later, when they might both speak more calmly with so much of the experience behind them. She thought she knew what it would mean to her mother. But with the terrible ruthlessness of youth, combined with her own hard common sense, she told herself that her mother had had her chance, and that age had no business to cripple the impulses and desires and plans of youth.

She knew that so far her mother had had nothing but suspicions to go upon. She had learned from David Bruce *the night* before that he had till then said nothing, and she had supposed he would go on saying nothing, although she had not asked him to.

Alice had seen for some time that Asia was managing her. Sometimes it had amused her; sometimes it had hurt. She had made up her mind several times that she would not let it go on, but she had always succumbed weakly in the end, feeling that for the sake of peace she might as well, that it didn't matter. Now she saw that it might be the easiest way out of this crisis, that if she let herself be managed they might avoid the break that she dreaded as much as Asia did. She could not smile back at her, but she looked past her inquiringly at her dressing-jacket hanging over the back of the chair.

"It's going to be a hot day, Mother. You'd better not work in the garden," said Asia, as she reached for it.

"Oh, very well."

"Don't you want to sit up?"

Mechanically Alice drew herself off the pillows, while Asia helped her into her negligee.

"Now, don't let your coffee get cold, Mother," and with that she was gone, closing the door behind her.

"Don't work in the garden, Mother. Don't let your coffee get cold." The words rang on in Alice's ears with the dominant insistence of drum beats on a march. Alice had often been comforted by these expressions, which seemed to her the outward and visible sign of an inward care that she loved to think her children felt for her, but now she wondered how much it meant to Asia to say them, whether it mattered at all.

She did let her coffee get cold while she drifted into another conviction of failure so devastating that she would gladly have died as she lay there in bed.

Nothing but the fear that Asia might come in drove her finally to choke down as much as she could. In dismay she saw that there were four slices of toast when she could eat only one. As if she had been destroying criminal evidence she wrapped up the other slices in some paper and hid them in a bureau drawer till she could dispose of them later.

She dressed slowly and absent-mindedly, doing things in the wrong order, and fumbling as if she were recovering from an illness. After she had aired and made her bed and tidied up her room, she went out to sit in her veranda rocker on the shady side of the house, outside her window. The day was not yet far enough advanced for the heat to be uncomfortable, and a morning freshness still lingered above the river, which lay without a ripple below her. The scent of roses and honeysuckle filled the air about her. Plants and creepers grew and trailed about the veranda posts, so that she looked through a leafy frame away over the low lands into the western haze. The noises from the mill, the eternal reminder of the preëminence of her husband's brains, the embodiment of his vitality and his success, seemed to beat upon her ears with a more than usual arrogant aggressiveness.

For a long time she sat feeling too crushed to face or analyze the thing that had beaten her. All she could feel was that she was beaten.

By degrees she thought backwards over her life, but not in any sort of order or association or logical connection, and out of scrappy scenes she pieced an arraignment of herself, and some kind of explanation for her failure.

She was staggered to realize how little she knew of the people with whom she had lived. "You do not know human beings," Bruce had said. Now that she was alive to this fact she began to remember things that strengthened it. There flashed among others into her memory the story of a girl who had been found dead in a gully at the foot of Pukekaroro some years before. The case had come before Harold Brayton, and Mrs. Brayton had hinted to her what the girl had died of. But the story had been told her only in a guarded way. She had never taken in the full force *of it.* She had learned nothing from it. She saw now that owing to her own attitude stories had always been told her in a guarded way, the decent way, she had supposed.

She wondered if there was any tragedy going on now under her unseeing eyes. "You do not know one-half of what has happened round you in this little place," Bruce had said. She began to review her life in its relation to the village about the bay. She had seen it all grow out of the rushes and the coarse grass. She had seen every plot staked out. She had marked the progress from day to day of every little home—the planting of the houseblocks, the rapid running up of the frames, the weatherboarding, the roofing. Then she had watched for the families to come in. As it had been her duty to call on them she had always done so early in the first week, making herself as pleasant as she could, especially to the brides and bridegrooms, for whom she always felt an absurd sympathy, as if they were heading for some sorrow which she saw and they did not.

As Tom Roland had prospered, her sphere of benevolence had enlarged. The presents she took to the new babies became more ostentatious. She sent cakes and presents at Christmas time to the poorer families. When the bay school opened she became its patron. She went to the picnics and concerts, and gave out the prizes with nervous little speeches. She had been the Lady Bountiful of the village. She had been pleased to feel that she had entered into the lives of these people, that she had meant something to them in the way of an influence towards refinement and righteousness. She had liked to know that she was welcome in every house, that the children ran to meet her, that chairs were specially dusted for her to sit upon.

But now she saw that she had known only one side of these people, the side that mattered least, the party manner side. She had prided herself that people always behaved in her presence, that they took no liberties with her. She saw now that this meant that no one had ever come to her with a story of sin and shame, that no one had ever come to her with the cry "Help me" hot upon trembling lips. No one had ever come to her for the understanding that in desperate moments saves souls from despair.

She saw that every one had lied to her and she saw why. She saw that every one had conspired to shield her and she saw why. She saw that because she had shut herself off from life life had closed its gates to her. And she saw that she did not have to flee from life because life had maimed her, that she should have done as David Bruce had done, that she should have reached out to it, taken it with both hands and used it.

Slow tears ran unheeded down her cheeks as she saw that the scheme of respectability that she had preserved in the face of cruel odds was all wrong, that she had laboured for twenty years to build something that had been no real use to anybody, except, perhaps, as a comforting delusion to herself, that it had been merely a pleasant fiction to her, and that others had passed it by because it had touched their lives only in their lightest moments.

She wondered afterwards how she managed to face lunch. Fortunately for both her and Asia, Mabel and the children always came home from the bay school, and in the fuss of looking after them and getting them off again in time strained silences and forced conversations were eliminated.

Alice lay down afterwards for an hour or two, and then, drawing her chair to the east side, she sat down to continue her investigation. She was determined to see herself now as she was. She had thought she had become emancipated from much of her past. She had come home from the plays stirred about many things, her mind a ferment about the "intellectual assent," the "special case," individual rights. But her emotional reaction to the situation she had found in her own home had plunged her back into the arguments of Puritanism, to fixed principles, to inevitabilities, to all the bogies that follow in the train of fear and prejudice.

The more she thought about it the more she craved to get away from the people she had failed. She wondered how she could face them again with the full truth of her own futility crushing her. She asked herself what she meant to the members of her own family. Would Betty or Mabel come to her with their secret thoughts? Physically they were women now. How did they feel about it? She did not know. She had told them one or two essential facts. She suspected Asia had added to their knowledge, but what they realized of life she had no idea.

What was she to Bunty, a healthy roystering boy, at the intolerable age when everything feminine was beneath his notice, when a mother was the dragon who ordered him to wash his face, clean his boots, and go to bed at unkind hours? Would he come to her when life began to puzzle him?

What was she to Elsie, a sweet and gentle child, who played much alone, and never gave anybody any trouble. Did she see her mother as a remote personage who was not to be bothered, as somebody who occasionally graciously condescended to play with her, but who could never play her way? She remembered the child had been taught by Asia and the girls not to trouble her mother with her childish griefs.

What was she now to her husband—an attractive figurehead for the respectable family structure that in his own way he seemed to value, a woman admired by people whose education and position he was bound to respect because he knew they ran the world? If she meant any more to him than this she did not know.

What was she to Asia? She knew that Asia loved her; that she recognized "the bond," and that she always would. She knew Asia valued her powers of endurance. She knew they were knit together by a common experience that meant inexpressible things to both of them. But what did she really mean to-day to the girl whom yesterday she thought she knew, and to-day saw that she had never known and perhaps never would know? What had she ever done for Asia except question every new move she had made, shake her head with the advent of each new idea, and oppose more or less openly her free and fearless ways?

She saw herself as an automaton who droned "don'ts" monotonously whenever any one pulled its string or poked it with an inquiring finger. In her imagination she conjured up the figure she thought she must now be in Asia's eyes—a sort of demon of caution enclosed in a wet blanket, with ominous arms pointing ever to disaster. She exaggerated its forbidding aspects till it became a Frankenstein.

She went over the things that she and Asia had talked about in the last few weeks—the garden, the weather, a summer cover for her bedroom chair, her new clothes, the sunsets, and meaningless gossip about people in Auckland and at the bay. She saw now that only bitter personal experience had brought her to realize the truth of Mrs. Brayton's words, spoken years before. In the throes of a momentous experience, torn by doubts and indecisions as her mother knew she must have been, Asia had chattered to her of flowers and the weather.

She began to wonder what she really was now to David Bruce. How could he love her if she was what she now seemed to herself to be? What had kept his affection the warm and beautiful thing it had been? Did she know him? She had been stunned the night before to think he would do the "infamous" things he said he had done. If she did not know David Bruce whom or what in the world did she know?

She asked herself what she was now to believe. She saw she would have to take stock again of her faith. Could she believe that a thing that Bruce would do was wrong? If she did believe it was wrong what was to be her attitude towards him? If she did not condemn him for doing wrong things could she condemn anybody else? How did one judge? What constituted the "special case"? Were Asia and Ross to be classified under that heading? And supposing it really was certain that they would never be found out, would she be so disturbed about their wrong-doing then? Further, would she not even be prepared to tolerate an action that would prevent their being found out? No, never, she told herself, and then again, yes.

Through all this torture of indecision she wanted passionately to do the right thing. She prayed that she might not settle into indifference, into the easiest way. Though she no longer prayed to gods who were abstractions in the sky, she cried out to something not of herself, to the god in a blind and struggling humanity, the something that keeps it struggling in spite of the blindness.

When David Bruce came to dinner he found her in the front room beside the window. In her eyes he read much of what she had been through, and he saw that she turned as she always had to him for the way out. It was a minute before she saw that he, too, had been scored by the night before.

"Oh, I hope you did not worry about me, David?" as she held out her hands to him.

"I thought about you. I could hardly help that."

She noticed that his voice sounded tired and that he looked as if he had not slept. She forgot herself in thinking of him.

"Don't worry about me," she commanded. "You have all got to stop worrying about me."

A smile flitted across his eyes as he caught the new note of resolution.

He motioned to her to sit down, and took a chair near her. But he made no attempt to talk, knowing they would soon be interrupted. They both sat looking at each other wonderingly, but with the certainty that they meant the same to each other. Bruce was still asking himself how she had kept her story from him. She was still wondering what else there was about him she did not know. But the answers would have made no difference.

They did not talk much at dinner, but the children were accustomed to their quiet moods, and seeing that he was tired they thought nothing of it. Even Asia, absorbed in her own story, saw nothing unusual about their silence.

The sun was setting as they walked out to the veranda and drew chairs to their favourite place behind the rose-trees outside Alice's window. It had long been an accepted fact that they sat here undisturbed, unless it was by Roland, who occasionally sat there too, when he was at home. Asia had instilled into the minds of the rest of the family that the "elders" liked to be alone after dinner, and it was to her training that Bruce and Alice owed much of the privacy they enjoyed, a privacy they could not have arranged for themselves without attracting attention. Bruce had wondered many times whether it had been done innocently or with design. It was one of the things he admitted he did not know, and he admired Asia the more for being clever enough to keep the knowledge from him.

Soon after they settled themselves they saw her go down past the store, and along the spit to the little bridge that now spanned the channel to the other side. They watched her disappear into the bush, evidently to make her way up to the road and down to the cottage without passing through the mill grounds.

Bruce expected that Alice would make some appeal for sympathy, but she did not. She continued to stare into the sunset while he filled and lit his pipe. Presently he leaned towards her.

"Have you decided what you are going to do?"

She did not move as she answered, her eyes still fixed on the sunset:

"I suppose I must not speak—I see it might be no good—but I don't know what to do. I still feel I ought to do something. How can I sit on here and see her go every evening—and know—and know——" Her voice fell away to a whisper.

"My dear," he began very softly. "Don't you think that is just conceit? We are all such infernal egoists that we can't conceive that anything ought to go on without our assistance or resistance. We will think that we personally are so important to the march of progress, to the defeat of evil. We don't see that sometimes the best thing may be the elimination of ourselves."

She turned her head slowly, and looked into his questioning eyes.

"You are right, David. That is one of the things that is the matter with me—oh, dear, so much is the matter with me." Unexpectedly her voice ended in a sob.

He closed his hand upon her arm, and smiled at her.

"So much is the matter with most of us. You have no monopoly over the muchness."

She recovered herself. She determined to keep her mind clear of emotionalism, for there were many things she wanted to ask him.

"Wouldn't you tell her, David? I have always felt that if a man came into her life she ought to know."

"Why?"

"Well, it would make a difference to most men."

"It would make a difference to most of us if we knew everything about everybody. If we didn't have delusions about most people we could not endure the sight of them. Considering we cannot see the whole of people, by all means let us see as much of the pleasant side as possible, and remain in ignorance of the things that might hurt us. I'm not so grim a realist that I would not throw dust in my own eyes if I could. The trouble with me is that I can't, so I have learned to take the truth as pleasantly as may be. But the Lord forbid that I should always be ramming so uncomfortable a thing down other people's throats. I only do it to avoid what looks like something still more uncomfortable. Now, why tell Asia? What good would it do her or Ross to know? What would the knowledge save them from? It would hardly stop them doing what they want to do, which would be your chief object in telling them."

"But if you wouldn't tell them, David, you must think it would make a difference," she persisted.

"Supposing it would. I should call that a good reason for not telling them. If they were likely to find out from others, I might think differently, but they will never know unless you or I tell. What right have we to drop a useless and unpleasant fact upon innocent people?"

She looked at him without attempting to answer.

"The right thing in cases of this kind is the kind thing. And don't let the deception worry you. Deception is one of the kindest methods man ever used. It covers up more ugly sores, helps more people to fresh beginnings, and sees more people into peaceful graves than anything else on earth. There is hardly one of us that could afford to part with it. Could you? Could I?"

She sat very still considering his words. Watching her as he puffed at his pipe, he realized how much she had aged in the past week, and he saw that if she could not be roused she was likely to let herself be crushed. He remembered that she had not worn the brown dress since the dinner, that she had appeared only in her oldest clothes. He contrasted her with other women he knew, who, faced with disasters, got some subtle comfort from their gayest gowns.

"Why don't you wear that brown dress?" he asked abruptly.

"Why, David," she began, startled, and then her eyes fell before his quizzical gaze.

"You know, you are acting as if there had been a death in the family, when it is instead a matter of life seeking to renew itself. It ought to be an occasion for gaiety. Yes, I mean that. Now you wear your brown dress every second night if not every night, from now on, whether I'm here or not. If you have decided to let them alone, you may as well be pleasant about it."

Her attempt to look shocked was a failure. Although she would have curbed any desire to laugh outright, she could not help smiling at him. But she was in no mood to be light for any length of time.

"David, I am going to leave them alone, but I cannot be happy about it, not even to please you."

He closed his hand over hers.

"All right, but you will wear the brown dress?"

"Very well. I will do that to please you."

He smiled again, and patting her hand, returned to his smoke.

After some silence she returned to her questions.

"David, you think they are making a mistake, don't you?" She sat up straighter in her chair, and looked at him with almost a judicial air.

"Why, how do I know? Only time can decide that about any action. If they win the world to respect their friendship, it's a success; if they don't, it's a mistake. We will be able to decide in ten years' time."

"But you think something." She would not be put off."

"My dear, I know what you want to know. You want justification for leaving them alone, for perhaps helping them. You want something to say aloud in the night to that conscience of yours. Well, this is what I learned to say long ago to mine. When I am faced with a human being in a mess I am not faced with the problem of compiling rules and regulations for the whole human race for all the ages. That is the thing we forget when we get off our ridiculous remarks about public morality and social order. What have I to do with cumbersome abstractions when I am faced with a specific instance of the cruelty and injustice of ignorant human judgment? If I were lecturing in public on morals, or helping to frame a code, I should talk very differently from the way I do when a girl comes to me with the prospect of a broken life hanging over her. I prevent all the harm I can. I've kept some girls out of it here when I knew in time, and guessed they could be frightened out of going with men by a good talking to. But I did not preach to those who came to me with the harm done. That would have been very useful, wouldn't it?"

Alice dropped her head unexpectedly into her hands.

"Oh, David, what a failure I have been," she choked. "I have never helped anybody."

He tried to comfort her, and to convince her that her self-condemnation was extreme and absurd. But he returned to his shanty feeling that he had not succeeded, and that she would have to work her conviction out of her system in her own way.

CHAPTER XXIX

ALICE awoke one morning a few days later with a feeling that something was in the air. The first thing she remembered was that her husband was leaving early for Auckland, and that she must get up and pack his bag, one of the few wifely duties left to her. Then she remembered that she had heard the girls say the night before that Lynne was going by the same boat to meet a Sydney friend who was on a visit to New Zealand, and that he would be away a week or two.

Without waiting for Asia to call her she began to dress. Whenever she was well she rose for breakfast if Roland was leaving early to be away for any length of time. Along with a few things that she always did for him, such as darning his socks and putting his clothes away, she had carefully preserved certain courtesies. She accompanied him to the gate when he left for more than a day or two, and came to the door to meet him on his return. If she was away she telegraphed to tell him the day she was coming home. She continued to consult him about small purchases about which she knew he was now generous and indifferent. He had never remarked upon these things, nor had she. She did not know whether he would have missed them if they had been left undone.

The whole family sat down together to breakfast, which was in itself a sufficiently uncommon occurrence to brand the day as unusual. When he was home Roland rarely arranged his habits to suit the hour the children had to eat in order to get off in good time for school. As he was either early or late he usually ate alone, though when she felt like it Asia took pity on his loneliness and ate with him. But she had never made a habit of doing so. When she was away Betty and Mabel together shouldered the task of looking after him.

Breakfast with him had always been a difficult and unsatisfactory affair. Although he was not hard to please at dinner, his morning appetite was as uncertain as a choppy wind, and the person who had waited on him always had a sense of failure at the end of the meal, and a feeling of thankfulness when he left the table. He was more than usually irritable this morning because he had not been able to find his cheque-book, and a twenty minutes' search on the part of the whole household had failed to locate it. He swore he had not left it in the store—where it was found just as he was leaving—or in the bush, or with David Bruce. So they all sat down with the disagreeable sense that they were under suspicion for gross carelessness. The one person who did not really mind was Asia. Any sort of fuss or diversion, pleasant or unpleasant, meant that nobody noticed her, or made her more conscious of what lay ahead of her.

Alice minded the breakfast atmosphere less than she usually did. Once she would have allowed the pressure of her husband's irritability to weigh upon her. Now it struck her as being trifling and unreal. What did a lost cheque-book matter? The scene moved before her as if she were looking at a picture. She felt an extraordinary detachment as she watched the members of her family. Tom Roland fussing every few minutes about his book, Betty and Mabel hurrying nervously because they were a little late, Bunty subdued and sulky because his father had accused him of mislaying the lost property, Elsie meek and silent because she shrank into herself in an uncongenial atmosphere, and Asia, the most unreal of them all, outwardly calm and managing, trying as she always did in such scenes to pour oil upon the troubled waters.

That two streams of events, the known and the unknown, could flow together under the same roof in the manner they were doing there before her eyes seemed to Alice to be incredible. She saw they were all mysteries to each other.

She began to wonder what kept them together, whether anything ought to keep them together, whether "the bond" were not the most artificial of ties. And speculating about it, she ate more composedly than any one else. Though she did not dare to scrutinize Asia, she was aware of her poise, of her apparent elimination of herself, and she wondered how she could possibly be so normal with such a personal crisis hanging over her head.

An hour later Alice sat on the front veranda to watch Tom Roland and David Bruce leave in the launch. She followed them till she saw them stop at a point below the mill where two men got aboard. That puzzled her till she guessed that Ross would accompany Lynne to Point Curtis, and then return with Bruce. But when she saw the boat coming up the river again there was only one person in it, and it did not stop anywhere. It was not till the afternoon that she saw that this was part of a plan arranged beforehand.

She stayed out all the morning, making a pretence of gardening in the shade. She heard Asia humming and whistling as she worked inside, and wondered if she were doing it to keep her courage up, or to impress her mother, or whether it were the spontaneous overflow of real happiness. Alice felt no anger now against the lovers. Though she would still have stopped them if she had believed she safely could, she had made up her mind to be blind. She was now like a puppet; she would not move till they moved; and when they pulled the string she would dance to their tune, not enthusiastically or energetically, but, still, she would dance.

At lunch-time she managed to be more normal than she had expected she could be, and the quiet meal with Mabel and the children was such a contrast to the restless breakfast that both she and Asia remarked upon it with smiles. But they both avoided looking directly at each other, and each hoped the other did not notice it. Asia remembered vividly afterwards that her mother was pathetically gentle and soft, and that she had looked a great deal out of the window. They were helped to keep up by Mabel, who was in a vivacious mood, and talked of what she had to do for the school concert and picnic that was soon to close the term and inaugurate the summer holidays.

After lunch Alice lay down for an hour, but she could not even doze with the suspense hanging over her. She had to make an effort to stay in her room for the time she usually spent there. Then she took some sewing to the eastern veranda, and sat down facing the village and Pukekaroro. But she could not sew. Her hands fell limply into her lap, while she stared vacantly at one thing and another moving about the bay. She saw women take in their washing from the yards. She saw two men lazily fixing something on the tramway under the hot sun. She followed a rider down the road beside the line until he disappeared behind a low rise beyond the kitchen. She saw him reappear on the crest of the slope and ride slowly to the stables and dismount. Although she saw men ride thus every day, she wondered idly who he was.

She heard the children screaming through their afternoon recess in the school grounds, and the noise of hammers about the boat shed on the spit, and as a background for these sounds, the mill, its belts and saws and chains. Once, when a truckload of logs broke from the bush near the base of Pukekaroro, she roused herself to a keener attention. It seemed to her it was coming too quickly. She had learned to know the different kinds of roar made by the load coming fast or slow, and she always listened in some anxiety, for some of the worst accidents had occurred at the curve at the foot of the hill to men driving carelessly. But she saw she had anticipated as usual. The trucks disappeared behind the rise only to come merrily on across the flat and be braked to a standstill beside the booms.

Alice wondered how everything could be going on just the same. It seemed to her incredible that nothing should be altered there now that she had seen something of what *went* on below the surface. She wondered if any other mother there were facing the tragedy of seeing a child plunge into uncertainties.

After four o'clock she heard steps through the house and the front gate click. Stung to wide-awakeness she swung her chair round. She saw Asia go down the path to the store. But she was still wearing the blue print dress she had worn that morning, and she went hatless, with nothing in her hands. Presently she returned laden with packages of groceries. Instead of taking them straight inside she came round the veranda to her mother. She was breathless, apparently from hurrying up the hill.

"Mother, a man has just come up from a new family below Point Curtis to ask for help. His wife is very ill. I said I'd go."

She said it so naturally that for the moment Alice believed her.

"Oh, dear"—she raised her face from her sewing—"who is it?"

Asia did not hesitate as she looked into her mother's eyes and down at a slipping package.

"Haywood; he said the name was. Uncle David said I could tell what it was, and send for him if necessary."

"Oh, yes." Alice bent over her sewing with a curious feeling of perplexity.

"Mother, if it was typhoid or pneumonia or anything like that I might stay for a few days. You can get Mrs. North or Eliza King. But there won't be much to do. I did some cooking this morning."

Then Alice saw.

She ran her needle into her finger, and leaned down while she put it in her mouth. Prepared though she thought she would be to meet the trial when it came, she felt a rush of pain through her body. But she was able to answer in a voice that did not betray her state of mind:

"Certainly. You must stay as long as they need you." Something in her rose to play the game. "You will need some old linen, and you had better take some jelly—I'll get it."

She got up quickly, dropping her sewing in the chair. She felt she had to move, to do something. Asia turned with her, walking a little ahead. Her face was flushed, and she could not look at her mother. She kept arranging the packages under her arm as if it were difficult to carry them.

"Now, don't do any work, Mother. There's no necessity——" she began, as they entered the hall.

"Oh, Asia, will you cease worrying about me—I—I—really—I can look after myself."

Asia was arrested by the irritation in her mother's voice, and she was misled by her manner into thinking she suspected nothing. It had the effect of diverting her for the moment, and clearing the air between them. She really thought her mother was becoming more independent, and that she now disliked being fussed over.

"Oh, all right," she answered, in a tone meant to placate, and walked on to the kitchen.

Inside her room Alice pressed her fingers into her temples to ward off the blackness that swept before her eyes. She took up her smelling salts, which helped her to steady herself. Mechanically she began to look for old linen, with a reactionary feeling that she need not have gone so far in aiding and abetting the lovers. But she made up a bundle, and taking it to the kitchen, she found two pots of jelly, and placed them with it on the table. Calling out where she had left them, she returned to the veranda, praying that Asia would get ready and go quickly. She hoped this would be one of the times when Mabel and the children would go up the Kaiwaka road to meet Betty, and that it would be over before they got home.

A quarter of an hour later she heard Asia come to the front door, put something down, and come on round the veranda. As she turned the corner Alice saw that she had changed into her plain old navy suit, and that her hair was neatly arranged under a sailor hat. She was dressed and looked exactly as she always did when she went on such visits as the one she had described. Alice dared not look directly at her, but she was stupidly conscious of her carefully quiet manner and her extraordinary poise.

Steeling herself, she determined to be equally calm.

"I hope you won't find it very serious." She looked past Asia's face, pretending to be attracted by something on her hat.

"I hope not." Asia could not elaborate the statement. Cool though she appeared to be she was inwardly seething with emotion, and anxious to get away as soon as possible without seeming too abrupt. "Good-bye, Mother. Don't garden in the sun, and don't bother cooking hot meals for the children. Give them cold stuff till I come back."

This further solicitude almost upset Alice. She dared not speak; she merely nodded her head as she put out her cheek for Asia to kiss. The caress was one of the most perfunctory they had ever bestowed upon each other. Hardened by the dread of reaction neither of them dared make even a show of affection. Without another word Asia turned quickly and disappeared round the veranda.

Alice stood in a daze watching her go down the path. She saw that she carried a light straw case, and that she walked as she always walked, with a free swinging stride. Just before she reached the blacksmith's shop she turned round, and seeing her mother looking after her, she waved her hand.

Tears gushed from Alice's eyes as she waved back. That the familiar greeting should not have been forgotten in that tragic moment touched her to the core. She began to sob, and, sobbing, walked inside to her room. She did not want Asia to think she was watching to see where she went. She saw her cross the spit bridge and enter the bush at the accustomed place. She did not know that once she was alone out of sight among the ferns and trees Asia sat down on her case and shed sad tears, not on account of anything ahead of her, but of sorrow for that she had left behind.

Alice had stood staring into the bush for some time before she felt the deathlike stillness of the house creeping upon her like some ghostly invisible presence. She tried to put it out of her mind. She told herself the house was just the same, that the children would soon be home, that everything was as it was that morning. But an incurable restlessness seized her. She went out into the hall, meaning to go outside, but instead something drew her to Asia's room.

As she looked round it she could not see that a thing had been changed. There was no sign that its owner had departed in a fever of unrest. Flowers freshly cut the day before filled several vases. The windows were open and the blinds fixed to let in the sun and breeze. The evidences of Asia's taste and individuality impressed her as if she were seeing them for the first time. She looked round at the pictures, the furniture, the books, the ornaments. She began to wonder why she had always associated certain material things with certain modes of thought, certain ways of living, as if one would commit murder or not according to the kind of furniture one owned, be immoral or not according to one's taste in colour and line.

She had expected to feel in Asia's room as if she had seen her coffin carried out of it, but there was something so reassuring about its sunshiny freshness that she could not cry. She walked to the window looking out upon the river to lower the blind, as the sun was streaming straight in. Her eye caught the light sparking from a bit of the zinc roof of the cottage across the river. It fascinated her. She wondered if Asia had reached it. Then she saw she had no business to follow her there, no business to try to visualize the lovers, no right even to think about them.

As she turned back into the room she wondered what clothes Asia had taken with her. On a sudden impulse she turned the handle of her cupboard, to find it locked. She tried the drawers of the bureau. They, too, were locked. It was the first time, as far as she knew, that any of her girls *had* locked up their things, for she had taught them such respect for each other's property as to make the precaution unnecessary. And she had never heard that the trust had been abused.

It struck her with the force of a blow that she was the person Asia had suspected, and there she stood convicted. And although Asia would never know that she had spied, she had believed that she might, and she was right.

Hot from head to foot with humiliation she hurried from the room out into the garden, and, unseeing, along the back path among the vegetables. There were mean things in her life of which she was ashamed, things she could not bear to think about, but she had never felt worse about anything than she did then. Her self-condemnation roused her out of the insensibility she had been cultivating for days to a determination to redeem herself in her own eyes, to redeem herself not by passivity, but by something positive, both in attitude of mind and action.

With her eyes hard and bright she made a contract with her soul that henceforth she would be no man's judge, and the censor of no one save herself.

Mechanically she stooped down and pulled a little clump of weeds from a carrot bed. When she raised herself she saw Betty and Mabel and the children coming along the path behind the cottages. She hurried inside to get tea ready for them. When she opened the cupboards she saw that Asia had cooked a stock of food to last for several days. She wondered why she was surprised and touched at this further evidence of consideration. She saw she had been supposing that Asia's whole character would be altered because she had chosen to do one thing forbidden by the conventions.

At tea she told the girls that Asia had been called away to a sick family. As this had happened before, they asked no inconvenient questions, nor did a suspicion enter their minds. In answer to a question, Alice told them they could not under any circumstance call upon Allen Ross in Lynne's absence, and she forbade Bunty to cross the river or go near the mill till his father returned.

After tea, as Alice went to her room to change, she remembered that it was the turn of the brown dress. She knew she had to wear it, for David Bruce was coming to dinner. But almost guiltily she took it out and laid it on the bed and looked at it. To wear her best finery on such an occasion looked at first like sacrilege to her. Then she told herself it was part of playing the game she had determined to play. Still, it was not without a few regretful tears, tears for the pity of it all, that she put it on. However, when she looked at herself later in the glass, she felt a little glow of triumph that she had so far conquered herself as to keep up appearances in that manner.

She rose on the front veranda as David Bruce came up to the gate. He kept his eyes upon her as he entered and mounted the steps. Without a word he took her hands, held her off at arm's length, and looked at her. She saw by his eyes, where laughter and the mistiness of tears were mingled, that he understood the criss-cross of her emotions and decisions, and her feeling about the dress, and that he knew what the day had meant to her.

It was not till they were in the sitting-room that she turned to him with the words that had been on her tongue as he came up the path:

"You know she has gone to him, David?"

"Yes, I know."

That was all they said about it before dinner.

CHAPTER XXX

THE autumn set in late after the unusually hot summer, remembered afterwards as one of the worst for fires that the north had ever known. For two months Tom Roland kept bands of fighters ready for any emergency, and he was fortunate in escaping with nothing worse than some bad scares, two small burns, and the loss of one camp outfit. For weeks at a time the pall of smoke rolling up from the fires started on the gum-fields, in clearings and on waste lands, obliterated the horizons. The low, scrub-covered ground opposite the mill inside the turn of the river below Roland's house, had blazed for one week, raising showers of sparks that were watched anxiously lest they should carry across. The smoke from this section filled the houses about the bay so that everybody tasted it on their tongues when they woke in the morning.

There had been one weird period of several days when the late afternoon sun had seemed to step out of the great curtain behind it and to be rapidly approaching the earth with the awful ominousness of some bulging blood-red eye in a monster mad with the lust for wholesale destruction. Men stopped work to look at it, and women shivered as with a presentiment of evil. Its appearance was so extraordinary that the newspapers sought to find causes for it, and concluded that the huge fires going on in Australia at the same time accounted for the phenomenon.

As she sat much alone Alice felt there was some correspondence between the behaviour of the seasons and the happenings in her own little world. It seemed fitting to her that that particular summer and autumn should be out of the ordinary. The constant anxiety about fire on the part of her husband and David Bruce paralleled her restlessness.

Those abnormal suns intensified the sense of unreality she had had about her life since the day she knew that Asia and Allen Ross had begun to live together.

It was not until more than two months of the relation had gone by that she began to accept it as something more than an excrescence on her experience. Then it began to fit in, to flow along with other things in her daily life.

She had managed to be so noncommittal after Asia's first return that they had both started without embarrassment upon the course they had since pursued. Alice had accepted without question the tale Asia told about the Haywoods. She had met Ross at tea two days later, taking her cue from the normal behaviour of the lovers. As time went on she had had relapses into amazement at their unruffled demeanour, moments of fear that they might be discovered, short periods of envy for their youth and courage, every kind of ebb and flow of emotion and decision about them. But all through she had outwardly preserved a serenity that completely deceived them, and that was praised as wonderful by David Bruce.

The lovers had been most discreet. Ross had come alone or with Lynne to dinner many times. He had never betrayed himself, nor had Asia. They had not shut themselves up to each other. They had joined in trips to the bush, in fire-fighting expeditions, in parties of various kinds. When they had gone alone in the launch up the river they arranged their start so that they were not seen leaving together. Ross always waited at or near the dell. When they went sailing down the river Lynne accompanied them so far, and landing below the gap, walked back through the bush. Bruce assured Alice that they might go on for a year like that, and that no one would suspect. If Roland thought anything about them, he never mentioned it.

This elimination of immediate danger affected Alice. She saw that it was bringing her to think differently of their action. She found herself wondering if, after all, the spiritual values they got did not justify them. She usually fell back from heresies of this kind into questions as to where it would end if everybody did as they were doing. But she watched them as much as she dared with interest, and sometimes with fascination.

One night towards the end of March she felt her loneliness and restlessness more than usual. It was the brown dress night, and she had almost come to believe that it had an uncanny influence over her. As she would have expressed it, it gave her the fidgets. If she had been a different type of woman she would have said it made her feel "naughty," "wicked," or "like the devil"; but, though she had heard such expressions on the mischievous lips of Dorrie Harding, it never occurred to her to use them, even in fun.

She had dressed carefully, knowing that Ross was coming to dinner, and hoping that Bruce would get down from the bush. But his failure to appear had put a note of disappointment into the meal, which seemed to her to have been unsatisfactory to the lovers also, because Roland, who was in a garrulous mood, monopolized the conversation with tedious repetitions of his fire-fighting exploits. She thought Asia and Ross were unusually quiet. She knew that Ross was soon to return to Sydney, and she rightly guessed that they hated to think that that summer of romance had to end. As she saw them go off together afterwards she could not help feeling sorry for them, seeing the inevitable changes they had to face.

After Roland had departed for the evening to visit the captain of a timbership that had arrived that afternoon, Alice sat down outside her window, leaving her children studying as usual in the dining-room. The night, heavy with smoke, was sultry and enervating, and yet had a curious goad in it that prevented one's giving way to it with pleasant limpness. There was also a haunting foreboding of winter, intensified by the crickets, that in keeping with the other exaggerations of the season were that year more numerous than ever. They seemed to Alice to chirp with a mournfulness worse than anything she had ever heard.

She had not sat long before they and something in the night got on her nerves.

Getting up, she walked off down the front steps and round into the back garden, where she began to pace backwards and forwards along the centre path. The night settled down quickly, hastened by the smoke. Stars were visible only vaguely at the zenith. She began to stop at intervals to listen for sounds that might tell of Bruce's return. But though the night was very still she could hear nothing that resembled a horse's hoofs down the road.

She could never tell afterwards what it was that drove her out of the garden and along the path to his shanty. She knew that unless it was very late when he returned he would come to see her, for she had not seen him at all that day. Although it was long after the time when she had ever gone alone in the evening to see him, she felt she could not wait. All that was in her mind was the idea that she would see if he were there, and that if he were she would bring him back with her.

When she got near his shanty she paused at the sound of scrappy whistling. Then she saw a faint sheen of light radiating from his doorway. She listened to hear if he had any one with him. As she did so a shadow crossed the light, and a stream of water thrown from a dish careered out into the night and splashed upon the dry earth. Hearing no other sounds, she was reassured and went on.

David Bruce was standing in front of his mirror adjusting a tie when he heard her step on the porch.

"You," he said, "I was just coming along." He gave her a quick, curious look, wondering what had happened.

She stood in his doorway as if she were waiting to be asked in.

"I didn't hear you ride down, David." Though her voice was natural she felt uncertain and nervous.

"No? I came slowly. The road is very dusty."

"Have you had your dinner?"

"Yes, in the bush. Aren't you coming in?" He turned from the mirror.

"Oh, yes." She moved forward a few steps, and then stood hesitating.

As he put on his coat he wondered again why she had come. But he treated her unusual action as if it were a common one. He left her to seat herself while he lit his lamp, blew out his candle, put away his soiled clothes, and hunted for his pipe and tobacco.

Absent-mindedly Alice sat down on his bunk watching him, and looking aimlessly about the room. Her eyes stopped at one of his windows.

"You need a new curtain, David," she said solemnly.

He surveyed the article she disapproved as if it had been an affair of state.

"Oh, do I? I hadn't noticed."

When he had finally cleared his clothes away and collected his smoking materials on a little table, Alice stood up.

"I just came to meet you, David," she said, as if it had suddenly dawned on her that she had to give a reason for her visit.

"Good gracious,"—he smiled easily—"sit down. Now that we are here we can stay here surely." His amused eyes helped her to lose some of her nervousness.

"What's the matter?" he went on lightly. "Is it just the dumps, or something more serious?"

Seated in a chair opposite her, he smiled approvingly at the brown dress. But though his manner was airy he was sympathetically conscious of her restlessness. He had helped her to laugh at herself many times that summer. He had brought her to shed the remainder of her stock phrases about morals. He had seen her undergo transformations as the result of her clearer self-analysis. But he knew she was still a long way off peace of mind.

"I don't know what's the matter with me, David. I'm beginning to wonder if I'm getting like these modern women who revolt against domesticity." Her troubled eyes looked into his and then over his shoulder at the wall.

"What!" he laughed softly. "You a feminist! What next?"

"Don't make fun of me, David. Do you really think my life now is a satisfactory thing? Do you?"

He saw she was bent on being serious, but he hoped to mitigate the intensity of her mood.

"Well, what do you think of doing? Do you propose to start a Browning club or a mothers' circle at the bay, or what?" Then he saw he had hurt her.

"David, don't, please."

"Oh, don't mind me, my dear. Now I'm ready to listen. What's the trouble?" He leaned forward.

"I've been thinking this summer, David. And I'm beginning to hate my useless life. I've been asking myself what I do that is any good." She paused.

"Yes? Go on." He began to fill his pipe.

"I don't do anything that means anything in the house—you know that. I used to love the children all taking care of me, but now I hate it, and they will go on treating me as if I were an invalid. They turn me out of the kitchen, they fuss about my getting tired, they seem to live in dread of my headaches. Oh, David, I hate it! I hate it! I'm nothing to any of them, and it makes me so lonely. I haven't anything to do. I'm no use to Tom—I'm only half a woman to you——"

She stopped because his hand had closed her mouth. Impulsively slipping to his knees, he threw his arms about her.

"Oh, my dear, do stop that half-a-woman business. Start a movement, anything——"

He threw up his head, but before either of them could move there was a step on the porch and Roland stood in the doorway. His rubber shoes had not heralded his approach upon the dusty path. He had a yellow piece of paper in one hand.

He blinked in the light from the nickel lamp, caught sight of the two at the bunk, and quickly drew back.

"Beg pardon," he exclaimed, startled. "I didn't mean to intrude."

Alice turned white in spite of the reassuring look Bruce shot at her as he drew away from her. It was the first time in all their experience that Roland had come upon them in anything like a compromising situation.

"You are not intruding," Bruce said, getting to his feet. "Come in, Tom."

"It's all right," muttered the boss. "It'll do in the morning."

"No, it won't do in the morning," answered Bruce quietly. "Come in."

But it was obvious the boss did not want to. He entered uncomfortably, and only when Bruce repeated the words almost as a command. He crumpled up the paper in his hand, bit his lips, and stared at the floor.

"Tom, this looks bad"—his partner looked straight at him, speaking with significant slowness—"and I'm afraid you won't believe me when I say that your wife and I have never been unfaithful to you in the conventional sense."

As Roland looked up Bruce saw incredulity in his eyes, but not the anger he had expected to see.

"Well, then, you're a mighty strange pair," was his blunt reply.

At these words Alice rose mechanically from the bunk. She, too, was amazedly conscious that he was not angry.

"I don't understand you," said Bruce.

"Do you mean you've never made love to my wife?" Tom Roland stared at him as if his not doing so was a matter for investigation.

"I mean that, certainly."

"You don't love her?"

"That is another story," answered Bruce, in the same calm tones.

"You love her, and you expect me to believe that you

haven't made love to her?" Roland stared again at him as if he were the sensational novelty at a circus.

"That is the truth."

And the boss saw it.

"Well, I'm jiggered!" he muttered, looking at the floor again.

Alice dropped back on to the bunk, struggling for breath.

Even Bruce could not at once get the significance of it.

"Do you mean you have supposed your wife and I were lovers?" he asked, after a moment of dead silence.

"Yes."

"For how long?"

"Oh, I don't know exactly." The boss bit his lips again, and kicked at the end of a rug. "Ever since you spoke to me about her anyway."

"What!" exclaimed Bruce, raising a hand at Alice, who had turned to him in astonishment.

"Well, what else could I think?" The boss looked up with a simple air of inquiry.

"God!" exploded Bruce. "Look here, Tom. You have the morals of a barnyard! But have you never met a man who could keep his hands off a woman?"

"Precious few. And there was something wrong with them," retorted the boss grimly

"Good God, man! There is some decency in the world. I've been in a position of trust. What the devil do you mean by thinking I would abuse your confidence in that way?"

Alice felt the world turning round her as she saw the two men face each other without hostility, without anger, with nothing but amazement in their eyes.

The boss was the first to lower his.

"Well, I thought you'd see I was giving you chances——"

"Giving me chances!" repeated Bruce.

"Yes," spluttered Tom Roland. "I'd had mine and failed. I came to see I wasn't her style, and never would be, and I *knew* you were, and I owed you a lot——" His voice cracked, but he went on brokenly, "I thought about it—I had always done what I damn well pleased—I thought I could give you a turn. I wasn't in a position to judge anybody, and when you spoke about her health I thought that was what you wanted, and that it was up to me to let you alone. I knew she didn't love me—I don't think she ever did—it was just hard luck——" His voice broke, and bursting into hysterical sobs, he dropped into a chair.

As she listened to him Alice got to her feet again, and she stood staring at him, her throat dry and burning, and tears running unheeded down her cheeks. She did not know why she was crying. She still felt as if she were in a dream.

Bruce also looked at him as if they were all puppets in a show. Roland's words were as much a revelation to him as they were to Alice. He could hardly credit that the man he had worked with for years could have kept a thing like this from him.

When he recovered his full consciousness he stepped to the chair and put his hand on the boss's shoulder.

"Tom, get up," he said hoarsely.

Controlling himself with an effort, Roland scrambled to his feet, and the two men looked at each other again, ignoring Alice, who stared stupidly from one to the other.

"You were willing to let your wife and me be lovers?" said Bruce slowly.

"After I'd thought about it, yes. And I stayed away a lot, and never came back without notice, and now you tell me you never saw it."

He felt that the one great, magnanimous thing he had ever done, his secret pride for three years, had been thrown away.

Bruce saw. He held out his hand.

"Tom, I don't know what to say to you."

Most uncomfortably the boss took it, wishing himself out of this. Then for the first time he took notice of the presence of his wife.

"Do you want a divorce? You could get plenty of evidence."

These words, shot at her, startled her out of her daze. She jumped, put out her hand, searching for something to hold on to, and turned beseechingly to Bruce.

But he did not look at her. Instead he walked to the door, leaned against it, and stared out into the night.

Roland looked impatiently at his wife, wondering why she did not answer.

"You must know by this time whether you want it or not," he said. "If you do I'll give you no trouble. I've lived on and off with Mrs. Lyman for years. She'd make no fuss; she'd like to marry me."

Alice felt as if she would choke. Words strained painfully out of her throat were strangled at birth. She turned agonized eyes on Bruce, but he never gave a sign. Her lips moved like those of a paralytic.

"What?" asked Roland, unable to hear.

"Do *you* want the divorce?"

Bruce only just heard her question.

There was a short pause, in which the room was as still as a vacuum.

The boss fidgeted, his hands working nervously.

"I can't say that I do," he mumbled.

"Don't you want to marry Mrs. Lyman?" Her voice was a little stronger.

"Not particularly."

"You have lived with her on and off for years, and you don't want to marry her?" she asked, not understanding.

He mistook the meaning of her tone.

"Well, that ain't remarkable," he snapped. "Lots of men live with women they don't want to marry. Why don't you learn something about the world you're living in? You saints! You don't know what goes on under your nose. I'm no worse than other men. I'm not half as bad as some of them that you've met and been very pleasant to. If you knew more about life you wouldn't condemn me."

"I'm not condemning you," cried Alice passionately, her face set in an effort at control. But she could not help herself. She sat down on the bunk and burst into tears.

"Oh, for God's sake," he exclaimed impatiently. He hated any scenes he did not make himself, and he wondered why on earth they had all got into this.

His tone stiffened Alice. She pulled herself up, and rising, faced him again.

"Do you want things to go on as they are?"

"Yes, I suppose I'd prefer it," he answered truthfully. "I don't hanker after any scandal. But I'm willing to go through with it if you both want me to." He kicked again at the rug.

As she looked at his lowered face and nervous movements, Alice grew steady with resolution.

"I will not get the divorce unless you wish it."

Her voice rang round the shanty. She fancied she saw Bruce move in the doorway. Her husband did not realize what that decision cost her, nor did he regard it as final.

"You don't have to decide it to-night. You can talk it over. You can live with each other, anyway, all you want to, as far as I'm concerned."

He swung round as if he'd done with it.

Alice stood frozen, dry-eyed, looking from him to the man in the doorway.

Bruce turned as the boss stumbled towards him.

"Tom," he began hoarsely. Roland raised a twitching, distressed face. "I hope you don't think I did things for you with this in view."

"Holy Moses!" exclaimed the boss, with an impatient gesture. "Do you think I don't know better than that? That's why I'm willing—here, I don't want to talk any more about it. But what you two do in the future is no business of mine. You know what I've been, and you've never preached to me. Well, I'm grateful. I'll agree to anything you want to do. Only settle it soon. I hate suspense."

He moved towards the porch with only one desire—to get away from this emotional strain.

Bruce caught sight of the crumpled yellow paper, still in his hand.

"You wanted to see me," he said, diverted by it.

"What?" jerked the boss.

"You came to see me about something." He pointed to the paper.

"Oh, yes." Roland was instantly relieved to come down to the comfortable subject of business. His manner brightened. "The Kauri Timber Company has telegraphed, urgent, to know how soon we can have a quarter of a million feet ready to ship to Australia. But I'll see you about it in the morning." Fortified by this break he looked back more cheerfully at Alice. "Now, I don't want to chew this over. I've said all I want to say. For God's sake don't be tragic about it. I'm not blaming you or anybody."

And with that he left them.

With the world turning dizzily around her Alice dropped back on to the bunk. For a minute or two, while Roland's rapid steps grew more and more muffled in the dust, she was unconscious even of Bruce's presence. She felt absolutely vacant, as if her whole mind had been swept clean of its contents. Her eyes were turned in the direction of the doorway, but it was some minutes before the still figure leaning there took form and meaning. Then its continued silence seemed to charge it with significance.

With her eyes glued upon him she remembered that she had refused the divorce, and that she had not seen his face since she had done so.

"David," she called sharply, feeling herself growing sick with the fear that he would misunderstand her.

He turned at one, and to her amazement she saw that there was a smile—a smile that screwed up his eyes—on his face as he came towards her.

Stupidly she saw him drop into his chair and stretch out his legs. Then he looked straight at her.

"There seems to have been an awful waste of good virtue somewhere, doesn't there?" he drawled.

She looked at him as if she had not heard him aright. She could not understand why his eyes held that expression.

"You think it's funny!" she exclaimed.

"Yes, my dear. I think it's one of the most humorous things I've ever known—and one of the most pathetic."

Then it dawned upon her that he was seeing things in the situation she did not see, and that what was tremendous to her was merely incidental to him. She had not begun to think of her husband or his attitude; she had thought first of herself and Bruce, and how they might be affected by this new element in their situation. She saw that he did not seem to be taking seriously the fact that Roland had offered them the chance of a divorce, and that she had refused it. His power to remain undisturbed by such an emotion-raising proposition astonished her. She suspected that for some reason best known to himself he was bluffing.

"I couldn't ask him for a divorce, David, not so long as he wanted me for anything at all." Her eyes searched his hungrily for the corroboration she wanted.

"That is right for you," he said quietly.

His use of the pronoun puzzled her. He saw that it added to the questions crowding upon her mind, and to the look of distraction in her eyes. Seeing clearly himself that nothing would in the end be altered by Roland's liberality, he meant to keep her as unemotional as he could.

"I mean that," he went on, as if they were discussing some simple matter. "You had to act as you felt. I understand perfectly why you feel as you do. Now you have decided that. Let it alone."

But he knew she could not and would not dismiss it as easily as all that. He wondered how long it would take her to come to the alternative, which, to his thinking, was a much more complex and difficult thing to dispose of; and, though he knew her well enough to be sure, even then, what her final decision would be, he knew she would not reach it without a dovetailing of desires and prohibitions that would bring upon her another period of mental torture. He was pretty sure that nothing that he could say would prevent that period of suspended resolution.

He watched her as she sat uncomfortably perched on the edge of his bunk, her face lowered, her eyes fixed on something on the rug. Her hands were gripped in her lap. She looked singularly young. Her cheeks were flushed, contrasting vividly with the white skin of her neck and forehead. Her graceful figure gave no sign of age. After all, she was only forty-three, and in spite of all that she had gone through, her inherited vitality had triumphed, and had brought her to the master years crowned with an attractiveness that held all who looked upon it.

It was seldom that Bruce allowed himself to think of the power of her physical allurement for him. He had always known that if he began to make a habit of that he would have to go away. He knew she was not conscious of the amount of physical quality there was in any man's feeling for a woman. He knew she would have denied the amount of it in her feeling for him. He had wondered lately if she recognized the source of much of her recent restlessness, if she would admit it frankly when she surmised it. He guessed that Roland's words would bring her to realize it in some degree.

He was curiously impersonal in his speculation about her, as if it were some man other than himself who was affected. He was helped to this detachment by his amazement at and interest in Roland's behaviour, which had astonished him more than anything had astonished him for years.

As she sat, Alice felt his eyes upon her. For some time she tried to resist their clutching reach. She tried to think. She tried to drag some definite statement from the blurr of words that travelled with the speed of an electric fan through her brain. At last she got something, the memory of her husband's permission to live with Bruce, and once she got that there was no room in her mind for anything else.

When at last she could no longer resist Bruce's scrutiny, and when she raised her face, he saw that she had come to the alternative.

The gripping, questioning look that passed between them was a strange one to happen between two people who had been as intimate as they had been for years. Only for a second did Bruce allow anything of his physical hunger for her to show in his eyes, but short though that revelation was it stirred her to hot confusion. He shut down at once on his own feeling, seeing that she would need his help to find herself in this new struggle.

Drawing himself up in his chair, he leaned forward, while she gazed at him, fascinated.

"Well, he has given you something to think about," he began quietly, "but you do not have to do all the thinking to-night, you know."

His impersonal manner amazed her.

"David," she burst out, "he said we could live together." She said it as if she thought he did not realize it.

He smiled.

"Does his saying so settle it?"

Then she saw that in this first stage of her reaction she had actually thought that it might.

She did not answer, but dropped her face.

"This is something you have to decide," he went on.

He saw her lips moving in a pitiful attempt to say something.

"What is it?" he asked gently.

"You would like me to live with you, David." She did not look up.

As he drew himself up again she raised her eyes full of storm and stress. She was surprised to see that he appeared to be calm.

"Look here," he began, in level tones, "you are not to allow what you know to be my desires unduly to influence you. There are times when a man's desires would make a prostitute of any woman. I want you to understand now that I will not have you at any time as a sacrifice, as a compromise, as anything that is not spontaneous and happy. If you ever come to me you will come to me as Asia went to Ross, and in no other way."

Unconsciously he had raised his voice, and his words rang round the room.

He went on with her eyes glued on his face.

"You will have to think about it, and I cannot help you. You know how I feel, but you have to decide on your own feeling as well as mine, and your feeling is something I have no right to force. And, please, remember that until you decide there must be no playing with our emotions. We have to go on as we have been doing. It will be hard now that the possibility of change has come on us like this. I have not lost anything by growing older, and, you know, you have been growing younger lately."

As he had talked her eyes had lit up with fire. She threw out her hands to him.

"Oh, David, I love you, and I want to do what you want."

"I dare say." He coolly ignored her hands. "But I won't have you that way."

She shrank back, hurt that he had taken no notice of her impulsive gesture. But she knew he was right. She knew her cry was the cry of a creature desiring the mate it had chosen, the primitive hunger for the pleasure in sight that takes no thought of the uncomfortable reactions that may come to-morrow. Then she was fired with admiration for the man who knew her better than she knew herself, and who would not take advantage of her lapses.

"Oh, David," her lips trembled, "I want to love you. I don't know whether I can—but I want to——" She looked as if she were about to move forward into his arms, but she stiffened herself up.

David Bruce rose to his feet.

"My dear, I want you to go home. I am likely to become irresponsible if you stay much longer. Now this is going to be the devil for both of us. Tom's words have removed one of my strongest incentives to virtue, and if you begin to be shaky and to talk of your wants, well——" He made a comical gesture of helplessness.

Again his light tone helped her. She stood up, but she could not dispose of her emotions as easily as he could.

"David, I don't know what to do——" she began helplessly.

"You don't have to know to-night, my dear girl. You can't settle things of this kind in an hour. It will take you weeks—months. One day you will tell yourself that you can come to me, and the next you will know you can't. And you will have to fight it out alone. The one thing you must not do is to talk about it to me. It's a queer situation to come up between us now. I wish you would take my word for the end of it, but you won't."

"What do you mean, David?" she asked, calmed by his positive words.

He looked at her with an inscrutable smile in his eyes.

"You can't do it," he said.

But the subtle perversity that sleeps in human beings till the prick of opposition stirs it to life woke up in her at the prod of his words.

She flashed a look at him that was almost a declaration that she would. It was the primitive provocative feminine again. Recognizing it, she flushed and turned her face away.

"Come on home," he said quietly.

She followed him out with a queer feeling that it was all a dream, and that she would wake presently, and be in a familiar world again.

They were half-way along the path before he spoke.

"Think about Tom a little," he said. "I can't get him out of my head, and I don't believe you've thought about him."

Then she saw that she had not.

At the back gate he took her hand, raising it to his lips.

"My dear, I'd rather you did not think about this than worry. Remember I love you. I shall go on loving you whatever you decide. I don't expect you to do what other people can do. You can only be yourself. I shall be in the bush for a day or two. Try to say something to Tom; praise him a bit, if you can do it without being upset. Write him a letter if you can't say it."

Resting his hand on her shoulder for a minute, he kissed her forehead. Then he turned and walked quickly back along the path.

Alice did not know why she began to cry, or why she cried on till she stopped from sheer exhaustion. When she got into bed she began to cry again, and she cried without thinking until she fell asleep.

CHAPTER XXXI

WITHOUT seeing Alice, Roland and Bruce left together in the morning for the bush. Though he saw at once that the boss did not want to make any reference to the night before, Bruce could not let it go at that, and as soon as they had cleared the kitchen grounds he said he wished to say something about it.

"Go ahead, then," said Roland uncomfortably, looking in front of him. "But I've nothing more to say. I said all I think about it last night."

Something about this blunt discouragement and the boss's comical discomposure amused Bruce. He laughed, but rather harshly.

"Upon my soul, Tom, do you think you can finish up things like that? Good God! You must have done some thinking to come to this, and some suffering. And all I want to say is I know it, and I thank you for feeling about me as you do. There are things that can't be put into words, and I don't try to put them there, but common decency demands that one show something occasionally. And whether you like it or not, I'm going to say I understand and appreciate your attitude."

The unemotionalism in his tone relieved Roland, who was more pleased by his words than he could have showed. He was perfectly willing to be praised. His childish vanity was capable of lapping up oceans of honeyed words. But he did hate anything that upset his comic-opera view of life.

"That's all right," he grunted. "There are things I could say if I knew how to say them, but I can't."

"All right," smiled Bruce. He saw he would have to find other ways of showing how he felt about it, if any such were left him. All day his thoughts reverted to the boss, and to his curious inconsistencies. He speculated about his mental processes, his preoccupation with action, his absence of any power to analyse motives or tendencies. Roland had always appeared to settle things easily, guided by some secret spring of intuition that took him straight to a conclusion while other people wrestled painfully with their souls about it. Bruce had always admired his inexhaustible fund of common sense, and he suspected that it was his common sense combined with his sense of fairness, rather than any reasoned philosophy about morals, that had brought him to the point of view he had with regard to himself and Alice.

When they returned to the bay on the third evening Ross and Lynne were staying to dinner, and nothing in the situation was allowed to obtrude itself upon that meal. Bruce noticed, however, that Alice seemed dull, and that she looked at him from eyes that gave signs of sleeplessness.

Afterwards Roland took Lynne off to one of the timber vessels to see a captain who had some good stories to tell. Asia and Ross disappeared. Telling Alice that he had to finish up something at the store and would be back presently, Bruce also went off down the path. When he closed up the office, about half-past eight, he found the lovers sitting outside on the tramway, waiting for him.

"Come on the beach a minute. I want to ask you something," said Asia.

Wondering what it was, he turned with them. They all walked the few yards to the end of the cliffs in silence. But as soon as they reached the sandy beach, and were screened from sight, Asia stopped.

"What is the matter with Mother? Has she found out about us?" she asked, her eyes fixed inquiringly upon his face looming over her in the dark.

"Why do you ask that?" He returned her questioning look.

"She has been dreadfully worried for days. You have

been away, so you haven't noticed. I don't know of anything else that could have upset her. But I didn't want to say anything until I was sure, for I would have preferred to wait till Allen went away. But if she has found out we both feel we would rather talk it out with her at once. Allen insists on doing his share of it."

Then Bruce saw that they had both screwed up their courage to face the trying ordeal. He looked away from them, but even in the dark they were conscious of the smile that lit up his eyes.

"Uncle David, why do you look like that?"

As he turned to them again, his glance fleeting back and forth between them, they realized that he had something to tell them.

"Asia, my dear, your mother has known about you and Allen from the beginning. She knew you were going to him that day you left for the mythical Haywoods. She knew when she got you the linen and the jelly."

He saw plainly how astonished they were.

"What do you mean?" exclaimed Asia.

"Just what I say."

"She has known all along!" she repeated.

"She has."

"And you knew she knew?"

"Well, why not?" he smiled.

Asia and Ross looked at each other, and back to him, and back at each other again, saying nothing, but thinking the same things.

"Did you tell her?" she asked, after an eloquent silence.

"I did not."

"Then she only suspected."

"No, she really knew. There are some things you can't keep from the people who love you, you know." His eyes still smiled at them.

"She knew!" she repeated slowly, looking at Ross. "Then she knew when she met us at tea and dinner all the time. I can't believe it. And we thought we were so smart at putting her off the scent, we were so careful how we behaved, how we looked at each other. And she knew! Uncle David, really——" She broke off, seeing that he was enjoying her amazement.

"And after all, you were the deceived party," he drawled. "Your poor benighted, out-of-date mother was clever enough to fool you."

He wished Alice could have seen their faces at that moment. Ross looked humbly at Asia.

"I always felt there was something about your mother we were missing," he said.

With a flushed face she turned to Bruce.

"I think you ought to have told me about this before," she said crossly.

But he was obviously amused.

"Why should I? You know I have never talked back and forth between you and your mother. You thought it best she shouldn't know, and she thought it best you shouldn't know she knew. And there you were. What was I to do?"

Ross nodded his understanding.

Asia looked down at the sand, and dug her heels and toes into it for some minutes.

"How does she feel about it then? You can tell me that now." Her eyes searched his.

"She has left you both on the lap of the gods," he replied quietly.

He was amused to see that these two people who had been so sure of themselves, so ready to defend their rights and principles, should be so subdued at this information.

"'There are more things in heaven and earth, Horatio,'" he quoted lazily.

And to that they had nothing to say.

"I would talk to her about it when you feel like it," went on Bruce, looking at her. "You might find out something if you did, and I have come to think it would be a pity if you went away without knowing her."

Then he said good night and left them.

It was not until they had talked for some time that Asia remembered that the cause of her mother's recent worry was still unaccounted for.

"There's something else," she said, puzzling about it. "I wonder what it is."

"I'm willing to predict, dear, that there are things that you will never know about that mother of yours," said Ross.

Bruce found Alice, as usual, outside her window. They had not been alone since they had said good night by the gate after Roland had thrown his book of revelations at them. He began without any preliminaries.

"My dear, I have just learned from Asia that you have been badly worried while I have been away. She came to me to know what the matter was. I gave her something else to think about. Now, what do you mean by worrying?"

"I can't help it, David."

He felt rather than saw that she was torn still by indecision, and he knew that, after all, he would have to help her to settle it. Leaning forward, he peered up into her troubled eyes.

"You must put what Tom said out of your mind," he began firmly. "I told you then and I tell you again that I will never let you do anything with a doubt in your mind. I believe you will always have a doubt in your mind about living with me. That is the end of it for me. It must be the end of it for you, for uncertainty would put a strain upon us at once. Now to help me, as well as yourself, you must stop worrying about it."

She looked away from him through the creepers into the night. He did not know that as she sat so still she was overwhelmed with a passionate desire that he would carry her off and force her to do the thing she could have done in no other way. For that mad moment she wished he was not the masterpiece of insight and control that he was. She thought that once the initial plunge was taken she could settle down to the compromise with a fairly comfortable conscience. It was the plunge she could not face. But if the responsibility had been taken from her she felt she could have been carried along on the wild winds of adventure with a fierce joy. Her heart cried out against its long lean years of hunger and suppression. It beat against the bars of training and tradition. But even while it raged it realized that it would succumb in the end to the something that chained it.

As she sat still and tense, struggling with intoxicating visions, Bruce took out his pipe and began to smoke. Something about the sight of his pipe always restored her sense of proportion. She realized that they were not a cave man and woman, but a pair of persons on a veranda, with a group of innocent children in the house behind them, and all the other appurtenances of a well-regulated environment. She knew she was not finished with mad moments, but she guessed that they would always trail off into safe periods of submission.

"You will say something to Tom," said Bruce, turning to her. He saw that he had brought her back to earth rather suddenly.

"Oh, yes—that is, I may not say anything, but I will write him a letter. That will be easier," she stammered.

Late in the evening she asked him to what Roland had referred when he mentioned his reason for thinking they wanted to live together. Bruce told her, and they saw that it was natural that he should have come to the conclusion he had about it.

When they said good night they both wondered if this was indeed the end of their beginnings, if they were not destined for the peaceful ways of middle-age. Neither of them could see that there was anything left to happen.

Alice lay awake most of that night wondering what on earth she was to make of the rest of her life. She could not understand why, now that she seemed to have disposed of almost all the things that could hurt her, she should remain restless and unsatisfied. She was at peace and would remain so, she knew, with her husband. She would keep her "beautiful spiritual" friendship with David Bruce still unspotted from the world—and however much she might relapse in mad moments she knew that was the only way for her. She was resigned to Asia's plans; resigned to losing her; resigned to seeing her go her own ways, whatever those ways might turn out to be. But all this resignation left her stranded on a desert strewn with the dry bones of missed adventure, with no finger-post to point the way to the high places of a new experience. It seemed to her that her life stretched out before her a drab and colourless thing fading off into a vacuous old age, wherein she would continue to play her ornamental part, to dress up for dinner, to play the lady bountiful, to sit out so many evenings in the week with David Bruce, to play his accompaniments less and less ably every year, and to be to her girls some sort of a pretty picture of nice old motherhood.

Listening to Asia and Allen Ross that summer had been responsible for much of her intellectual unrest. It was not only her physical energy that had been restored. The *Weltgeist* that was moving hundreds of thousands of women of her age all over the world to repudiate an ornamental middle-age had got her. She had been stirred by the eager talk of Asia and Ross about socialism and the labour movement. Indeed, their interest in such things at a time when she would have expected them to be oblivious of everything but themselves had had a good deal to do with her changed attitude about their unconventional ways. They had talked with design to distract her attention from themselves, but none the less they were in earnest, and their enthusiasm affected her more than they knew.

Alice had always known that there was a good deal wrong with the world, but she had had no idea that it was in the awful mess it was till she heard Ross and Asia outline its horrors of unemployment, wage slavery and economic inequalities. She had paid little attention to the subject before, though she had listened to many a fruitless argument at her own table between Roland and some passer-by. When she had asked Bruce questions, he had answered lightly, knowing she was not really interested. She had unconsciously adopted in the matter her husband's point of view, judging from his business success that his opinion must be of value. She had seen that there was little to reform at the bay, for apart from occasional emergencies it was one of the most prosperous places in New Zealand. Though Roland snorted at the very word socialism, feeling that its advocates planned to kill just the kind of brains and initiative that he himself possessed, he had been a most generous employer, often paying more than the standard wages, charging only a nominal rent for his cottages and land, making little on the cost price of the goods purchased by his employés at his store, and lending money without interest to those of them who needed to borrow. He had built the school and the dancing hall, had given and prepared the football and the cricket field, and had never opposed a single improvement asked for. No employer in the colony had taken more precaution against accident, or had provided more safeguards for his work-people. When socialism was mentioned in his presence he naturally pointed to his community as a convincing example of the benefits of capitalism, as if that settled the subject for the whole world and for ever, and he always resented and fought in ways at his command such socialistic legislation as was proposed from time to time by the Government.

So Alice saw, as she lay awake that night, that the bay had little need of her awakened desire to start something. She saw that she would continue to sit upon the carefully dusted chairs, to give out the school prizes with a gracious smile at the flushed, upturned childish faces, to be a charming hostess to her husband's clients and distinguished visitors, and to be to the working people that vision of refinement and righteousness that had once been a source of pride. And she saw that every time she got a letter from Asia in

Sydney it would bring home to her her own futility. And she saw that not a week would go by, in spite of all her efforts, without her wishing she could go to David Bruce with all she had to give him.

So it was no wonder, after such a night, that Alice was not ready in the morning to give to Asia's discovery the importance that in Asia's mind it occupied.

Asia, too, had slept little. She thought over the whole summer, seeking to have a complete picture in her mind. She was deeply hurt and humbled to think that she had failed to see how much her mother had altered. She hated to think she had been so absorbed in herself that she had not seen things that she felt must have been obvious. She determined to talk to her mother at once, but now that she was not buoyed up by the thought of principles to defend, now that she had to play the ignominious part of trying to explain her own misunderstanding, she was, for her, uncertain and uncomfortable.

She screwed herself up to face it with two cups of strong coffee, and guessing the time when her mother would have finished her breakfast, she walked in to her, shut the door, and sat down on the bed facing her.

Alice did not even see that she had something important to say.

"Mother," Asia plunged, "Uncle David told me last night that you know about Allen and me—that you have known all the summer."

"Yes, I—I have known," said Alice lamely, with almost the air of having been detected in some questionable occupation. Then she wondered why Asia wanted to bother her about it at that moment. She was almost too tired to think. She looked back at the girl sitting in her fresh blue print dress as if she were something on the wall. She did not notice the significance of the look in her eyes or of her unusually uncertain manner.

Her dispassionateness startled Asia, who saw her face outlined against the pillow as if it belonged to some one else.

For once she felt as if her tongue were glued to the roof of her mouth. She did not know how to go on.

"You have known all the summer, Mother," she repeated, looking down at her hands.

Then Alice saw that the advantage was hers, but she was so little of a player of a game that she did not know how to use it. She could only look at Asia, wondering why her sureness and decision had deserted her. She felt no sense of triumph at conquering even for a moment so redoubtable an enemy in the battle of wits.

"Yes, I know. I understand," she said simply, as if she had disposed of it long before, and wondered why the question should have been reopened.

Then Asia saw that something else had swamped the importance of her behaviour in her mother's mind. For a moment that was a shock to her vanity, but she was quick to see the pathos of the whole situation, and she was determined to show her mother how she felt about it.

"Mother, I didn't know you knew. I have misjudged you. I would have told you if I had thought you would understand—I didn't want to deceive you. I thought it was the best way. I had to do it. You could not have stopped me, and I thought it was better to wait——" She stopped, feeling that she was saying something superfluous, that her mother knew it already.

"My dear, I think it was better to wait. Now we can talk about it quietly. I could not have talked about it at first. It hurt me. But it does not hurt me now. I see it all differently. I have learned many things this summer. I shall never worry about anybody again. I shall never worry about you or what you do. I know you are going to Sydney. I shall not worry about that. Now you see that I have altered." Alice had looked out of the window as she spoke in dull, even tones, but with her last words she turned her eyes upon Asia with a sad little smile. Then she saw that she had astonished her. "You are surprised?" she said questioningly.

Then to her amazement Asia fell forward on the bed with her face in her hands. Never for years had Alice seen her shed a tear, and she did not see why she was crying now. She stared at her golden head in that unprecedented position for some seconds before she spoke.

"What is it? What is the matter?" she asked stupidly.

Asia made an effort to control herself. She sat up, wiping her tears away with her hands. Despising weakness in herself, she was ashamed of this breakdown.

"Mother, what has happened to you?" she asked, trying to steady her voice.

"To me?" Alice looked at her and away again. "Why, nothing. I just see things differently."

And that was all that Asia could get from her that morning. But the conversation thus begun lasted with breaks and interruptions for a week, an illuminating week for Asia. She had always loved her mother. She had always passionately admired some things about her, and passionately deplored others. She had suffered more in her sorrows than she would ever suffer in her own. She had prematurely matured in the grim crucible of her mother's experience. She had always known that her mother had had a tragedy in her youth. She had always believed it to be the tragedy of some worthless husband. But she could not see why it should have been allowed to darken her life, and she blamed her introspective temperament for much of her reserve and her fear. She thought all the things she did not understand about her mother were accounted for by that temperament.

They asked each other no personal questions. Asia volunteered a lot of information about herself and Ross, what they meant to do, how they proposed to live, but at the end of the week she was no wiser as to what it was that was troubling her mother, or had been troubling her. There was a curious ebb and flow of emotion between them that week. Sometimes they felt very near to each other, and then something dropped like a wall between them. Alice felt she had got Asia back again—how, she did not know. But Asia felt at times that she had lost her mother, and it was she, who now made the advances, who tried to follow into that lone land of intimate personality that is created out of pain and the thoughts one thinks in the terrible hours before a slow dawn.

But at the end of the week, though they were not yet clear as to what it was that had happened between them, as to how far it was an emotional or an intellectual change, they did feel an immense gain in mutual interest. Alice saw that Asia now asked her questions with a real desire to know how she felt, and the subtle flattery in this was afterwards one of the pleasant memories of that groping week.

CHAPTER XXXII

THE sun was setting in a sky cleared by recent rains and fresh winds, which had carried off the smoke clouds and left the hills sharp against the horizon. As Alice waited on the veranda for Asia to tell her that dinner was ready, she watched the colours flame up and deepen in the sky, and as she watched them she felt again the curious vacant feeling that had haunted her during the day. She wondered why the departure of Ross and Lynne two days before had left the place so empty, and she knew that if she noticed it as much as she did that Asia must have been feeling it much more.

The Australians had had a part in her awakening that summer. They had been interwoven, unknown to themselves, into the new material of her aroused interest in the world about her. She had been stirred by their vitality and their enthusiasm. She had begun by resenting them. Now she was sorry to see them go.

She had been ready to sympathize with Asia, but she soon saw that she desired no appearance of mourning. To be suppressed in this direction gave Alice a strange feeling of the artificiality of their relations. She had been in a mood to go deep, but Asia had preferred to dabble in the shallows, and pretend she was unconcerned, and that she was not lonely. This was because she was afraid her mother would over-emotionalize anything that she might say. All day Alice had had a suspensive feeling which she remembered vividly afterwards. She had wondered how she would get through the month or so before Asia left, and still more how she would live on the years ahead.

But the thing that troubled her most was that with David Bruce still left to her, as much hers as he had ever been, she should be afraid of the future. The "spiritual friendship" had filled her life once. She could not understand why it did not fill her life now.

As she watched the mackerel sky change from gold to rose she saw David Bruce coming along his path, and she was glad that he would be there to dinner. She went down to the gate to meet him.

"Is Tom coming?" she asked, knowing they had been together in the bush.

"He said he was when I left him two hours ago." He mounted the steps beside her.

"I gave him the letter this morning, David."

"You did," he smiled. "I wondered what was the matter with him."

"Why, what——"

"Oh, he was unusually quiet, that was all."

They sat down. He began to tell her of a cave one of the men had discovered the day before in the bush. As he talked they heard the beginnings of a rumble about the base of Pukekaroro, and turning their heads, they saw a load of logs break from the low bush and come on down the tramway.

"That will be Tom," he said, and brushing aside the thought that the boss was driving too fast, he continued his story. "There may be some valuable greenstone in it. It's an old burying place——"

His head shot round, and he sprang to his feet.

Startled, Alice jumped up with him.

The dull roar of the trucks down the hill had suddenly ceased. An instant's sharp silence was followed by a crash of splitting wood, mingled with the snapping and jangling of chains. There was one short echo round the bay and then a piercing stillness.

Straining their eyes, they could see nothing, for the load had disappeared behind the rise.

"My God!" muttered Bruce underneath his breath, as he sprang down the steps.

As he swung through the gate he saw that she was following.

"You stay here," he commanded, looking into her frightened eyes. "I'll let you know as soon as I can."

Asia and the girls rushed through the house as he spoke. Waving them back, he started to run.

"An accident?" Asia looked at her mother's white face.

"Yes," said Alice faintly, "on the line."

Asia knew that no man but Roland ever braked a load down so long after knock-off time. She looked after Bruce racing to his shanty for his first aid case. She saw men rush out of the kitchen and out of the cottages, and along the road over the slope that hid the foot of the hill from view. She saw Bob Hargraves and others dash out of the store and run too. She saw women gather in groups on the paths.

"Mother, I'm going, and I will come back and tell you. Go inside, all of you."

Asia knew she had a right to go because she had helped at many an accident, and had bound up many a cut and broken bone. But she wondered even as she ran if she would be of any use. There had been two wrecks at the curve with men driving recklessly. One of them had been killed outright, and the other had died in a few hours. There had not been wanting predictions that Tom Roland would some day pay the penalty of his carelessness.

Mechanically Alice led the girls indoors and asked them to give the children their dinner and take them outside.

Then she sat down in the sitting-room to watch for the first sign of a messenger. She could not think and she did not try to. But though she could neither imagine nor anticipate a fierce excitement burned her.

Roland was more than half-way down the hill, driving recklessly but not dangerously, before he saw a group of children on the track at the curve below him. The utmost care had always been taken to keep people off the tramway, and during the day a guard was stationed at the tool depot at the foot of the hill to watch the coming and going from the school. Every family had been warned, and there were signposts at frequent intervals. But after hours the precautions were not taken, as only the boss drove late, and that but rarely. This evening the children of Bob Jones, the head contractor, returning from a birthday party at a neighbour's house, were not known by their parents to be near the line.

Roland jammed on his brakes, but at the rate that he was going they did not hold. He yelled at the children, and the eldest, a boy, started to run, for he knew they had no business there. But the two little girls clutched each other, paralyzed with fright, and stumbled and fell between the rails.

Roland saw that he would be on them before they could get out of the way. As the brakes did not grip, there was only time to do one thing—wreck the trucks and jump for it. He saw that, and knew the risk. But he did not waste a minute.

Hearing the yells, Bob Jones had rushed from the veranda of his house close by. A clump of bush trees that had been left standing because they were ornamental hid his children and part of the line from his sight. But as he ran he saw Roland swing a loose chain end down in front of one of the hind wheels. He saw the load rise over it and sway and keel over. He saw the boss's feet catch as he turned to jump, and he saw one of the two big logs strike him and carry him down, and pin him to the earth. It all happened before he had time to cry out.

Then he saw his crying children, saved with only a few yards to spare.

"God!" he groaned, realizing the cause of Roland's madness.

In a sudden reaction he swore frightful oaths at his terrified children, and roared for his wife, who had run after him, to get them away. Then he ran madly for the tool shed at the curve.

The first runners from the kitchen and from adjacent shanties reached him as he was dragging out the heavy jacks and levers, and they were about to raise the load when Bruce reached the scene.

The men worked like maniacs, but with faint hope, for one look at Tom Roland's face, which had fallen clear and was unscarred, told them the truth. The rest of him was under the log, something that the most hardened bushman dreaded to see. And when it was, after a few desperate moments, bared to their sight, that terrible lump of clothes and flesh and crunched bones drove most of them to blasphemy to stop the shock of nausea that curdled their stomachs.

But every voice was stilled as quickly as it had been raised. No one of them had ever seen Bruce overcome before, and when he sank on the ground and dropped his head into his hands the men set their teeth on their oaths, and a hush fell upon them, a hush that was broken first by the sobbing of Bob Jones, who began to cry unashamed as he told how and why the boss had done it. In a minute there was not a dry eye left, and other men running up looked and saw and broke down too.

Asia ran up to the group unnoticed. She was the only woman present, and her eyes were the only ones that stayed dry. With one glance round she took it all in, but though she was shocked and sickened she could not cry. She was by no means heartless, but even in that moment she saw that it was a fitting way for Tom Roland to die, that it was the way he would like to have died, and then in a flash she remembered what his death would mean to her mother and David Bruce. Then she looked at him, still sitting with his head in his hands. She saw that all the men stood helpless, stunned as such men are seldom stunned, and that they were all waiting for Bruce to raise his face and lead.

And when at last Bruce did raise his face almost every eye was upon it. They all knew that as Roland's sole partner Bruce was now their head. But they were not all thinking of their future under him, or fearing changes. So far as they were able to think at all they remembered the whispers that now and again had arisen in the past and died away —just occasional remarks that Roland was away a lot and made things easy for his wife and his foreman, just vague suspicions arising out of nothing but the situation. This and the influence that he had always had over them made them all turn to him.

There were no signs of tears upon Bruce's face, but there was a desperate calm upon it, the result of a fierce struggle for control. He was white under his tanned skin and his eyes looked as if they had tried to retreat back into his head. But what he had been thinking no man ever knew.

He saw no one in particular as he got to his feet. But he was attracted to the man nearest him, whose shoulders were still shaking. Seeing that it was Bob Hargraves, he put his hand on his arm a minute. Then he looked at one or two others, meeting strangely unfamiliar expressions in familiar eyes.

"Get the stretcher, boys," he said hoarsely. With the words his lips trembled, and he stood still struggling for composure, while sobs broke out again around him. Then when he raised his face he saw Asia. As he walked up to her every one drew away from them.

"You see," he said, looking calmly into her eyes.

"Yes, I see. What shall I tell Mother?" There was nothing in her tone or her eyes to show that she thought of more than the obvious elements in the tragedy.

"Just tell her he has been badly hurt," he answered quietly. "I will come as soon as I can. I will have him taken to my shanty." He gave no more sign than she did that there was anything to think of but the effect of his death upon others.

They both thoroughly understood that any expressions of personal sorrow were unnecessary.

Asia turned to hurry back. She felt much more than she could have showed a sense of shock at the sudden cutting off of so vital a creature as Tom Roland, but she felt as if it had no connection with herself. She did not even see then that it was pathetic that she should have lived for years in more or less intimacy with a person whose sudden death could rouse no more feeling than relief. She did not pretend that for herself it was any occasion for mourning. She could only feel his death in its relation to others.

Her thoughts ran far ahead of the present as she ran homewards. Her mind became rapidly possessed by speculation as to what it would mean to her mother, what difference it would make to her home. She wondered at once how soon she would marry, and made up her mind to influence her mother to be unconventional about the time of waiting. The more she thought about it the more excited she became. She knew Roland had died worth a good deal, that the quiet way they had lived at the bay was no criterion of his wealth. She knew David Bruce was his sole partner and sole trustee. She knew there would be money for all of them, and she foresaw that her mother would find herself suddenly rich as well as free.

She met Alice at the gate.

"He's very badly hurt, Mother," she said breathlessly. "Uncle David can't tell how much at present."

Stooping down, she pretended to take a prickle from her skirt. She had no desire to pry into her mother's soul, or to embarrass her by anything that looked like curiosity.

"We had better get the children away," she went on, raising herself. "They could stay at the Hargraves' to-night, and go to the Kings' to-morrow. The house will have to be still. I'll get the bed ready."

And so for the moment she threw her mother off the scent.

But a few minutes later, when Alice stood in front of the dining-room window to watch the procession come over the rise, she saw that it did not come on, but turned by the kitchen towards Bruce's shanty. The swift suspicion that darted into her mind was mingled with a sense of shame that as a matter of habit David Bruce should be saving her again.

She saw that the quickest way to get the truth was to go after it herself. While Asia was telling so much to Betty and Mabel and getting some of the children's things together, Alice went out of the front door and round to the side path.

One of the men who saw her coming told Bruce.

He met her half-way. There was still no room in his mind for more than the sense of shock and some realization of the grief of the people who had loved Tom Roland. When he had sat sickened with his head bowed he had seen what it would mean to Alice and himself, and seeing it, had dismissed it as something that could wait. He felt no more than this now as he looked at her. But he saw that she was feeling something besides anxiety.

"My dear, you must go back," he began gravely. "There is nothing you can do, and you cannot see him yet."

But she looked at him suspiciously.

"David, I will not be saved," she cried. "I need not see him, if you say not. But he is to come to his own home." Then something about his eyes told her. "What is it? Tell me the truth, David," she said very quietly.

"It is the last time he will ever come," he said, with a sadness he could not help but feel.

"He is dead!" Even though she had thought it, had hoped it and was ashamed that she had hoped it, it was a shock now that it was put into the hard frame of words. The full meaning of it she could not realize. She could not do as Asia had done, let her thoughts run on into the future. In Bruce's eyes she saw nothing personal, and in that first moment there was nothing personal in her own. She did feel even then that death was a thing so much bigger than the desires of any two people that it would have been sacrilegious to obtrude personal feeling upon it. She felt nothing but the shock of a life cut off, a sense of blackness, of inability to move or think.

"I can't think clearly yet," he went on quietly. "It will be a dreadful shock to everybody, the men and all. I shall have to think for others. You understand that?"

The light in her eyes grew sharp with a first glimmer of realization.

"Yes," she said, her voice trembling. "I understand."

Bruce took a folded letter from his coat and handed it to her.

"Your letter. It was in his vest pocket," he said eloquently.

A flood of tears blinded her. She sobbed helplessly.

"Don't cry for that," he said gently.

Then a question formed in her mind. She wondered what had caused the accident, if he were driving recklessly because of a mood brought on by that.

"How did it happen?" she choked.

"He died well, my dear. He wrecked the trucks to save Bob Jones's children who were on the line."

"He did that!" Her eyes dried as she spoke, and there was a new quality in her voice. Bruce guessed that the manner of her husband's death would greatly affect her feeling about him and her life with him in the past.

"Well, my dear, he never was a coward, was he?" he asked.

They looked into each other's eyes. Though they could not possibly pretend to each other that they would rather Roland had lived, they felt that in dying like that he had earned regrets that they would not otherwise have experienced in coming into their freedom.

"Go home now," he said after a minute. "I will come as soon as I can. But I shall have to go round the bay first."

Then Alice looked firmly at him.

"David, he is to be brought home, please, at once."

"There will have to be an inquest," he began doubtfully, "and the whole place will want to look at him. His face is all right, and there is no reason why they shouldn't see him if they want to. But you couldn't stand that."

"I can and will stand it," she cried.

"Mrs. Lyman might want——"

"Then she shall," she answered passionately.

His eyes lit up at her and then grew grave again.

"All right," he said gently. "I will have him brought home. You had better get the children away."

"Yes. Asia is doing that."

With one straight look, in which neither of them tried to show all they felt, they turned, knowing that now that the future was theirs there need be no unseemly haste in seizing it, and that for days at least they would both have to think of others.

CHAPTER XXXIII

LATE that night David Bruce stood alone in Bunty's room beside Tom Roland's body. Outwardly it looked like any other body laid out beneath a sheet, except that there were no hands to fold upon the breast. Bruce and one or two of the men had had a sickening task trying to make it look presentable, but they had succeeded so well that there was no aggressive sign of the mangled thing it had been. The white face looked extraordinarily dead, lacking the fierce eye fire of the living man. Only his reddish hair, now dulled with grey, bristled still as if it would make a fight for life. His square jaw was set in death as it had been in life, but there was a pathetic sensibility upon his strong features that now softened his expression, a something of appeal that arrested Bruce as he leaned over him to pin the handkerchief to the pillow.

Since the body had been carried there no one but Bruce had seen it. Alice, knowing she could not bear to look upon him, had stayed in her room, asking Asia to see that she was left alone. Not even Bruce was to be admitted to see her that night. Asia broke the news to Betty and Mabel, who, remembering only their father's more generous and cheerful years, were stricken with this first contact with death, and went to bed to cry in each other's arms. They were only too glad to be assured by Asia that no conventions required them to look upon their father's body. Asia saw no reason why she herself should see it. She would have done anything for it that had to be done in the name of decency and respect, but she could not pretend that she had any sentiment to spend upon it.

Bruce went in for more reasons than one. He knew the body had lain alone, and he had sentiment about it. He had just come from going round the bay. He had visited every family, had talked to most of the men, and had given such consolation as he could. He knew that if Tom Roland's body had lain in any house but its own it would have had a weeping crowd about it all night long, that the only dry eyes were those of the two women who had known him best, and that, while every other home about the bay was crushed with shock and helpless with grief, here there was already the sense of immense relief and the beginnings of readjustment.

This aloofness of his family from him in his death struck Bruce as one of the saddest things that he had ever known. The fact that he understood the reasons for it did not make it any the less sad. He knew well enough that any show of feeling on the part of Alice would have been indecent. All she could do was to be still. But he himself had been the boss's friend, curiously partial though that friendship had been. He had not yet recovered from the shock of seeing that dominant thing wiped out in an instant. It still seemed incredible that it should be gone. He realized that the stillness that hung over the house was more than the stillness of death, that it was also the stillness of the passing of Tom Roland.

And thinking of it, he wondered what Roland's death meant to himself apart from the freedom it gave to him and Alice. He did not feel personal grief of the kind that makes one wonder how life is to be faced without the friend now gone. He felt as if some landmark he had cared about with the affection one can bestow sometimes upon an inanimate thing had been suddenly destroyed by a storm. He had the sense of loss one has at missing a familiar object that one has had around for years. It was more physical than mental. Roland's energy had always been a stimulus to Bruce, like a strong wind ever blowing and forcing one to move with it.

Bruce surveyed their partnership as he stood there. They had had a certain kind of intimacy that went deep, that had rarely found expression in words. It was the understanding of two men, male animals, for the physical problems they had to face. Tom Roland had always felt that David Bruce understood as no one else did the goad of his own rampant vitality. For that understanding there was little he would not have done for his partner. But only on the evening in Bruce's room had any evidence of feeling on the subject come up between them. Now Bruce knew that the boss had loved and respected him with probably the finest feeling that had entered into his mixed emotions.

Their business relations had been their common ground of interest. In the main they had agreed about their plans, and they had readily compromised where they differed. They had the same sense of justice and of fairness. They had respected each other's judgment. They had been amused at the same things in the men, at the same incongruities in the happenings of everyday life. Business had inspired them with a mutual admiration for work well done, for promises promptly kept, for adjustments honourably made, for problems pluckily met and solved. In all their years of association they had never had a dispute. They had been a splendid working team. Bruce had supplied more of the ideas than any one ever knew, but he was more than willing to let Roland have the spectacular part of putting them into effect. Bruce was interested in the idea; Roland in getting credit for the result. Both had been satisfied.

Intellectually they had never met. As far as Bruce knew, the only book the boss had read in years was *The Letters of a Self-Made Merchant to His Son.* He had never had any ideals for humanity. Such improvements as he had made at the bay were those of the benevolent despot who finds a vast emotional satisfaction in the praise and gratitude of immediate dependents. Roland had loved doing good only where he could be sure of getting the eye-shine and hand-shake in return. The great movements of the world had left him not only untouched, but absolutely ignorant of their tendencies and power. But he had met what he called the fads of young people without hostility, with a good deal of tolerant amusement, and with the remark that they might as well do what pleased them for a while, because he was certain that as they grew older life would round them up and put them in the safe line of sober judgment.

Though Roland had responded, apparently without forethought, to his own impulses, he had been generous, as far as Bruce knew, in dealing with the results. He had paid well for all his fun, and he had kept his respect for the women and girls he had lived with, having, as his one radical accomplishment, a single standard for the sexes. He gave women the right to do as he did, and when it came to the supreme test of his philosophy, he was prepared to take, as he had shown, the same stand towards his wife.

These things David Bruce thought over as he looked upon him, and he wondered that with so much known so much should still remain unknown about him. After fixing the window and seeing that nothing would rattle or blow about if a wind arose, he went out, locking the door behind him.

He found Asia in the dining-room waiting to give him something to eat. They began to talk at once of how they were to manage the inquest and the funeral, and not a personal word was said. Then Bruce lay down as he was on the front room couch. As they all lay awake they could hear, at intervals, the sounds of hammering on the spit, where the head carpenter and his staff worked all night on a labour of love, the coffin, the most elegant coffin the bay had ever seen, made of the choicest bits of mottled kauri from Roland's private collection.

As Asia thought, and remarked only to Bruce, the boss would have been delighted with the stir caused by his death. Glorified details of his dying were telegraphed all over the colony, to become the subject of many a sermon. Resolutions of sympathy for the sorrowing family were passed by dozens of organizations. One man sat at the store telephone for two days taking down the telegrams that poured in upon Alice and Bruce. An urgent wire arrived the morning after his death from Auckland to say that fifty leading business men of the city would come to the funeral, and later in the day a message was received to say that a big delegation of timber men would come by launch from the Wairoa.

After breakfast people began to flock to see him. Asia took upon herself the task of receiving them and showing them into the room where the body lay, and of seeing that they did not stay too long, and of managing them generally. That was something Alice felt she could not face, and she spent the day sitting in her own room, listening to the ceaseless procession of steps up and down the hall. In the afternoon a party of fifty children from the two schools, with their teachers, all carrying wreaths and crosses of wild flowers, came awed and sobbing to look upon the face of the man who had always been the life of the school picnics, the donor of most of the prizes, and as an amateur conjurer the most applauded of their entertainers at the concerts at night. To many of them, in whose homes he had been a little god, he was Uncle Tom, the lovable deity who always had a threepenny bit to spare, and who made jumping bunnies for them and shadows on the wall. It was this procession of children that brought to Alice's eyes the only tears she shed that day. And she wondered how a man who had always been so irritable with his own should be so loved by the children of everybody else.

It was not till the evening of that first day after the accident that Mrs. Lyman appeared. As they sat trying to eat in the dining-room, they saw her drive up in her well-known little yellow gig. With a quick look at her mother, Asia got up at once. But she was surprised to see Alice rise and wave her down.

"I will meet her," she said quietly.

Asia shot a look at David Bruce, who refused to see anything, for Betty and Mabel were no longer oblivious of signs. So she was left to her own speculations.

Alice and Mrs. Lyman had met at shows, where the florid, black-eyed landlady of the Hakaru public house had somewhat paraded her ascendancy over the boss in a manner that had more than once disgusted his wife with him as well as with her. Alice had seen in Mrs. Lyman nothing more than a vulgar harridan who was only one stage removed from a prostitute. She had felt at times in years gone by, when her husband's infidelity had hurt her, that she could have understood his carrying on with a beautiful or seductive woman, but she never could see how a man who had been attracted by her could also be attracted by a type so utterly different from her own.

But her feeling about Mrs. Lyman had altered. She knew she was as vulgar as ever as she looked at her standing in the doorway, dressed ostentatiously in black to show the world that she considered she had as good a right as any one to mourn for the dead. Once Alice would have called her mourning brazen, but now she wondered if it were not a sign of a real courage. The bay and the countryside had always forgiven the boss his sins in so far as it was aware of them, but Alice knew from Bruce that Mrs. Lyman had been pretty generally ostracised for years by all the members of the community who claimed to be respectable. Alice knew the bay would condemn her, but she herself felt only a pity for this primitive woman who was willing to take risks for the man she loved, and who was now left bereft of the one human being upon whom she had lavished her affections for years. She wondered if it were not greater to dare all deliberately for a thing beloved than to deny feeling as she herself had done. Who was to judge?

Mrs. Lyman glared at Alice. She had hoped Tom Roland's wife would be in retirement. She knew David Bruce would receive her courteously if he were there, but she had been a little afraid of Asia, even though Asia had never snubbed her, and so, partly in self-defence, she had brought a large cross of white hydrangeas that she had taken half the day to make, feeling that that offering could hardly be refused. She was amazed to see Alice come forward and hold out her hand.

"Come in, Mrs. Lyman," she said gently. "It was kind of you to come."

Kind! Mrs. Lyman wondered if she had heard aright, and her courage, ferocious in attack, evaporated immediately before the possibility of having nothing to do. She could not even frame the first sentence she had planned. All she could do was to hold out the cross.

"That is beautiful," Alice went on, "but you would like to see him, and put it with him yourself, wouldn't you?"

"Yes, please," choked Mrs. Lyman, dissolving into tears at this unexpected reception. Feeling that something had put her dreadfully in the wrong for the moment, she followed Alice to the door of Bunty's room.

"I will see that you are not disturbed for a while," said Alice, and as she spoke she put her hand for a minute on Mrs. Lyman's shoulder. Then she motioned her to go in, closing the door behind her. And for some time afterwards Alice felt as if she had at last got into the flow of the great human current that carries all men, great and small, towards some goal of understanding and goodwill which they see as in a glass darkly.

At the end of half an hour Mrs. Lyman stole out like a guilty thing, her veil drawn over her face. As she stumbled on to the veranda she came face to face with Asia and Bruce, who were talking to people waiting there to view the body. Asia at once held out her hand, and Bruce walked round with her to help her into her gig.

Suffering a reaction from her temporary humility, Mrs. Lyman tried to console herself as she drove home.

"I must say I didn't expect that from 'er," she said, "and 'er the cold thing she is. Oh, Lord! Why did 'e 'ave to die? The only thing I 'ad. I ought to 'ave been 'is wife, not 'er, if things 'ad been as they should be. And 'e knew it. It was me 'e wanted, not 'er, and 'e would 'ave married me if 'e could 'ave got a divorce from 'er. That's this world for yer!"

One of the things Mrs. Lyman had never learned from Roland had been his thoughts about his wife, other than the bare fact that she did not love him, nor had she ever heard from him a hint as to the possible relations of his wife and Bruce. Roland had had his delicacies of feeling and his points of honour.

"Poor soul," said Bruce, speaking of her later in the evening to Alice. "She loved him, and she never looked at any one else. She will be the loneliest thing in the place for some time. And she did something for him. She was a good cure for polygamy."

"David!" Alice was shocked, though she could not have said why.

"Well, my dear, she really has kept him monogamous, I believe, for the last three years. Don't you think that's a good thing?"

She gave him a strange look.

"I am glad he had her, David. I'm glad he had something he really wanted."

She looked down at her hands.

They were sitting in the front room, expecting no one else to come that night. Asia had retired a few minutes before, and the house was now still. It was filled with an overwhelming conglomerate smell of the flowers that had been brought in that day, and although all the windows were open the air was heavy and sense deadening.

Neither Alice nor Bruce had any intention of coming to themselves so soon, but the mention of Mrs. Lyman had brought to her mind something she had thought of many times that day.

She had guessed there would be plenty of money, and already her thoughts had turned to it and to what she could do with it. Although she had never seen her husband's will she knew from Bruce that he had made one, and she knew that whether he had or not, under the New Zealand laws the bulk of his money and property would belong to her and the children.

"David, do you know if he left her any money?" she asked, raising her face.

"Mrs. Lyman?"

She nodded.

"Not in the will I've seen, the only one so far as I know." He looked curiously at her. Her face looked whiter because of the black dress she was wearing, but there was something about her eyes that held him. He was interested in the way in which she was keeping herself and him in the background.

"There's plenty of money, isn't there?" she asked, and he saw what she was coming to.

"Plenty."

"Then, David, I'd like her to have some, to think he left it to her, quite a good sum, please. Can you manage that?"

Full of her own thoughts she did not see the significance of the light that shot across his eyes, or notice the quality of his tone as he answered shortly:

"Yes."

Soon she saw that his thoughts were not concentrated as they should have been upon the carrying out of her designs. His eyes were fixed upon her face with one of his inscrutable expressions, a compound of hunger and tenderness and the sternness of voluntary renunciation. She looked back at him doubtfully till his eyes flamed suddenly, and then she rose with him and felt herself melt into his arms.

But he had not held her crushed against him for many minutes before he remembered. Stiffening, he stood still, merely holding her face against his. Then he drew away from her.

"Oh, Lord!" he exclaimed, disgusted with himself. "Poor Tom. I did mean to wait till after the funeral." Then he regarded her reproachfully, as if she had been to blame.

"Keep away from me," he said with a comical sternness. "It will be at least two weeks before I have time to deal adequately with you."

For days he carried with him the memory of the smile with which she had answered his words.

Roland's funeral far outshone that of Mrs. Brayton. To the people she had been a vision, a luxury; but the boss had been a plain fact, a necessity, something that went with their food and clothes and simple pleasures.

The entire population for a radius of twenty miles came to it. In the mellow warmth of the still late autumn day they sat out in the field, and along the spit, and on the tramway. Those who drove were in charge of a committee of men who placed them in the order of their coming to fall later into line for the Kaiwaka cemetery, where, as the day was fine, Alice and Bruce decided that the service should be held so that more could hear it.

It took Bruce and Harold Brayton and Bob Hargraves and Asia, and a committee working under them, four hours to arrange a programme that should provide for all who had not seen the coffin to see it, and to place all with some attention in the funeral procession. By midday everybody had been disposed into groups and their order fixed. Then they waited only for the arrival of the Auckland merchants, who had telegraphed their progress at intervals along the road. When at last their three big brakes drawn by teams of four horses were seen swinging round the base of Pukekaroro, there was a stir through the whole crowd of mourners, and a feeling of relief at this break in the tension.

At one o'clock the procession started.

Roland's coffin, loaded with flowers, and followed by three buggy loads of wreaths and crosses, was carried in relays on the shoulders of the oldest workers. The first eight, which included Shiny, were men who had grown grey in his service, all having been with him since the month of his beginnings in that bush. Round them in a sort of square marched the other pall-bearers. Immediately following them walked David Bruce, Harold Brayton, Bob Jones, who sobbed at intervals, Bob Hargraves, and Asia, the only member of his family who was present. She did not want to go, but she felt she ought to represent her mother, to whom it would have been an ordeal so trying that they decided she should not go.

Following this little section of the people nearest to the dead man walked the Auckland and the Wairoa delegations. Then came the lines, over a quarter of a mile long, of engineers, saw men, mill and bush hands, tramway and general workers, and behind them their families. The school children with their teachers followed, and after them the general public, among whom Mrs. Lyman drove, heavily veiled, in a long, straggling wave of vehicles. Seen from the house on the cliffs the coffin was out of sight on the road at the base of Pukekaroro before the last buggies had fallen in from the field.

The ministers of four of the local denominations assisted to bury Tom Roland, and to hold him up as an example of a noble and successful citizen, pointing a moral for all in the heroic sacrifice of his end.

Immediately after the funeral a public meeting was arranged to consider plans for the erection of a monument to his memory. At this meeting it was decided without argument that the anniversary of his death should be a public holiday in the bay school for ever, and that the story should be told every year of how and why he died. There was a three months' dispute as to whether the monument should be erected on the spot where he had died or above his grave. Finally the advocates of the cemetery won the day.

CHAPTER XXXIV

ONCE again Alice watched by her western window for a boat to come through the gap on the river. It was the first week in May, when in the southern latitudes nature calls a halt between the anticipative melancholy of autumn and the winter's onslaught of wind and rain, and gives a consolation prize of a week or two of days filled with crystal sunshine and clear stillness, days when life carries one along on winged feet, days of dreams and visions and those wonderful ambitions that are too vast to be ever pinned down afterwards within the narrow limits of action, days when one forgets death and disruption, pain and disillusionment, and sees only that the world is very good.

It was the afternoon, but there was no haze anywhere, and the hills high and low stood out sharp against the sky. There was no motion among the forest trees and only the suggestion of a ripple on the river. Tom Roland had been buried over two weeks, and the bay had taken up its daily round again, so that outwardly it seemed the same. The mill hummed and screamed its dominance through the days as it had done before. New vessels had come to take the places of the loaded ones beside the wharves.

As yet nothing had been altered, but to Alice it had taken on a new form and meaning. It now belonged to her, to her and David Bruce.

As she looked at the low hills that lay like a band of indigo on the western horizon, she remembered the times she had cried out to them, seeing in them the guardians of the water highway that was to her the way out, the road to a vague land of promise about which she had sometimes allowed herself to dream. She had looked at them as a prisoner in a valley dungeon might look through bars at a neighbouring mountain pass, wondering if he would ever go that way to life and freedom. Now that she knew she could go any day she chose, she wondered why the keen edge of her desire had gone from her.

In that fortnight Alice had shut down her mind for ever upon the past. Apart from the shock of it, her husband's death had given her little to think about that she had not thought already during that summer of revelations. She had made her last review of the past and its blunders. It was to the future she now turned.

And in that turning she was aided and abetted by Asia with an energy and disinterestedness that amazed and delighted her. The day after the funeral Asia had descended upon her mother with an avalanche of common sense and frankness that crumpled up most of Alice's remaining reserves. When she saw her come into her room after breakfast and close the door behind her she knew she was in for it. But these interviews had been shorn of most of their terrors. Alice merely raised herself on her pillows, and then looked expectantly at Asia, who sat down facing her on the bed.

Asia, who had put her own affairs into the background, was now obsessed by her mother's future prospects, and she was not afraid to show how she felt about it. Alice was to learn with much surprise in the days that followed that the years and her absences had made no difference to the girl's realization of her mother's life, that the apparent difference was due to wider comprehension, to a knowledge that even mothers have to work out their own salvation for themselves, and to the fact that the older one grows the more one sees the two sides to every question.

Asia tried not to be flippant or over-decisive, and to remember that the flowers had not yet faded on Roland's grave. But she could not keep her joy out of her eyes as she looked back at her mother's face against the pillow. She did hope that her mother had not got beyond realizing what the future might mean. She did hope she could begin again with some of the glow of youth in her heart.

"Mother," she began, "I hope that now at last you are going to be happy. Don't pretend you don't know what I mean. I know you can't announce your plans to the world, but you can at least tell me when you mean to marry Uncle David. I want to be at your wedding."

And having it thrown at her like that, Alice had blushed like a girl, and had turned her face away.

"Really, Asia, it is too soon——" she stammered.

"Oh, don't be conventional with me, Mother, please. I can't be quiet about it. I can't pretend to be mourning. You know your husband was nothing to me, though I appreciated his good points. We both did all we could for him while he was alive. Now we can leave him. And you don't have to wait a year to marry Uncle David, or any of that rot. Three months at the outside——"

"Oh, Asia," gasped her mother with a touch of impatience, "do let us arrange that for ourselves."

Then Asia had the good sense to see, even while it hurt her vanity, that this was really her mother's affair, and that she ought to be left to plan for herself.

But that started them, and now that the future had got into their blood they found it difficult to keep up before Betty and Mabel that air of soberness that they decided should be preserved before them for a week or two at least. In the days that Bruce came to dinner before he went to Auckland they tried to do the things that the bay expected them to do. They went round the little homes trying to make everybody feel that their world would not be wrecked. They listened humbly to eulogies of Roland that even he could hardly have heard without a blush. And then when the girls and the children had gone back to school, and they had seen Bruce off to Auckland for a week of preliminary arrangements about the will and the boss's estate, they began in good earnest to plan what they would do with their money.

Roland had left Asia a sum independent of her mother's trusteeship, but as his own children were all under age Alice had the control of the rest of his property, and was, with Bruce, trustee for them. Asia was surprised to discover that her mother had already formulated well-defined plans for the future, that she had thought of a maternity home in Auckland for unmarried mothers, and a scheme for sending them to Australia and starting them in places where no one knew their story. In these evidences of her modernity Asia saw much more of her own influence or the effect of her own actions. That week completed the *rapprochement* begun before Roland's death.

At the end of it they knew that judgment was at last entirely eliminated between them, that any sense of ownership that might have lingered on was dead for ever, and that now their youth and age might clasp hands across the bridge of years.

The only thing that had troubled Alice in that week of waiting for Bruce to return was that she could not be as sure of Asia's future as she now felt of her own, but before she could frame a complete sentence on the subject Asia stopped her.

"Now, Mother, you can't settle our future because you are settling yours. Allen and I are just as likely to be happy with uncertainty as you are with certainty. At any rate we can't tell beforehand. And whatever happens to us we won't wreck society or let ourselves be spoilt. That's all we owe the world. And if the experiment doesn't work, whether we can marry or whether we cannot, we will hurt each other as little as possible in the ending of it, and we will come through with understanding and respect."

And Alice heard her without any smile of superiority, or any predictions of disaster.

Now, as she sat by her window waiting for the first sign of a boat beyond the gap, Alice knew that she was happy. She felt an immense contentment in thinking of her future life with David Bruce. She thought it was curious that the mental and physical restlessness that she had felt for months had entirely left her. She was by no means in the fine frenzy of emotionalism that Asia would have had her show; as far as her marriage was concerned she was calm. The sex relation had no longer for her that glamour of mystery that so stirs and fires the feelings and imaginations of youth. She knew that though it promised to be in the future a very different thing from that of her life with Tom Roland, it would be incidental, balanced as it had never been in her life before.

She hoped as she sat waiting for the boat that in working and planning how best to spend her money she would lose finally the sense of wasted years that had so troubled her that summer. The real great passion of her heart now was the idea of work with David Bruce, and, realizing that, she understood more than she had before the cementing element in the friendship of Asia and Allen Ross.

When at last she saw something move against the right cliff, like a fly at the bottom of a wall, her speculations suddenly ceased. She snatched up a field-glass and strained her eyes through it. She could easily distinguish the launch and two heads above the gunwale.

Then for a minute her heart leapt to her throat. In all the times she had watched for returning wanderers there had been no craft laden with the promise of this—no time when love, peace and happiness together sailed the swift current of expectation.

She knew by the sign of the foam-crested wake billowing up from the bow of the boat that Asia was driving it at full speed. She could hear the sharp pit pit of the engine above the conglomerate noises of the mill. As they came racing on, something about the impudent fury of that little American machine screaming its effectiveness at the hills got into Alice's blood, and she sprang to her feet, her eyes aflame.

After watching it tearing at her she turned to her mirror to see that her cheeks were scarlet. She smiled at herself like a girl. She powdered her nose. She rearranged her best old lace about the neck of the brown dress, which Asia had insisted on her wearing that day instead of black. She told herself that she was still young, that the years that the locust had eaten were no more now than an ugly dream.

When she looked out again the launch was level with the point below the mill where Ross and Lynne had lived that summer, and just for the minute she wished again that she could see the end of that story too. Then she saw that Asia was standing up by the engine.

She ran out on to the veranda, forgetting that some one might see and interpret for himself the reason why she waved her handkerchief. She waved harder than ever when she saw Bruce swing his hat above his head. She would have liked to have gone down to meet them, but she decided that would be too conspicuous. When they reached the landing-stage beside the booms she went into the hall. She found she could not be calm now, that anticipation could still raise a ferment in her. But the minute she heard Bruce's voice outside the gate she became still again.

Asia walked off round the garden path, leaving him to enter alone.

It seemed to Alice that his brown eyes held only the old quizzical smile as they met hers, that he came to her with the calm assurance of a husband rather than with the fire of a lover, and the wish half formed in her mind that he would seize her. But she forgot it as he drew her into her own room, that one room in the house in which he had always forced himself to be impersonal.

There as he looked at her before throwing his arms around her she saw in his eyes what no words can ever adequately express, that fierce longing of the human soul for something that it can never get in itself, that something part physical and part mental that completes itself, that tantalizing something that one-half of humanity is always searching, and that the other half is always questioning when found.

Alice and David Bruce sat in a luxury of silence, and it seemed now to her that there was more magic in the language of his eyes and of his hands than there could have been in any words. After all, what had they to say to each other that could increase the emotion of that hour of freedom? The phrases common to lovers in the first stage of mutual soul searchings would have been stale, flat and unprofitable.

Sounds in the hall first arrested their attention.

"The children home," he said, raising his face from hers.

"Don't move. Nobody will come in," she said.

They sat on till they heard steps outside the door.

"Mother," called Asia. "I'm putting dinner for you and Uncle David in the sitting-room. Now do eat it while it's hot."

"Oh, Lord!" groaned Bruce. "Dinner! We can't even get through a day like this without dinner. And it must be hot too." He sat up in disgust. "No use, dear. I've been dreaming of freedom here with you in my arms. But we are not free; we will have to eat dinner every day of our lives. Even if we want to go without it some idiot will impose it on us. And if it isn't that it will be something else."

She laughed so spontaneously as he drew her to her feet that he looked at her.

"I see," he said, "I must make you laugh oftener."

CHAPTER XXXV

IT had been a fancy of Alice's, after they had decided that they would move to Auckland to live, that they should leave the bay in the spring, on the anniversary of the day they came down the river in the black punt. Even Asia said it was a nice idea, and Bruce, who was determined that Alice should now have a few of her whims gratified, said it should be arranged that way if it meant chartering the *Ethel* specially for the occasion.

And it did mean that in the end, for the anniversary did not fall on a regular steamer day. The imaginations of the captain and the crew were fired by the magnitude of this enterprise. It was the first time the little steamer had ever been hired for a private undertaking. They cleaned her up for the occasion, and flew the New Zealand flag, which they displayed only for such events as the King's birthday, Empire Day, the owner's birthday, Labour Day, and the anniversary day of the Auckland Province. And for long afterwards they dated various happenings as so many days or weeks before or after "the week we took Mrs. Roland and the family from the bay. Special trip, Mister. Nobody else on board. Cost 'em thirty pounds."

Almost the entire female population of the bay and a few of the men gathered about the private landing at the side of the tramway and the booms to see them off. The *Ethel* was to get away about nine o'clock, on the top of a high tide which allowed her to get up to the launch wharf over the mud flat.

The morning was fresh and clear, with a winter tang still in the air, and the river rippled to a light western breeze charged with ocean ozone. The zinc roofs of the cottages glinted in the sun. The shallow waters of the bay sparked in patches where they were torn by the hurried movements of shoals of little fish fleeing from some enemy, real or feared. The white line of the sandspit glowed from the narrow channel by the mill side to the foundations of the store. All round the horizon, the hills, high and low, cut sharp into the rain-washed sky, not yet warmed up by the sun. Pukekaroro and the bush walls behind the mill were brilliant with spring colour, clumps of rata red and kowhai gold and new fern greens. But nowhere now was there silence, and rarely could one hear the song of a solitary bird calling for its mate. Not a tui had been heard about the bay for years, and even the enterprising wekas had been driven further into the forests.

Everywhere that morning the daily business of the place was going on as usual, with its accompanying agglomerate of sounds; for, however much the women of the bay were interested in the departure of the late boss's family, David Bruce had not seen that it was an occasion for sentimental interest on the part of the men. Only those who could, like the old head carpenter, conveniently leave jobs on the spit or about the store, and Bob Hargraves, now promoted to be local manager, were there for last words or final instructions.

While the last of their baggage was being put aboard, Alice sat in a chair on the *Ethel's* deck with a favoured few gathered about her. In her arms she held a huge bunch of spring flowers that Harold Brayton, with nice feeling, had gathered in the now neglected old garden in the pines. His quiet presentation of them had brought to Alice's eyes the first of the many tears she was to shed that day. Hovering over her, divided between tears and jokes meant to sustain her own and everybody else's courage, was Mrs. King, white haired and fatter than ever, and sure of her supreme right to claim most of the last moments of the whole family. In contrast to her, her daughter Eliza stood silently by, still in deep mourning for her drowned lover, but trying to smile at her mother's sallies. Mrs. King had a powerful rival in the person of Mrs. Bob Hargraves, who had been trying vainly for a week to hide her immense pride in her husband's promotion, and in the fact that he was now to have the house on the cliffs as a residence, with a good deal of the old furniture and fittings intact. She now stood on the other side of Alice with an air of owning the whole family almost as pronounced as Mrs. King's. On the fringe of this familiarity, with a somewhat precarious hold upon it, stood Mrs. Bob Jones, who was uncomfortably aware that the boss's wife had never liked her, although Alice had always courteously acknowledged her position as the wife of one of her husband's most important and trusted heads, the second, indeed, only to David Bruce. Mrs. Bob Jones felt in her secret soul that her husband should have had the boss's house for residence, and she also felt in her secret soul that he would have had it but for the unfortunate fact that Roland had on and off throughout the years paid her certain attentions in her husband's absence, until his final complete absorption by Mrs. Lyman. She had seen sadly in the last weeks that her chickens were coming home to roost, and she wondered how much of what she had called mere flirtations with the boss had got to Alice's ears and how.

On another part of the deck Betty and Mabel held court with some of their elder pupils, and with those few of the better class younger country folk, who as old school-fellows had some claims upon their friendship. The two girls, who had resigned their positions as teachers to follow their mother's desire that they should get degrees at the Auckland university, were wildly excited at the prospects of life in the city, which they knew only from short and tantalizing visits.

To a little group of boys Bunty outlined with flourishes reminiscent of his father the impression he intended to make upon the town school that would be favoured by his attendance. Listening to him, but not with that amount of admiration he would have liked, stood Elsie, shyly holding the hand of Lily Hargraves, her favourite playmate.

Asia alone had no particular group to smile upon, but went from one to another on the wharf, shaking hands, promising not to forget them, and telling them that she would write, because it was kinder to lie than to tell the truth. The bay knew that she was the person it was really saying good-bye to, for she had told all frankly that she was going to Australia to live, and that she might never see the place again. Bruce had not packed up, or said a word about going except in the ordinary course of business, and Alice had said that she would often return, so that the farewell emotions really centred on Asia, who saw that she had meant to the place more than she ever imagined.

There was more than grief and a sense of coming loss mixed in the emotions of that farewell. Nobody had told the bay that Alice and Bruce were to be married soon after they got to Auckland, but everybody felt in their bones that something of the kind was to happen, and their whispered speculations and their anticipations added a pleasant excitement to their other feelings, and caused them to look for signs. But in this respect they were doomed to disappointment, for Bruce talked on the wharf to Bob Hargraves till the captain called out "All ashore" as the last box went aboard. Then in the scramble of final hand-shakes and good-byes, the excitement of seeing the gangway drawn and the ropes thrown off, they forgot to see if Bruce looked at Alice or if she looked at him, for they were trying as people do at a circus to see every way at once, and to catch the eyes of all the family in turn for that last look and smile of recognition that seemed at the moment to be so important.

Alice stood, unashamed of the tears in her eyes, looking back at the faces blurred before her, and hoping that she had really been something more than a pleasant picture for them to talk of after she was gone. If she could have seen into their hearts and realized how much they really did reverence her as a pure, wronged and gracious lady, even though their estimation of her meant an unconscious criticism of her dead husband, she might have felt, as Asia did, that it was pathetic they could feel so about a person they did not know.

The family group stayed still while the *Ethel* moved out into the channel. Betty and Mabel and the children continued to wave to their friends on the wharf till they were opposite the mill. Then there was a diversion. The mill siren blew three long blasts as a salute, and the mill flag was run up and dipped in their honour, while the men gathered on the wharves cheered loudly as they passed by.

Swelling with pride at the greatness of the hour, the captain of the *Ethel* answered with such steam power as his machinery could muster, and there ensued a duet of laughably uneven quality till they had passed the mill grounds.

"We came in fear and trembling; in glory we depart," murmured Bruce, as if he were quoting something, as he turned his amused but sympathetic eyes upon Alice.

"Oh, David, don't make fun of it. I'm sure they mean it," she said, wiping her eyes.

"Of course they do," he answered.

He had looked on at the whole morning scene, seeing with amusement the rivalries that had crept into the leave-taking, the local jealousies, the obtrusion of claims upon his and Alice's favour, all the ebb and flow of ordinary human feeling and motive into any situation, humorous or tragic. But outwardly he had shown no favours, but had given as usual the impression that he was the same to every one, that supreme achievement of diplomacy among average people in a small place.

When the *Ethel* reached the main channel out in mid-stream, and the faces on the wharves were no longer to be distinguished, the family group dissolved. Bunty and Elsie went off to explore the steamer in the care of the first mate, and Betty and Mabel found seats that suited them where they might flirt unseen with the second mate, who was a fresh good-looking boy they had met before.

Alice, Asia and Bruce continued to stand near the stern, looking up the river. They had forgotten the people, and were thinking of the place. They looked at the mountain cleaving the sky like a giant wedge of earth driven into the heavens, at the gap through which Tom Roland had brought his dreams of wealth and glory to fruition, at his self-made monument, the mill, roaring and screaming its efficient way through the crystal morning, at the long streamers of smoke drifting away from it on the breeze, at the cottages clustered by the water, and at the house above the white line of cliffs, now half buried by shrubs and trees.

"I never thought I should feel like this about coming away," began Alice.

"We are not leaving it," he smiled. "We never really leave anything behind."

"No," she admitted humbly. "I am bringing away all it has taught me. Why are you smiling, Asia?" she added, catching a gleam flitting across the blue eyes. "I suppose you want to tell me not to be sentimental."

"Wrong, Mother. I was thinking of the secrets locked up there in that little place, the whole of life in a nutshell," nodding her head back at the bay in general. "I guess you are the only person who knows them all, Uncle David."

"Probably," he smiled.

"Let them die," said Alice quietly, looking out over the low swampy southern bank at the Brayton pines that were now coming into view behind the green hill.

She thought of some that Asia did not know, and Asia thought of some that her mother did not know, and Bruce thought of some that neither of them knew.

Thinking of one in particular, Asia moved away from them to a place where she was out of sight for the moment. She wanted to look her last upon the place in the bush above the point they were now passing where the two men had lived that summer. She thought of the story the little cottage hid, and of the tale it would never tell. Her eyes softened as she looked up into the fresh spring greens, and at the dark rocks reaching out unevenly into the tide below. She felt passionately that her summer story had been a great thing to her, and she could only hope that it was a story that would never be spoiled. She had learned, perhaps too soon, that lives are not finished performances, or any series of rounded-off experiences, but a flow of endings dovetailing into fresh beginnings, of abortive experiments, of searches, of reachings out after alluring signs, of retreats, hurts and disillusionments, the whole apparently bound by a cohesive thread, sometimes lost sight of, a thread that seems to lead somewhere, but about which no wise man will dogmatize.

She stayed alone till they reached the gap. Then she looked for her mother and Bruce, who were still where she had left them, looking back up the river.

"I wish," Alice was saying, "that I had a picture of the old black punt. I always meant to have some one take one before it broke up."

"For a family crest?" inquired David Bruce, amused at her sentimentality.

"What more appropriate thing can you suggest?" she demanded, her grey eyes lighting up.

His story-telling eyes alone answered her.

And then they turned with Asia to see the last of the bay. They did not speak as bit by bit the gap cut off the familiar features of the place. The mill side of the river went first; then the bay, their old home and the mountain; then the green hill, the Kaiwaka heights behind it, with the spot where Tom Roland lay buried; and last, the black pines of the Brayton farm.

But they knew, even when the gap had cut it all out of sight, that they had not left the river and the hills behind them.

Asia felt that she would carry the freedom of them with

her to Australia, into her work with Allen Ross for the intellectual dynamiting of the unthinking masses.

Alice told herself that she would carry the inspiration of them with her into the refuge she planned for the remaking of broken lives.

David Bruce had a fancy as he stood there that he would like to come back to them to die, if only he might be buried as lost diggers were by the sweet fern on some hillside under the open wind-swept sky. But even as he pictured to himself that free and pleasant ending for his bones, he suspected that Alice would see to it, if he died first, that every horrible trapping that civilization has devised for the disposal of a defenceless corpse would be heaped upon his in the name of reverence and respect.

And smiling at his fancy, he drew Alice with him towards the captain, who was beginning to think it was time somebody recognized the importance of his part in the events of the day.

THE END

CPSIA information can be obtained
at www.ICGtesting.com
Printed in the USA
BVHW042137040720
582969BV00002B/43

9 781375 466561